**Warning**:

**Wonderland** is a
Magical **world**
**where** the most
far-**fetched** *dreams*
come true.
**Alas**, it is also where
**intoxicating**
*nightmares*
run rampant.

# Death of the Mad Hatter

## Sarah J. Pepper

Published by Neximus Publishing
ISBN-13: 9781492823919

Editors: Deb Lebakken, Heather Banta, Emily DeHaan, Sandra Long
Proof Reader: Mercedes Roth
Photography: Josh Wilcoxon of Wilcoxon Photography
Cover Design: Sarah Storm of Design Monkey
Hair/Makeup: Angelique Verver of Platinum Imagination
Model: Amanda Boer of Amanda's Imagery

# Young Adult/New Adult Novels by

# Sarah J. Pepper

*Of Course the World is Flat*

*Devil's Lullaby – Ringer's Masquerade Series #1*

*Death's Melody – Ringer's Masquerade Series #2*

*Angel's Requiem – Ringer's Masquerade Series #3*

*Forgotten – The Fate Trilogy #1*

*Twisted Games – The Fate Trilogy #2*

*Fallen Tears*

*Death of the Mad Hatter*

**I will not follow rumperbabbits down dirty holes.** I will not follow rumperbabbits down dirty holes. I will not follow rumperbabbits down dirty holes. I will not follow rumperbabbits down dirty holes. I will not follow rumperbabbits down dirty holes. I will not follow rumperbabbits down dirty holes. **I will not follow rumperbabbits down dirty holes.** I will not follow rumperbabbits down dirty holes. I will not follow rumperbabbits down dirty holes. I have a story to tell if you have time. I will not follow rumperbabbits down dirty holes. **I will not follow rumperbabbits down dirty holes.** I will not follow rumperbabbits down dirty holes. I will not follow rumperbabbits down dirty holes. I will not follow rumperbabbits down dirty holes. I will not follow rumperbabbits down dirty holes. I will not follow rumperbabbits down dirty holes. **I will not follow rumperbabbits down dirty holes.** I will not follow rumperbabbits down dirty holes. It's a juicy story! I will not follow rumperbabbits down dirty holes. I will not follow rumperbabbits down dirty holes. I will not follow rumperbabbits down dirty holes. I will not follow rumperbabbits down dirty holes. I will not follow rumperbabbits down dirty holes. *Cross my heart and hope to die* You will want to hear it. So listen up and pay attention. I will not follow rumperbabbits down dirty holes. **I will not follow rumperbabbits down dirty holes.** I will not follow rumperbabbits down dirty holes. I will not follow rumperbabbits down dirty holes. I will not follow rumperbabbits down dirty holes. Listen good! I will not follow rumperbabbits down dirty holes. I will not follow rumperbabbits down dirty holes. **I will not follow rumperbabbits down dirty holes.** I will not follow rumperbabbits down dirty holes. I will not follow rumperbabbits down dirty holes. For what you don't know will hurt you. I will not follow rumperbabbits down dirty holes. I will not follow rumperbabbits down dirty holes. **I will not follow rumperbabbits down dirty holes.** I will not follow rumperbabbits down dirty holes. I will not follow rumperbabbits down dirty holes. I will not follow rumperbabbits down dirty holes. I will not follow rumperbabbits down dirty holes. **I will not follow rumperbabbits down dirty holes.** I will not follow rumperbabbits down dirty holes. Rabbit holes are fun, even if they are a little dangerous. Don't let anyone tell you otherwise, not even me! I will not follow rumperbabbits down dirty holes. I will not follow rumperbabbits down dirty holes. I will not follow rumperbabbits down dirty holes. Just remember to take your dirty shoes off so you don't track mud around the house because that's how you get caught. **I will not follow rumperbabbits down dirty holes.** I will not follow rumperbabbits down dirty holes. I will not follow rumperbabbits down dirty holes. I will not follow rumperbabbits down dirty holes. I **will follow rumperbabbits down dirty holes.** Yours Truly, AL.

# A *Wondrous* Prologue

The Queen of Hearts kissed the King one last time before the Joker ripped his head from her hands and tossed it alongside his body. The queen's guards picked up the royal pieces and clumsily carried the dead king away. No one spoke. Only the sound of a ticking clock interrupted the stunned silence of the night.

Standing next to a bloody guillotine, Hearts let a love-letter the king had written slip through her fingers. Appearing out of nowhere, a Cheshire kitten, affectionately named Chez, distinguished by his purple and blue stripes, playfully pawed the letter until it was a shredded mess of paper. The queen simply watched. When the Joker reached for the remaining pieces of the letter, the kitten bit him, drawing blood.

"If you want to play dirty, may I suggest a play date, Chez?" the Joker asked, inspecting the bite mark. His voice was as innocent as a child's, but the look in his beady eyes was that of a psychopath's. "I have all sorts of modified toys collecting dust in the dungeon."

"Don't antagonize the Joker, Chez. He is a bit of a schizoid," Hearts said, picking up the kitten. She stared at the pieces of the love-letter for so long that her eye twitched. "Burn it so that no one finds out the king had loved a seamstress."

The Joker picked up the pieces and fisted them. The recipient of the letter showed through his fingers: *Dearest Genevine*— He held his hand up to his mouth and blew. Pieces of the letter flew into the air and burst into flames. They flickered until they reached the floor; where they turned into ash.

"I'm required to scold you for leaving your sharp toys scattered around, Joker. It's a pity the king had to pay for your untidiness," Hearts said, glancing at the guillotine that was drenched in royal blood.

"Then I shall only take out my biggest toys when you order me to do so... again," the Joker said with a wink. "Since this is a hush-hush operation, I assume you want me to kill Genevine? Oh! Perhaps, she could have a *misfortunate accident* as well?"

"No, that would be far too coincidental," Hearts stated. "Keep Genevine alive. It's fitting that she must live, knowing her lover is dead. Oh, and see to it that she never leaves Wonderland. All things considered, she is still the most talented seamstress in the court, and I'll need someone to sew me a black dress to wear at the king's funeral."

*The Jack had prophesied: If the king loses his head, then the Queen with a Bleeding Heart would rule the Red Court until Time ceased to move forward. When a second carried on for infinity, every creature in Wonderland would tip their Hat to the misfit girl with a Boy's name (or was it a boy with a Girl's name?) who'd end the Reign of Terror. However, it all hinged on the One-Eyed Hare being able to convince an uninspirable Heir that the impossible was indeed possible—like stopping time—and that Love was worth a Beheading.*

*Heads would Roll...*

*Hearts would Break...*

*In the end, would it matter who Reigned?*

"Reign of Terror—everyone acts like it's a *bad* thing," the Queen of Hearts said, reading the script that Jack of Diamonds, a.k.a the prophesier, had scribbled on an ingredients page of a violet book entitled,

*Sweets for the Rabbit Hole Voyager.* The Mad Hatter's crest, M.H. and a top hat, was printed on the bottom of every odd numbered page inside the book.

Hearts tore the last stanza from the *Bleeding Hearts Prophecy*, crumpled it into a ball, and smashed it between the pages of *The Lazy Killer's Poisons*, another of the Mad Hatter's works.

What a silly notion—dying for love. Ugh! (Cue eye-roll)

Nevertheless, the faux love of her life did "misplace" his head, and he was king, until today. These two happenstances made Hearts believe that the *Bleeding Heart Prophecy* was about her and that *her* head would roll. And furthermore, it *always* mattered who reigned!

She pushed both of the Mad Hatter's editions back onto the shelf, but made sure the one about poison was flipped upside-down, just to see if any of her feline servants would notice the disarray of her library. With her hands behind her back, Hearts stepped down from her golden step stool and paced around the library, which was filled with more books than anyone could read in a single lifetime.

"I have no heirs," Hearts said, thinking out loud. "And I've never been fond of hares. Hence, it would behoove me to damage the reputation of all the rabbits in my court, just in case this *Bleeding Hearts Prophecy* holds some weight."

Wandering aimlessly around her library, she spotted a speck of dust on the third shelf. She walked over to the fainting couch and rang a silver-plated bell. Quickly, a *glaring* of cats raced through the door. They stood at attention on a glittering line that Hearts drew years prior, when she still loved the king.

But, that was a long time ago.

All of the cats toed the line, except for the Cheshire kitten, Chez. His butt was high in the air as he got ready to pounce on a hopping bug that was hiding in the shadows next to the king's personal chambers.

"It's filthy in here," Hearts said as she walked past each cat, giving them a look of severe disapproval. She stopped in front of a black cat whose tail fluttered whenever she passed. "You have forty-eight seconds to remove the dust I located in this room, or you'll spend a week in solitary confinement with the Joker."

In a panic, the cats raced around the polished library, frantic to locate the speck of dust that the queen had spotted. The smaller cats flipped onto their backs and let the bigger cats use their furry bodies as dust rags. In the meantime, the queen collapsed onto a scarlet colored couch. The Cheshire kitten, who missed the formation on the glitter line, pounced on the cushion beside her. A feisty grasshopper wiggled in his mouth.

"What did you bring me, Chez?"

Chez dropped the grasshopper on the queen's lap. The bug wore a tiny dress coat with a broken heart and the King's initials on them: E.E. The bug wheezed, which made the kitty's incisive purr grow louder.

Chez pawed at the grasshopper and said, "I found this hoppy creature snooping around the king's chamber."

"Spare me from this vile kitten, my Queen! I did nothing wrong," the grasshopper begged. He held up a miniature violin and a mangled rod. "I was only near the king's chambers tonight because he enjoys my music before resting. I barely cracked his bedroom door when this feline attacked me! The king would never allow such behavior; so unbecoming!"

Hearts petted Chez behind his ears and talked in a baby voice. "Haven't you heard? The king had a misfortunate accident earlier this evening."

Every single cat in the library skidded to a halt. Their eyes glowed in the darkness of the night. The grasshopper swallowed noticeably hard.

"The Joker's guillotine broke his fall," Chez said.

"Accidental beheading," Hearts recited. "I was beside myself with horror as it happened. I've already spoken to the Joker about leaving his toys around. It shall never happen again."

"Eddie, the King of Hearts, is not clumsy," the grasshopper said and cleared his throat. He glanced at the other cats. One shook his head 'no' to caution the bug not to disagree with the queen, but the grasshopper

4

wouldn't listen. "Eddie would never have *accidentally* tripped on the weapon. He had to have been pushed!"

"Are you calling me a liar, grasshopper?" Hearts spat.

"Eddie was not a klutz," the grasshopper said, nervously.

"The king's proper name is *Edward*, not Eddie," Chez corrected, "And he wasn't *pushed!* He *tripped* over me and fell onto the Joker's big boy toy."

"That's right," the queen said, giving Chez a quick pat on his head.

"That's not what I saw when I was on my way to play for the king," the grasshopper said, then slapped his hand over his mouth.

"Did you see something to contradict my claim?" Hearts lowered her face so that she and the grasshopper were eye-level.

The grasshopper shook his head. The more visibly his legs trembled, the wider the queen's smile grew.

"Leave us, my glaring," Hearts demanded. "The grasshopper and I have much to discuss regarding this unfortunate accident involving my dear, late husband."

The cats scampered out of the library, leaving Chez behind. The grasshopper's eyes darted to the exit as the last cat closed the door.

"Well, the king tripped over an *unsuspecting* kitten right before the Joker lost his grip on the guillotine rope, but Edward took the risk of *death* when he broke my heart!" The queen blinked away a nonexistent tear. "Edward wanted to leave me and our so-called loveless marriage, for a seamstress! Leave me? For a seamstress? Can you imagine my humiliation?"

"Why are you telling me this?" the grasshopper asked.

She affectionately petted her kitten. She smiled an appeasing smile, but it quickly turned into a sneer. "Because Chez will make sure that you never tell a soul."

5

The grasshopper took off hopping toward the room belonging to the Prince of Spades. "Robby! Robby! Help me!"

"Sic him, Chez!" the queen ordered.

Chez disappeared, only to reappear in front of the grasshopper. The kitten flicked out his claws. He fixated on him with blood thirsty eyes.

The grasshopper gulped and with his last breath, he shouted, "Hearts killed the king, Robby! She pushed Eddie over Chez so he'd land on the guilloti—"

# CHAPTER ONE

(Ryley: Present Time)

I narrowly escaped the house before my mom attacked me with her pair of kitchen scissors—well, actually, it was my hair for which she was gunning. *Any distinguishable young man shouldn't have a mop of hair for the first day of school*—her words, not mine.

"What happened to the appointment I made for you at *A Little off the Top?*" shouted my mom, Lauren, as she followed me onto the rickety porch.

An old ceramic frog just outside the front door shook with each of our steps. Etched on the suit was a spade and my dad's initials: R.E. The frog was a novelty house key holder. Before the proverbial shit hit the fan, my dad had presented the frog to my mom. In its mouth was a silver ring that she *still* wore on her ring finger, regardless of everything that had happened.

The vibrations from our steps caused the frog to fall onto its side. My mom stepped over it, not letting the frog steal her attention away from me, even though—for some unknown reason—she still cared about it.

She said, in her perfected motherly tone, "You look like a girl, Ryley!"

7

"Mom, it's not like my hair is halfway down my back." I slipped on my baseball cap.

"It's covering your ears and neck," she said flatly, eyeing the hair.

"That's all part of my plot so when I get this massive neck tattoo I can hide it from you. I was leaning towards a spider tatt," I teased and gave her a quick peck on the cheek.

"You hate spiders."

I put my hands on her shoulders. I still couldn't get used to being taller than her. "I'm practically an adult now. I can make my own hair appointments."

"Clearly you can't," she said. "And I don't care if you turn eighteen in a couple months. You will always and forever be my baby."

"Love you too, Mom," I said, acting exasperated.

She fought to keep a smile from spreading across her face, a sure sign that I'd won this battle. So, it was my most effective verbal ammunition. She was a sucker for the "L" word.

"You know, you could drive to school if you fixed up the old beater in the garage," she said. "It's not like your father will notice."

"Someday, Mom."

I turned to leave, taking the steps two at a time. Slinging my backpack over my shoulder, I walked the few blocks to Rockingham High, home of the mighty Ravens. One more academic year left before I could ditch this backwoods town and head off to a big-name college; hopefully, on a full-ride baseball scholarship. I kept my fingers crossed, but I'd settle for any university with a decent physics department. Even then, I wasn't too picky in choosing a university to go to, as long as it was at least a hundred miles away from here. Of all the towns I'd lived in since my biological father checked out, I couldn't believe my mom settled down here; in this dump of a town.

I peeled open a cherry breakfast bar I'd snuck out of the kitchen when my mom was scraping off the burnt eggs and maple syrup from a frying pan—a breakfast experiment gone bad. The flavor of the bar reminded me of the sucker I'd *commandeered* from last year's Miss Rockingham High, Courtney Frick, after a baseball game this summer. I hadn't been able to land a date with the infamous redhead yet, but my chances were improving with each one of her giggles. Since my antics were lame—one notch above a knock-knock-joke—it *had* to mean that she was into me… or that I sounded so stupid she couldn't help but to laugh.

Before everything went to hell, my dad told me to keep a girl at the edge of her seat so that she wouldn't be able to walk away when I finally made my move. It was the last "normal" advice I could remember my dad giving me—

"Stop!" yelled a girl with an ear-piercing scream.

Startled, I dropped my second attempt at breakfast and stopped in mid-step. Expecting to be hit by a car or blindsided by a football, I was stunned when a girl raced over and snatched up a stuffed bunny that was inches from being squashed by my Converse shoe. It was a dingy white rabbit with a Sharpie 'X' in place of its missing eye.

"I almost peed myself! I thought I was going to eat the sidewalk after a car crashed into me, not trip over a stuffed animal!" I yelled at the eccentric girl.

Since the entire high school had an enrollment of less than two hundred kids, I knew every girl in the female student body. This particular girl *had* to be new to the roster, but she looked familiar—déjà vu familiar.

There was the type of girls who dressed for guys, the type who still played dress-up, the type who lived in sweatpants, and then there was an entirely different breed who wore mismatched socks with pride. This chick fell into the last category. Why would anyone possibly think bright orange and blue would go together, unless they were a Boise State fan? Her shoes were quite possibly handcrafted a hundred years ago, and her tattered skirt looked as though she found it in a dusty box tucked away in an attic. However, the zebra patterned gloves actually appeared to be from this decade.

"Well, it's rather fortunate that you didn't dribble. Mr. Ruth would have a fit if he became familiar with the underside of your pee-soaked shoe," the girl said, petting the stuffed animal's head. Her accent was none that I'd heard before—and I'd lived in a lot of different places. She sounded like a British gal impersonating a southern bell. "It'd be quite regrettable if anything happened to him on the first day of school. He must have fallen out of his hidey-hole."

"You named your stuffed rabbit, *Mr. Ruth*?"

She covered the bunny's ears. "Rutherford is his proper name, but he *hates* it and makes all the other rumperbabbits call him by his nickname."

"Rumperbabbits?"

"Bunnies, rabbits, hares—rumperbabbits. Same thing," she said with a wink. She had the most volatile light-blue eyes that were so electrifying I couldn't look away.

Time out—just for reference, I didn't believe in juvenile notions, like love at first sight. In my book, time didn't cease to move forward when two people fell in love. As a matter-of-fact, I'd have to be drunk (not on love) for such an irrational idea to enter my mind.

But, there was no denying the euphoric disposition of this girl; she had a mischievous charm. I wouldn't have said that I necessarily liked it, but it was intriguing. *She* was intriguing… and new. For a town whose newspaper's biggest story was the harvest report, having a new girl in school would most likely be headlined on *The Gossiper's* front page.

She crammed the animal into a mesh, side pocket of her backpack that had been intended for a bottled drink. After securing her rabbit, she dug into her pocket. Pulling out a bright blue candy wrapped in wax paper, she introduced herself as Alice Mae and then popped the candy into her mouth.

It brought my attention to her outlandish lipstick. I didn't know much about makeup, except that it itched like the dickens. Last spring, I participated in the One Act Plays. It was the *only* reason why I knew the difference between lip gloss and lipstick.

Scout's honor.

Clearly, Alice Mae wasn't a makeup connoisseur either, judging from her bright purple eye shadow that she paired with the light blue lipstick smudged halfway on her lips. The illusion looked like she was in a perpetual kissing state. She had the genetics to be naturally beautiful—high cheekbones, porcelain skin, pouty lips, and that silky, blonde hair that drove most men into an aphrodisiacal state of desire. Yet, she painted over it to create the illusion that she wasn't as attractive as the girls who made this year's homecoming candidate list, like Courtney. Remember her? I thought. Again, I couldn't emphasize enough my disbelief in soul-mates or that meeting Alice Mae was in no way prolific. Courtney mattered, not this random girl. But, I couldn't dismiss the fact that I'd literally stared at her lips for the better part of a minute, so I shot up a prayer hoping that she hadn't noticed.

"You're new here," I said.

*Good one, genius.*

"Do you always point out observations, or are you simply worried about this particularly crucial day of the educational system?" Alice Mae asked.

"Huh?"

She stuck her thumb out over her shoulder, pointing at the brick building that had our school mascot, a fighting raven, embroidered on a green flag that was hanging on a white chipped flag pole. "You're going to be late for the first day of school if you don't hurry along."

Almost everyone had left the school parking lot and had made their way inside the turn-of-the-century building. I glanced at the worn wrist watch that used to be my dad's. Once upon a time it was bronze, but those days were long past for this timepiece. The spade etched at the top was almost worn away. Three minutes passed eight—two minutes until the second bell would ring. My usually levelheaded mom would flip out and transform into this berserk tyrant if Wittrock, the principal, called her because of my tardiness.

"Save me a seat in the detention office, buddy!" Dax yelled from his *Yota* as he drove to a vacant parking spot a block down. The *T* and *O* had long since fallen off the clunker of a car, but it ran great considering the odometer had rolled over twice. Dax was a loyal kind of guy—even to beat down cars.

11

"Dax doesn't move very fast in the morning. He has a love affair with his snooze button," I explained to Alice Mae. It wasn't that I owed her an explanation, but she had given him the most perplexing look.

"I used to be BFF's with the snooze button too," Alice Mae said. "But that was before I understood the importance of a ticking clock, and nonticking clocks."

"Is that supposed to be a metaphor about wasting time?"

"No, to convince a ticking clock to stop is just an unattainable ambition I strive to attain to end what has already been set in motion," she said absent-mindedly. "Of course, it's been predicted my wrongness will overshadow my accomplishments so my impossible endeavor is just another pathetic, traitorous attempt to sway the unrelenting, apocalyptic reign of Hearts."

*Huh?*

She turned her attention back to me, giving me a quick once over. I brushed the breakfast bar crumbs off my shirt and tried not to let Alice Mae know that her visual inspection had thrown me.

"*You* look like you've been up for hours, dressed so impeccably in your ripped jeans and stained t-shirt," she said.

I hadn't exactly gotten a clean shirt from my closet this morning; but in my defense, I had given my shirt the Sniff Test. No BO, so I figured I was good to go. "A little food never hurt anyone."

She flicked the bill of my cap up. "Attire aside, you have *his* eyes, and that's all that really matters. See you around, Ryley."

I grabbed her arm when she turned to walk away. She didn't tell me to take my hand off her, but she cocked an eyebrow and glared so viciously I was sure she'd left a number of dead in the wake of that stare.

"I don't like to be touched after traveling from..." she said, clearly bothered that I'd infiltrated her personal bubble. "It just stings, okay!"

"How do you know my name?" I loosened my grip on her a little. Since I hadn't squeezed hard, I figured the wincing pain in her eyes was an act. "Have we met before?"

"We've never been formally introduced." Her eyes glossed over, like she was seeing me, but not really. The brilliant blue of her eyes lightened, which was physically impossible and eerily chilling. Batting away my hand, she spat, "Your auburn hair is as untidy as Mr. Edgar's. He'd be pleased you two look so alike, especially since you have a *girlish* name."

She smiled a fierce little smirk and turned away just as Dax approached me. Her step was light and bouncy, dancing to the theme song of her life.

Dax slapped his hand on my shoulder. "Who's the new dame?"

"Her name is Alice Mae," I said without taking my eyes off of her. "She knows about my dad, mentioned him by name."

"No one in Rockingham knows about your old man except me and your mom. That secret is locked down tight—Secret Service style."

"She said I have his eyes."

"It's not like he is suddenly going to walk back into your life. He'd have to find you first," Dax said, reassuringly. "Too many years have passed for him to be a part of your life again."

# CHAPTER TWO

(Alice Mae: Present Time)

Closing my assigned locker door behind me, I stood up inside of it as much as I was able. My head skimmed the metal top. What I'd give for a sip of *Drink Me* juice so I could fit properly inside.

The locker wasn't nearly big enough to provide everything needed for proper education, much less to conduct surveillance. This was my eleventh school I'd attended in my search for a boy named Ryley Edward Edgar. He and Lauren jumped ship and moved more frequently than a band of fugitives on the run. But, I supposed they were just that; persons of interest, being hunted by a royal twat. I wondered if Robby dropped the bomb and told them about the nightmare he escaped from, or the life he left behind in Wonderland.

After my most recent incident with the Queen of Hearts, I'd been "encouraged" to complete a search and rescue mission for the boy. Along with everyone else in Wonderland, I desperately needed to please Hearts. If I somehow screwed up this assignment, I feared that the next time I returned to Wonderland, I'd be in two separate pieces—my head and my body. Thus, my obligation to the queen was clear: Bring Ryley Edward Edgar to Wonderland using *any* means necessary.

I was ninety-nine percent sure that I'd finally found the infamous boy that Hearts wanted. Even so, I had to be one hundred percent sure this dorky boy was the one she wanted. I wasn't taking any chances, not anymore.

"After I take his photo *and am sure he is the one*, you'll need to deliver this to Hearts, Mr. Ruth." I held up the white rabbit and looked him square in the eye. The bunny didn't move. Yet, I knew he heard me. "But not until I'm confident he is the one she wants. I don't need another lesson in tactical reconnaissance from the Joker."

I carefully set Mr. Ruth down so I could get to my camera. My fabulous, perfect, fashionable heels barricaded the bunny between my ankles. I didn't care if he wasn't animated when he was in the form of a stuffed animal. I knew from past experience that the moment I wasn't paying attention, he would transform into a living mini lop and hop away faster than I could say *runaway rumperbabbits romp around in ridiculous rendezvous residences.*

Peering through the locker vents, I memorized the hallway since I hadn't much time to study the school's layout before enrolling so had to study the blueprints in more depth tonight. Nevertheless, I knew my locker was nowhere close to his, and I needed to document his existence without too many watchful eyes. So I needed to get creative. Thus, I'd stalled to keep Ryley from making it to class on time. I hoped my efforts weren't in vain and waited for the young man with a disheveled hairstyle to stroll by my locker from the principals.

Not more than ten minutes later, Ryley walked by with a pink slip in his hand. I squealed then slapped my hand over my mouth, hoping to prevent more noises from fleeing. He eyed my locker, and I swore that he could see me spying on him through the metal slits. His russet colored eyes darkened in the same way his father's had when suffering with male-PMS.

Even if I hadn't "befriended" Robby Edgar, I'd know Ryley was a *wondrous* specimen. His chameleon-like eyes darkened and lightened, depending on his emotions. It was a trait only known to people who had associations with Wonderland. Mine changed too, but it was only by happenstance from spending so much time in that realm. *A big thank you to the Joker for that,* I thought bitterly.

I snatched my vintage Polaroid camera from my backpack. "Smile pretty for the camera, you nincompoop."

# CHAPTER THREE

(Ryley: Present Time)

Insanity—plainly defined as a deranged state of mind or lacking the ability to rationalize. Hands shot into the air when the half-deaf literature teacher, Mr. Blanch, asked for the interpretation of Ernest Hemingway's deteriorating mental condition. He circled the desks with his hands behind his back. Wrinkles lined his button-up shirt and there was a stain on his pants that had to have been there since spring semester. It was one of the many markers that made me believe the rumors that "wife-number-three" skipped town. Also, a tan line encircled his finger where his ring had been.

Mr. Blanch stopped circling the room and leaned against his desk, which never had a single paper on it. As far as I was concerned, the desk was purely decorative.

"Care to explain what mental illness the infamous author suffered from, Miss Frick?" Mr. Blanch asked.

"Dementia," Courtney said, flipping her red hair over her shoulder—her signature move. "The infamous author was clearly deranged, even though he was brilliant."

Most buddies in my class deemed gingers to be either smokin' hot or ugly as sin. Like with most stereotypes, I didn't take much of a stand, but

I bet that a gang of starving vampires wouldn't eat her because she was so drop-dead gorgeous. She batted her ridiculously long eye lashes that framed her bright green eyes. She was beautiful and smart—if you were into that kind of thing. And judging from all the sideways glances the guys in my class were giving her, I wasn't the only one wanting to call her *mine*.

"—do you think? Ryley Edgar, am I boring you?"

Verbal diarrhea, coming out in the form of an "umm," was my reply. Mr. Blanch crossed his arms over his chest. He could have called me out, since it was completely obvious I had no clue what he'd asked, but he had *some* tact. I swear he could sense when his students were losing focus, or perhaps he just singled out the male students who had drool dripping down their chins.

Courtney turned around in her chair and mouthed me the answer. For all I knew, she was speaking French because I was god-awful at reading lips, especially hers. I was as functional as a brain-dead sloth when I looked at her lips.

"Speak up, Ryley," Mr. Blanch said. "You know I can't hear out of my right ear after the IED detonated in my Humvee."

Had I mentioned that this teacher was a decorated war hero? I'd never seen him in anything other than a long sleeve shirt, even though summer in Rockingham felt about as refreshing as huddling in a blast furnace.

A knock at the door saved me, or so I thought. In walked the last girl I expected to see, Alice Mae. She strode in with a sense of confidence most girls would never have wearing her getup. She had to be color blind.

Alice Mae handed Mr. Blanch a note. He read it quickly and said, "Ah yes, Miss Liddell, I heard through the grapevine that the Mighty Ravens were expecting a new student."

Mr. Blanch pointed to a seat next to me and said that he needed to continue with class if we were going to stay on track for the school year. I fought the urge to leave the second Alice Mae's keister touched the plastic seat beside mine. I won't admit that I was checking out her butt, but she did lower her hand and waved until I looked up.

Great, now she probably thought I was into her. This day couldn't get any worse. Mr. Blanch continued on with his lecture, but I wasn't listening. Every one of my brain molecules was focused on Alice Mae. My mind was spinning trying to figure out she knew my name before I mentioned anything, and how she knew my dad was alive.

She smiled apologetically. As if reading my mind, she said, "Your father is—"

"Don't bring him up, not again, not ever," I said in a low voice and glanced up at the teacher. Mr. Blanch armed himself with a dry erase marker and was standing in front of the newly furnished white boards that had been screwed in over the old black boards. There was still chalk on the ledge. Apparently the school budget provided for new state-of-the-art paraphernalia, but wasn't going to be bothered to clean out the old technology—like chalk and erasers. That was a small town for you. When Mr. Blanch turned around to write, I leaned over to Alice Mae so I wouldn't have to speak loudly. "If you cherish your reputation at all, you won't mention him in public ever again. Or I'll make it my personal mission to ensure that your life is so miserable your nightmares give you warm-fuzzies."

She mumbled something that sounded like "get in line."

"Ryley, let's have another go at this," Mr. Blanch said grimly.

There were times I thought he was faking the whole part-deaf bit. Or the last decade of teaching had conditioned him to the signs of when his students weren't paying attention. I sat up tall in my seat.

"Do you suppose all his brilliance led to Hemingway's untimely death?" Mr. Blanch asked.

I shifted nervously. I didn't like to discuss such matters of insanity, especially not in class. I guess it wasn't like anyone knew about my family history of mental illness, except for Dax, and apparently Alice Mae. I was determined to keep everyone else in the dark. There wasn't any need for them to know my dad wasn't playing with a full deck.

"I suppose," I said, keeping my voice even. "Eccentric people are prone to insanity. It is believed that musicians, writers, and artists are susceptible to psychosis. That's why they can create such great works, but it

18

comes at the price of their sanity."

"I beg to differ." Alice Mae fiddled with her pencil, not the standard number two. Oh, no—she held a purple colored pencil with several bite marks.

Mr. Blanch said, "Enlighten us why."

Alice Mae opened her mouth to explain further, but then jumped in her seat like someone startled her. She kicked her backpack and cursed under her breath. From the bunny reference, I assumed that Mr. Ruth had upset her somehow. The stuffed animal was by her feet, but I hadn't seen her take him out.

"Your departure is premature," she scolded so quietly, I was positive I was the only one who'd heard her. "I said to deliver it to Hearts *after* I was sure he is the one."

When our eyes locked, she smiled. It wasn't the kind of smile that one wore for a camera. No, she smiled like she was committing a crime and was going to thoroughly enjoy it.

She nudged the rabbit with her foot. "Fine! Deliver it to the queen when no one is looking, but if I'm mistaken, it's your head, Mr. Ruth."

Inside the mesh pocket where Mr. Ruth belonged was a trademark square-picture of an instant photo. On the picture was me. Me!?!? When had she taken a picture of me? A heart was scratched around my face. I glanced at her fingernails; the photo residue was embedded in her nails. She grabbed her stuffed animal and shoved it back in the mesh pocket, hiding the Polaroid.

Mr. Blanch tapped his desk, using the red marker he had used to make the whiteboard bleed ink. He asked again, "Why do you disagree with Ryley's observation, Miss Liddell?"

Alice Mae looked like she was surprised to see him still in the room. She shook her head, clearing her mind. When she spoke again, she was as self-assured as ever. "Crazed or disillusioned—people know they are certifiably insane, or they haven't come to the realization that they belonged in a straightjacket... yet."

19

I cringed when she said *straightjacket*. No one else in the class seemed to notice my adverse effect to *that* word, except Alice Mae. She tilted her head to the side and sucked harder on whatever candy she had in her mouth.

"That's an interesting perspective." Mr. Blanch went on with the lecture, discussing the various authors who had mental illnesses. Marquis de Sade, Leo Tolstoy, Sylvia Plath, and others made the list.

I couldn't disagree with Alice Mae's definition of insanity—not completely. Everyone was a little bit nuts, in their own way, but we all weren't completely bonkers. Granted, some people were a wee bit crazier than others. Usually, most kept their madness hidden, but it was clear that Alice Mae chose to embrace her lunacy. She should try out for the One Acts this spring. She was theatrical, to say the least.

As soon as the bell rang I asked, "When did you take my picture?"

"A photograph? Of you?" she asked, picking up her backpack. The rabbit and the photo had vanished. She shrugged her backpack over her shoulders and smiled innocently. "To which photo are you referring?"

"You can play dumb all you want, but I know that you have a Polaroid with my face on it," I said. "It was behind that stupid rabbit."

Alice Mae winced when I said *stupid,* but recovered quickly with an inviting smile. "Why Ryley, aren't you a little full of yourself?" she said, and rolled the candy against her teeth. "If I wasn't mistaken, I'd say that you imagined the photo and the bunny."

"Right, I made the whole thing up," I said sarcastically.

"A confession. Fabulous! I didn't think we'd get to this part of the game so quickly," she said, and glanced at the watch my father gave me. She stared just a little too long to be merely curious. The edges of her lips tugged when she noticed the spade etched into it.

Why shouldn't I be surprised that she picked out the *only* thing that had belonged to my father—a man that no one else knew was alive? "What game?" I said, covering the timepiece with my hand.

"Let's pretend we're playing a Who's Who game but everyone's a

20

liar," she whispered flirtatiously. "It is rather curious why you'd fantasize about me taking your picture, don't you think?"

"What do you want with me?"

She wiggled her finger. I stood up and stepped as close to the girl as I could manage. She glanced over her shoulders to make sure no one was listening, and then she stood on her tiptoes to whisper in my ear.

"It is not *me* who wants anything from you."

With that, she turned around and pranced out the door. I stood numbly by my desk. It took a bit for me to process her comment. She didn't want anything from me, but someone did? What the hell did that mean? I grabbed my backpack and chased after her. However, Courtney was waiting for me in the hall. Normally, this would be cause for celebration. Now, it was just irritating. Alice Mae had gotten away.

"What's up?" I asked, stealing a look down the hall to see if Alice Mae was still in sight. Maybe I could still catch up with her.

She walked as close to the hall lockers as possible. When she passed a lock, she tapped it with a bobby pin. If the lock was opened, it closed. If the lock was closed, it opened.

Was she a witch casting spells on the locks? I rubbed my eyes; I had to be seeing things.

"—my parents are going to the lake house this weekend," Courtney's fingers were turning white from holding her books so tight.

I rubbed the back of my neck and stole another glance at Alice Mae. More unbelievable than the unlocking locks business was what I saw next. She was chatting with Becky, Courtney's best bud and co-captain of the cheer squad. Becky was the Asian version of Courtney: fit, pretty, and smart, and had just a little too much sass.

*What could those two possibly have in common?*

Courtney cleared her throat. "So do you want to come over to my place on Saturday and watch a movie or not?"

"I have other plans this weekend."

"With Alice Mae?"

I laughed, "Not in the foreseeable future."

Becky and Alice Mae parted ways. What had they been talking about? Becky was head cheerleader and Alice Mae... well, I couldn't picture her with pom-poms.

Courtney asked, "Then why are you still looking at her?"

I snapped my attention back to the redhead. "I'm not." Obvious lie, but what was I supposed to say?

Courtney didn't look convinced either. "I'll be right there, Becky. Ryley was just blowing me off."

I pulled out my phone and recorded a voice message to Courtney. "I swear that I am not interested in Alice Mae. She is a pathetic attempt for a girl—for a human being. You're the one I want, Courtney. So how about I take you out another weekend? We could check out Aftershock." I hit the send button. Her phone buzzed a second later.

"You can say what you want, but that freak still turns your brain into mush," Courtney said wounded.

I knew I was being a simpleton, but I couldn't pinpoint the reason why she was so miffed. "Ummm, I'm sorry? You think you have competition with her? You're the hottest thing in this building!"

"For someone who is supposed to be a genius, you can be very dense." She snapped her fingers in front of me and then made a face. "You suggest hitting up a club *after* I asked you to hang out with me without *parentals*?"

No parental supervision?

It *just* registered that Courtney had asked me to come over to her house—alone. What was I thinking? Why was I acting so stupid? I opened my mouth, hoping that sounds would come out in a coherent sentence. Instead, I made an unmanly sound that I'd rather soon forget.

22

# Chapter Four

(Alice Mae: The First visit to Wonderland)

"A world where the impossibilities of our most far-fetched dreams come true—that was the essence of Wonderland."

M.H, my mentor but more commonly known as the Mad Hatter, had said those very words during my first visit to the wondrous world of Wonderland, nearly eleven years ago. What he should have said was: Wonderland was a magical world where the most far-fetched dreams come true. Alas, it is also where intoxicating nightmares run rampant.

The best times of my life happened in Wonderland, and also the worst. But, I was getting ahead of myself. It all started with a rabbit, a sly rumperbabbit to be exact…

… A pesky white bunny had been munching on my best carrots, which I appreciated as much as being hit over the head with a swab of used toilet paper. Thus, it was the reason for the garden pursuit. I tracked down that rabbit, following it into a hole next to my aunt's apple tree.

My first fall down the rabbit hole—a porthole to Wonderland—was a painstaking one. It wasn't so much because the drop felt like a free-fall from a five story building, or that I had been so sure I would be a splat in the center of the Earth, but because I kept reaching out with my arms in an effort to slow my descent. The rock walls scraped my skin and bruised my bones. The dirt embedded under my nails. I crashed to the bottom of the hole, but I hadn't died, so I called it a win.

None of this dirtiness would have happened if I hadn't chased a rather uncatchable rabbit in the first place. My parents had sent me to live with my overly stern aunts because of unruly behavior that was unbecoming of a woman. At least that was what my aunts told me, but I had another theory. My folks sent me to live with them in hopes I'd straighten up out of sheer boredom.

It didn't work…

… And so the story went: After I drank what needed to be drunk and ate what needed to be eaten, I had unlocked a mouse door that was guarded by a ceramic toad wearing a suit with a spade and the initials R.E. sewn on it. In its mouth was a bronze key that unlocked a mysterious realm I thought was possible only in my dreams. The colors of the sky and land were all wrong. The blue sky was too dark and was littered with dozens of sun dogs, like it was a dumping ground for rainbows. The ground beneath my feet was dark as mud but wasn't wet. The leaves growing on the trees were multicolored like flowers, but the flowers were too big. One petal was the size of my head. I felt like an ant that crawled out from the dull dirt and into a spray painted world of wonders. The door I'd squeezed through was covered by bright yellow vines, essentially trapping me in this place.

A purple caterpillar lay on a branch of a white magnolia tree, munching on a blue leaf. He looked at me, and I swore the little creature raised its eyebrow as if it was unimpressed with me.

"Where am I?" I asked, talking to myself.

"Where you are, is a state of being, a place in your head and a location in Wonderland—far, far from your own," the caterpillar said before taking another bite of the leaf. "But more importantly, where you are standing is on private land. You're trespassing on my property."

My mouth dropped open. "You can talk!"

He spit out the leaf bits he'd been chewing and stuffed them into the tiniest hookah in the known universe. "Did you think you were the only privileged creature who had the ability to communicate using fancy words, stupid girl?"

"Ester, stop bugging the discombobulated girl." A gentleman walked over to me. He was dressed in a new white suit and tipped his top hat. The price tag was still hanging from the hat. His white soul patch matched the color of his hair, though the locks upon his head were more peppered gray. Gold rimmed goggles covered his eyes. A bright orange scarf was tied around his neck. His black-polished fingernails were tinted a slew of different colors. Traces of pink powder the size of sugar dusted his clothing. He smelled like apple pie and gumdrops.

I wondered if the man had been baking. "Who are you, sir?"

He took off his goggles, revealing the kindest eyes I'd ever seen—they looked like chocolate chips. There was a little bit of a fanatical look in them as well. The eye shadow was flicked on his eyelids, like he had been trying to recreate donut sprinkles with makeup. "My name is far too complicated to say and gets quite boring to listen to. Simply saying it will give your tongue a workout that is unnecessary. Far too much time will be wasted by constantly addressing me by it. Thus, I go by M.H, my dear girl. What is your name?"

"Alice Mae," I said.

The caterpillar groaned. "The One-Eyed Hare brought a *girl* with a *girl's* name to Wonderland, not a *girl* with a *boy's* name. Did Rutherford even bother to read the prophecy he found in the *Sweets for the Rabbit Hole Voyager* recipe book?"

"There is much still to uncover. The white rabbit has excellent intuition," M.H. said. "And you know he prefers to go by Mr. Ruth. He'll get his tail in a twist if he hears you utter his proper name."

"Rumperbabbits are oversensitive about what the other creatures call them. They should be lucky they have names at all, despicable creatures."

Having trouble following their sidebar discussion about degraded rabbits, I asked, "What does M.H. stand for? I'll still call you by the abbreviation, but it has made me curious. Perhaps it would be okay to tie your tongue to say it, just this once?"

"Marco Hickerns? Marian Hoff? Oh! Perhaps Massive Human?" The caterpillar lit the hookah and took a drag. A blueberry aroma accompanied the smoke that Ester blew out his nose. "M.H. Has never told a soul his name. So we call the Madman the Hatter."

"I will, and have always preferred to, go by M.H. instead of indulging in the silly nickname given to me by the critters of this realm. Mad Hatter, can you believe it? Silly name," M. H. said, but then pressed his finger to his lip. After a moment of pondering, he licked his finger and made a face like the colorful substance lining his fingers wasn't to his liking. "I do suppose that nicknames hold the utmost significance, at times. Or is it the time that makes the nicknames significant?"

"When would nicknames ever hold any value?" I asked.

"When they are given appropriately!" M.H. placed his hands on his knees so that we were eye level. "My name is nothing of importance to you. Still, your name is one that *may* matter, but we'll get to that in due time. Would you like some candy?" He held up his littlest finger to me like I was to lick it.

I gently pushed his hand away. "My parents told me never to take candy from strangers."

"Well, they are quite smart! It's a shame the Maude sisters stole you away from them."

"They didn't. They told me I was a troublemaker and needed proper watching over," I said, mimicking Vida Maude.

"I suppose it doesn't matter why you came to be in their possession. But a more significant point is that you are in fact a trouble maker, or at least I hope you are. And you will not be eating candy, my dear girl," he said, and wrapped his hand around the finger he offered me to lick. With a quick jerk, the finger came off. I wanted to scream when he handed it to me, but I kept my emotions under control. "It's a caramel shell, my dear girl. One lick and you won't feel like asking so many questions; a defense tactic of sorts."

I didn't know exactly what he meant by that, but I took his word. "Then why make candy if you aren't to enjoy them?"

26

"I make candy because I have a bit of a sweet tooth, but sometimes others need them for unconventional reasons. I can show you if you want."

I didn't know what I was getting myself into, but I knew I didn't want to spend any more time with a bug that called me stupid. I handed him back his caramel finger, which he tucked in his coat pocket.

"Who needs camouflaged caramel?" I asked.

"A dear friend of mine—Robby. He needs all the help he can get, which weighs heavily on my candy making abilities," M.H. said and looked at a pocket watch. The numbers were written backwards. The second hand turned clockwise, but the hour hand ticked counterclockwise. "We're going to miss our flight if we don't get a move on."

"Are you trying to turn back time?" I asked, ignoring his comment about flying.

M.H. gave me a hard look before sliding on his goggles. His kind, brown eyes shimmered like the ocean when the sun shone upon it. "It is not the reversal of time I strive for, my dear girl. It is to prevent it from moving completely; an impossible feat that is yet to occur."

"If it's impossible, then why try?"

"Because then the Reign of Terror shall end," M.H. chuckled and exchanged a knowing look with the caterpillar who had been munching more leaves for his hookah. "A world where the impossibilities of our most far-fetched dreams come true—that is the essence of Wonderland."

Looking around the upside-down realm, I certainly agreed that things were possible in this world that were not in mine.

"I promise you that you'll never have more exciting adventures than the ones you'll have in Wonderland. It is my greatest hope that you fall in love with this place and the people who live here," he said, and offered me his hand. "Come and see for yourself. I'll give you the bird's eye view of Wonderland before I show you my candy shoppe."

M.H. wiggled his charred eyebrows and dragged his hand through his singed hair as he inspected the ruins of the discarded seating contraption that had been strapped to Omar, an oversized, flying egret. However, the seat had been intact before the bird had antagonized Lowery, a penguin splashing in a nearby cold spring.

The flying adventure was promptly cut short after the argument as to which bird was more suitable for flight—an egret or penguin. The ratchet straps broke promptly after Omar nosedived to duel the lowly penguin. When the seat came loose, it sent M.H. and I spiraling out of control. We collided into a cluster of hot rocks, where the dragon lizards socialized.

"You madman!" A purple lizard screamed as it raced toward us.

Other lizards came out of hiding when rocks were no longer shooting through the air. They went to work collecting the rocks and putting them into piles. Apparently there was a dispute to which location would be the best since M.H.'s flying apparatus was burning in their original place.

"Calm down, Liz," M.H. said to the infuriated purple lizard. He took off his broken goggles and tossed them into the fire.

"Calm down? Don't you see what you've done?" Liz yelled. "You've caused anarchy in our village. Get that flying contraption off the rocks now!"

"But it's on fire," I said.

"Do you think I'm blind, stupid girl?" Liz yelled. "I don't care if your pants are on fire. I want that pile of junk off my property!"

"In due time," M.H. said, glancing at his pocket watch.

"In due time, he says," Liz mimicked, as she eyed M.H.'s backside.

It was in that moment that I realized these lizards were actually fire breathing amphibians. Liz set M.H.'s pants on fire. He took off running like a rocket ship, patting his butt as he ran. His top hat fell off as he hopped over the sizzling rocks. Since I didn't particularly want to keep the rampant lizards company, I chased after him, grabbing his hat along the way.

"Stop, you stupid girl! You and the madman must stop!" Liz shook her fist at me as I raced across the hot rocks after M.H.

I giggled, recalling the absurdly tall M.H. running away from the wreckage, slapping a fire from his buttocks. Fortunately, he wore suspenders to keep his trousers from falling to his ankles, since the fire had eaten away much of the material around the waistline. The hole revealed his bright blue underwear with his initials sewn on with green thread.

"Well, I suppose a visit to Miss Genevine is of the utmost importance," M.H. said, inspecting his backside.

"Who's Genevine?" I asked, handing him his hat that had fallen when he was distracted by his fiery pants.

He dusted off the hat, which had no dirt on it, but paid no attention to the charred edges. After shoving it on his head, he bent down to my level. "Genevine is a nasty old lady with the longest ear hair you'd ever imagine. But, such thin hair is essential for what she does, especially since her spiders are on strike. Oh! Never mention her oversized anklet."

"That makes positively no sense."

"It will, my dear girl. One day our ways will be of the complete absolution, and your ways will become positively senseless." He gently took my hand. "The Jack of Diamonds wrote to me before my existence ever came into being."

"Who is the Jack of Diamonds?"

"Once he was a very rich man but that was before Hearts demoted him to a glorified butler," M.H. said scornfully. "And his great-great-grandson, the Joker, is a poor substitution as a forecaster… Jack had made mistakes in his predictions before, but not as often as the Joker. Conversely, the old man was known to be missing a few cards in his deck, which is probably because the Joker constantly steals his playing cards to practice his demented magic."

"So the Jack was a rich prophet before he became butler?" I asked, thinking of the only logical way a man could write another before being born. "Did the Jack say anything about me?"

M.H. pulled the 10/6 price tag from his hat. Taped to the back was a yellowed note. After carefully unfolding it, he handed it to me. Written in red ink was the Jack's prophecy.

*BackWards Wanderer Prophecy: A strong-Willed child shall set the time-stalemate into motion, but only if a tWo-eyed hare can lure her to the Wonderful World of Wonderland. She Will be given a choice to live Wondrously forever or be banished to Weep in her homeland. Seconds Will tick forWard and backWards until her decision no longer Wavers. HoWever, she Will choose Wrong.*

# CHAPTER FIVE

(Ryley: Present Time)

*The crazy ones have the most fun.* That was the reasoning of most warm-blooded males. Well, it was my friend Mick's, logic anyway. He was the one who'd brought it up.

"I thought it was blondes who had the most fun," Dax chimed in innocently, looking at Mick's light colored hair. But, I knew better than to think that Dax's sideways glance was purely innocent. So would anyone, if they took two seconds to see how he looked at Mick.

"Well, then it's a double whammy!" Mick laughed, and put his arm over my shoulder like we were going to have a version of a father/son pep talk. "Alice Mae is nutty *and* a natural blonde. I would know—I sat behind Becky and Courtney during second period algebra. For the entire hour, they had a heated discussion about hair. Hair! I didn't realize there was so much to discuss. Anyway, by the time the bell rang they agreed—no, *swore* to high-holy-heaven—that Alice Mae's hair was indeed a natural blonde, but Becky was sure she saw extensions, whatever that means."

"Maybe you should go for her," I said, shrugging off Mick's arm.

Dax metaphorically kicked me in the shin.

31

We walked through the halls to our sixth period class. Weight Training. It filled the physical education requirement and freed up an hour after school. Just because it was baseball's off-season didn't mean we got a free pass for the school year. Our coach required us to train year-round if we had any shot at state next summer. After changing in the locker rooms, we headed to the school's basement; a glorified storage closet where all the old sports uniforms and band suits went to die. Before my time, the school council agreed to put up a false wall in the middle so there would be somewhere to put the new weights.

It'd been decades since anyone could call the weights new, but the old metal fulfilled its purpose. Dax lay down on the old, red pad that had been donated a decade ago by the aerobics instructor when her gym went out of business. He began knocking out the second set of our pyramid workout.

"You hear anything about what Alice Mae and Becky were talking about?" I asked, nonchalantly.

"No," Mick said, crossing his arms. "Why are you so interested in what Alice Mae does and who she talks to? You interested in shackin' up with the new girl?"

"I have my eye on Courtney."

Pushing the bar up, Dax grunted. "Maybe the both of you should leave the poor girl alone."

"Let the poor girl be?" Mick said. "And rob her of the experience of dating a good looking guy like me? Besides, someone's got to show her around Rockingham."

I guided the bar to the rack when Dax completed his eighth repetition. "You act like it's your civic duty to—"

"Scar the girl for life," Dax interrupted as he sat upright. "When was the last time you dated a girl for longer than a month?"

Not wanting to get in the middle of Dax and Mick's nonexistent love affair I bailed. "I'm going to grab a drink."

On my way to the drinking fountain upstairs, I overheard Alice

Mae's voice. I froze. While Alice Mae might be bat-crazy, I had to admit she had a mesmerizing voice. So when I was able to convince my legs to move, I took on the role of a creeper. I'd never admit it to another soul, but I peered around the freshman hallway and searched for her. I rationalized it; if she had some sort of scoop on my dad, I needed to prepare for a possible retaliation. Everyone had dirt—I just had to figure out hers.

She leaned against the furthest locker, next to the girls' bathroom, and pulled on the ruffles of her skirt while Mrs. Dotson, the music director, bragged about the Raven swing choir. She'd taught at Rockingham for twenty four years and hadn't lost her spirited enthusiasm.

"Of course, you can use the classroom during your free period! And, I think you should really consider joining the choir," Mrs. Dotson said eagerly and handed her a stack of papers. "You have the natural octave for All-State soprano."

Alice Mae shoved the papers into her locker. It was the second day of school, and her locker was already crammed full with random junk— plastic soldiers, dozens of torn folders, a monocle, fingernail polish, one striped sock, two empty water bottles, a bungee cord, sparklers, and a vintage camera... A ball of purple yarn bounced out before she was able to shut the door. It rolled on the floor, zigzagging sporadically, as if an invisible cat was pouncing on it.

While Mrs. Dotson chatted on and on about the glory of the Rockingham choir, Alice Mae stopped the ball with her foot. I was ninety-nine percent sure that Alice Mae sneered at the ball, but I was too far away to know with *absolute* clarity. While Mrs. Dotson talked about Alice Mae's future music career, the girl looked straight at me; like someone had tipped her off that I was creeping from around the corner.

Possible reaction strategies included: tiptoeing backwards, playing the total stalker role and stare back, or manning-up.

Alice Mae was clearly up to something; she had admitted it; we were playing a game. Who's Who—whatever that meant. And she confessed to being a liar, in passing anyway. If she wanted to play games, I'd give it a go.

Wearing a smug grin, she bent over and picked up the ball. While she slowly twirled the string back around the ball, she never took her eyes off of me. I pretended not to be unnerved by her glaring stare as I approached her.

"What's up, Mrs. D?" I asked.

"It's Mrs. Dotson," she corrected. Her hands were on her hips like my mom would do when she was scolding me, but there were the makings of a smile on her face. "I was just trying to convince Alice to join—"

"I prefer to go by *Alice Mae*."

"My apology, I'll give you a few days to mull it over, but I think you could really be phenomenal in the choir. Maybe you'd consider singing the National Anthem before one of the football games."

"I'll ponder it," Alice Mae said.

*I'll ponder it?* Who talked like that nowadays?

Mrs. Dotson said, "Keep on her, won't you, Ryley? Alice Mae has a charismatic voice, wouldn't you agree?"

What was I supposed to say? Yeah, she sounded enchanting, but then again sirens lured unsuspecting sailors to their watery deaths with their alluring song. Thus, I shrugged my shoulders. "She sounds like a girl."

"A girl?" Alice Mae repeated. "Was it my hair or my makeup that tipped you off that I am a female? Or possibly you noticed my dress when you were staring at my arse? Shall I give you a sticker for identifying me as a girl by the sound of my voice?"

"Ummm," I said and then turned my embarrassing, audible response into a cough.

Mrs. Dotson fell for Alice Mae's infectious smile. The teacher beamed. "Your vocabulary amazes me as well, Ryley. For someone who's gunning for a highly coveted physics scholarship, one would think that you'd have more well-rounded language skills," Mrs. Dotson said with just the right amount of professionalism mixed with motherly assertiveness.

"I'll work on it," I said.

"Good," Mrs. Dotson said, looking at her wristwatch. After commenting that she had to get to class before the freshmen staged a heist, she walked away.

"A physics scholarship?" Alice Mae asked when Mrs. Dotson was out of hearing range. She squeezed the yarn ball into her locker. A few of the music papers slipped halfway through the bottom crack of her locker. Instead of opening the door, she shoved them back through the crack.

Since she only cracked the door, I highly suspected that there was more in her "Misfit Locker of Random Crapola" that she didn't want me to see. A racecar fell out of her locker and scooted across the floor like someone had pushed it. When I stopped it with my foot, some invisible thing smacked into my shoe as well—or I was losing it too.

Alice Mae glared at my foot like I'd somehow lured the toy car from her locker. I lifted my foot just enough so she could retrieve the vehicle. She picked up the car, careful not to touch me as she pulled the car out from under my foot.

"So what's it like being a brainiac?" she asked.

She fiddled with the car. If I had a vivid imagination, I'd have said it was a miniature replica of my dad's old beater. With her fingernail, she scratched the side, directly under the right fender. I didn't get a good look at it, but it looked like a top hat crest.

"I'm not that smart, just one of the only students who comprehends theoretical physics," I said and leaned against a random locker in an attempt to look casual. "What about you? I don't consider you to be very stupid, even though you'd like me to believe it."

"My stupidity…" she trailed off, losing herself in her thoughts. The blue in her eyes turned frosty, and she pressed her lips into a thin line. Her baby-blue eyes made her look naive, but I wasn't going to fall for it. She wasn't a moron. "My level of intelligence is dependent on who you ask. I'm not known for my remarkable noggin'."

"So you have a reputation of being dense," I said, more than asked. "I'm not really into labels, especially intellectual ones that stem from rumors."

I looked her up and down, searching for any clues that would give me a reason to how and why she knew my dad. I didn't know exactly what I was looking for, eyeing the particularly outlandish girl. She definitely wasn't trying to blend in, which had to mean she wasn't trying to hide. It exemplified her confidence, prancing around in a chic clown getup.

"I noticed your vintage camera was being crushed by a bungee cord, take any pictures lately? I mean, other than the ones of me?"

She gave me a knowing smile. "I am a sightseer."

"And a risk taker if you bungee jump," I said.

She smirked. It was a subtle gesture, only the very corners of her mouth twitched, but it was screamed *evil*, thus it was noteworthy. "You understand theoretical physics. A man who comprehends theories would be apt to make a few said theories himself. So, my question to you, Ryley, is what theories have you made about me, other than that I'm an adrenaline junkie and an amateur photographer?"

"They're inconclusive."

Alice Mae pushed the car through a vented slot in her locker. It fell to the bottom with a clang. How did the toy miss all the junk in her locker and hit bottom? There had been a solid layer of junk on the bottom of her locker.

After looking me up and down, she rolled her eyes and sighed heavily. "Did you need something, or were you only spying on me?"

"We're overdue for a chat."

"What topic would you like to have a little heart-to-heart about?" She asked while she reached into her pocket and retrieved a tiny pop bottle. She bit the top off and poured a blue substance into her mouth and took a bite of the bottle. It smelled like cherries. Instead of swallowing it, she chewed the bottle like it was gum.

"You know."

"How in the world would I possibly know what you want to discuss? I'm not a mind reader."

"What do you know about my dad?"

"You made it perfectly clear we weren't to discuss *that* person, *ever*," Alice Mae said. "It's really difficult to follow your thought process. First, you don't want to discuss family matters, and now, you seek me out like some scoundrel and demand that we discuss him."

I wanted to shake the answers out of this girl. "What do you know about him?"

"Who?"

"My dad!" My fists were balled up by my sides.

She covered her eyes and shook her head. "So I'm privileged enough to speak his name now? Oh dear, Vida Maude was right. You people change your minds more often than not! I've only talked to you once, twice if you count the very rude, interrupted conversation we had in literature class, and yet you've changed your mind in the matter of a single day."

"How do you know him?"

"He lit Zola Maude's hair on fire," Alice Mae said as a matter-of-fact. And then her expression changed from Miss Smarty Pants to a halfway-scared look. "I swear to the Queen of Hearts that if you come at me with a match, I'll kick you in your man bits."

"I'm not going to light your hair on fire," I said, even though the idea sounded appealing. "Why would I set you on fire?"

"I don't know how you people think," she said, looking over my shoulder. "I really should get going. I do believe a hall monitor is making his rounds. It'd be a crying shame for you to get another pink slip on the second day of school."

How did she know I got the first one? "Us people?" I asked, refusing to get distracted with the possibility of detention. It was what she wanted. How she knew I had gotten a tardy didn't matter. She was trying to throw me, which meant I was onto something. I stepped closer so I towered over her, hoping she'd be intimidated.

37

"I can't quite follow Otherworlders thought processes anymore," she said, and then trailed off like she revealed too much information. "You're an odd duck, you know that?"

The feeling was mutual.

She suddenly looked on top of the lockers like something had caught her eye. The soft echo of a cat's meow resonated. It was so faint I *had* to have imagined it, until I saw Alice Mae's eye twitch. Did she hear it too?

"What do you want now?" she said, not bothering to hide her annoyance.

Seriously? We were back to the beginning of our conversation again. I was getting a tension headache just from talking to this girl! Apparently migraines came with the territory. A hissing sound echoed in the hall. Since I saw no cat, the only logical explanation was that the school's pipes were malfunctioning.

"So Hearts did like the photo that Mr. Ruth delivered?" she asked.

Trying to follow the conversation detour, I said, "The photo that wasn't of me?"

"Precisely," she stated absent-mindedly. It was like she was having a conversation with someone else. Maybe her invisible friend? When she finally looked back at me, she wore a bored expression. "I hate to cut our unproductive conversation short, but I must go at once. I've been summoned and don't like to keep people waiting, especially the Queen B. I don't trust her around Mr. Ruth. They have a bad history," she said, and then slit her throat with her finger.

"You're not going anywhere until I get some answers."

"Let me know how that works out for you," she laughed and expertly turned on her heels.

"Answers. Spill!" I grabbed her arm. A whimper escaped her throat. My stomach dropped at the sound, but I pretended it didn't crumble my heart.

Her tiny hands were clenched so tight I actually thought she was going to backhand me. But she didn't move; she was frozen still. I could see the hardened look of pure anger in her eyes. Time was irrelevant as we had a staring contest. "Next time you touch me, you'd best be better prepared."

I smirked. "Better prepared? For what?"

"For me," she said under her breath and stepped closer so that our shoes were touching. "Because I fight dirty and don't care who knows it."

With one swift movement, her knee got friendly with my manhood. I dropped—instantly. I lay on the cold floor, crumpled in a ball. I cursed. This little thing of a girl just got the better of me! She knelt beside me and put her finger to my lips, stopping the slew of R rated words coming from my mouth. Her skin tasted like caramel. Instantly, I licked my lips and immediately regretted it. I'd licked her finger. Her finger! My reaction made me want to face plant into the floor—oh, wait, I already had.

"You stupid, stupid boy," she said, tucking my hair back. "You won't make it a day in the Red Court."

I opened my mouth to rebut, call her out on the cheap shot, or at the very minimum spit in her face, but my mouth became sticky, like I had caramel sticking to my teeth. The more I moved my jaw, the stiffer it became. The little wench probably hit a nerve when she kicked me!

"I. Will. Get. Even," I said through gritted teeth.

Her comeback: A raised eyebrow. Her grin deepened as she watched me writhe in pain with my hands clutching my pants. I wanted to scream at her, but my jaw was now locked shut. She patted me on the head like I was a dog. I couldn't be happier the hall was empty so no one else could witness this humiliation.

"Next time, think twice about making me mad. I won't hesitate to nut-drop you again. So, be a good boy and think about that while Hearts and I take care of the adult stuff."

# CHAPTER SIX

(Alice Mae: Present Time)

Getting the dirt on others—that was my civic duty to the Queen of Hearts, but I hadn't always been her minion. After a particular misfortunate event that ended with a death, I had been appointed as the Queen of Hearts' informant, for lack of a better job description. I took care of her dirty laundry, not because I particularly wanted to be a part of her Reign of Terror, but because I was talented at manipulation. I understood what people wanted to hear and see so I used it against them. When I was growing up, this little talent led me into juvenile trickery, but now that I was older, a slap on the wrist was a desirable punishment.

M.H. could attest to that... if he still had the ability to speak. The queen was quite imaginative when it came to punishments. Her methodology usually involved the Joker and a very pointy object.

Dressed in black clothing, trimmed with crimson red lace, was the queen. Hearts was shorter than most. I'd be surprised if she was five feet. A black brooch in the form of a heart with a dagger sticking through it was pressed on her collar. Her bright red hair was pulled up into a loose bun. Hearts fanned her face with the snapshot I'd taken of Ryley. Pulling Mr. Ruth out from the side pocket of my backpack, I thanked him for delivering the photo yesterday. Secretly, I was just pleased that he'd done it without any catastrophe occurring between him and the queen. I pulled out the white frog stool that was placed across from her throne and sat down. I kept Mr. Ruth safely on my lap and placed the monocle over his good eye. He trembled in my hands, but at least he wasn't leaving little poop balls like he usually did after losing his eye.

The One-Eyed Hare had a few run-ins with the queen. When I first met him, he was a two-eyed Hare, but that was a long time ago.

I glanced at the faded red, heart-shaped clock that hung next to the massive portrait of the deceased king, who was affectionately called Eddie by most everyone in Wonderland. Yet, she sneered his proper name—Edward—whenever possible. He had the same hue of brown eyes as Ryley, warm with a streak of darkness.

The queen caught me staring at her late husband and slapped two pictures on the table to draw my focus back to her—attention hog. Tea splashed over the edges of two tea cups. A yellow-eyed porcupine, wearing a white uniform, almost tripped over his own two feet when he raced onto the table in an effort to quickly clean up the mess.

It only lasted a second, but a blood-red line encircled the greens of her eyes. It faded quickly. "If you insist on taking your sweet time, I'll tie catnip on your sleeve and let Chez loose."

The porcupine's mouth dropped, and his yellowish eyes faded so that they were stark white. As soon as he regained the ability to blink, he wiped up the rest of the spilt tea and ran away so fast that he looked like a blur.

Studying an old photo of Eddie and then the Polaroid of Ryley, Hearts said, "You've finally found Robert's son."

I nodded and reached for the teapot. Very little tea had splashed out from my cup, but I knew from personal experiences that miniature spies, or big people with a little Drink Me juice in them, could hide in the most creative places—like a tea pot. So, topping off my tea was purely a preventative measure to make sure there were no eavesdroppers.

Hearts took a sip of her tea only after I did. "You know what you have to do next, don't you?"

"A plan is already in place," I said. "I was able to convince Becky, a girl classmate of his that he was keeping secrets, dangerous secrets that may be devastating to her friend, Courtney. I consider it a sidebar plot to keep him on his toes. It probably isn't necessary since the boy is already quite curious about me. He thought his secret about his father was well kept, and now he is surely plotting a way to get me to spill the beans about how and what I know about his dear old dad."

"Another shenanigan? I do hope you don't plan on luring him to Wonderland using a damsel in distress method or by threatening the underprivileged boy." The queen's light tone was laced with a pungent threat. Mess up her plan, and she'd find a way to extend my debt to her. Got it.

"Nothing so juvenile." A sideways smirk grew across my face, mimicking hers. "I actually got the idea from rumors the Otherworlders whispered in the school halls."

"Don't be so pretentious. Just tell me your plan."

There were times that I hated being so good at being dirty. "Make him fall so irreversibly in love with me so that he'll chase me anywhere— even here, to Wonderland."

# Chapter Seven

(Ryley: Present Time)

"I'm a moron."

The words flew out of my mouth like I had some sort of self-incriminating Tourette's. Why, you may ask, was I talking so fast, or that my palms were drenched in sweat, or why I'd suddenly developed an eye twitch? Yes, an eye twitch. I had taken on the personality of a deranged ogre.

Tugging on my baseball cap to hide the twitch, I hoped that Courtney hadn't noticed the symbolic drool hanging from my mouth. But really, how could she not know the effect she had on me, or any warm-blooded guy, when she wore her skin-tight cheerleading outfit? I mean, come on! She couldn't have looked more... *Come hither*, with her rosy red nose, as she blew warm air into her cupped, cold hands.

I had to take a personal time-out on life and look away before I attempted anything foolish, like to try to warm her with my ice cold hands. Intruding the "person bubble" of a peeved woman was *never* a good idea. I glanced around the stadium. It was jam-packed with fanatic football fans, witnessing my pathetic excuse of an apology. Some girls on the stand pointed at me and giggled. If their response was any clue to my foreseeable future with Courtney, I was going to strike out big time.

Dax sat in front of the band with two steaming cups. He nodded to the scoreboard. I had exactly four minutes and seventeen seconds to convince Courtney to give me a second chance before she picked up her pom-poms and cheered the Ravens to victory.

I stuffed my hands in my pockets and waited for her to either forgive me or send me away. Courtney exchanged a sideways glance with her Cheer captain and BFF, Becky.

Becky's expression was one that I'd seen many times before. More often than not, I saw it when I was dismissed and instructed to 'go to hell.' She looked me up and down. I'd accept that there wasn't much to take in, but the girl sure took her time giving me the once over. "There are at least six other football players, *and John Luke,* who promised me that they'd take you out of the picture if you do something stupid or rash, where Courtney is concerned."

John Luke—the quarterback and homecoming king—yeah, I was "vaguely" aware of who he was. Pretty sure he was the extra-large version of a "non"-steroidal guy who was glaring at me from the football field. He also happened to be Courtney's ex. *Yippee.*

"And I'm sure *none* of them are looking for a way to get into her pants," I said, sarcastically.

"Are you planning to de-pants Courtney?" Becky said and then popped her gum. "Because I can guarantee you a black eye if you break Courtney's heart."

Three minutes and forty-two seconds left. "Courtney, can you call off your guard dog so we can talk in private?"

Becky's mouth dropped. "You're calling me a dog?"

"Yep."

"Tell me why you were checking out the new girl, and I'll leave," Becky said, looking past me.

I glanced over my shoulder. Alice Mae hid in the shadows underneath the bleachers. She clutched to the support beam like she was convinced that she'd fall off the face of the Earth if she let go. Her dress was covered in dirt and her skin was muddy. Her smile lit up her eyes. It was that kind of a smile one wore when she was about to prank an unsuspecting bystander.

"Becky, you can't tell me Alice Mae isn't something of an interest to look at, prancing around in a 1950's outfit and looking like she got into a fight with a garden gnome using a bungee cord as a hangman's noose," I said.

"You've got two minutes," Becky said and then left to join the other cheerleaders.

"Why should I give you a second chance, Ryley?" Courtney asked.

I did something rash—I tucked her hair behind her ear. She didn't swat my hand. She was giving me a green light?

"Because I do want to hang out with you," I said.

"You're a horrible apologizer. I'm pretty sure if Becky was a witch, she'd do some voodoo stuff to you tonight."

"Then I'm over-freaking-joyed that she's *just a bitch.*"

"Hey, she is my best friend!" she said, and turned away to go fetch her pom-poms.

"That may be, but you know I'm not lying about her." I called out. She didn't slow her walk. Okay, name calling probably wasn't the best idea, but it was the truth. "I'm sorry! Forgive me?"

"No." She didn't look back at me.

I couldn't have been misinterpreting her body language so poorly… could I? I ran up next to her. I nudged her shoulder. She nudged back.

"So next Friday, do we have a date?" I asked.

"I've got an out-of-town game."

"Saturday?"

She bent over to snatch up her pom-poms. Beside them was a hot chocolate and her phone which she picked up and then opened her schedule app. I stole a peek. There was nothing booked the day after her game. "It looks like I'm busy washing my hair that night."

"Fine, I can take a hint," I said and turned away.

Before I was two steps away she called out. "The next weekend I'm free."

I didn't look back. Instead, I just raised my hand up in the air and gave her the thumbs up. I finally did it! I landed a date with *Courtney!* As soon as I had rounded the corner, I threw my hands up in the air in victory.

… And walked right into Alice Mae.

I quickly inspected my now-muddy clothing. I knew, without a shred of doubt that if Becky saw my dirty clothes, she'd start rumors that Alice Mae and I had been neckin' under the bleachers.

"What hole did you crawl out of?"

"A filthy one," Alice Mae said. She bit her bottom lip and tried to wipe off the mud that had ingrained into my jacket.

She was only making it worse. I grabbed her shoulders and held her away from me. "Just stop and stay away from me."

"You're the one holding me still."

Swearing under my breath, I let go of her. This girl would be the end of me! I had every intention of walking away, but the desperation in her eyes stopped me. I didn't know if it was the sparkling light from the football field or if there was a lunar eclipse, but her blue eyes turned to the darkest shade of midnight blue I'd ever seen. A tear trickled down her dirty cheek.

"I'm truly sorry, Ryley."

Oh, hell. A muddy jacket wasn't worth tears, even if I didn't like her. "It's fine, Alice Mae. It's just a jacket. Nothing a little soap and water won't get out."

She frowned. "What are you talking about?"

*My jacket*, I wanted to yell. Why did this girl make everything so damn confusing? Was my dismissal about the dirty clothing so baffling? Hadn't she just tried to clean it? How could she not connect the dots? She got me dirty, tried to clean it, teared-up because she couldn't fix it, and I told her it wasn't worth crying about—then she gets confused?

I took a deep breath before speaking. "The jacket—it's not worth crying about."

"Oh, that." She glanced at the smudged stains. "I thought we were past that incident. I was actually—"

She stopped talking when a stray, orange cat crawled out from under the bleachers and rubbed up against her leg. She nudged the cat with her foot so it would bother someone else, but the feline wasn't taking the hint to get lost.

"I'm truly sorry for making a mess of your life, Ryley."

47

# Chapter Eight

(Ryley: Present Time)

The first period literature class was missing one unforgettable student. Second week of school and Alice Mae already skipped, though rumors had spread that she'd gotten the kissing disease and had to stay home. Becky had a stellar glare and didn't mind using it on me when she saw me walking down the hall to get to second-period chem.

She raced up to me with her algebra books in tow. "Rumor has it that Alice Mae and a "mystery man" were making out during the football game."

"I feel sorry for Mister X," I said dismissively, and picked up the pace in hopes to keep the conversation short.

Becky matched my step. "And then it dawned on me that I did not, nor anyone else in school, see you until the end of the second quarter."

"Your point?"

Becky grabbed my arm, stopping me from escaping into the classroom. "Are you Mister X?"

I've had it! "Why do you care?"

She acted like I had truly embarrassed her. Okay, I hadn't been particularly quiet, but she seriously needed to back off.

"I don't like you," she said.

"I'm pretty sure that Ryley got the memo," Dax said, approaching us. He walked between Becky and me and stopped to face her. "You're acting like a scorned woman. Dare I say that you are like totally in love with him?"

"In love with Ryley? Please! I'd rather lick a maggot infected goat's butt than kiss this loser," Becky said.

"Yet, you find reasons to speak with him *in private.*"

"We're in the middle of a hallway."

Dax didn't miss a beat. "So why do you insist on inserting yourself into his and Courtney's conversations?"

"Because I'm looking out for my friend," she said.

"So am I," Dax said.

She rolled her eyes. "I heard rumors about you, Ryley Edward Edgar. I visited my cousins in Alabama last year and they remembered you and your mom from when you were in grade school. My cousins said that you and she skipped town in the middle of a night for no reason whatsoever."

I smacked my forehead. "Oh, that's right. I forgot to mention that we were being chased by a zombie serial-killer that murdered my dad and had to ditch that redneck town before it ate us."

She narrowed her eyes. "I'll be investigating you."

"Don't forget to put on your detective hat," I said.

If she heard the mockery in my comment, she pretended not to notice. "You know of my uncle—the probation office for the county. Well, he's a computer illiterate and had some technical difficulties over the weekend. Since I know all of his passwords, I did a little digging on the Edgar family. Turns out, there is no death certificate for your dad."

I looked around and spoke in a hushed tone. "My mom and I are under federal protection services."

She stepped closer. "Why?"

"Because Dad was killed," I said. "The records were expunged, but every once in a while some naïve high school girl uncovers the truth and we have to skip town again."

"Do you ever tell the truth?"

"I like to mix it up. Keep you on your toes," I said and then wiggled my finger closer. "If you dig deep enough, you'll find that there were other members in my family who bit the dust prematurely."

Thankfully, I wasn't the only person to recognize Alice Mae was off balanced, so it wouldn't be far-fetched to think she called in sick to avoid being picked on. Still, rumors about her and a mystery man couldn't possibly be good for me. I definitely didn't need anyone, especially Courtney, thinking that I was into the crazed girl. Nonetheless, when she graced us with her presence after lunch, I was secretly pleased. *Only* because I needed to make sure she didn't go off and tell everyone that the rumors were true and I was the mystery man.

"Where were you at first?" I asked, trying not to make a face because of her outfit.

Faded pink tights should never be worn—period. Nevertheless, it was easier to overlook that fashion no-no because she wore an oversized tie-dyed shirt. At least she made it a little more stylish by tying the shirt's back into a knot with a ponytail holder. A navy blue duffle bag hung from her shoulder.

"Chez wouldn't get out of the oven, and my aunts were trying to bake sweets." She held her finger along the wall, tracing the brick line as we walked down the hall to the freshman hall.

"Who's Chez?" I asked, walking alongside her.

"A spy. He doubles as an annoying, super-villain feline. It would seem that making sure I received a tardy slip on week two was on that cat's top priority list."

There were far too many oddities about her comment. "Why was there a cat in your oven?"

"He was *curious*."

"Is this cat real or is he a figment of your imagination?"

That earned me a slap across the face.

"Do you think I'm dumb as well as deaf? I know when I'm at the butt of a joke, so I'd advise you to choose your words wisely, or one day they will get you into trouble not even you can talk your way out of, Ryley, or should I say *mystery man?*" she paused to take in my reaction. I kept my face as blank as possible. "So you heard that one too? Here's your warning Ryley, make me mad and the whole school will think that we were swapping spit."

I bit my tongue, not addressing that topic. She knew she had me so I changed topics. "You think I'm a smooth talker?"

She made a one-eighty so we were no longer walking in the same direction. "Edgars are notorious smooth talkers, until they meet their demise because of their slick words... Speaking of which, I heard a rumor that your family is in the witness protection program."

I couldn't stop a grin from forming. Becky could never keep her mouth shut, especially if the secret was juicy. It had been too easy, putting the idea in her head that my family had a murderous past. Whatever. I didn't care as long as it got her looking somewhere other than at my old man. The entire town of Rockingham didn't need to know that he was chilling in a straightjacket on the other side of the state.

Instead of following Alice Mae like I really wanted to, I left for the men's locker room, changed into my gym clothes, and read the daily weight lifting program.

When the bass drums went off in the classroom above the weight room, I assumed that some of the basketball players or wrestlers commandeered a room. The bass was cranked. A rap song played over the speakers. Surely, the music teacher would realize that someone was seriously blowing off some steam upstairs. I knew something was afoot after three techno songs. I finished my last squat set and decided to get a drink, and do a little investigation. I took the stairs two at a time, bounding up the steps.

I peered in Mrs. Dotson's secondary music classroom which used to be the home-ec classroom. Inside was Little Miss Unconventional. I would have expected to see a giraffe dancing to the beats before I could convince myself that Alice Mae was performing—with her eyes closed at that. Light-pink ballet shoes were laced up around her ankles, making her pink tights no longer ridiculous; they matched the mood. Her blonde hair was pulled into a bun.

I leaned against the door frame and watched. Ten seconds of observation made it clear that Alice Mae was a talented dancer. Her balletic movements were excellent. Her legs went on forever. She spun on her toes. I was never one to be hypnotized by any kind of dance, but the way Alice Mae moved was so graceful and fluid. She twirled on her toes effortlessly. I crunched mine. It looked painful. The music didn't match the style of her dance, but at the same time it did. She was able to hit the beats with impression stances as well as move gracefully between challenging poses. I caught my breath when she leaped into the air and both legs were perpendicular to the floor. But what was truly earth-shattering was when she pulled her leg up straight beside her head.

"Pick your jaw up off of the floor." Dax nudged my shoulder.

I hadn't heard him come up behind me. I didn't think too deeply about what that meant.

Alice Mae was still in her own little world, oblivious to the fact that she not only had drawn Dax and my attention, but Mick's as well. He stood behind Dax and glanced over his shoulder.

"I don't think there's a tighter derrière in the entire school, but to be fair, I haven't been able to check out all the new freshmen yet," Mick said, rubbing his chin.

Falling onto her heels, Alice Mae rested her hands on the small of her back and looked up at the ceiling. Her hairline was dripping wet, and she was breathing heavy. My jaw literally fell open when she stripped her shirt so that she was only wearing a fitted sports top. I predicted that girls everywhere went on yo-yo diets or worked their tails off in the gym to get a stomach like hers.

Dax left, I think...

My feet were unmovable. Mick didn't budge an inch either. Hidden under her baggy t-shirt was this perfectly sculpted woman. It wasn't like she had a six pack, but she could eat cupcakes for the rest of the year and still not have a muffin top.

What alarmed me more than my own drool was that the entire length of her arm was battered and bruised. Half the dark spots there was ripped flesh. I'd had similar injuries from sliding into home base, but I sincerely doubted that she was much of a ball player. My stomach twisted into knots. I imagined the worst. Was she okay? Hell, I didn't care if she had kicked my family jewels, no one deserved to get slapped around.

"You're still gunning for Courtney, right?" Mick asked, seemingly oblivious to Alice Mae's injuries.

"Got a date with her next Saturday."

He grabbed my shoulder. "I never thought I'd be glad you were hooking up with the hottest redhead in school."

With that, he pushed away from me and approached Alice Mae. His walk screamed confidence. When he reached the podium, he grabbed the remote for the speakers and turned down the music.

Alice Mae stopped instantly. Her face turned three different shades of red. I wasn't buying it. The girl could act.

"Was I intruding?" she asked weakly, looking from Mick to me. "Mrs. Dotson gave me the impression that the classroom was empty this hour, and I could use it for my free period."

"It is," Mick said and sat on the edge of the teacher's desk. "You have some wicked moves, girl."

"My name is Alice Mae, not girl."

Mick extended his hand to shake her hand. She grabbed her arm, just above the elbow and below her bruising. She stared at his hand like she didn't know what to do with it. It couldn't have been more awkward. He finally lowered his hand.

"I'm Mick."

"Alice Mae," she said. She walked over to her duffle bag and unzipped a small compartment where she pulled out a homemade Tootsie Roll. After unraveling it, she popped it in her mouth and discarded the wrapper. She shot it Anny-Anny Over style. It missed the trash can by a solid foot, landing next to a crumpled wad of paper.

"I didn't mean to intrude," Mick said. "I just wanted to invite you to a dance hangout a lot of us go to. It's called Aftershock."

"Who is *us*?"

"Bunch of kids from school," he said. "I'd introduce you to them if you wanted to go together."

"I'll take that under consideration."

"Do you have plans this Saturday night?"

"Yes."

"Maybe next weekend?" Mick asked.

"Maybe."

He handed her back the remote. "Let me know."

He walked out of the room, not bothering to talk to me before leaving. Striking out was never pretty. I shut the door when I was sure he was down the hall. I walked past her to the trashcan and picked up her wrapper and the paper ball. I tossed the paper in the trash but held onto the wrapper.

"Where did you get that bruise on your arm?" I asked, hoping to keep her distracted from my hand.

"You can see them?"

"I'm not blind."

She narrowed her voltage blue eyes. "I fell."

Textbook batter woman syndrome. I wanted to do something, anything. I was about four seconds from alerting the school counselor. "You fell?" I repeated.

"Down a rabbit hole."

"It must have been a pretty big rabbit to dig—"

"I'm not lying, not about this Ryley, so you can get off your white horse and stop trying to save me. I don't need to be saved. I'm perfectly fine managing my own life." She crossed her arms and glared at me like I'd done something insulting. "Why am I defending myself to you? Something's seriously Wrong with me! But if you must know, rumperbabbit holes are particularly exorbitant in this part of the country."

The corners of my mouth twitched. "Of course they are."

She turned away from me and slipped on her oversized t-shirt. I sniffed the wrapper she'd thrown away. A faint cherry scent lingered. I tasted some of the residue. It wasn't particularly sweet, but I quickly had the biggest sugar rush of my life.

She grabbed her duffle bag and headed for the door. Instinctively, I reached for her bruised arm to stop her, but I hesitated. She stared at my hand, like she was looking for a reason to fight.

"You are really okay? You really just tripped?" Regardless of her answer, I made a mental note to alert the school counselor.

"It's not me you should be worried about," she said, and sighed heavily. "It's a pity, really."

"What's a pity?" I asked.

She gave me a wide berth as she walked to the door. I thought for sure that she'd walk out without answering me, but when she reached for the handle, she turned to face me.

"That Mr. Edgar didn't tell you more before he became trapped inside the prison of his mind."

That was it! I raced toward her and slammed the door shut just as she was opening it. "You know nothing about my dad!"

She gave me a sympathetic look. "No Ryley, it's you that knows nothing."

"What do you know about him?"

"Many things, but none of it really matters, not anymore."

What was that supposed to mean? "Who is Zola Maude—the lady whose hair he lit on fire?"

"Vida Maude's sister."

"More information would be abundantly helpful!" I said and slammed my fist against the door, next to her head. She pinched her eyes shut and braced for impact. "For years, no one knows about my dad and then you show up and act like you've known him for years! Explain!"

"Zola Maude and Vida Maude are my aunts," Alice Mae said, and slowly opened her eyes. "And my legal guardians when I stay in this part of the country."

"Where are you from?"

Sucking harder on her candy, she nervously picked up the edge of her shirt. "I might as well live in a completely different world from you, Ryley. We're obviously different to understand each other, much less communicate with any measurable civility."

Suddenly she jerked her head toward an opened window on the far side of the classroom. She rolled her eyes like it annoyed her that it was open in the first place. "Chez, I don't need a babysitter!"

She looked from the window, to the floor, until she stared at her shoes. It was like she was watching an invisible person crawl through the window, onto the floor and stop at her feet.

"I've already made too many fatal mistakes, I shouldn't tell him anything else," she mumbled to herself and then looked back at me like she forgot we had been in the middle of a discussion. "I shouldn't have piqued your curiosity. It was cruel because I can't tell you anything else."

The door opened. Mrs. Dotson dropped her sheet music when she saw me and Alice Mae unaccompanied in the classroom. "What are you two doing *alone?*" she asked, suspiciously.

"Practicing," Alice Mae said at the same time I said, "Just leaving."

I quickly shoved my hands into my short pockets and stepped over Mrs. Dotson's fallen papers. I was halfway down the hall when Alice Mae called out my name. She peered from the door frame.

"Did you like my dance? I've been working on it for years, per the Joker's request," she said and bit her bottom lip like she was trying to seduce me.

"I don't like you."

"That's not what I asked."

"Frustrating isn't it? Getting answers to questions you didn't ask, but are noteworthy nonetheless." Why couldn't I get this girl out of my head? What was I doing? I asked the first, random question that popped into my head. "Do you like me?"

She smiled, but I couldn't tell if it was an *I like you back* smile or *I enjoy messing with you* smile.

"I never really knew my father, or my mother for that matter," she said. "I came to live with my aunts when I was just a girl, but I know if I had the chance to see them again, I would take it."

"You have no right to tell me how to run my life," I said, cynically. "You don't know up from down, so that you have the audacity to offer unwanted advice is comical."

"Why would my sense of direction matter when we are discussing family members? Besides, I just thought you might need some advice—you know, from a friend to a friend."

"Let's get this straight right now. We are *not* friends."

"I just thought that since you were finding reasons to hang out with me…" Her voice trailed off. Her bottom lip trembled. She pulled out another piece of wrapped candy and popped it in her mouth. The sugar seemed to calm her. When she was no longer shaking, she turned around and walked briskly in the opposite direction. The halls echoed, so I could hear her arguing with Mr. Ruth about the theory of relativity and where jerk-faces fit into the time and space grid.

"I disagree, Mr. Ruth," she said, dramatically talking with her hands. "Ryley absorbs more space every time I talk to him. I would suggest that he's a catalyst, like a black hole to which we will all get discombobulated if we aren't careful and keep our distance."

I wouldn't have thought Alice Mae had the cognitive ability to understand Einstein's time and space relativity theory. Discovering that offset my awe because she discussed that theory with a toy.

# CHAPTER NINE

(Ryley: Present Time)

The masonry work that had been used when building the brick wall next to the AP physics class door was well done. I'd know. I just walked right into it. It hadn't budged. If I had been walking any faster, I'd probably have a goose egg. Conversely, if I weren't inspecting Alice Mae's homemade candy wrapper like it held the secrets to the universe, I probably would have noticed the gigantic wall that had always been there. I heard a few snickers but pretended not to notice and found my way next to Irwin, the smartest guy I knew.

Dumping my bag on the floor, I shot up a quick prayer that, the physics teacher wouldn't ask me to read anything. My algebra book wasn't going to do me much good. Fortunately, I'd grabbed the right notebook. I convinced myself that it was the candy wrapper that had distracted me, not Alice Mae. I tore out my notes from yesterday and handed them to Irwin who was scribbling on his tablet.

"T-t-thanks," he said, taking my notes. "I think my oo-orthodontist is trying to run my f-family dry with all these appointments. M-most p-p-p-people don't have to g-g-go once a week."

I felt sorry for the kid. He might as well have a bull's-eye on him. He was the epitome of a nerd—braces, glasses, curly long hair, plaid shirt with a vest, pants too short and distinct stutter. If we'd have a debate team, he'd be on it. But instead he played chess, was the backstage man for plays, and used his study period to teach mathematics to younger classmen. I had a soft place in my heart for Irwin. If I wasn't good at baseball, we'd basically be the same person—a geek who was into physics and liked performing on stage.

"You're in advanced chemistry, right?" I asked. After he nodded, I handed him the candy wrapper. "Can you tell if there is any substance laced in with this candy?"

He pushed his glasses up after they had slid down when he inspected the wrapper. "Of c-course I can. Just g-g-give me a few d-a-ays."

# CHAPTER TEN

(Alice Mae: First visit to Wonderland Continued…)

An old hag, whose white hair with purple streaks stuck out in every direction, slammed the door in M.H.'s face. He leaned against the indigo door, chipping the sun-curdled paint with his pointy fingernail. The door was the most presentable aspect of the entire makeshift house. It had been pieced together with twine and duct tape, and painted with giveaway samples from a paint store.

"You'd have me be publically humiliated rather than help out an old friend?" M.H. asked, so painfully pathetic that I wouldn't have wasted another minute to open the door.

"We are not friends," Genevine called out.

"Friends. Confidants. Buddies… Foes with a common enemy— they all mean the same thing. It's no secret you and the Queen of Hearts had a falling out," M.H. said, speaking in his typical happy-go-lucky tone. He enjoyed covering up his true intentions with giddy commentary. "We're on the same side."

"We're on the same side?" she said, mockingly. "And which side would that be? Clearly not the same side of this door."

61

"The side that is against the Bleeding Heart."

Genevine cracked the door, but only enough so I could see one of her sea green eyes. Her soft green eyes turned dark. A parlor trick, no doubt.

She wore enough makeup to supply a model convention for a year. But she didn't look out of the ordinary, in this realm. Even M.H. had a particular fondness for the facial application that seemed to be accepted.

"Admit that I'm the most skillful designer, seamstress, and fashionista in Wonderland—including hat making—and I'll consider helping you," Genevine said, peering through the peephole in the door. "You should really just stick to Candy Making. You don't suck at that."

"You make candy?" I asked.

"Who do you think created the recipe for the *Drink Me* juice?" he said, rhetorically.

M.H. turned around and bent over so the grumpy woman could see the fiery hole in his pants. "I just need a patch for my bottoms. It wouldn't take more than five—six-stitches—tops."

"Then drop trou and hand them over," Genevine said.

"And prance around half dressed? What will the girl think?" M.H. said and gestured to me.

"What girl? Does she have a boy's name?" Genevine asked.

How hadn't she noticed me standing next to M.H? "I do not have a boy's name," I said when her gaze dropped to me.

A discouraged expression showed on the woman's face, which she quickly covered up with a sneer. "Well, the girl must not be very bright if she's hanging out with the likes of you."

"Brightness is not a measure of brilliance, Genevine."

After an epic eye roll, she opened the door. M.H. wasn't kidding when he mentioned that Genevine had a particular fondness for eight legged creatures, or that she wore a large ankle bracelet. It was quite literally a ball and chain. However, M.H. told me not to mention it, so I didn't.

While the exterior of her home was patched together, inside was a Fabric Snob's dream home. Fabric, sewing materials, and thread cluttered the interior... as well as a horde of spiders.

While Genevine went to work finding a fabric that matched M.H.'s slacks, I clung to his side. Creepy crawlies weren't exactly my top choice when it came to animals. Most of the spiders sat on the outer edges of the windows and between the cracks in the walls. A few even held picket signs demanding better working conditions. One read: *Sweeter sugar water for flippin' Flies.* The next read: *More Fly Swatters.* The last read: *Sick of eatin' flies. Better lunch plan!*

"Why do you work with spiders, Genevine?" I asked.

"What are you saying, stupid girl? That we're not good enough for you?" The spider who spoke threw down his sign. After stomping on it with one of his many feet, he crossed two sets of arms.

"I didn't mean to offend anyone," I said.

"Well, who would you recommend I work with, if not spiders?" Genevine gasped, as if no other creature could compare to the magnificence of her tiny helpers.

I shrugged my shoulders. "A human?"

"All high and mighty is she," a spider said, dangling from the ceiling by a purple colored string. "She should meet the queen. It would be interesting to see whose ego would be bigger. Hers or Hearts'."

"Maybe a rabbit," I said, ignoring the spider's insult. They were my favorite animal when they weren't munching in my garden.

"A rabbit!" The spider gasped, disgusted with my choice in help.

"Calm down!" Another spider said. It hung from the ceiling just above my head and held the end of a string-like leash that was tied to a pet-fly. A tiny purple ribbon was tied around the flying insect's neck. It buzzed over the heads of many disapproving spiders. "She can choose whatever figurative helper makes her happy, even if it's unconventional. Can't you, little girl. What's your name anyway? Certainly other humans had given you a proper name?"

"Alice Mae."

Each spider's hopeful expression immediately dropped into a discouraged frown at the mention of my name.

"My-oh-my have mercy! That's a mouthful of a personal identification word," M.H. said as if it was the very first time he'd considered my name at all. He giddily clapped his hands together like he'd just stumbled upon a marvelous realization. "Let's call you Al! It's the most perfect perfected perfectest nickname! Al for Alice Mae. And it uses the first letter in your first name and the last. Don't you just love it?"

Al? That was a boy's name! Ugh, I hated it! But since I had already infuriated a family of lizards, two birds, and offended many dozen spiders, I wasn't jumping at the bit to lose my only friend in Wonderland by vetoing the awful nickname.

"It really is excellent," I lied.

The spider holding the leash to the pet fly whispered, "You are quite a horrific liar—a poorly chosen competitor to the queen's wits, but you are a girl with a boy's name, now Miss Al, and that is important!"

"The chosen one might still be a boy with a girl's name," one of the spiders said. "The Jack was not sure of the identity."

The clutter of spiders considered this information like it was crucial on some level. I was still clueless as to why any of it mattered, but the morale of every spider in the room heightened at my new nickname.

"She looks like a trouble maker," a spider holding a picket sign said. "We'll certainly need to keep our eyes on her."

I didn't understand why my wits and the queen's were being compared, and it seemed I'd entered into a real life chess game, but I didn't understand the strategy.

"Why, that she is! The greatest trouble maker in all the land!" M.H. exclaimed, like it was a good thing. "Al is to be my apprentice. Even the white rabbit approved. The tWo-eyed hare lured her here."

I thought the fall down the rabbit hole had been a sheer accident. "The white rabbit lured me here on purpose?"

Genevine stopped rummaging through her fabric to laugh at my question. "You're desperate to make the *Bleeding Hearts Prophecy* come true."

M.H whispered to Genevine that I wasn't ready to hear the prophecy yet, even if everyone in the court had read the script in the *Sweets for the Rabbit Hole Voyager*. "The white rabbit is a wonderful messenger. That's all that you need to know for now."

I sighed. What I did know and understand was limited. Maybe he was right. I shouldn't worry about what I didn't understand. I glanced at the picket signs. "Why don't you give the spiders better working conditions, Genevine?"

"Oh, they don't appreciate my organizational skills," Genevine said, throwing a ball of yarn across the room as she continued her search for the material.

"I could help you clean up the place."

"Clean all you want, but I'm not going to owe you anything for it," she said.

That was fine with me. After a few hours of straightening I understood Genevine's organizational process. Sticky cloth goes with the non-sticky thread, but only when it was a prime color. The pastels were to be crumbled into balls and shoved into the closets and dark corners of her shack because then the sun wouldn't fade them. Threads were to be knotted so the integrity of the strings stayed in place. This was her reasoning, not mine. But I understood, and found it particularly marvelous.

I would catch the spiders watching me. Minute after minute, more and more began fetching things for Genevine. The cleaner I got the room, the more spiders I recruited back for the seamstress.

Once M.H. was patched up, Genevine turned to me. "I can't

believe this madman let you prance around looking so asinine. He has positively no fashion sense."

"We don't have time for a makeover," M.H. said, pulling out his watch. "We have a schedule to keep."

"And I'll never forgive myself for letting this girl out of my sight looking so silly. It's clear she's too stupid to know any better, and I owe her for tidying up my shop," Genevine said, opening up a drawer full of eye shadows, lipsticks, and containers that I didn't even know the names. She handed me a tube of blue lipstick and a rose-shaped compact mirror and told me to put it on.

"I've never worn makeup before," I said. She pretended not to hear. I half-heartedly applied it. I glanced in the mirror before handing it back. I hadn't gotten the edges very well. As a matter of fact, it looked like I'd drawn a heart on my lips with expertise.

Genevine smiled approvingly. "Madness looks good on you."

She stopped digging through her makeup and told me to take off my shoes quickly. She handed me was a pair of antique shoes. "These will never go out of style, and my anklet is much too distracting to do these shoe justice."

# CHAPTER ELEVEN

(Ryley: Present Time)

In literature class, I was behaving, sitting at my desk, hands clasped on top, and staring at the chalk under the dry erase board. My eyes were glossed over, but at least I was looking forward, which was better than some of my classmates who were half falling asleep. Alice Mae was shuffling a deck of cards absent-mindedly. Every so often, the corner of a card would spark, but it was probably just the light catching it. It couldn't have actually been a flame. Every time I got the inkling to ask her why she was carrying a deck of playing cards around, I clenched my hands. I didn't care what that girl did… Ten minutes into class, my hands were white knuckled.

"—Ryley?" Mr. Blanch asked.

I blinked back up at the board. There was a long list of names of infamous American authors.

"Don't you think that would be a grand idea?" he asked.

There was a fifty/fifty chance of answering correctly. "Sure."

A unanimous groan echoed throughout the classroom. Alice Mae's cards scattered around her desk. She picked them up as fast as possible, like it would be less of a distraction. Mr. Blanch grinned and snatched my cap off of my head.

"Hey!" I said, reaching for it.

"Just because you won state last year doesn't mean you get a free pass to wear hats, Ryley. You know the school's policy: no headwear on school premise."

Mr. Blanch instructed all of us to write our names on a piece of paper. Since I still didn't know what I'd gotten us into, I didn't understand why I was writing my name, but I followed the instructions anyway. He asked us to pass the pieces of paper to the front where he collected them there and tossed them into my cap. He walked around the room, letting each student drawn a name.

One by one, names were drawn. I held my breath when Courtney reached into my cap. When she pulled out a piece of paper, it *had* to have been mine.

"Alice Mae," Courtney groaned.

The girl in question looked up, acknowledged that Courtney had spoken her name, and looked back down at her notebook. I drew Irwin's name.

"Ryley Edgar." Alice Mae read from the paper she drew.

"Now that everyone knows who they have to interview, you can choose any one of these authors. Read any one of their novels. You can check them out from the library if you don't have access to a book otherwise," Mr. Blanch said and tossed me my hat. "You'll interview your classmate and write a research paper on the author they chose as well as their perspective of the story chosen. You have until the semester break to do the interview and write the essay."

When the bell rang, a crumbled paper smacked me on the back of my head. I picked it up. Written on the college rule paper with pink pen was a list of ten generic questions about literature and instructions to return it to Alice Mae Liddell as soon as humanly possible.

"Don't you want to know what book I'm going to read before

giving me interview questions?" I asked, facing her.

"Does it look like I care?"

She actually looked insulted. "I thought so. The school counselor and a social worker came to my house, asking questions pertaining to these outlandish bruises you said I had." She pulled up her sleeves, revealing much smaller black and blue marks than she had before. Surely, they couldn't have healed so quickly. "I didn't figure you to exaggerate, but it was nice to know that you cared."

"I would have done the same for my archenemies, so don't make it a big deal."

Crumpling her questionnaire and shoving it into my backpack, I made a solemn vow that it would be there until the end of the semester so that she'd only have a week at most to finish her essay.

She glanced at the name I drew. "Irwin. Isn't he that physics guru friend of yours?"

"Why do *you* care?"

"Don't mistake my curiosity for caring, Ryley." She dug out a tube of blue lipstick and then applied it. She smacked her lips together. "If you must know, he's in my chemistry class."

"What's your point?"

"Well, he's been preoccupied lately. Examining what looks like a Tootsie Roll wrapper," she said. "I don't suppose you know anything about that?"

She knew. I could tell that she knew, without a shred of doubt, that it was her candy wrapper that he was examining. I didn't bother denying it. I was a pretty good liar, but I figured Alice Mae would see right through it.

"I didn't think you were smart enough to be in advanced chem."

"Do you want to know what happened to the last person who implied that I was stupid?" She looked about as nice as a dog with rabies. "He ended up all alone in a psych ward."

# CHAPTER TWELVE

(Ryley: Present Time)

I hated Alice Mae's grandma shoes. What was she thinking anyway? Wearing those clunkers was committing fashion suicide—even I knew that, and I wore stained t-shirts. During lit class, she used her lime colored pencil to count invisible insects in the air. I swear she was doing it to antagonize me, like everything else she did. At lunch, she sat alone. Most of the loners chose the far corners of the cafeteria, but not Alice Mae. Nope, she sat smack dab in the center of the football players' table.

Mick didn't look particularly disappointed that she'd joined their table. Though, whatever moves he was busting out, Alice Mae wasn't going for it. Even John Luke, the guy that had girls in the tri-state area drawing hearts around his name, couldn't get much of a rise out of her. With a semi-bored expression, she picked off everything except for the pepperonis on her supreme pizza. The girl ate enough candy to sustain an army, but she chowed down on her mutilated slice like she hadn't eaten in days.

"Snap out of it, Ryley!" Dax said. He sat across the table from me and had eaten all of his pizza. "It's not like Alice Mae enrolled in Rockingham High simply to annoy you."

I doubted that. "I can't ever get a straight answer out of her. She's particularly unfocused when it comes to how she knows about my old man."

I needed an excuse to talk to her, no matter how pitiful. I dug out the crumpled paper with the list of questions for English class on it out from under my books. After smoothing it out, I wrote answers to each one of her questions with short, clipped phrases.

"You two should hook up already. It's getting old listening to Mick go on and on about how hot she is," Dax said.

"I don't like *her.*"

"You don't like who?" It was Courtney. She walked up behind me, tray in hand.

"You," I teased. "Are we still on for Saturday?"

"I'm looking forward to it," she said. "Listen, I know you and Becky don't get along, but she's just worried about me. My breakup with John Luke was not good for my mental psyche."

"Your relationship with John Luke wasn't good for my mental psyche either," I said, and then caught sight of Alice Mae's notorious blue and orange overcoat. She dumped the pizzeria entrails into the trash and walked toward the exit. "Please don't take this the wrong way, but I have to talk to Alice Mae about something. It's kind of important and a bit ludicrous."

When I stood up to follow Alice Mae out of the cafeteria, John Luke made his way over to where Courtney was sitting. Super. Still, it wasn't like I was going to go up against John Luke. I'd just watched him pummel a receiver during the last football game.

I slipped on my red Raven baseball cap when I walked outside to the football bleachers. There were only a few people hanging around, but since it was an overcast day, most people opted to eat inside. After sitting on the metal seat, Alice Mae patted her lap like one would for a dog or cat. She then began petting the air.

When it was clear she wasn't going to ask why I followed her, I told her that I had finished her list of book questions. She reached for the paper, but I jerked it away, just out of reach

"What you know about my dad," I said.

"Are you really going to detain your lit answers until I tell you what you want to know about your father?"

"Yes."

She glanced at the paper. "Don't you think I could make up a few silly responses for a research paper? Obviously you didn't try very hard. I am pretty sure you wrote less than ten words total. I can make something up. I'm pretty skilled at that."

"So put 'skillful liar' on your resume."

"You're not very funny."

Okay, this paper wasn't going to get me anywhere with her. "I'd rather not have the entire school knowing about my dad's condition."

"I'll keep your secret so it doesn't ruin your reputation—I suppose that is why they call them dirty little secrets. Rest assured, no one will know," she said, and then zipped her mouth shut with her fingers.

*"Off with his head!"*

It wasn't Alice Mae; whoever said that I should be beheaded wasn't a girl...unless she was also a ventriloquist.

"Hush, Chez." Alice Mae brushed her legs, like she was pushing something off her lap.

"You're certifiable!" I said.

"And you are finally beginning to make sense," she said, leaning forward. She propped her elbows on her knees, which made her look younger than she actually was. Black and white pin-striped gloves covered her hands. The fabric that would have covered her finger had been snipped off. She tapped her chin like she was pondering a deep thought. "No wonder you can't be my friend. You're apparently allergic to people you deem deranged!"

"I thought you were going to leave my dad out of this!"

She leaned back on the bleachers. Her arms spread out like she was trying to tell me she had nothing to hide by using her body language. "I only brought up insanity in general. You are the one who assumed that I was referring to your dear old daddy. By the way, when was the last time you visited your father?"

"You're impossible!"

"And you're insufferable," she said, closing her eyes. "Please leave so I can soak up some sun in peace."

"Rain clouds are rolling in, you nut-case!"

She opened one eye and smirked. "Are you telling me that the sun's rays aren't strong enough to wiggle through a cloud?"

"You're wearing long sleeves."

"And, your zipper is down."

I checked. She wasn't lying.

"Shall we continue this discussion, Ryley, or have you had enough embarrassment for today?"

A loud bang stole our attention. We both turned our heads in the direction of the sound. A stray, orange cat had climbed out of the dumpster, causing a ruckus. Its head was stuck in a soup can.

"For heaven's sake, Chez!" she said, agitated.

When I turned back to Alice Mae, she had disappeared. I hadn't even heard her leave. The only evidence that she'd been on the bleachers was that Mr. Ruth had fallen between the bench seats. I picked up her beloved stuffed bunny. Her vanilla scent lingered in the fabric. I inspected it. One eye missing and the other was loose. The stitching was coming apart at the feet. It didn't take a genius to deduce that Alice Mae spent little time away from this animal. She loved it. I finally had some leverage.

73

# CHAPTER THIRTEEN

(Ryley: Present Time)

Space time continuum. Blonde hair. Pin-stripped gloves. Otherworlders? I rubbed my face. I couldn't get the image of her putting her damn leg straight in the air out of my head. Even cherries no longer made me think about Courtney—the girl I had a date with later tonight. *So why couldn't I get the 'other girl' out of my head.* I stared at Mr. Ruth. I'd stuffed him in the first baseball hat my dad had given me. Years of grit from the dugout had become one with faded blue fabric. The white embroidery appeared more cream than white.

"When was the last time you visited your father?" I said, mimicking Alice Mae.

I hated how that girl got under my skin, especially when she was right. My excuse for never visiting him, besides that he always told me never to come back, was that West Harbour Psychiatric Treatment Facility was three towns over, a two hour drive from Rockingham.

I didn't know how long I gawked at *her* stupid bunny before I just couldn't stand the mere thought of Alice Mae. For lack of a better word, I was being a girl (forgive me), and a needy girl at that. I was practically waiting for her to call me and give me all the answers I needed willy-nilly. No, this was a game to Alice Mae, Who's Who. And since she kept bringing up my dad, dodging every question I ever had about him, and nonchalantly questioning me about seeing him, I figured that she wanted me to go to him. He had to be a significant "Who" in this game.

I couldn't let Mom find out I wanted to see Dad because she'd make a big deal about it. That meant that I couldn't take her car, leaving me with the old beater that had been collecting dust in the third stall of the garage.

I propped up Mr. Ruth, who was still in my ball cap, and went to the garage. Inside was my pop's '56 Corvette. A high pitch squeal screamed when the engine rolled over. I pulled the key back out and opened the hood. It wasn't long before my hands were covered in grease. The engine was in serious need of a new belt and an oil change, along with a laundry list of other things. I kicked the tires for good measure when I noticed scratches by the right fender. It looked significantly like the crest Alice Mae had scratched into her toy racecar. It was a crest of a top hat with the initials, "M" and "H."

After grabbing my mom's credit card and commandeering her car, I headed off to the service station to order some new parts. The bell chimed when I entered the gas station. Two old ladies were bickering at the checkout lane.

"Mikado!" A bald lady wearing a faded house coat slammed down a brown speckled banana and some change in front of a clerk. She carried the same orange cat who got its head stuck in the soup can like it was a football. The cat looked less than pleased, but hung there nonetheless.

"That's entirely too dark, Zola Maude. Mustard is a more suitable color for a perfectly ripe banana," the other lady said. Her shoes matched Alice Mae's. I supposed that was the fashion statement of the early 1900's.

"What do you think, boy? What is the best color for eating a banana?" the bald one with the burn scars that scourged the top of her head asked. She grabbed my arm like lonely, old people sometimes do. Her eyes widened, which were magnified by the massive glasses she wore. Dropping the cat, she covered her mouth. "Edgar?"

75

"Who are you?" I asked, glancing at the cat that slapped the old lady's leg with his paw. Apparently it didn't appreciate being dropped.

The other old lady, who smelled suspiciously like Aqua Net, picked up the cat and held it like a football. "If he were the original Edgar, then he finally figured out the time-warp continuum. Don't you think Robby would be a little older? Certainly this is his son—the one Hearts is searching for, Zola Maude."

"You're Alice Mae's aunts?" I asked.

"And you're that bratty son of the man who deformed me!" Zola Maude said, gathering up her fruit. She barged out of the shop.

"Are you going to hold me responsible for something my dad once did, too?" I asked Vida Maude.

"My gorgeous hair is still intact, isn't it?"

"There's not a hair harmed on your head," I said. "It's much like your niece's hair... speaking of which, Alice Mae is quite a peculiar girl. And, she seems to have quite an interest in my family."

"You are *interested* in why she has an *interest* in you?" Vida Maude asked. "That is *interesting*, young Mr. Edgar."

"Why all the interest?"

"It's been prophesied by the Jack that if the King loses his head then the Queen with a bleeding Heart would rule the Red Court until Time ceased to move forward," Vida Maude whispered like she were reciting a script. "When a second carried on for infinity, every creature in Wonderland would tip their Hat to the misfit girl with a Boy's name (or was it a boy with a Girl's name?) who'd end the Reign of Terror. However, it all hinged on the One-Eyed Hare being able to convince an uninspirable Heir that the impossible was indeed possible—like stopping time—and that Love was worth a Beheading."

This whole damn family spoke in riddles.

"What are you talking about? And you didn't answer my question, which must be a family attribute. Why is Alice Mae interested in me?"

"This prophecy is every reason why she's interested in you," Vida Maude said. "But, I'm sure at least part of the prophecy is wrong. Insane Love isn't worth a Beheading."

At least we were on the same page about one thing—love wasn't worth dying for.

"Listen lady, I don't know what prophecy you are quoting, but what does it have to do with me?"

"Perhaps everything, perhaps nothing," she said. "Did your father not tell you a thing? You might as well be an authentic Otherworlder."

She grabbed my arm to hold me still while she leaned in close enough to kiss me. Our noses practically touched. I pushed away when she plucked out a strand of my hair from my head. She backed away and inspected my hair like it held the secrets of the universe.

"I suppose your father had his reasons for not telling you," she said, dropping my hair on the ground.

The cat jumped out of her arms and swatted the strand as it fell to the floor. Using both his paws, he picked up my hair and sniffed it. I swear the cat actually smiled.

"I always suspected that your father had snuck you back to your true birthplace, for the sole purpose that you wouldn't be blindsided when the queen came looking for you. A shame. Games are more fun when everyone knows the stakes," Vida Maude said. "A word of warning, sonny—don't tell anyone else about us, not a word you hear. It's up to the Queen to keep our secrets safe. Beheading is still practiced in our realm, if subject to the Wrongdoing Law."

"Your realm?"

The cat meowed. Vida Maude picked it up and scratched behind its ears. When it began purring, Vida Maude talked to the cat in a baby voice, "Would you allow the boy to know, Chez?"

The cat stretched out in her arms. It yawned; our human conversation had completely bored it. Vida Maude's eyes turned icy blue, just like Alice Mae's did when she was going full blown irate.

"We are from Wonderland, young Mr. Edgar," she whispered pleasantly, but her smile turned to a sneer. Her white dentures transformed into points—surely a circus trick. Her brightly colored clothes transformed to dull colors. She chuckled in the way I imagined every comic book villain would. "We are from the wondrous world of wonders."

# CHAPTER FOURTEEN

(Alice Mae: Second visit to Wonderland)

My second visit to Wonderland was a bit more productive than the first. Once again, the white rabbit was eating in my garden like it was a veggie buffet. He munched on the lettuce like it was his personal salad until he saw me. I was tempted to hit it over the head with a shovel, but M.H. had mentioned that the white rabbit had chosen me. Chosen me—for what I hadn't a clue, but I figured the animal wouldn't appreciate me clubbing it over the head with my garden tool. So instead, I followed it down the rabbit hole...

I descended through a dirty porthole, landing hard on my bottom in the *Waiting Room*, as I came to call it. The *Waiting Room* was the aphotic, round chamber between the Otherworld and Wonderland. Aside from my muddy footprints, the floor was polished, checkered tile and the walls were made of granite. Honeysuckle vines crept in from a wooden mouse door that the white rabbit had run through. A ceramic figurine of a frog guarded the door. Sewn on its tiny jacket were the initials R.E and a symbol of a spade. A table made completely of glass was in the center of the room. When I say glass table, it would more accurately be described as an ice sculpture of a mermaid holding a tray. On the tray was a small glass bottle with the words *Drink Me* etched on it.

"So, M.H. created this," I said, inspecting the bottle. On the back side of it was a crest. I was surprised I hadn't noticed it before. The Mad Hatter's initials were etched on the bottle as well.

I drank the potion. Today it tasted like maple syrup and cotton candy. The ground came up at me like I was on an invisible roller-coaster. When my insides had settled down, I walked over to the frog which was now the same height as me (or me the same height as it?) I had shrunk to the size of small critters. I knocked on its head. The ceramic frog burped up a skeleton key made for the mouse door.

I shoved the key through the door and crawled into the Wonderful World of Wonderland. I expected there to be a cupcake with the words *Eat Me* on the other side of the door, or at the very least the aggravated caterpillar with the hookah. However, the Wonderland that I walked into the first time was not a vast forest like it was before, but rather a well-manicured lawn with a gigantic mushroom house. M.H. was there dressed to the nines, flaunting a new pair of gold rimmed goggles. He held a tiny flowered dress and tea pot. The designs on the dress matched the pattern on the teapot exactly

"Genevine insisted that you would have the perfect camouflaging clothes for today's events," he said, lowering the tea pot and dress to the ground. "Get inside and change quickly."

"You're kidding me."

"I have a tea time with Hearts. The queen, more than any other Wonderlander, whispers the best kept secrets. But we must hurry if those whispers are to occur. Hearts is quite unsympathetic for tardy goers, and we are to meet at high tea."

I climbed up the handle and peered into the spout. "What happens when someone pours hot water in here?" I asked, not loving the idea of eavesdropping via tea pot.

"The Queen of Hearts *never* drinks from someone else's china, and she *only* drinks after someone else has sampled the brew. She's quite certain that someone is out to poison her and has every right to be suspicious. My candy operation is just a cover for my... anti-antidotes."

"You make poisons to kill people?"

"Money is in the ones that only take one sip to…" he said, and then made the movement of slitting his throat. "Ever since Eddie Edgar's *unfortunate accident*, there is a market for the ones that only make you ill too, but those aren't going to make me rich. I need one that will kill with a single drop."

"Eddie Edgar? He wouldn't by chance be brother to a Robby Edgar?" I asked, sliding to the bottom of the pot.

Handing me the matching dress, M.H. nodded. "You catch on quick. The white rabbit chose well. You were always a top candidate since your folks live far-far away and you live with your *wondrous* aunts. It is of miraculous happenstance that you are the same age as Robby's son. So, it made you quite the candidate indeed."

"Robby's son?" I said.

"He goes by Ryley. Although with such a strong upbringing, I thought Robby would have chosen a manlier name, less universal. The name Ryley can be both ways—boy or girl," M.H. stopped to ponder that idea a bit further. "Maybe Robby chose the name to keep the queen from knowing too much about his child."

Sitting cross-legged in the bottom of the teapot was where I heard the Queen of Hearts' voice for the first time. The demeanor in which she spoke made it evident that she thought highly of herself.

"I've heard rumors that a girl from the Otherworld was spotted in my court," Hearts said. "Can you imagine? An *Otherworlder* in my court without my knowledge!"

M.H. gasped. "Surely not your court!"

"I was appalled as well. I was hoping that you knew some information about the girl. I'm told she goes by the name of Al—silly name for a girl. Such a silly name, that I could be convinced to put the girl out of her misery."

"'Hall 'ai prepare t'the gilly?" a man with a rough voice asked. He spoke as if his tongue had been cut out.

"Yes, Jack," M.H. said. "Or at the very least, see if the Joker has his weapons prepared."

Carefully, I climbed up the spout of the teapot to get a closer look to whom M.H. was speaking. Standing next to a red-haired woman, wearing a golden crown and pushing a racecar, was the oldest butler known to man. Gray hair stuck out of his ears, yet not a single hair was on the top of his head. He raised his bushy eyebrows, which seemed to help him see. His beady black eyes looked like they belonged to a bird rather than a person. To say he had a few crow's feet was an understatement. He wore a red and black uniform. The colors were so faded and worn it looked like he'd put on the uniform sometime during his late twenties and didn't bother to take it off—ever. He looked like he could be my great-great grandfather. He walked like a great-great grandfather. I would have timed how long it took for him to leave the room if I had a watch. I was guessing close to a full minute.

Watching the old man leave, Hearts smiled. It appeared pleasant, until I noticed her pointy teeth. As I studied them, they turned back normal only to turn pointy again. A crimson line outlined the green in her eyes.

She asked, "Dare I say that your sources slipped up on the gender of this trespassing Otherworlder?"

I wanted to smack myself, for I just caught on to why M.H. had given me the dreadful nickname. It was to keep me protected! This way, the queen didn't know if I was a boy or a girl! If it kept me from getting well acquainted with the guillotine, then I'd gladly go by Al. I was beginning to like the abbreviation more and more.

"Fine, then I'll put the word out that I'm looking for a… child named Al. I don't very much care if it is a boy or girl; I just want the Otherworlder out of my court!" Hearts said, and mumbled a string of words I hadn't heard before. *"Every creature in Wonderland would tip their Hat to the misfit girl with a boy's name (or was it a boy with a Girl's name?) who'd end the Reign of Terror."*

"Quoting the *Bleeding Heart Prophecy*?" M.H. said. "Are you worried, my queen?"

"I must take everything with precaution," she said, and pushed the racecar off the side of the table. "After the Joker informed me of this Al character, he then advised me to close all of the rabbit holes."

"The Joker does foresee the potential future, just like the Jack," M.H. said. "If he advised you to do something, I would recommend you to heed it."

"I assume that Robert had a child by now, even if I can't pinpoint where in the Otherworld he and Lauren live," Hearts said, still in deep thought. "The Joker's spell to track, manipulate and control, that he cast on Robert's car only works if the person holding the racecar replica is close to the original vehicle. And Robert has been staying far, far away from here."

"If he stays far away from Wonderland, what is the problem?"

"He tarnished my good name!" Hearts exclaimed. "Banishment was not a fitting punishment. Misery is what he deserves. So I've changed strategies. I'm asking you as a dear friend, M.H, to convince the white rabbit and his rumperbabbit friends to dig several holes."

"But that would go against the Jack's advice," M.H. said. "Why the sudden change of heart?"

"Isn't it obvious? Wait for the child named Al or Roberts's son to fall down a hole." The queen laughed, growing louder and louder as the seconds trickled by. "I'll tell the Joker to get his sharp toys ready because we are going to kill the *Bleeding Heart Prophecy* before time stops."

# CHAPTER FIFTEEN

(Ryley: Present Time)

I Googled Wonderland. One small town in Arkansas showed up on the search engine as well as a few places in the United Kingdom. Few places in the world still practiced the art of beheading. A family conspiracy was the only answer I could fathom. Alice Mae and the Maude sisters *had* to be jerking me around.

"Well, if Alice Mae was from another dimension, it would explain her accent," I said and looked up at Mr. Ruth who was perched on the kitchen table. Until I conducted amateur background checks on the Liddell family via the World Wide Web, he was under close surveillance. Why was the innocent looking stuffed animal under observation? Because when I returned home from the gas station, my mom's ceramic frog was gone. It vanished.

I glanced at the wristwatch my old man had given me. It was a quarter to four, and I still hadn't figured out what Courtney and I were going to do for our date. I mean, I knew what I *wanted* to do with Courtney—kiss and not stop until I ran out of air. But, I couldn't get a particular blue shade of lipstick out of my head...

"Is this stuffed rabbit giving you any good advice?" my mom asked, walking into the kitchen.

"He's not much of a helper."

"Rumperbabbits usually aren't."

"Did you just call rabbits rumperbabbits?"

Mom blushed. "It was just something your father used to say. He used made-up words often and sometimes spoke in riddles. He kept little secrets, but that was a long time ago. What's troubling you?"

Mom sounded like Alice Mae. I shook her from my mind for the nine hundredth time that hour. "I have a date with Courtney, and I haven't a clue of what I'm going to do."

Sitting down beside me, she said, "The standard dinner and a movie is a failsafe."

I pushed my phone toward her so she could see the screen. The night showcase was on it. "A solid line up of chick-flicks, and I want this date to be unforgettable."

"Your father used to take me to the movies all the time."

"Your point?" I asked, and then winced at my insensitivity.

My mom took her time to respond. Usually, I kept my personal opinion of my dad buried deep, but sometimes it showed its ugly face—at my mom's expense. Times like this I wished there was a rewind button to life so I could take back what I had said.

"Robby wasn't all bad you know."

"So why did he insist that we move towns so often?"

"You know Robby was diagnosed with paranoia, but that didn't mean he wasn't brilliant."

"So we moved all over the country because he *once* was a smart man and you followed his lead?" I took my mom's hand and gave it an extra squeeze. "He's not the man you married, Mom. Dad isn't there anymore."

"Ryley, he asked me to relocate often to keep you hidden."

"From who? The boogie monster?"

Her stern expression stopped me from saying anything more regrettable. "He asked that of me *before* you were born, Ryley. It wasn't a request made after his mind broke. Someone wanted revenge, and your father had it in his head that they were going to take you away—far, far away from us."

"Why?"

"He said that I was forbidden to know. Years later, right before he was institutionalized, he rambled on about beheadings and prophecies. It was one of the few promises he asked of me, and I wasn't going to let him down—no matter what."

# CHAPTER SIXTEEN

(Alice Mae: Third visit to Wonderland)

Candy factories were popular in Wonderland, but the most notorious one was named after M.H. *The Mad Hatter's Ooey Gooeys*. His mushroom house was made up of chocolates and seemingly endless sugary snacks. The outside looked like an oversized mushroom, but the inside might as well have been a gingerbread house.

I traced a purple licorice trim on the wall and then licked my finger. An explosion of grape flavor erupted in my mouth. It was the greatest sugar rush of all time. I picked up a colorless bottle and gave it a sniff, expecting some heavenly aroma. But there was nothing. It was absolutely odorless.

"Snakes go berserk for that," M.H. said and picked up a bottle similar in size to the *Drink Me* ones. A snake wrapping around a skull and cross bones was etched onto the glass. "And they, along with frogs, toads, lizards, any other reptile or amphibian loathe this. According to my research, it acts like repellent."

"Research?" I repeated. "Is candy really significant enough to justify research?"

"Candy is vital to Wonderlanders and VIP Otherworlders," M.H. lectured. "Without it, our people couldn't travel to the Otherworld and live normally."

"Wonderlanders live in my world?" I asked, eyeing his kitchen table that had been made up entirely of red gumdrops.

M.H. laughed, "My dear, your aunts, the Maude sisters, are from Wonderland!"

My mouth practically hit the floor. This place—Wonderland—was *my* place. It was *my* escape from the reality. They knew about it?

"They suck on homemade candies, like these, to keep their thoughts straight and keep from seeing imaginary people and things," he said.

"What's a VIP Otherworlder?"

"A person who spends a lot of time in Wonderland. Normal Otherworlders don't react to our candies, unless they spend a lot of time here," M.H. said, kneeling down beside me. "The more time you spend in Wonderland, the more you become a part of it. People weren't meant to live in two worlds. One day you must choose which one you'll live in—one day. But, today is not that day."

I remembered the *BackWards Wanderer Prophecy* he showed me: A strong-Willed child shall set the time-stalemate into motion, but only if a tWo-eyed hare can lure her to the Wonderful World of Wonderland. She Will be given a choice to live Wondrously forever or be banished to Weep in her homeland. Seconds Will tick forWard and backWards until her decision no longer Wavers. HoWever, she Will choose Wrong.

"I will choose Wrong," I said.

"There is no use fretting about what cannot be done, but only act on what can be done. The Jack made one for me too." M.H. lifted his hat and peeled out a piece of burnt newspaper. Scribbled on it with orange ink were the words of a *Comings & Goings Prophecy*: *You're a HATed fool to believe the Bleeding Heart won't find out your Comings and Goings. Some come. Some go. But one fool cannot do both... unless he is in two separate pieces. Come & Go. Come & Go. Come & Go.*

"If you separate into pieces, you'll die."

"Death will come for us all," he said. "Like I said, there is no use fretting about the inevitable."

"What can I do?" I asked.

"I'm in search of an apprentice," he said. "Someone who's smart, cunning, and who has a VIP pass into both realms. Someone like you."

A smirk so evil widened across his face. He looked to the far corner of the room. Shadows cast on the walls, making it nothing like the rest of the rainbow-colored room. There was a black door so small only a mouse could pass through. It was almost unnoticeable.

"Have you ever wondered why you get a tummy ache after eating a lot of candy?" He didn't wait for a reply. "Because too much of a good thing is actually a bad thing. Candies can be poisonous. Thus, they can become a weapon more hazardous than a guillotine."

"Are you planning to hurt someone?"

"Hurt? No," he said, speaking technically. "But there is someone I want dead, which is where you come in, Al—my sweet, sweet girl who has a boy's name."

Al. He was talking about me! "What do you want me to do?"

"My candies will only make a person sick. I need to create one that will be deadly but tasteless, especially shall we say, if one unknowing queen were to drink it in her tea."

"You want to kill the queen? Why?"

"Many reasons, but the most important is because she is not the rightful ruler of this court. She banished the only man who is fit to rule."

"And who is that?"

"Robby, my colleague in this devious candy making business. When he finds a way to stop time, he'll need a deadly sweet," he said, and stood up and walked to the little black door. "Will you help me create a candy weapon, so poisonous yet sweet that no one will suspect foul play?"

# CHAPTER SEVENTEEN

(Ryley: Present Time)

Standing in front of the mirror wearing stone washed jeans, black boots, and a dark gray button down shirt. Courtney would instantly know that I was trying hard to impress her the second she noticed that I wasn't in a t-shirt. Only when forced did I wear a button down shirt—usually at a funeral or a wedding. I grabbed one of my twenty three baseball caps. It was a green university one that I'd visited last year when I checked out the physics department. It was a little snug.

Mom was right about my hair getting out of control, but to give in now would mean that she won this battle. After our intense heart to heart, I wanted to keep things from getting faux pas. Lifting it up off my head just a little, I turned it on to the side—yep, even more lame. Wearing it flipped back looked no better, so I just wore it like usual: propped on my head like a train conductor. A gust of wind would easily blow it off.

The last item in my wardrobe was the stuffed bunny, which I tucked in my back pocket. I wasn't letting it out of my sight again.

A red silk dress——that was what Courtney wore. Her lips were such a dark crimson color that I couldn't look away. I just stood on her doorstep staring at her like a baboon… until her dad stepped out from behind her. I expected to see a .22 or some shotgun in his hands. There wasn't.

He had the same red hair as his daughter, but his facial features would never be described as feminine. Even though he sat behind a desk for a living, I doubt he'd think twice about rolling up his sleeves and acquainting his fists with my nose if I tried anything ignominious with Courtney.

"I expect my *only* daughter to be home by midnight," he said.

"Really, Dad?" Courtney asked and held up three fingers. "So I suppose those *three* other girls living in the house aren't my sisters?"

"Let me rephrase," he said, staring me down. "Courtney is to be home at a quarter to twelve."

"Seriously Dad?" Courtney demanded.

He crossed his arms. "Eleven thirty."

I snagged Courtney's hand and led her away. At the going rate, I'd never get past the front steps before Courtney's curfew was up.

Supper at Little Italy went smoothly… until Courtney's food arrived. She took one measly bite of her salad, and her face paled. She spit out the lettuce in her napkin. "I think I'm going to puke."

Courtney hurried off to the bathroom. What was the protocol for something like this? If I followed her into the bathroom to hold her hair up (or whatever gesture was considered appropriate) any other person with lady-parts inside the women's bathroom would surely freak. Predicting that the night would end with a mob of dismayed women chasing me out of the restaurant would surely add to the gossip.

Well, the threat of vomit answered any question about if I was to get a good-night kiss. "I hope she's alright," I said to the waitress who had brought over two iced waters. The perfume she wore was familiar. I just couldn't put my finger on it. Cherries and vanilla?

"I'm sure she will be, but I'll bring over a glass of 7-up, just in case she's taken a turn for the worse," the waitress said and hurried away to the kitchen.

I took my eyes off the women's bathroom door just long enough to thank the waitress—Who was Alice Mae, wearing the waitresses' trademark black uniform. That's why the perfume smelled so familiar! It was Alice Mae's! That nitwit seriously sabotaged my date? I took off running toward the kitchen. Shouting her name, I burst through the metal swing doors and grabbed her.

"Why did you poison my date?" I demanded, shaking the girl by her shoulders. I was ready to strangle Alice Mae, but there were far too many witnesses.

One of the cooks pulled me away from her. Holding me up against the wall, he pressed his gigantic forearm under my throat.

"You burst into my kitchen and spread rumors about food poison—that will put this place out of business," the cook said in a not-so-nice manner.

"Not food poison, *poison* poison," I clarified. Stop talking and think about the words jumping from your mouth, I thought. I was sounding like an idiot. "That waitress impersonator did it!"

I was ready to let her have it, but there was one pesky problem. The waitress wasn't Alice Mae. She didn't look even remotely close to Alice Mae—other than her blonde hair.

I owed this random girl a well thought out apology, but all that came out was a pathetic, "I'm sorry."

Needless to say, the on-site-manager "subtly" instructed me to leave. He promised that my mom would hear about my behavior. Twenty minutes later, Courtney joined me outside the entrance. Water dripped from her hairline and her makeup was rubbed off—not a good look for her. Clutched in her hand was the 7-up can the waitress had promised.

Mortified would be the best word to describe my level of horror.

"A waiter told me you'd been escorted out. Why?" Courtney asked. Her voice wavered.

"There was a gigantic misunderstanding."

I took her hand, even though I didn't want to get sick, and guided her back to the car so I could take her home. Unforgettable was what I was going for on the date, but this wasn't it. Perhaps, by some chance, the whole world won't know about my impulsive actions tonight.

"I heard you grabbed a waitress," Courtney said. "Why?"

So much for keeping this a secret.

"I thought it was Alice Mae," I said and rubbed the back of my head. What I was about to say sounded like a line in a bad horror movie. "I thought that she poisoned you."

"Who poisons people nowadays?"

Desperate people, very desperate people.

# Chapter Eighteen

(Ryley: Present Time)

"You deserve a makeup date," I said, pulling the car into her driveway. "Unless your sickness was actually an exit strategy and you want nothing to do with me."

She looked like a wreck and needed a bathroom *stat*. But she managed a polite smile. "I heard rumors that you were a good kisser."

Time out: How does one respond to that?

"I'd like very much to see for myself," she said, and then made a mad dash for the house with her hand over her mouth.

When I pulled into the driveway, Mick and Dax were walking up the front steps. Mick had a stack of papers in his hand. I honked twice, gaining their attention. I met them on the porch.

"I was just going to drop this off with your mom," Mick said. "I thought you had a date with Courtney tonight."

"She got sick."

"She bailed on you, huh?" Dax said.

"Something like that," I said, thankful that they hadn't heard about my accusation yet. I glanced at a stack of papers in Mick's hand. "What's that?"

He shoved a "missing poster" into my hands. Drawn with colored pencils was an animation of Mr. Ruth. Scribbled at the top of the missing poster was Alice Mae Liddell's phone number as well as her address. Clearly, this girl hadn't heard of a computer since everything was handwritten.

"Alice Mae called me today, at six thirty in the morning. She was freaking out because someone had stolen her stuffed bunny," Mick said. "I thought it was a crank call, until I went to her house to calm her down. She was ballin' her eyes out and drawing up these posters. She asked me to pass them out."

Dax leaned against the porch railing. "And Charming here called me up to hang out—aka, tricked me into helping him."

"Alice Mae had your phone number?" I asked.

"No girl can turn me down, but I will admit that she took more persuading than most," he said. "But, it's no longer an exclusive number. Most everyone in town that didn't slam their door in my face now has her digits."

"I'll let you know if the critter hops into my life," I said, keeping my back to them since Mr. Ruth was still stuffed in my back pocket. With my hand on the front door, I asked, "Dax, do you want to keep passing out posters for a girl you have no interest in or chill out with me for a few hours?"

"You have anything to eat?" Dax asked, and pushed past me.

"You're just going to let me pass all these out by myself?" Mick asked as the screen door closed.

"I'm not the one who wants in her pants," I said. "But if you want to hang out and then tell Alice Mae you passed out all you could, I won't rat you out."

For a half a second, Dax looked hopeful that Mick would agree. The prospect of a video gamer night—a gamers' dream evening—was an offer that few guys could turn down.

"Naw, I'll just drop these off and offer her an arm to cry on," Mick said and left.

My knuckles cracked. I'd balled up the missing poster without realizing it. I seriously needed to get control of myself! Why did I even care?

Grabbing a bag of spicy potato chips and little weenies, I got the television in my room set up. It'd been far too long since I'd been able to veg out in front of the big screen. I grabbed my staple drink of iced tea and a Coke for Dax.

"Is this all part of your evil plan to get Alice Mae to tell you how and what she knows about your dad?" Dax said, holding up Mr. Ruth that I had put on my nightstand. "Why are you, and every straight male, fixated on Alice Mae?"

"I don't like her," I stated and grabbed the bunny by the ears and shoved him under my bed sheets. "Why would I bother with Courtney if I was—"

"Oh, I don't know," he said, sarcastically. "Maybe because you're *madly* in love with her?"

I held the crumpled missing poster and tossed it into my trash can. It hit the rim and bounced out. He still didn't look convinced so I pulled out my cell phone and sent Courtney a text, saying that I hoped she felt better and that I'll be thinking of her tonight. I held up the screen up to Dax before I pressed send.

"Do I have to quote Shakespeare?" he asked.

"Huh?"

"You protest too much."

"I don't like Alice Mae."

"Then why are you carrying around her rabbit?" he asked, glancing at the bunny ears sticking out of the sheets.

"Leverage."

"Light bulb!" Dax said, looking up at the metaphorical light above his head. "Instead of kidnapping her things to get her to talk, maybe you should ask your dad what he knows about Alice Mae instead of the other way around."

# CHAPTER NINETEEN

(Ryley: Present Time)

The West Harbour Psychiatric Treatment Facility—aka my dad's home sweet home—might as well have been a lone brick building constructed on top of some hill, with bats flying over the towers, and overgrown grass on the walkways, but it didn't have any of those psych ward stereotypical characteristics. In fact, crab apple trees lined the road up to the white painted hospital. The grass was manicured like a golf course. Blue birds chirped in the blue sky.

A lady at the front desk asked me to sign the facility's register. I adjusted my North Carolina hat so that my eyes barely showed. I kept my head down and waited in silence for the staff to let me in. I was forbidden access into his personal room. So, when the nurse led me into a large recreation room, I wasn't surprised that I barely recognized my dad.

His gray hair stuck out in every possible direction. His brown eyes were hidden under the mop that was his hair. His leathery skin was sagging and more wrinkled than most fifty year olds. He wore a white t-shirt that had a grid drawn on it with paint. In the center of the grid, there was a black circle. It looked similar to Einstein's theory of relativity. He used to be a profound physicist, back in the day, which was possibly why I wanted to go into that area of expertise. It would give me some way to connect to the man who fathered me until his schizophrenia stole him from my mom and me. But then again, his drawing could just be a botched tic-tac-toe board.

Rocking back and forth on a wooden chair, he reached out to the nurse. "I must speak with M.H! Urgent business. Tick tock, time is running out! Unless I find a way to stop it, and stop her—stop them. I must find a way! It's the only way! I have to stop her and Hearts! Where is she? Where is Al? She will know where M.H. is hiding!"

"Al isn't your visitor today, Robert," the nurse said in a calm, passive voice.

"Robby! How many times do I have to tell you to address me as Robby? Only one despicable person calls me Robert, so I don't want to be reminded of *her*." My dad scanned the room. "If Al isn't visiting me, then who?"

"Ryley is your visitor," the nurse said.

"I have a son named Ryley," my dad said, looking straight at me. "Or was it a girl? Girls have boy names, boys have girl names. It's all somewhat confusing. Fetch me the girl with the boy's name, my young lad."

Young lad? I wondered what century or geographical location he thought he was in, talking like that.

I sat down in the chair beside him. He stared at me before his eyes drifted to the floor. Mr. Ruth rested on his shoe. I hadn't even realized it had fallen out of my pocket. If I didn't know better, I'd swear it hopped out; but that would be absurd. I snatched it up and shoved it in my coat pocket. Staring at the stuffed animal, Dad mumbled a word that sounded too much like rumperbabbit to be coincidental. Mom was right. He knew something; the same something that Alice Mae knew. Secrets were locked in his mind; I just had to find a way to retrieve them.

I kept my hand in my pocket with a tight grip on Mr. Ruth, I said, "Dad, there's this girl—"

"That belongs to my son!"

He grabbed my wrist that had the watch and jerked it. Keeping a tight grip on Mr. Ruth's ears while my father pried at the watch, I tried to gently push my father away.

"Give it back! It's his! That belongs to my boy!"

"Dad, I'm your son. I'm Ryley. I need you to concentrate. Do you know an Alice Mae or her two aunts? Vida Maud—"

"Get your hands off me, you heathen!"

The nurse pulled me aside. When we were out of hearing range, she said, "I am really sorry, Ryley. He's showed few signs of improvement of late."

"Who is Hearts?" I asked.

"I'll have the doctor explain."

She escorted me to a private conference room and told me that a doctor would be in soon to explain my dad's deterioration. A crusty old man entered about thirty minutes later. He pulled up my dad's records on the computer. From the notes, he told me that Hearts was some sort of royalty.

"A queen?" I asked.

"That is the conclusion we had come to."

"Who is Al? And why is he visiting my dad?"

"Al is actually a young girl." The doctor paused a moment to let me absorb the information. "A young, blonde haired girl."

# CHAPTER TWENTY

(Alice Mae: Fourth visit to Wonderland)

The white rabbit—an unsuspecting curious creature in the Otherworld—was the animal at the bottom of the Wonderland totem pole. That piqued my interest, if I dismissed that it was my favorite animal. Nonetheless, the white rabbit, along with every other rumperbabbit, was regarded as a lower class citizen. M.H. acted like the animal was just a messenger of sorts, but I was beginning to think the creature was a much bigger role in the story than M.H. had led me to believe.

So when the white rabbit showed up in my veggie garden for the fourth time, I decided not to chase it. "What's your name?" I asked.

The white rabbit made no indication that it understood a lick of what I was saying. It just stared at me with its two little eyes and twitched its nose.

"I won't hurt you," I said, pushing a carrot toward it. "I just want to know why M.H. thinks you to be only a messenger."

The rabbit's nose stopped twitching—for a half a beat. Then, it took off running. And so the chase quickly ended with me falling down the rabbit hole that was next to my aunts' apple tree.

M

My entrance to Wonderland didn't open to a vast forest, or to M.H.'s mushroom house. I peered out of a grandfather clock. The dials turned forward very slowly. Springs and screws were laying all around the clock. Climbing out of the clock, I was knocked on the head by the second hand, and then stumbled to a floor. It was composed of white marble and black granite. I was in a hallway fit for a king. Red drapes hung from the windows, blowing with the night wind. Gold trim framed the hallway.

Entranced by the sparkling black chandelier hanging below a ceiling painting of an abstract winter scene, I screamed out when a gigantic white monster hopped up beside me and stepped on the hem of my dress. I swallowed a scream. When my eyes adjusted to the dim lighting of the closet, I noticed that it was the white rabbit, only that it was the same size as me—or rather, I was the same size as it.

"My name is Rutherford but I will terrorize your garden if I ever hear you call me that, and I have good hearing," the rabbit said and pointed to its long ears.

"What shall I call you then? The white rabbit?"

"Mr. Ruth," the white rabbit spat. "Everyone else might know me simply as the white rabbit—like I'm not important enough to have a name. But it doesn't mean I don't have a name… Just because bunnies lost the queen's popularity contest it doesn't mean we are insignificant."

"It's nice to meet you," I said, holding out my hand.

The rabbit gaped at my hand like I had sneezed onto it. My palm was dirty—I was dirty. Covered in the stuff actually. Water and mud dripped from my clothing and gathered on the floor, creating quite a sopping mess.

"If you keep sticking your arms and legs out like you are going to slow your descent, all you'll do is get dirty and quite bruised, stupid girl," Mr. Ruth said.

Why did everyone insist that I was stupid? "Tell you what little bunny; I will never address you by the white rabbit if you agree never to call me names again. I don't appreciate being called stupid."

"Fine," the rabbit said. "M.H. said I was only a messenger? Calling me a messenger is a demotion that I will not allow! If he thinks that I will hop around doing his bidding just because he's buds with Robby, he's got another think coming!"

"What is the big deal with this Robby fellow?"

The rabbit's mouth dropped. "You seriously don't know anything, about anything, do you stupid—do you Al?"

"It's becoming quite obvious I know little about Wonderland," I stated, trying to keep my frustration under wraps.

"Robby is the only living member of the Edgar family..." he said, and then added. "Or so we thought."

Footsteps sounded. The white rabbit took off; hopping like its fluffy tail was on fire. I raced after him, leaving a trail of tiny footprints on the checkered tile. Unable to keep up with the rabbit, I made a beeline for the window, planning to hide behind the drapes.

"Moon burn is a real threat, Al!" the rabbit said from behind a closet door. "In here, with me!"

I darted behind a door along the hallway. Just as we pulled the humongous door shut, I heard the queen. If I hadn't spent an afternoon trapped in a tea pot listening to her, I might not have believed that she was the queen. Her voice was high and shrill. She had the body of a child, but the face of an adult. And the curly red hair of a doll I played with in the Otherworld.

Behind her was a boy my age, being dragged by M.H. If I hadn't known better, I would have thought that he was a loyal servant of the queen—a double agent. The boy had wild brown hair and eyes that looked like russet chocolates. The boy's eyes changed darker, which was an indication of the Wonderland creatures.

"I knew Robert's child would stumble down a rabbit hole, M.H."

Hearts said, pleased with the good fortune.

"You're working for the queen, Mr. Ruth? You dig holes for her?"

"There is more than one rabbit in Wonderland, so don't go making accusations that I sided with the queen. She'd just as quickly behead me as help me in a pinch."

"I'd help you in a pinch."

The rabbit scrutinized me, like he was trying to find the lie in my statement. "I heard a rumor from Alfred that you said you'd prefer the company of a rabbit than to a spider."

"I did."

The rabbit's nose twitched. "You... you actually like rumperbabbits?"

"What's not to love?"

He shook his head in confusion. But, he did scoot a little closer to me, even though he didn't answer my question.

"Do you really think Robby Edgar would take the chance of coming back to Wonderland?" M.H. asked, looking at the boy.

"My dad knows this place?" the boy asked. His voice squeaked at the end.

The queen walked over to him. Every floor tile she stepped on flashed and then quickly dimmed. Following her was the old man, Jack, and a younger version of him. A man wearing a dunce hat and striped black and white leggings sat on the floor beside the table. He had the same beady black eyes as the butler. The family genetics were uncanny. He looked like a much younger version of the butler. Judging from the playing cards that he shuffled in his hands, I assumed him to be the Joker.

"Where did you think he came from?" the Joker asked, staring at the boy.

The boy crossed his arms and stared at the queen. If his glare was any indication, he was not happy about being regarded as unintelligent. "A stork?" the boy said, mockingly.

The Joker stopped shuffling his cards. Without warning, he thrust his arm in the air and released the cards. Fire lit from each card as they changed from playing cards to tarot cards. White smoke filled the air. The Jack walked around the boy, observing every single card. He managed to keep watch on each card as it hit the floor. Some sizzled as they made contact. Others burned into ash. But a few others shined brilliantly like blood on a knife.

"Pick up three cards, child," the Joker said, speaking pleasantly to the boy.

"You pick them up!" the boy exclaimed. "*You* made the mess!"

The Jack knelt beside the boy. A word wasn't spoken, but after he snapped his fingers the boy carefully chose three cards and handed them to the Joker.

"What's your name, boy?" the queen asked.

The boy hesitated. He shifted nervously from foot to foot. The boy gaped at the queen, like he wasn't sure of what had just happened.

"I only ask because I do not know how to address you," Hearts said and smiled the most trustworthy smile a person could replicate.

"You may call me Sir Underwear Superpants," the boy mocked.

Even I knew that wasn't his real name.

The Joker showed the queen the cards the boy had chosen. "The card of death. And…" the queen stopped looking at the cards. "How is this supposed to be an accurate reading when there are still playing cards mixed in with the tarot cards?"

"What did he choose?" M.H. asked, looking at the Jack like the old man had all the answers.

"Deuce of hearts," the Joker said. "A king of spades."

"Robby favors the spade symbol. This boy is his son," M.H. said.

"Stop acting like you know anything about prophesying!" Hearts said. "Jack, what do you make of it?"

The Jack walked over to the queen and took the card. He grabbed a pencil from somewhere in his pocket and scribbled on the card. After he was done, he tore it in half. One piece he handed to the boy and the other was given to M.H. Without uttering a word, the Jack walked away.

"What does the prophecy read?" Hearts asked.

"The HATed fool will die," the boy said.

The Joker snatched up the card and read the words. "The HATed fool will die *twice*," the Joker said, making an amendment to the prophecy. The Joker handed the torn card to M.H. "Another incomprehensible prophecy given by a senile old man. Anyone with a seeing eye knew there was supposed to be a 'twice' at the end of that phrase."

M.H. read what the Jack wrote on his half of the card. "Before the MADness stops. It's a *Madmen's Prophecy*."

"So the entire prophecy states that the HATed fool will die twice before the MADness stops," Chez repeated. "Tell me, Joker, how does someone die twice?"

"How am I to know?" the Joker said. "But I'd love to play with the fool whose death can be repeated. My play dates would last much longer if someone could be killed over and over again."

"Enough of this rubbish!" Hearts said, rubbing her temples.

Just then, a man dressed in business clothes ran into the room. An army of card soldiers and two white painted women with red hearts marked on their faces followed. The man looked like an older version of the boy. He exchanged a quick glance with M.H. but neither man spoke a word to the other.

"Dad!" the boy shouted.

The Joker flung a card in front of the boy. Normally, a thrown card wouldn't have given me pause, but the paper card shimmered and glistened as it twirled. From the sparks, dozens of spikes protruded from the paper. The boy stopped before it grazed his face. The card hit the floor with a loud thud. It stuck, unmoving, because one of the spikes jammed into the tile.

The Joker sneered, "Dare I say that this boy belongs to Robert Edgar—commonly known as Robby the Banished Prince?"

The queen clapped her hands. A door, a fifth the size of the human door, snapped open. Four frogs wearing a bellhop uniforms raced in, carrying a golden stool.

"My, my, what a pleasant surprise, Robert," Hearts said condescendingly as she stepped on the golden stool—still being held by the four frogs. They raised her so she was just high enough to be face to face with the intruder.

The man winced as the frogs' legs began to buckle and shake under the queen's weight. However, he quickly regained his cold, hard composure. "My dear sister-in-law, it's been a long time since I've seen your ugly face."

"I was hoping it'd be another decade or two before we met again. Since you accused me of the unspeakable last time we were together." The queen inspected Robert. "Your eyes aren't dilated. Someone has been slipping you sweets. Who?"

M.H. flinched. Immediately, an orange cat appeared beside him, floating in the air, like gravity dared not pull it to the floor.

"Nervous for some reason?" the cat asked, contemptuously as it showed its claws.

"Oh Chez, M.H. is mental, but he'd never betray me," Hearts said, but never took her eyes off Robert.

M.H. took off his hat and placed it on the boy's head. The rim fell over his brown eyes, keeping him from seeing anything disturbing.

The queen spoke in a diplomatic tone, "I'd never in my wildest dreams consider the possibility of leading the—"

"You tricked my son into coming to this place!" Robert yelled, advancing toward the queen.

The card soldiers blocked him with their paper mache swords and battle axes. They looked like they could be taken out by a heavy duty squirt gun, but I wasn't confident enough they would become soggy to put my theory to the test. The two, white painted women wearing the red, facial hearts stepped in front of the queen. When it was clear Robby was not going to harm her, the queen stepped in front of them. It didn't take a genius to figure out they were her personal guards.

"Thank you, LeDee and LeDum, but Robby is no match for me, not anymore," Hearts said to the painted women.

Robby said, "Did you think my son would like his head to be detached from his body like his Uncle Eddie?"

"Don't speak about my beloved late husband that way!" Hearts shouted. "You should consider yourself fortunate that I didn't order you or your son to be beheaded the moment I heard of your arrival to my court."

"Then allow us both leave, and we will never return again."

"You already promised never to return," Hearts said, dryly. "Yet, here you are."

Robby swore. "I'll give up all my candy."

"All of your candy?" Hearts said. She grinned a horribly evil smile when he nodded. "Tell me the boy's name, and you have a deal."

Robby's jaw tightened. He spoke through clenched teeth. "My son's name is Ryley."

"Your child's name could be that of a girl's or a boy's," Hearts said. "When a second carried on for infinity, every creature in Wonderland would tip their Hat to the misfit girl with a boy's name (or was it a boy with a Girl's name?) who'd end the Reign of Terror... I don't suppose you gave your son a girl's name on purpose? Tempt fate?"

"Quoting the *Bleeding Hearts Prophecy*?" Robby said, laughing comically. "After all these years, you're still afraid of a silly fortune?"

"Being scared is not the same as being mindful. I'd keep a closer watch on your son. For the next time I find him in my court, he'll see the Joker's blade," Hearts said, stepping off the golden stool. "Joker, please escort the Edgars out."

M.H. tossed Robby a piece of checkered candy, for which he received an earth-shattering glare from the queen. Her eyes turned blood red.

"It's only an Eraser Tracer, an unforgettable-forgettable sweet to make the boy lose recollection of this night," M.H. explained. "To make Wonderland seem like it was only a dream."

"So be it," she said after a long pause.

I couldn't believe that she let them go! Why would she do such a thing? What was her plan? As she and M.H. were leaving, she stepped on a tiny, muddy footprint. She howled so fiercely that one would think she was dying. The frogs that had been carrying the stool dropped it to tend to their queen, wiping her shoe clean of mud.

Chez appeared beside it and gave it a sniff. "A muddy footprint."

Mr. Ruth shifted nervously beside me. "This is another spectacular reason to keep your legs and arms tucked close when you fall down the rabbit holes—it's harder to track what is clean!"

The cat followed the prints closer and closer to the closet door. Once her feet were rid of any mud, the queen followed her kitty with the utmost curiosity.

"Run away while you still can, Mr. Ruth," I said. "You're faster than me so you might just get away!"

"She'll wring your neck!" Mr. Ruth exclaimed.

"I'm not afraid of her," I said.

"I owe you my life, Al. If you survive—"

"Just go!"

He darted away so fast that he looked like a white blaze. I couldn't even pinpoint his shape; much less make out that he was a rabbit. The flash caught the queen's attention. Fearing that she'd order her soldiers to pursue it, I pushed the closet door open.

The orange cat didn't bother hiding its hunger. "It's just a defenseless, little creature, a girl."

Sometimes the most delicate creatures can be the most violent, little kitty. Though, I didn't say this, but the thought echoed in my mind as the cat clawed me out of the closet.

# CHAPTER TWENTY-ONE

(Alice Mae: Fourth Visit to Wonderland Continued…)

I can still remember the hateful look in the Queen of Hearts' eyes when she found me hiding in her coat closet. I'd dismissed the possibility of monsters long ago, but I could see the blood thirst in her eyes. She grabbed me by the shoulders after Chez dragged me out via his claws. Bright red marks lined my arms.

"What is your name, little girl?" Hearts asked.

I didn't make eye contact with M.H. He was on my side, but, for all intents and purposes, he had to stay in character in front of the queen. In her presence, he was her ally, not mine.

I spoke in a soft voice, pretending to be scared. "Al."

"Al?" Hearts repeated with a laugh. She grabbed a piece of my hair and inspected it. Commenting that another dumb blonde had fallen into her court, she asked, "What are you doing here, stupid girl?"

"I fell."

"How convenient that you just so happened to fall down the hole the same day, the very hour, that Robert's boy arrived," Chez said. His yellowed eyes narrowed. "Are you spying for the traitorous Mr. Edgar?"

"I've never met him," I said. "And, if you didn't want me coming here, then why did you order for so many rabbit holes to be dug?"

M.H. winced at my last comment. I suppose that was something that I wasn't supposed to say.

Hearts asked, "Where did you hear of such a thing?"

"A little bird told me," I said.

Chez licked his lips. "Was it Omar, the cockatoo?"

"No!" I crossed my arms. "I snuck up on you when you were having a tea party. I heard everything you said about digging holes so that a wannabe prince would take a stumble into this realm."

"Then you are in need of a punishment," Hearts said, stepping away from me. Her voice carried, echoing through the hall.

The door at the very end of the hall cracked open. I could barely make out the Jack's beady, black eyes before his kin pushed past him. In the Joker's hand was a sword that looked like it had been intended for a toy soldier. As he flipped it in the air, it grew bigger and bigger until it became the largest blade I'd ever seen! Only when it was the size of my body did he hurl it in my direction.

In sheer panic, I froze.

Out of the corner of my eye, I saw the Jack take a pair of dice out of the Joker's pocket. When he threw them on the ground, a puff of smoke erupted. The Jack disappeared. He reappeared in front of me and grabbed the blade. But it was too late. The weapon cut me, scratching the side of my face. The blade disappeared from his hand.

"Hands off my toys, great-great-grand pappy!" the Joker screamed, digging in his pockets. He ripped out a handful of jacks and threw them at the Jack. Every jack missed, ricocheting around us. No one moved a muscle as the pointy toys stuck into the floor and walls.

Somehow, only the LeDee and LeDum had been hit; the redness of the blood was brought out by the white paint. I suspected that no one else was harmed because of Jack's doing; he had sorcery powers. Eyeing the toys, I knew one thing. If I was going to make it out alive, I was going to learn some of the Joker's tricks.

Hearts reacted as if the Joker just dumped a gallon of pimple pus on her. "I swear I'll use those jacks to drain you dry if one stabbed me, Joker!" she screamed and then looked at me like I'd instigated the ruckus. "Off with her—"

"T-t-the'th a c-child," the Jack whispered, stepping in front of me. His lisp made it difficult to understand. But it was only when I looked more closely did I see that the tip of his tongue was actually cut off.

M.H. gave me a look that screamed his fear, but it was concealed in the blink of an eye. "The Jack is right. You know the Rightdoing Law passed down from the White King before you. No beheadings for children, no exceptions."

"Stupid law," Hearts said. "I should have done away with that as soon as I became ruler, but it would be poor public image since the king… tripped on the guillotine and died by accidental beheading."

"Accidental beheading?" I said. "Do Wonderlanders really believe that was what happened to the King?"

… I should have stopped talking while I was ahead.

# CHAPTER TWENTY-TWO

(Ryley: Present Time)

Mr. Ruth's missing posters papered the school's halls by Monday morning. All of Alice Mae's fingernails had been chewed off by the day's end. Come Tuesday, most of the posters were torn, thrown in the garbage, or being stepped on after falling to the floor. A few still hung, probably because Alice Mae worked on them non-stop in her spare time. *A little piece of me* felt guilty—okay, I was fully willing to admit to my crime by the time Wednesday rolled around. Or at least slip the stuffed animal into Alice Mae's locker, but I wasn't sure what would fall out if I tried it. When Thursday rolled around, most of the Mr. Ruth drawings had mustaches and sombreros.

On Friday, I copied the phone number on the only poster left hanging (which happened to be next to Alice Mae's locker) and sent off a text message while walking to lit class. *You should always put a reward on a missing poster.*

I expected my phone to immediately beep with a text message reply. It didn't. I don't know how many lockers I passed while staring at my screen. Only after I shoved it into my pocket did the alarm go off. Figures.

Alice Mae: *How am I to know what reward to offer to a stranger?*

114

Me: *You will get your bunny back when I get some answers.*

I hit send, and then was attacked from behind. Alice Mae swung her backpack at me—something pointy jabbed my side. I jerked the bag from her hands. I caught a glimpse of her icy blue eyes when she jumped on my back and swatted me. I dropped her bag and my phone, and subsequently stepped on it, while I pried the crazed lunatic off me. She was a feisty one! I slammed her into the wall before she retracted her claws and let go.

It wasn't like this went unnoticed by our classmates. A crowd of students formed around us. Courtney was amongst them. Her wide eyes and dropped jaw only added to her horrific expression, but I didn't care—not then. Alice Mae demanded my attention, and I was going to let her have it.

Furthermore, it wouldn't be long before the teachers caught wind and passed out detention slips. Alice Mae must have drawn the same conclusion. Tears pooled in her eyes. I rubbed my head; she'd ripped out a few chunks of hair. A few strands fell loose and drifted to the ground.

"I should have known that *you* are holding Mr. Ruth hostage!"

"It's just a stupid bunny!"

She grabbed my baseball state champion's cap off the floor, picking out a few of my hairs, which had been pulled out during the tussle. She twirled it on her finger.

"Give that back you damn infuriating minx," I said, ready to pry the hat from her fingers.

"It's just a stupid hat!" She tossed it on the floor and wiped her dirty antique shoes on it. Her snooty smile spoke the words she dare not speak.

"You're not going to get Mr. Ruth back now. You are terrible at negotiations," I said, jerking my hat up from under her shoe.

We stood so close I could smell her cherry-vanilla perfume. I'd rather she smell like a wet-dog covered in skunk spray than a not-so-sweet girl.

"Blanch will give you detention faster than any other teacher here. It's time to make your exit. She's not worth it." Dax grabbed my shoulders and pulled me away. He handed me my phone. The screen was cracked. Great.

We didn't utter a word to each other in the first period, but I sincerely doubted she was going to bow down now. This was war. Even though "the line was drawn," I hadn't realized how high the stakes were until seventh period. My locker had been suspiciously covered in shredded, red fabric. String hung from the door handle and pieces of fabric were strewn across the hallway. It wasn't until I unlocked it, that I realized the shredded material was my state championship hat!

"That miserable hussy!" I yelled, slamming my door shut and fisting a handful of red fabric.

I marched toward the freshman hall, but stopped dead when I caught glimpse of her outré blue and orange coat. She was leaning against the wall by the water fountain, absentmindedly painting her fingernails bright green. The same M.H. crest that was scratched into the side of my dad's car was drawn on her hand with blue ink. I started several different insults, but none seemed callous enough to explicitly describe the horror she'd done.

"Use your words," she said without looking up at me.

I growled. Yep, growled. I tossed the remaining hat pieces at her feet. "You underhanded vixen!"

"Something upsetting you caveman?" she asked, innocently.

"And you vandalized my dad's car!" I said, staring at the hat crest on her hand.

My accusation didn't faze her. "Prove it."

"That rabbit is toast!" I said, thinking of the ways I would destroy Mr. Ruth. Fire. Industrial sized paper shredder. Hacksaw. Maybe I'd dismember it, take pictures, and send them to her.

Screwing the top back onto her bottle of nail polish, she looked up at me and smiled. It wasn't a pretty 'take my picture' kind of smile. No, it was a suggestive, yet threatening one. She blew on her nails. The blue lipstick and the form of her lips made it look like she was attempting to kiss her fingers.

She pushed away from the wall, staring at me like I was harmless, like she could win this fight. She acted like I was her target, instead of the other way around—she should fear me, not mock me! Hell, I was keeping my hands clenched tight at my sides so I wouldn't do anything rash. I stood my ground, shaking with rage. I wanted to backhand her, and do things to her with my fists that I'd only do to a guy. She pressed her pointer finger on my chest. Dragging her finger down my shirt, she smiled pleasantly—in an evil, twisted sort of way. Green polish smeared onto my clothes.

"If anything happens to Mr. Ruth, you'll never uncover my secrets, and I assure you that they are dirty and juicy." The soft, beautiful tone of her voice changed into something more menacing. It was wispy, like an old man's, not a young girl. "Robby told me *so much* during my visitations in his padded room."

"You're Al?"

She curtsied and then turned on her heels, walking away merrily. Before she rounded the corner, she added, "How are my negotiation skills now, Ryley?"

My fist collided with a locker. An instant burn radiated up my arm. Not the smartest move but brighter than strangling the blonde broad. The bell rang. Students filed into the hallway, putting more and more bodies between us. Meaning that she was going to get away scot-free—I had no way of proving that she purposely destroyed my irreplaceable cap.

I raced after, bumping into people in my chase. They didn't look particularly pleased with being barrel rolled, but I refused, re-effing-fused, to let her get away. She'd made it to the stairs before I caught up to her. I took the stairs two at a time until I was in front of her, blocking her.

"You're not going to get away so easily!" I said. I edged to the end of the step.

Raising an eyebrow, she laughed, "Think of it this way, Ryley. I saved you from the humiliation of wearing such an ill-fitting hat. It was much too small for you anyway. I did you a favor."

"Out of all my ill-fitting hats, one has never given me a headache like you do."

"I've only begun to give you a headache," she whispered and turned around and walked down the steps.

She got to the landing before I was close enough to grab her wrist, stopping her escape. She wiggled, freeing her hand. When I refused to back off, she moved her leg like she was going to knee me in the groin again, so I completely closed the gap between us, pressing my hips against hers. She had no room to strike.

"I'm done with this charade!" I yelled even though we were millimeters away from each other. "Everything you say doesn't make a lick of sense. Why did you come here? Surely it wasn't just to annoy me."

"Just because you don't understand my way of thinking, it doesn't mean that I don't make sense!" she yelled. "You're such a—"

"A what?" I interrupted. "An Otherworlder?"

She stepped closer, even though I hadn't thought it possible, making it clear that I hadn't intimidated her. Even though I was taller than her, she stood on her tip toes, making us closer to the same height.

"Actually, I was going to say that you are such a *boy!* What's an Otherworlder, Ryley? I'm not sure that word even has a definition, or did you make it up? Now, who sounds crazy?" she said, spreading her arms wide.

I'd forgotten about everyone else in existence. They were all staring. Judging from the context spoken, I did sound more insane than she. I seriously hated losing this game to her!

"What is Wonderland, Alice Mae?"

"Do you not remember anything?" She seemed genuinely frustrated. "Sometimes I wish you never ate that Eraser Tracer!"

118

"I'm not in the habit of remembering places I have never been, you stupid girl!"

"Don't call me that!" She socked me in the gut. Normally, I would have thought it cute that she tried to attack me since she was so feeble, but today it only aggravated me.

"I was alerted that your father's car had moved," Alice Mae said. "Was he able to answer any of your questions?"

The hall got so quiet, not a single person coughed. I wanted to rip the damn rabbit's head off, but it was in my backpack that I'd dropped when I noticed the hat carnage in my locker.

"My dad is not around," I said.

"Interesting phrasing," Alice Mae said, analyzing my comment. She tapped her finger on her chin like she was deep in thought. "You didn't say he was dead, nor did you confirm it. Perchance you and your mom made up a series of lies about him?"

I had to shut her up before she told everyone the truth! I hated how she could completely destroy me with a few simple words. She knew my deepest secret, and now she was telling the whole school about my whacked-out dad!

"—where does he live Ryley? I can't seem to remember its name. It was some kind—"

I slapped my free hand over her mouth. She bit down. I pulled my hand away. Teeth marks were embedded in my skin. Smirking at me, she licked her lips.

"You instigated this war!" she said. She spoke more loudly. She was right. Her voice did carry. "Your father isn't dead. He's insa—"

In a stated of extreme panic, I did the only logical thing I could do to shut her up.

I kissed her.

# CHAPTER TWENTY-THREE

(Ryley: Present Time)

Our lips met, silencing her. The sweet flavor of Alice Mae's strawberry gum filled my mouth. I kissed her harder than I'd ever kissed a girl before. Usually, I hoped to leave them breathless. I wanted her to be completely and utterly speechless.

I figured she was as likely to bite me, but she caught me off guard; she kissed me back. She moved against me like she danced—smooth and gracefully—but fiercely, nevertheless. She wasn't backing down. This had to be just another game to her, and I wasn't about to let her win.

Without letting her come up for air, I walked her back against the locker—or wall, I wasn't sure and didn't care. She tasted… her kiss… it was hypnotic.

Her lips should have a warning label posted: Highly addictive. The kiss manifested high concentrations of rhapsody. Her hands slipped up around my face and then into my hair. She pulled me harder against her, using my hair as leverage. I wrapped my arms around her thin waist as she sucked on my bottom lip. Right when I thought she was going to break the kiss, she bit down. A moan slipped from my throat.

Her voice wavered when she spoke. "You were right all along, Ryley. We weren't destined to be *just friends.*"

Her electric blue eyes sparkled like jewels. Her pouting lips made me want to shut her up with another kiss. My plan backfired. I'd gotten her to stop talking about my dad, but she'd infiltrated my mind. I was buzzed. It wasn't just the happy go lucky adrenaline rush—it was so much more than that. I stumbled. The gravity seemed to have taken five, because it felt like I was flying, even though I was still planted on the floor. I know this because I checked. The black and white tile squares appeared to grow and shrink. There wasn't a particular rhythm to their shifting. Every single lock on the lockers sparkled like metamorphic rocks. The ceiling wavered like water. My stomach flipped.

"May I have my gum back?" Alice Mae asked.

Until then, I hadn't noticed that her strawberry gum had made its way into my mouth. I fished it out and dropped it into her palm. She quickly popped it into her mouth. The floor stopped shifting, but a few black tiles still shimmered. I had the sudden urge to step on each and every one of them.

Alice Mae cupped my face and directed my attention back to her. She looked at me—hard. "Oh dear."

"What's in that gum? Hallucinogens?" I asked. My words didn't slur, but it didn't exactly sound like me either.

The distant sound of the bell rang, indicating that we were late. I'd forgotten we still had another class to endure.

She said, "I have to go."

"Where?"

"Away."

"Away *where?*"

"Just away," she said, pushing me back. She twirled away and hopped down the hall, stepping on each black square that flashed.

# CHAPTER TWENTY-FOUR

(Ryley: Present Time)

Standing in the middle of a mostly empty hall, I scratched my head. I wasn't sure what had happened—how the series of events had progressed from her shredding my beloved hat to us having a semi-intense make out session in the hallway.

"You're not going to get that second date with Courtney, not anymore." Becky stood in the hall, arms crossed, and glaring at me like I had committed the vilest of crimes.

I didn't deserve a second date, and yet I didn't feel completely heartbroken. It was probably because my lips were still swollen.

"You led Courtney on," Becky said.

"No, I liked her." I looked down that hall that Alice Mae had scampered. Seriously, how had my life changed so much between sixth and seventh period?

"Liked being the correct tense," she said. "Stay away from my friend. Or I'll tell her the truth."

Now, she had my attention. "What truth?"

"Well, I put on my detective hat—like you suggested—and found something rather interesting."

"What's that?"

"Your dad developed nomadic traits after Edward died."

"Listen Becky, I was just pulling your leg. My dad doesn't have a family. He was adopted. I don't have any uncles, or aunts, or weird cousins," I said. "It's just me and my mom."

Becky dug in her pocket and pulled out a piece of paper. She crumpled it up into a ball, threw it at me, and left. I picked the paper up and unfolded it. It was a copy of my dad's health records from the first university he taught at, over a decade ago. Under family history, written in blue ink, was my dad's handwriting. Brother: Edward Edgar—heart condition.

"Where did you get this?"

She glanced over her shoulder. "I told you I have family connections in law enforcement. I was able to dig up a few old documents… still haven't found a death certificate for your dad."

# CHAPTER TWENTY-FIVE

(Alice Mae: Present Time in Wonderland)

I didn't know what a heart attack felt like, but if I was to guess, I'd say it was the pounding sensation in my chest that almost paralyzed me when Ryley's lips met mine. Resting my elbows on the queen's table, I buried my head in my hands and willed my heartbeat to slow. My palms were sweaty. My legs were shaking. Even so, none of my physical ailments had anything to do with my impromptu fall down the rabbit's hole.

"Why do you insist upon sticking your arms and legs out when falling down through the rabbit holes, Al?" Chez said. His fuzzy tail swept across my hands.

That cleared the butterflies from my stomach. I lowered my hands and glared at the damn cat. "Because I'm just a stupid girl and won't learn," I said, sarcastically.

Rolling onto his back, Chez chuckled, "I think you secretly like tracking mud into the castle. You know it annoys the queen."

"It's no secret," Hearts said, walking into the room. "How many times have you scrubbed the floors clean of your mud prints?"

"Two hundred and forty eight times," I said, smiling like it didn't bother me, even though I hated the ancient sponge (a glorified germ factory) and the bucket of bleach.

Hearts stepped up a series of short stairs and then sat down on a chair, much higher than mine. She lifted the black and crimson colored tea pot and poured herself a cup. After dropping two sugar cubes into it, she looked me over.

"Your lipstick is smudged."

Blushing, I covered my mouth and immediately regretted my reaction. I needed to appear unemotional. I lowered my hands and smirked, just like Hearts inadvertently taught me so many years ago.

"I told you my plan was to get the boy to fall in love with me. Obviously, it's working," I said.

I poured myself a splash of tea. I blew into the cup and pretended not to notice that my hands were still shaking.

The queen raised her cup to her lips, but from a lower angle, I couldn't tell if she actually took a drink. "It appears to be working quite well."

I waved her comment off and lowered my cup without taking a drink. I trusted the queen about as much as I trusted a starved flesh-eating deadman. Besides, Hearts' paranoia of poison spread throughout Wonderland, me included. Over the years, she'd banned most poisons, especially after her roses died, which was why M.H. had developed a less concentrated potion. It simply made a person ill——not dead.

"The reason for my unplanned visit is because Ryley reacted to the wondrous candy," I said. "I thought only those who spend a great deal of time in Wonderland, or call this court their birthplace, reacted to the sweets."

The queen and the cat exchanged a look. "The boy reacts to our sweets because he is—in essence—one of us, even if he was born in the Otherworld for he is the only Heir to the throne. Wonderland must always have a ruler."

"Well, that settles that," I said and stood up to leave. My legs wobbled. "Next time I return, Ryley will be with me."

"Not so fast," Hearts said. She pointed to the mud tracks. "You're not leaving this court until the floor is clean enough to eat from."

I bit my tongue before I said anything unpleasant, or commented about eating off the floor. I didn't want to plant that seed in the queen's head. I would not be the one to have a meal where people walked. That's where I put my foot down.

"If I stay here, that means that no one is watching the boy," I pointed out. "Do you remember Becky? She is now obsessed with finding out what Ryley is hiding. They might skip town, and the racecar is only now working! If they go too far away, I won't be able to track them. It will be almost impossible!"

"You did it once, you can do it again."

I clenched my sweaty, shaky hands. "But my plan! The ground I've made with getting Ryley to fall for me might be undone if I stay here longer than necessary."

Chez rubbed up against my leg. "Did you honestly not think the queen had plans of her own?"

# CHAPTER TWENTY-SIX

(Ryley: Present Time)

A half-full bucket of balls was spilled over the batter's box. My shoulders ached. Sweat coated my shirt. Dust covered my face. Yet, it didn't matter when I hit the ball with the baseball bat. The crunch took my mind off of Alice Mae—even if it was for a millisecond. The bat's vibrations stung my hands, which was also a nice distraction from the strawberry flavor that still saturated in my mouth. I was beginning to hate strawberries, even though until now they were my favorite fruit. But Alice Mae made a mess of that flavor too, just like she'd made a mess of my life.

I swore it was premeditated. Why else would she have apologized for *making a mess of my life* under the football stands?

Dax showed up. Saying nothing, he picked up my discarded glove, grabbed the half full bucket of balls and walked to the pitcher's mound. He didn't have an All-Star pitching arm, but he was pretty consistent at getting the ball over the plate without pegging me.

"I don't want to like her," I said, swinging the bat at a curve ball. I missed.

Tossing the next ball into the air, Dax laughed. "Do you think that I woke up one morning and decided to be gay? Do you think it's easy for me to like someone who is completely and hopelessly heterosexual?"

Point taken.

He nodded to someone behind me. "Speak of the devil."

Mick grabbed me by my shoulders and greeted me by smashing his fist against my nose. Tears filled my eyes as I cursed and defended myself. Mick socked me in the stomach twice before Dax was able to tear him away.

"You knew I was going for Alice Mae!" Mick shouted.

Blood dripped from my now-broken-nose. "It wasn't like I planned to kiss her!"

"Let me guess—you tripped, and your lips accidentally smacked hers?" Mick said. He pushed away from Dax, but since he wasn't moving to attack me again, Dax let him.

I pulled off my shirt and held it against my nose. "Honestly, I just wanted to shut her up."

"And kissing her was your genius idea?"

I shrugged my shoulders. "It worked."

Mick groaned, but the corners of his frown turned up. Rubbing his hand, like my face had actually done some damage, he commented that we were even. "You know Courtney is never going to give you the time of day again."

*Time of day*, I thought, looking at the watch that was once my dad's. It ticked on steadily. How was it possible for my life to get turned upside-down in a matter of seconds? One moment Alice Mae and I were sworn enemies—like a superhero to a villain. A kiss changed all that. If I could only turn back time, I was sure that I could fix everything. I'd be living in a wonderland. But I couldn't do the impossible, like turning the clock backwards. In the present day, here in real life, I reminded myself, I'd fallen for the Wrong girl.

# CHAPTER TWENTY-SEVEN

(Ryley: Present Time)

Edward Edgar—heart condition. Those four words, written in my dad's handwriting, were proof that he had a brother. It was evident that he and my mom had been lying to me, but why? After all these years, why hadn't anyone bothered to tell me about my long, lost uncle? To find out from Becky was a low blow.

If my mom wouldn't talk about this Edward guy, then I needed to pay my dad a visit (and probably leave without any answers) or ask Alice Mae, since she claimed to know so much about my family.

Plus, it would give me a valid reason to talk to her.

Not that I needed a reason to talk to her. I paced around my bedroom, clutching Mr. Ruth while trying to think of what to do next, when I stepped on a mushy ball. I lifted up my shoe. A small round bunny turd was stuck to the bottom. I stared at Mr. Ruth like he was to blame. I sniffed it just to see if my imagination was going haywire. It stunk of rotten, overcooked popcorn. The only reasonable explanation was that a kernel got wet and turned to mush.

Someone knocked at the door. "The principal called," my mom said, perceptibly annoyed, as she opened the door. "He said you caused quite——"

"Who's Edward Edgar, Lauren?" I asked purposely calling her by her first name, the name that every respectful son should never call their mother.

"Watch your words, young man!"

"I was named after my uncle, wasn't I? Ryley Edward Edgar."

"You have no uncles, Ryley."

I tossed her the crumpled paper, proof that she'd lied to me for years. She caught it and carefully unfolded it.

"Care to change your story?" I asked, folding my arms and squishing Mr. Ruth.

My mom pressed her lips into a thin line. Her face turned ghostly white. Tears gathered in her eyes, but none spilled over. The wetter her eyes grew, the worse I felt. I uncrossed my arms, tossed the rabbit on the bed, and walked up to her.

After a lifetime of seconds, she managed to speak. "Your father said that his best friend growing up was named Eddie. Never in my wildest dreams did I think he was Robby's brother," she whispered, tracing the paper like it was made of gold. "I didn't know."

I was ready to rattle off another ill-thought out question when she looked up at me. My heart broke instantly. Tears spilled from her eyes. She was usually so well put together that it took me off guard.

"I miss him, Ryley. I miss him every day, every hour."

I took her in my arms and rocked her like she had done when I was a child. It'd been years since I cried in front of her, and I couldn't recall ever seeing her cry. My gut ached listening to her weep.

"Why don't you go see him?" I asked. "I know it's not the same, but it's still Dad—somewhere in there."

Pulling away just enough to knock off my hat and mess up my hair, she said, "When we moved to Rockingham, I told Robby that you had a hard time moving from town to town. I told him we couldn't skip town anymore. He understood but said that if we weren't going to move as often then we can't visit him. He said he thought they were tracking him, and if we visited then they would eventually find us. So, I promised him because it was so hard for you... I made it a year before I went back to see him."

"What happened?"

"He went berserk and said if I ever come back to visit, he'd do what he should have done years ago. Return to Wonderland and go on a killing spree... he said that was the only way we'd be safe."

"Safe? From whom? Him?"

"From Eddie's wife, Hearts," she said. "and her minions."

# CHAPTER TWENTY-EIGHT

(Ryley: Present Time)

Alice Mae wasn't at school the next day. Or even the day after that. A whole week went by with no sign of her. It was like she'd been a figment of my imagination. And, I could almost convince myself that I'd made her (and the kiss) up, until I caught Courtney glaring at me. I couldn't blame her for being upset with me. I'd be pissed at me too if I were her. So when John Luke became glued to her side again, I couldn't be bummed out. And I wasn't. I just wished there was some way I could apologize to her; so she knew I wasn't just another guy looking for the hottest piece of tail in school. Of course, when John Luke offered to smash my face with his oversized, beastly hand if I ever uttered a word to Courtney, I was less inclined to speak to her again.

On a good note, Mick had moved on.

Dax hadn't.

When Monday rolled around, I couldn't stand it. I had to see Alice Mae again! She'd wiggled her way into all of my thoughts. I couldn't even veg out in front of the television without thinking about her. Why had she suddenly disappeared after we kissed?

And then there was the mystery-uncle, Edward, and his wife, Hearts. Was she the same Hearts that Alice Mae referred to? Was she really a queen? And why did Alice Mae go by Al when she visited my dad? Was she trying to hide from someone too? There were so many damn questions and even fewer answers. I didn't know what to think.

I sent Alice Mae a text, saying that we needed to talk. I purposely left it vague. There were a million topics we had yet to discuss, and I didn't want to scare her away. I never got a response. Nothing. Zilch. When Wednesday rolled around, I texted her again saying that I needed to talk to her— more accurately apologize—and that she didn't have to say anything. Just listen. Again, no reply. So I called her and got an automated message saying that the number I called was out of cell range. Not to be dismissed so easily, I sent her a text every day, for thirteen straight days. On the fourteenth day, I sent a rather desperate one.

*For all that is holy, if the kiss meant anything to you, text back.*

During the middle of the fifteenth night, I heard the unmistakable beep of a text message. Waking up from a daze, I rolled onto my side. I eyed my phone that was on my nightstand. The broken screen clearly confirmed that I'd received a text message. Alice Mae finally replied! My brain momentarily stopped working. All I could think that was I'd finally gotten some kind of communication from her.

*Text back.* That was what she wrote.

My body was still exhausted, but my mind was firing on all cylinders. I tried thinking about anything but the girl who'd just texted me. Her message didn't make any sense until I read the previous ones.

Me: *For all that is holy, if the kiss meant anything to you, text back.*

Alice Mae: *Text back*

Me: *Are you back?*

Alice Mae: *Back where? You really need to ask more specific questions, R. If you are asking about my current state of being—then yes, I'm back in Rockingham.*

Me: *Were you in Wonderland?*

Alice Mae: *Yes.*

Me: *What were you doing there for two weeks?*

Alice Mae: *Scrubbing floors. I'd rather not talk about it.*

Fine... Me: *What is on your mind?*

Alice Mae: *You.*

I swear my heart stopped beating. I re-read that single-word response over and over. I began to type another response when my phone exploded by a bomb of text messages from Alice Mae: *Stars. Candy. Always candy. Kitties. Decisions. Decisions. Decisions. Dancing. Many things are on my mind.*

Again, I tried to think of an appropriate response when another text came through from her. *The kiss.*

This was absurd. What was I supposed to say about that? Instead of texting back, I decided just to call.

"You really shouldn't call someone so late at night. It's half past four, Ryley," she said, in lieu of a greeting. "Most people have rules about phone conduct."

Here we go again... Why couldn't she be the slightest bit normal? Why was I starting to like the fact that she wasn't like everyone else I knew? "But texting in the wee hours is okay, especially after a two week hiatus?"

"I did have several messages from you. It seemed that you were in dire need to speak with me. So speak."

Before I could get a word in, she asked about the protocol on doorbell ringing in the middle of the night. I asked her why it mattered.

"Because I'm on your front porch," she said. "I thought that there was some sort of emergency since you'd left so many messages."

Two thoughts went through my mind. First, my mom would have my head on a platter if Alice Mae rang the doorbell this late on a school night. And Alice Mae was on my doorstep—*right now!*

"Don't ring the door. I'll come down."

Cradling the phone, I pulled up my jeans. She filled the silence talking about the importance of proper manners. Grabbing a shirt, I tried to think of how to slip it on. I contemplated just setting the phone down when she asked what I was thinking about.

I looked at my shirt and answered. "Clothes."

She giggled. It made me smile. She should really try out for the choir. Her voice was stunning, even if she rambled. Instead of shrugging it on, I balled it into my hand so I wouldn't miss anything she said. I kept the phone pressed up against my ear and walked down the hall, careful not to step on the few floorboards that whined when weight was applied. It was brutal, since I just wanted to run to her. I peered through the small window in the door. Standing on the front step with her back to me was Alice Mae. The moon shone on her skin, making it glow. Her hair glistened against her navy blue dress. The fabric actually stopped at her knees, revealing more skin than she usually did at school. Dirt speckled her pale legs.

I ended the call and set my phone on the counter. I cracked the door, pushing it open slowly so as not to wake my mom.

"Ryley? Are you there? It is horribly impolite to hang up on—"

"I'm right here, Alice Mae."

She turned around and her mouth fell open when she saw me. Her cheeks appeared to have been sunburned. Her stare swooped to my bare stomach. One would think that she'd never seen a guy shirtless before. A soft squeal resonated from her throat. Her eyes widened as she slapped her hand over her mouth. Her hair flung in the air as she spun around so her back was to me.

Her reaction was adorable (and a huge compliment).

I shrugged on my shirt. "I'm dressed now. You can turn around."

Without making a peep, she shook her head. I literally had to wipe the smile off my face as I approached her. She didn't budge when I stepped behind her, and she barely scooted over when I walked down the steps so I

135

could face her. We were eye level since she was still on the top step. She was as red as a cherry, and her eyes were pinched tight.

"It was probably inappropriate for me to walk out before being fully dressed, but to hang up on you would have also been rude," I said, hoping she understood that I wasn't purposely trying to embarrass her.

Nodding ferociously, she told me that she understood my reasoning, but she kept her eyes closed. I reached for her hand, but hesitated. Grime coated her fingernails.

"Why are you so dirty?"

"I've been told I'm not a fast learner," she said. "I'll forever stick my arms and legs out to catch myself when I fall. It's instinct."

Wow. That made no sense whatsoever. Instead of trying to follow her train of thought, I asked her if we could have a serious talk.

"You can talk to me with your eyes closed," I said, fighting the urge to lean in closer. "But we have a talk long overdue. I want you to listen to me. I want you to *hear* me."

"It is your logic that hearing improves with closed eyes?"

Well, it did, but I actually just wanted to keep her from seeing the desperation in my eyes when I took in her lips.

"A woman called Hearts was married to my uncle, who I've never met. Is it possible that the Hearts you know and Eddie's wife are one in the same?"

"Anything is possible," she said.

"Just answer the question. Are they the same person?"

She nodded. I edged closer. My feet were on either side of her shoes. They weren't the grandma shoes she wore at school, but they were vintage, nevertheless. Lime green stitching lined the cream shoes. The tips of her perfectly polished toes stuck out of the top. Mud clung to the sides, but for being light colored shoes, they were relatively clean.

"I've gotten the impression that Hearts and my dad don't, or didn't, see eye to eye," I said, desperate to touch her lips again. My mouth dried. "Why?"

"So much has happened in the past, it's rather difficult for even me to make sense of it."

"Do you know why Robby would want Hearts dead?" I asked.

She licked her lips. "Because he knows Hearts' secret."

"Which is?"

"If I knew, it wouldn't be much of a secret, would it?"

She was lying to me. I guessed that she knew exactly what the secret was, but her fingers grazed mine. It was highly distracting. Her skin was so soft. She traced her index finger over my hand. I closed my eyes as I memorized the feel of her touch. It was so faint; I could almost trick myself into thinking that I'd made it up. Leaning close enough to feel her breath on my skin, I fought the urge to grab her and pull her against me. She'd scare too easily.

"I don't want to be just friends, Ryley, and I am tired of this frivolous feud in which we have partaken."

She said exactly what I was thinking. "We'd make an awful couple. It'd be catastrophic if we indulged in these silly feelings."

"They are just silly feelings," I said. "No more than just chemical reactions blowing up in our brains."

Our foreheads touched. She didn't pull away. She didn't pull away! My hands were shaking as I slipped my hand around her waist. She placed her trembling hand on my chest. The realization that she wanted me as much I did her almost did me in. I tightened my grip around her waist.

"It would be ridiculous for us to be together," I whispered.

"Indubitably."

137

Reaching for her chin, I held my breath. A gasp slipped from her throat when I encouraged her to look up at me. I took the last step closer to her so that there was no space between us.

"Ryley? Don't kiss me. It will make such a mess of... I won't be able to clean up my chaotic emotions. I'll have to hire an emotional housemaid."

"I wouldn't dream of kissing a girl like you." My nose slid down. My lips were so close to hers. I could almost taste them. "I don't like chaos in my life."

She stood on her tiptoes. When her lips grazed mine, she screamed.

# CHAPTER TWENTY-NINE

(Ryley: Present Time)

That damn cat.

Three distinct bloody marks were scratched down Alice Mae's leg. Chez scampered off before I could catch him. I swore that cat sabotaged my chance with Alice Mae on purpose.

"Chez, the Super villain," Alice Mae said.

She inspected her feline inflicted injury. Her hands smoothed over her legs, checking the depth of the cut marks. When she caught me looking, she blushed and turned away.

"I should really get back home," she said, and headed off.

Just like that?

I raced up to her. With no shoes on, it proved to be difficult. My feet seemed to step on every rock in our yard. When I caught up to her, I reached for her hand. She stared straight ahead, but the edges of her mouth twitch when my fingers interlocked with hers.

"I should probably walk you home," I said. "In case any more crazed animals try attacking you."

She nodded and appeared to be actually considering the possibility of being attacked again. "It would be poor luck to be assaulted twice in one night."

She stopped when we approached a puddle. She pointed to my bare feet. "You don't have shoes."

"It's just water," I said, trying to sound tough even though I cringed every time I stepped on a pebble.

She released my hand and dug in her dress pocket. She pulled out a lemon drop. She popped it into her mouth and closed her eyes. I offered to take her wrapper, and shoved it in my jean pocket.

We continued our walk, hand in hand. I shouldn't have been surprised when her house was only a few blocks away from mine. One-oh-six looked like every other house on Sneve Street. There were white shutters on either side of the windows. It was painted a dull brown, so it blended in with all the other houses on the block. There was a line of shrubs along the sidewalk that separated the yard from the street. A single apple tree was in the front yard. A few fallen apples were scattered on the perfectly manicured lawn. Not a single board creaked when we walked onto the porch.

"Thank you for your escort, Ryley," she said, and opened the front door. She gave me a second glance before stepping onto the mahogany interior floor boards. The flicker from a candelabrum on an end table cast a soft glow on her face.

Refusing to end the night unsatisfied, I grabbed her waist. I jerked her against me and kissed her like I wanted to—like I *had* to kiss her. Her sweet and sour kiss, compliments from the residue of her lemon drop, made my mouth water. She made an eager sound and pulled on my shirt, dirtying it with the grime under her nails.

I walked her backwards up against the doorframe, sandwiching her between it and me. I tried to control myself, but her kiss was so incredibly tantalizing that I needed more—craved more.

"I'm not letting you out of my sight unless you promise me that you'll be at school on Monday," I said, gasping for air. I kept my eyes closed but didn't pull away.

"Kiss me again, and I'll show up every day next week."

I obliged.

She held onto me like she would fall without my support. What surprised me was that I wanted her to come to me for help. I wanted to protect her. I wanted her to feel safe, and I wanted to make sure she was taken care of. I'd never fallen for a girl like Alice Mae before. Maybe that was why those relationships had never lasted longer than a few months.

"You will be the death of me," I whispered, breaking the kiss.

When I opened my eyes, the world had transformed, blurring somewhat if I looked anywhere other than at Alice Mae. I untangled myself from her. She clung to the doorframe like she might fall if she didn't hang onto it. She walked inside. She closed the rectangular door but didn't shut it completely. Maybe it was because the frame no longer fit quite right. The top seemed narrower than the base; the door was built in reverse. Its top was wide but the base was narrow. There was a two inch space. Her explosive blue eyes seemed darker than usual, or maybe my vision was just messing with me. My mouth still tasted sweet and sour, from our kiss. Dropping my gaze to her swollen lips, I already knew that I would have a newfound love for Lemon Drops. Her lipstick was no longer drawn to create a pouty illusion. My cheeks warmed when I thought out how ridiculous I had to look with blue smeared on my lips. She bit her bottom lip. My stomach flipped. I clutched the offset doorframe for support. Forcing myself, I looked away from her delicious lips.

"You're making a mess of my plan."

"Good," I said even though I hadn't a clue what her plan was, but I didn't care, as long as she didn't take off for weeks at a time again.

She looked at me like she was trying to memorize exactly what I looked like—from my disheveled hair to my bare feet. I wiped blue makeup off my lips, staining the outside of my hand with her lipstick.

"My plan is... complicated and devious in nature. But that doesn't matter. The day I must choose is upon me. I can feel it. I'm no longer a girl learning about Wrongdoings in Wonderland. I'm no longer the girl strapped to a flying a bird, destroying lizards' homes, or talking to spiders. I'm no longer the girl in a mushroom house, weighing choices that no child should make. I'm not the same girl who painted the queen's roses with poisonous paint. I'm not the same girl who watched a father rescue his son from behind a closet door. I'm no longer innocent. I let my friends pay for my mistakes. I won't make only one Wrong decision. I'll make many, but it doesn't matter. Soon, I must choose where I'll live, even if it's the Wrong decision."

I didn't understand about ninety percent of what she'd just said. But the ten percent that I caught, I didn't like. She was going to move—choose a different place to live?

"People move all the time. I moved twenty three times before my mom and I settled in Rockingham," I said.

"I'm afraid my residency will be permanent."

Vida Maude flung the door open. For a woman wearing a nightdress, she was rather intimidating. "Did you give him any of your sweets?"

"No," Alice Mae said, sounding weak and pitiful.

Ever since I almost stepped on her bunny, Alice Mae had never given me the impression that she was submissive or weak. It made me wonder what relationship she and her aunts had.

"He's wearing your lipstick," Vida Maude said, eyeing me over.

"I'm aware," Alice Mae whispered.

"Well then he had a taste of your sweets!" Vida Maude glared at her niece and then me. "Drink something containing caffeine. It will offset the effects of the candy."

That made absolutely no sense. "What drug is in these candies?"

"None." Alice Mae and Vida Maude said, simultaneously.

I didn't believe either of them, but it didn't really matter. Vida Maude slammed the door in my face. I walked home, which would have been quite disastrous if a talking toad hadn't showed up to escort me back.

When I went for my morning run the next morning, the ceramic frog that guarded our front door was sitting in his usual spot. Grime and dirt covered the ceramic frog and floor boards around him. When I lifted him up, the floor that was covered by his body was spotless. It was as if the toad had never left.

# CHAPTER THIRTY

(Ryley: Present Time)

Monday morning couldn't come fast enough. Alice Mae waited for me at my locker. When I leaned in to kiss her, she pressed her finger against my lips.

"Both my aunts insist that I don't kiss you during school hours," she said, and then bit her lip. "They will know if we do."

"Because they have spies?"

"Well, there is Chez..." she said, trailing off. "But, it would be quite disastrous if I attended school without my candy."

Our classmates were watching us. I spotted Becky down the hall. She was holding up her phone, probably recording Alice Mae and me.

I leaned in close so I only had to whisper. "I thought you said that the candies weren't narcotics. Still, I couldn't fall asleep last night until I downed an entire jug of iced tea. Caffeine isn't supposed to make you tired. So why did it? Is this some sort of Wonderland spice or something?"

"The candy made in Wonderland is different from the candy here. Thus, the effects are different." She sighed heavily. "Sometimes, candy can be dangerous."

"To whom?" I asked, mockingly.

"Sleepy parents of rowdy, sugar-high children," she said, and stuck out her tongue. "But that's not to say all are that way. Some people react differently when tasting them. Some candy can be poisonous if the dosage is high."

Poisonous? I pulled away. It just clicked. My horrible date with at Little Italy…"Did you poison Courtney when we were on a date?"

She didn't respond. She didn't move. She just stood there as if she was suddenly frozen.

"You did, didn't you?" I said, pushing away from her.

She shook her head. But, it didn't go unnoticed that she didn't deny my accusation.

The first bell rang. Everyone around us walked through the halls like mice in a maze. A thousand questions bubbled up, but I knew she wouldn't answer them. Every single one I thought of sounded too vague, even to me.

"I hate being late," Alice Mae said and left for class.

Like a drone robot, I followed her to the classroom and chose a desk in the back. I thought about tearing off a piece of paper and passing it to her, but Mr. Blanch prided himself on note-catching, like a recreational sport. When his back was to us, I slipped my phone out of my pocket and sent her a text.

Me: *Why did you poison her?*

She jumped in her desk when her phone vibrated. Mr. Blanch stared at her, waiting for her to make a move indicating she had her phone on. She'd get detention for sure; it was against school policy to carry your phone, even though most everyone did. She waited ten minutes before retrieving it. She glanced at the message and shoved it back into her backpack. Instead of replying, she drew in her book. Was she purposely messing with me? She used each of her colored pencils to doodle. By the time she was finished with her drawing all her pencils were covered in bite marks; she was nervous.

I felt ill. I was totally and completely into the psychopath. And what was worse was that I jerked Courtney around. If nothing else, I owed Courtney an apology of epic proportions. So I flipped open my notebook and wrote that I was sorry—for everything. The more I inscribed, the less confident I became with my words. I shut the notebook, thinking that perhaps the words would come out better if I just told her the truth.

The bell sounded. I bolted out of my seat.

"Courtney, wait up!" I said, rushing over to her.

She acted like I had just called her fat. "What do you want?"

She turned around and walked out the door. That didn't slow me. "I'm sorry!"

"Sick of sucking on the blonde bimbo's jacked-up lips?" Courtney said, glancing back at me. She glared the kind of glare all women seem to have perfected by age ten. But, she wasn't looking just at me. Behind me was Alice Mae, close on our tail.

Without slowing her pace, Alice Mae grabbed my cap and took off running toward her locker. That girl—that infuriating girl—knew how to rub me the wrong way! It was idiotically annoyed that I was remotely into her.

Courtney's apology would have to wait. I took off running after Alice Mae. After a few strides, I easily caught up with her. But, she ducked into a janitor closet before I could wrap my hands around her neck.

"You could have killed her!" I shouted as soon as she slammed the door shut behind us.

"No, I wouldn't. I have all the calculations memorized. I know just how much powdered sugar to give you if I wanted your stomach to merely be upset, how much would make your heart race, how much to make you hallucinate, and how much to kill you." She handed me back my hat, which

146

I immediately put back on my head. "So if I wanted her dead, she'd be six feet under."

"Why did you poison her in the first place?" I yelled.

"She made me mad."

"Mad? How? Never mind, I don't care. You're going to jail for a very long time," I said, and twisted the door handle.

She grabbed my hand. I tried to pull away, but she sunk her nails against my skin. I wouldn't have been surprised if she drew blood, but I dared not look away from her eyes. She studied me with an intense curiosity. There was no blue in the world that could compare to the brilliance in them. I hated that they were so enchanting.

"If I'm to pay for any crime, it won't be because I poisoned some silly high school girl. I guarantee Hearts will be my *get out of jail* free card."

"You work for her?"

"If I was to answer that, you'd have a very different opinion of me," she said, and then released my hand. "Go. Tell your little friends and their law enforcement."

She didn't need to do any convincing. I pushed the door.

"But then you'll never know what I know."

I stopped. Weighing my options, I jerked the door closed. "I hate you sometimes."

"The feeling is mutual."

"Answer one damn question," I said in a low voice. "How do you know my dad?"

She smiled again, but it wasn't scandalous. It wasn't pretty. I needed a picture book to decipher the differences between her smiles. But, if I were to guess, her smile was the kind people wore at a funeral. She smiled the kind of smile people do when they are trying to hide their sadness.

"I met Robert Edgar on my first assignment."

Recalling everything I'd learned, about my dad, my uncle, the queen, and their murderous past I asked. "So you *do* work for Hearts. Why?"

"That's two questions," she said. "And this particular assignment was *before* my alliance with Hearts."

"But you do work for her now? Are you one of her minions?"

Alice Mae replied, but it wasn't an answer to my questions. "Regardless of which side I'm on, your dad and I do have one thing in common."

"Humor me."

"We both want Hearts dead."

# Chapter Thirty-One

(Ryley: Present Time)

Growing up I'd always been told that I looked like my dad. I used to love it, but when his mind began to deteriorate, I stopped finding the comment to be so enjoyable. Leaning against the far wall of the activities room of the West Harbour Psychiatric Treatment Facility, I tried to not think about the fact that even Alice Mae had said that I look like my dad. *He* looked like a crazy person, but *I* was the one who was going to bring up the topic of alternative worlds or realms.

I walked over to his table. He glanced at me and then stared off into space, like he was pondering life and death questions.

I set up a chess board. I made my first move and waited. He didn't even glance at the board. Minutes droned on. Finally, I took out a mint. At the sound of the wrapper, my dad jerked his head toward me.

"May I have one?" he asked.

"If you make a move."

He moved his pawn. I handed him a regular piece of candy. Pocket dust clung to the wrapper. He inspected it like a scientist would a Petri dish. He slowly unwrapped it and then licked the mint.

He sighed heavily. "It's not the right kind."

"The right kind of candy?" I asked.

"It's just ordinary," he said. "I don't suppose you have any *extra*ordinary ones? They help me think clearly and so I don't see the creatures that shouldn't be allowed here. Maybe the nurse has some. They really don't have the power to keep them from me. I just let them think they have me trapped here."

A nurse came over after my dad frantically waved his hands in the air. "Is something wrong?"

"I would like my medication, the special kind," my dad said.

She smiled and patted his shoulder. "I can bring the pills your doctor prescribed."

He shook his head viciously and dismissed her. After she left, I moved my piece on the chess board. He watched my movement like a snake tracking its prey.

"Do you want the kind of candy that keeps you from seeing?" I asked, thinking about Alice Mae's candies. "If I got you some, do you think you could tell me about Wonderland? Could you explain the nonsense about it?"

"Nothing good comes from Wonderland," he said in a hushed voice. He cupped his hand around my ear and pulled me close. "If there is a rabbit hole nearby, then you are already doomed."

"I'm screwed because a few bunnies are around?"

"Rumperbabbits work for *her*, which means that Hearts is close. Did the white rabbit accompany you again? He's listening to everything you say, a glorified spy and messenger. He reports everything back to her."

Right on cue, Dad snatched Mr. Ruth from my coat pocket. He tried to rip the bunny's head off. Alice Mae would have a heart attack if I brought back the stuffed animal with the fluff on the outside and a separated head. So, I jerked it from my father's hand. The soft tearing sound of its stitches warned me that it wouldn't be long before it was in two pieces, so I swung at Dad. My fist collided into his nose. Any questions I asked after that were met with a blank stare and incoherent mumbling.

# CHAPTER THIRTY-TWO

(Alice Mae: Present Time)

A single, red rose leaned against the bottom of my locker. The stem was covered with black thorns. I stroked a petal, smoothing it between my fingers. I half expected the red paint to rub away...

In Wonderland, I wasn't beheaded after the queen found me hiding in her closet. The laws were clear. Children are not to be beheaded, even if they are not protected by the Rightdoing Law.

Every creature in Wonderland was protected by the Rightdoing Law, until they commit a crime. Thus, on their first offense, they cannot be beheaded. The Wrongdoing Law stated that no beheadings shall be conducted until a second crime has been proven. Yet, punishments could still be rendered, and Hearts found quite a punishment for me.

M.H. and I leaned on her balcony rail that overlooked her rose garden, while Hearts stood behind me. The rose bushes that surrounded her castle were covered with silver thorns that were coated with black gel.

"One prick will *allegedly* put you on your death bed so I don't often get unexpected guests. No one has been stupid enough to prune them, so the lethal black poison has never been proven," Hearts said, handing me a paint brush. "M.H, it would be lovely if you'd show her to the garden shed. Al's punishment for trespassing is to paint all the white roses red."

So as the story went, M.H. led me to the shed where the paint was stored. Inside the lopsided shack were loads of chemicals.

"That was a very brave and stupid thing you said to the queen." M.H. picked up a bucket of red paint and a brush. "To suggest that Eddie died in any other way besides accident was quite bold."

"Well who is clumsy enough to accidentally trip on a guillotine?"

"You'll live longer if you refrain from making such comments to the queen," M.H. warned.

I grabbed a pair of working gloves, knocking over a few bottles in the process. I quickly picked them up, but stopped suddenly when I grabbed one with a skull and crossbones etched on the side.

"Why is this here?" I asked holding up the bottle.

"I told you, remember? It acts like a snake repellent," M.H. said. "Hearts doesn't like creepy-crawlies near unless she can control them."

I set the bottle down and picked up a jug of pesticide. "I wonder what would happen if all the antidotes and repellent were to mysteriously disappear or be replaced with something lethal."

"What are you thinking, Al?"

I looked around to make sure that no one was listening. "Remember the day you told me about your candy operation?"

"My memory is not at a loss," he said in a hushed tone. "I asked you to make a decision to help me and Robby create a delicious poison. You left me hanging for an answer."

"It seems like you are creating all of the potions, so what does Robby do?" I asked, unscrewing the top of the pesticide jug.

152

"One day will come when I create a tonic that smells and tastes like tea but is fatal from one drop." M.H. set the paint bucket down and sat on it. He took off his goggles and tucked them inside his suit pocket. "Robby is a dear friend and plans to do what no other creature in Wonderland will."

"Which is?"

"Find a way to stop time and then take the first drink," M.H. said. "Hearts never takes a sip of tea until someone else does first. Robby volunteered to be the one who samples the poisoned tea."

"But then he'll die too!"

"I've pointed out such consequences to him as well. Even so, he says that it is his responsibility to ensure the creatures of Wonderland are safe from her Reign of Terror. Hearts killed his brother, runs a dictatorship in the Red Court, tortures the seamstress, and has *dismantled* everyone who stands in her way. Even if he has to die, he'll do so because it will end her reign."

"Surely there is another way! If everyone in the court hates her, why do they allow her to rule? I'm surprised more creatures aren't plotting an assassination."

"Hearts has an army of soldiers and a loyal escort of women who will abide by her every order," M.H. said. "Besides, Robby would rather spare the creatures from a bloody war."

"And then who will rule if Hearts and Robby both die?"

M.H. shrugged his shoulders. "The rumperbabbit clan? There will always be a ruler and sometimes that creature is most unexpected."

"Oh, which reminds me, Mr. Ruth really doesn't like being considered just a messenger."

"I'm aware, but sometimes we have to be called names we don't like, for our own protection."

"So why do you need me?"

153

"Robby needs candies to keep his head on straight while he's in the Otherworld. The queen is watching the rumperbabbits more closely because of the *Bleeding Heart Prophecy*, and the Jack has warned me that the queen will discover all my comings and goings."

"So you need me to be a deliverer?"

"You've come to a crossroads. You must choose sides. So, I will ask once more, will you help us kill the queen?"

"Why does it matter if my ultimate decision will be Wrong?"

"Because not everything you do will be wrong." M.H. nodded at the pesticide in my hand. "What are you going to do with that?"

"I hope I make some good decisions, but since the Wrongdoing laws protect me from death, I'm going to enjoy committing a crime worthy of this punishment." I unscrewed the lid and poured the liquid into the paint bucket. "I'm going to do exactly what the queen wanted—paint the roses red and hope she enjoys my unconventional way of expressing myself."

Ryley pulled me out of my thoughts when he plucked the red rose from my hands. "Is there another guy that is pining for your attention?"

*Another guy* pining for my attention? Was he *still* gunning for that role? I thought my plan had failed when he figured out that Courtney mysteriously got sick on their date because of me. "You're not mad at me anymore?"

He stood as still as a statue, yet, I could almost hear the wheels turning in his mind. He was weighing his options. And then—for the first time—I thought that he might be trying to manipulate me. Work me like I had been working him. However, my job description had been "Liar" for much longer, so I was seasoned at outsmarting the amateurs.

I said, "When you figure out an answer—"

"Why did you want her sick?"

The truth flew out of my mouth before I could silence it. "I wanted to be on that date instead of her."

"That is the least amount of information you'd dare to give me," he said. "You're playing with my emotions. You're toying with me, and believe me, you are a good at it. I shouldn't even say this... But, I think you are telling me the truth, at least the part where you admit to liking me, which makes the lies you tell harder to decipher. So, you do actually like me, don't you?"

My cheeks burned. How did he figure that out? I'd excelled at being confusing and speaking in riddles. Instead of answering, I acted like he hadn't just frazzled me by getting on with my day. I opened my locker door. A spew of my novels tumbled out with my school books, along with an array of toys that I'd pillaged from the Joker over the years. If the madman knew I'd been behind the mysterious disappearances he wouldn't wait for the queen's order to execute me now that the Wrongdoing Laws no longer protected me and the Rightdoing Laws didn't keep me safe because of my past crimes. One more offense and I'd hear the queen yell, "Off with her head!"

"You're quite the reader," Ryley said, eyeing my books.

"I'd live in a library if I weren't keeping my aunts company," I said, glad to talk about anything besides Wonderland and my deceitful ways.

Reading the titles of my books, he sniffed the flower. "Why does this rose smell like pesticide?"

The corners of my mouth went up. "All the red roses in Wonderland smell like that because of an old prank I played on the queen before....before I knew better. Consequently, all red roses carry that scent now."

"You're not the sweet, innocent girl you try to make yourself out to be." Ryley examined the flower like it had otherworldly value that I wasn't telling him. "Who sent you the flower?"

"Hearts," I said. "It's a reminder."

"A reminder for what?"

I thought about lying to him. But I wanted to see what he would do if I told him the truth, even if I had to make it seem like a lie. I picked one of the dying petals off of the rose. "That I have a job to do no matter what the consequence."

"I know Hearts wanted something from my dad. That's clear. And, my dad is hell-bent on keeping me and my mom a secret, so I can't help but think that Hearts wants something from me as well."

"Hearts wants something from all of us."

"What do *you* want?"

His brown eyes turned so dark, I swore they stole the color of the night sky. He took my hand and pulled me up off the floor. Standing in the middle of some very dangerous toys, he kissed me on my cheek so lightly that I could have been made to believe it hadn't really happened. But there was no convincing my heart it hadn't. My plan backfired... How was I to lure him into the Red Court now?

"What do you want, Alice Mae?"

My confession came out airily. "Freedom."

"Hearts has something on you, doesn't she?"

Something? No. Try *someone*. "Yes."

"What?"

Pressing my lips into a thin line, I smiled weakly. I stepped away from him and shook my head. For being so smart, he sure was dim-witted. "What do you think, Ryley?"

# CHAPTER THIRTY-THREE

(Ryley: Present Time)

Sneve Street was like every other street in town. Yet, the Maude house was different than most, even if it did have a single apple tree in the front yard and a vegetable garden in the back. The once manicured yard was torn up with an array of rabbit holes. There was just something different about the house. The Victorian house was painted with bright colors, but the sun had faded them over the years, giving it an eerie vibe. I could have sworn that it was painted a dull brown before.

I walked up to the front door. Instead of a doorbell, there was a lion head knocker. The door knob was molded to look like a person's face when I swore that it looked like every other round doorknob before. Just as I raised my hand to knock on the door, it opened. Alice Mae's bald aunt barricaded herself within the doorframe.

"The young Mr. Edgar," Zola Maude said. "It's poor form to show up without an invitation."

"Is Alice Mae home? I found something that belongs to her," I said, digging Mr. Ruth out of my backpack. Alice Mae knew I had it, but I needed an excuse to get past her overprotective aunt.

"She lost the white rabbit?" Zola Maude said, reaching for it.

157

I held it above my head—out of arm's reach for the old woman. "Alice Mae papered the school with missing posters. I've come to give it back to her for a reward that was mentioned."

"That stupid girl would pay a pretty penny to get her precious little *One-Eyed Hare* back. There is a heavy price on his head in Wonderland—in this realm it's just another stuffed animal."

Vida Maude walked down the hall and opened the door enough to give me the once over. Sugar coated her hands, and she smelled of spice. She rolled her eyes upon noticing Mr. Ruth. "My niece is upstairs in her bedroom. Boys are not allowed there."

"I'm not a *boy*." I said, tossing the rabbit in my hands just to make sure they didn't forget about the leverage. Since they were rather interested in the rabbit, I knew it was my ticket in the door.

"Oh, I wouldn't have said that, young Mr. Edgar," Vida Maude said. "If you are not a child, then you can be beheaded. The Rightdoing Laws protect the behaving children, and govern the adults. Break one Wrongdoing Law and your head is as good as hers."

They must have been talking about the Laws of Wonderland. Beheading isn't a form of punishment—well, not anymore. Lethal injection or prison sentences were the accepted penalties here. Pointing out law differences wouldn't get me anywhere so I said nothing.

"Keep the door open. Alice Mae's room is the third on the left," Zola Maude said and then nudged her sister. "He sure does look like Robby."

"Attractiveness doesn't run in the family," Vida Maude said, turning toward the kitchen. Purple smoke was coming from it, followed by the distinct scent of burnt chocolate.

Vida Maude screamed, "You left the pot boiling without supervision!"

"Yes, yes. I made a mistake," Zola Maude said, slamming the kitchen door shut. I could still hear her scream at her sister. "Don't tell the queen. We'll just make a new batch of candies. Everything will be fine."

"Hearts may be our friend, but she hates burnt chocolate!" Vida Maude yelled back.

Note: My dad and Hearts hated each other (for some reason, maybe something to do with my uncle Edward's death). The Maude sisters are friends with the queen, thus they are not on my side.

What side was Alice Mae on? She wanted the queen dead. Yet, she seemed to do her bidding. Was she a double-agent? Or had I just watched too many espionage movies?

Disregarding the aunts, I shoved Mr. Ruth back into my backpack and took the stairs two at a time. The upstairs was wallpapered with blue flowers. The carpet was green, until reaching the first blue door on the left. After that, it was hardwood and white walls, which stopped at the start of the second door on the right. Then the wall color changed to dark blue, so dark that it appeared almost black. The floor was made of black stone, but I couldn't figure out what type. The third door on the left was covered in tin foil—no, not tin foil. Silver. Crushed, silver.

I knocked on the door. No one answered so I pushed it open.

Alice Mae sat square in the middle of a white room, surrounded by children's games. Puzzle pieces. Jacks. Dice. Clay. Half a dozen cards were cast around her. Some cards were fortune telling. Others were playing cards. Some were baseball cards.

She didn't bother to look up to acknowledge my presence, like a guy walking into her room was a common occurrence. It bothered me more than I liked.

"Zola Maude doesn't like me," I stated.

"If it makes you feel any better, I don't think Vida Maude is very impressed with you either."

Her bed was white, but stained with red paint and smelled of pesticide. "Another punishment from Hearts?"

"That was Zola Maude's doing," she said. "She wasn't exactly pleased with my behavior when she found out about the roses."

A white dresser with crystal handles was placed underneath the lone, small window in the room. It looked like any old dresser... that had been sawed in half with a chainsaw. On the dresser was a photo of Alice Mae when she was a young girl, standing next to a man with wild hair and a top hat. It was the same hat that my dad had worn for his wedding.

"Who is this man?" I asked, pointing to the picture.

"M.H."

Never in my life had I wanted to strangle a person I wanted to kiss so desperately. "Just initials? He doesn't have a name?"

"He has had many pseudo names. Most creatures refer to him simply as the Mad Hatter. He's never told me his God-given name, so I cannot tell you what that might be. You act like I am intentionally being mysterious and secretive, when in fact; you just don't like the answers."

"Why is he wearing my dad's hat?"

"Because he and your father were once great friends before I came along and ruined everything," she said, frustrated. Her lipstick and eye shadow were completely removed. She looked *natural*—beautiful without her makeup mask. She would always have the biggest, bluest, most spectacular eyes I'd ever taken in.

"Haven't you ever seen a girl without pretties on?" she asked, fidgeting in her cream dress. I hadn't seen many girls still wear full-length long sleeved dresses, but Alice Mae wasn't up to the twenty-first century fashion either.

"Not you."

"You think I'm ugly." She held up her hand to stop me from answering. "Let me guess. You just think I'm beautifully-handicapped and need assistance from makeup to be considered pretty?"

"Ugly isn't a word I'd use to describe you—ever."

"So then why are you staring at me?"

"Isn't it obvious?" I said and set my backpack next to her.

"No."

"Digging for compliments?" I said, sitting down beside her. My knee was approximately one inch from hers. It was the perfect distance for her to either scoot closer or lean away. She didn't lean away. "I didn't peg you to be that kind of girl."

"I'm not," she said, picking up the cards and slipping them down her sleeve. I watched them disappear, but I had to admit, it was an impressive trick. Her clothing didn't bunch up as she stuffed more cards in her sleeve.

One card in particular caught my attention. Two of Hearts. It had been torn but taped back together. She followed my line of sight, looking at her hand. Suddenly, she turned pale. Acting frazzled, she said, "Do you ever wonder what it'd be like to be so small that you could hide from all life's problems in a house made up of cards?"

"I've never really given it much thought," I said, not sure if it was a rhetorical question or not. I suspected that it was to take my attention off the card, which made me more curious.

I grabbed for the card, but she wasn't willing to surrender it. So there we were, sitting on her floor, surrounded by toys, and fighting over a card. I'd lose my argument with Vida Maude about not being a child if she saw me now.

"Hiding something?"

"No."

"Then why put up such a fight?"

She let go, but didn't look particularly pleased about it. The playing card looked like it was circa 1900's. Along the edge was a message written in pencil. "*The HATed fool will die twice before the MADness stops.*"

Déjà vu. The words were familiar, but I didn't remember ever reading them. "Who gave this to you?"

"M.H."

"What's the riddle supposed to mean?"

"It's not a riddle. It's the *Madmen's Prophecy.*"

Tears filled her eyes. She buried her face in her hands. Her cries were soft. It made my chest ache. We hadn't defined our roles; we had only kissed, but it didn't mean I was her boyfriend. Did I even want that title?

I didn't know what I really wanted, but her whimper did me in. I reached around her waist and pulled her close so that our knees touched. When she didn't pull away, I tightened my hug around her. She buried her face into my shoulder.

"Did I say something wrong?" I asked.

"Do you believe in ghosts?"

"I believe that some people are haunted," I said. "I don't believe that a misty substance manifests to scare people. But people can be haunted by their past, their family, their upbringing, their future or any number of things."

"Like prophecies?"

"Sure."

"I believe in ghosts," she said, and reached for the torn card. She traced her finger over the words. Her lip trembled. "I wish I didn't like you."

"I wish I didn't like you either. My life would be a lot less complicated."

She smiled as a tear ran down her cheek. It was such a sad, little smile. I couldn't bear it. I reached for my backpack. I pulled out the stuffed animal and handed it to her.

"Hello, old friend," she said, cradling it in her arms.

I let them bond a few moments before asking, "So are you going to deny that there is something up with the candy, or am I going to have to pull your teeth for answers?"

"I prefer my teeth attached," she said, and then sighed. "The candy helps keep me focused. It has that effect for true Wonderlanders, or anyone who spends a great deal of time there."

Did that mean I was a true Wonderlander? I wasn't born there; I had the birth certificate to prove it. "After we… kissed," I said and then coughed nervously. "I was anything but focused. The candy residue affected me. It gave me a sugar rush."

"Caffeine offsets the effects of the magic inside the candy."

"So you see the world all jacked up without candy, until you down a Coke?" I asked.

"Wonderland is a place of magical elements. Think of it this way. Wonderland clings to a person through and through. It gets on your clothes and skin. It ventures inside your body the more you eat the food."

"It's sticky. I got it."

"Even their odd way of thinking becomes your own. So when a person enters this realm, they still aren't rid of the magic that is the essence of Wonderland. Thus, in this realm, we tend to see things that aren't really there. Many Wonderlanders are considered paranoid lunatics. The candy keeps a person centered, offsetting the magic that is Wonderland. It allowed your father to focus too, before… well, that's a long story. A boring story. And doesn't have a *Happily Ever After* so I doubt you'd like it."

"Does the story about my dad and the candies have anything to do with M.H. or you?"

She didn't answer, which was answer enough. She knew my dad because of the special candy. The how's, why's, and what's were important, but I knew if I asked her outright, she'd never answer. So, I had to be a little more devious.

"Can we have a hypothetical discussion about Wonderland?"

"Anything is possible when Wonderland is concerned," she said.

"You speak like it's a different world, not just a place on planet Earth. Can you explain?"

"Do you have any paper?" she asked, placing the rabbit next to me. While I dug in my backpack, she whispered to Mr. Ruth. "Keep your good eye on him. The more he knows the bigger the flight risk he becomes."

I wonder if she purposely said that loud enough for me to hear or not. Of course she'd say that, just to mess with me.

I pulled out my notebook. The corner was torn off, looking suspiciously like an animal bite mark. Alice Mae didn't seem to notice or care about it. She just took my notebook and flipped it open to the middle. I cringed when she opened it to the note that I never gave Courtney. The one where I told her I was sorry and explained why she suddenly got sick. I tore it from the spiral, crumpled it into a ball, and shoved it in my backpack.

"We can use that, unless you still planned on giving it to Courtney," she said. A glimmer of hope resided in her beautiful blue gems.

I retrieved the balled-up note and handed it to her. I could tell that she wanted to smooth out the paper and read it.

"I used to like her," I said.

"You speak in past tense, but that's all wrong. What you should have said was *I like her*," she said, squeezing the ball tight. "I've seen the way you look at her."

"She's pretty to look at," I admitted, and then immediately wanted to smack myself. I couldn't believe how dense I was acting. "But looks aren't everything. If they were, I might as well date a mannequin because the conversations would be just as dull and boring. *You* are not boring to talk to, infuriating maybe, but not boring."

"So you do think I'm ugly, but at least I'm interesting so you won't succumb to boredom?"

"I'd like to be around you even when I'm not bored, if you wanted to hang out with me."

164

"Is that your way of asking me out?"

This wasn't a conversation I was prepared to have. "Can we please get to our theoretical conversation about Wonderland?"

"Do you believe in aliens?"

That caught me off guard. "Do I think they are living amongst us? No. The possibility of life on another planet is possible. There are countless galaxies and the universe is infinite."

"That was a politically correct answer, which tells me little about your actual opinion. But, I'll play along and pretend that answer satisfied me intellectually."

She reached for the clay and rolled it into a cylindrical object. Then, she tugged on a loose string from her dress and pressed it on top of the clay. After placing it on the floor, she pulled out a card from her sleeve. The Joker. She flicked it in the air so quickly my eyes could barely keep up. A flame flickered from the corner. She used it to set the string on fire. It quickly burned until reaching the clay and then the fire slowed. She'd created a candle.

She tore another paper from my notebook and held it over the flame. It soon burned the paper, creating a hole in the middle. After it took off, she blew out the flames. In the center was a hole a few inches wide.

"This represents Earth's ground," she said, holding up the paper with the hole in it. She spoke about how Earth had specific laws of gravity. The physics was logical and straightforward here. "Everything on Earth is orderly. Every action creates a reaction. Up is up, down is down. The circle of life keeps the world in perfect balance. Even time is linear."

Holding up the crumbled note, she informed me that it was Wonderland—a much smaller, more secretive place. "The physical laws there used to be orderly, like Earth. But then as the world changed, so did the logic. It's a very illogical place, and our laws became unconventional. Up may be up, but only for a little bit. Down can seem endless. People live and die, but don't always stay dead. And time... well, there will come a time when a second will carry on for infinity. It is my greatest hope that I will be in Wonderland to witness the stopping of time."

"What's with the hole in the Earth's ground?" I asked.

"A rabbit hole. Think of it as a vortex," she said, and scraped the burnt particulars off the side of the hole.

She wiggled Wonderland through the hole. It got stuck partway through. "Earth's gravity sucks up Wonderland. They are like sister-realms. Thus, creatures from either side can go back and forth."

"You honestly believe this?" I asked.

"Why is it that when I willingly give you answers, you insist that I'm making them up?" she said, and tossed the papers into the air. *Earth* shriveled up like it was still on fire whereas *Wonderland* floated in the air like a hot air balloon. Standing up, I poked it with my finger. It popped. Pieces rained down on me like confetti. When they touched the floor, they disappeared.

"How did you do that?" I asked.

"Magic," she stated and waved her hand over her face. Her perfect, porcelain face changed so that she looked like the waitress at Little Italy. She waved her hand over her face again and she once again looked like her usual self.

My mouth hung open. "Impossible."

"I told you the essence, the magic, of Wonderland is sticky. And it would behoove you to remember that nothing is impossible in Wonderland." She walked over to the small window and rested her elbows on the ruined dresser. "You believe in the possibility of aliens, yet the theory of different realms is too farfetched to consider? For being someone who claims to be a genius, you are quite simple minded."

Try this for being simple minded, I thought. "Did Hearts have anything to do with my Uncle Edward's death?"

"Did your dear old daddy tell you that?"

"It's a suspicion," I said. "I understand that my dad and Hearts don't play nice together. Your aunts and the queen are BFF's. If I can believe you, then he and this M.H. character used to be friends. I just don't know where you stand."

"I didn't hear a question there."

"I didn't ask one," I said, approaching her with unwilling feet but with a willing heart. I knew she was trouble. I shouldn't get involved, but tell that to my heart. It raced faster than it ever had during a baseball game. I swear my ribs would crack from the break-dance my heart was doing. Why was it that this girl twisted my logic? She distracted me, making a mess of my thoughts. What had she done to me? "Take me to Wonderland."

"Not even if you beg me," she said, impudently. "Besides, you can barely manage yourself when you have a taste of my candy. How would you survive a visit to a place that has no logic?"

"I'm not getting down on my knees to beg," I said.

She turned around and rested her arms on the dresser. Without any makeup to hide behind, there was no denying her fierceness. Residing within the blue gems of her eyes, there was a sense of craftiness and brilliance that couldn't be measured.

"Would you rather date me or a mannequin?"

My mind went blank. We were back to the dating question? My mouth opened but nothing came out. I rubbed my eyes, hoping to buy time for my brain to start working again. She had bitten the bottom of her lip. I settled on a headshake since I couldn't convince my voice box to work.

She grinned. I wished that I had a directory of what each one of her smiles meant.

"I'm not saying I'd say yes if you asked me out. I'm merely curious to what you'd say."

"You wouldn't say yes?"

"You're quite full of yourself, aren't you?" she said, teasingly. "And no, I don't know what I would say."

"What if I did?"

"Ryley, you are quite a horrific date-asker-outer." She pushed off the dresser and walked past me. She picked up Mr. Ruth and kissed the top of his head. I swear I could feel the faint pressure of her lips on my cheek when she kissed her bunny. When she pulled the rabbit away from her lips, it felt like she was pulling gum off my cheek. "Magic is very sticky."

I rubbed my jaw. The moment my fingertips touched my skin, the sticky sensation of a would-be kiss was gone.

She handed Mr. Ruth to me. "Keep him safe."

I don't know if she was telling the rabbit to keep me safe or vice versa, but it didn't matter. I'd take that rabbit everywhere because it was what she wanted.

I was done for.

# CHAPTER THIRTY-FOUR

(Ryley: Present Time)

A gang of misfits—Irwin, Mick and Dax—were waiting by the school's front doors when I arrived. They were my friends, and I couldn't ask for better ones. Still, I didn't exactly love the expressions they had. They were up to something—something fishy. Speaking of pesky things, Chez was perched on the trash can beside the school. A swoon of girls petted him. I could hear his purring. I had half-a-mind to back-hand the little devil. His yellow eyes turned golden as he watched me.

"You're on my radar too, cat," I said, under my breath.

Chez eyeballed Mr. Ruth who had hitched a ride in my jeans pocket. If cat's lips could curl, his did.

"We were just reminiscing about the good-old-days," Dax said when I reached them. "Actually, I was and have been epically disappointed with our final year at Rockingham. See, I have had a lot more time now that you are distracted by Alice Mae. Mick is busy chasing off all the freshmen girls—"

169

Sarah J. Pepper

"A-and I've b-been busy s-s-s-studying for my SATs," Irwin interrupted and pushed up the glasses that were sliding down his nose.

"Remember when the class above us got that hundred pound pig and a few chickens through Blanche's window last homecoming? Why hadn't we planned something out there? It's our senior year and it's already halfway through the first semester. We have to do something," Dax said, like it was our God-given right to terrorize the school.

"So Irwin had this ingenious idea to follow the animalistic trait and use critters again," Mick said. "So we were thinking that we'd go down in school history if we got a boatload of frogs and let them loose in the school."

"Going down in the record books for being suspended because I unleashed frogs in the school isn't something I want to be remembered for," I said.

"Then we won't tell a soul that we were the ones behind it," Mick said. "Think of it as thankless pranking. Besides, we have the perfect plan! Mr. Wang's chemistry room window is on the first floor. Irwin will simply leave it open one night and—"

"And the school will know that it was a senior who did the prank. It was the very same strategy the previous class did," I pointed out. But, it was an excellent idea, leaving the window opened to break into the school. Most people wanted to get out of the building as fast as humanly possible. A category I usually fell into, but there was something intriguing about the idea. I put it in my mental file of good ideas.

"T-then what's-s your-r p-plan?" Irwin said, looking over his shoulder like we were conducting a secret covert operation. "You ow-we me, for c-checking out that c-c-candy. I *have* to do s-something s-s-scandalous at least once in my l-life."

"Do it during the day," I said, and then told them my idea involving the frog unleashing extravaganza. "We won't use Mr. Wang's window to get them in, but he'll be a benefactor. He won't have to purchase frogs for the big dissection project at the end of the year."

"The women folk are gathering," Mick said, nodding to a group of girls that were petting Chez. "We'll talk later."

170

The cat walked up next to Becky, rubbing up against her legs. Courtney had arrived. She was talking fervently and using her hands.

Courtney handed Becky a piece of paper. My blood pressure shot up. I hoped it wasn't more documentation about some family member I didn't know existed. Courtney pointed to the school door and shook her head. It didn't take a mind reader to know that she didn't want to be anywhere near me—even walking into the school was too much. She waited, armed with a bunch of girls, while Becky walked away from the group and approached us. Chez wasn't far behind.

"So Alice Mae has you carrying around her stuffed animals?" Becky said, glancing at Mr. Ruth who was still in my jeans pocket. "Can someone say *whipped?*"

"What do you want Becky?" I asked.

"Nothing much. What are you boys up to?" she asked.

"Nothing," Irwin said, quickly—too quickly.

Becky picked up on the not-so-subtle response as well. Her eyebrow raised, but she said nothing. Instead, she showed me a paper.

"Can you give these questions to Alice Mae? She needs to fill them out and give it back to *me*. Courtney would rather not have anything to do with your new squeeze, but doesn't want that dumb, blonde girlfriend of yours to ruin her GPA in lit class," Becky said.

"Tell her yourself," Dax said and pointed to the girl in question. "She's right there."

Alice Mae unwrapped her scarf and shooed the cat off the school property. "Scat, Chez! I thought we'd been over this. You are *not* to spy on me at school!"

The cat meowed.

"I don't care if you are bored!" Alice Mae yelled, whipping her scarf at the critter.

Chez hissed.

"Well, tell Hearts my plan is still in place and working better than expected. She doesn't need you to check up on me," Alice Mae said and tied her scarf back around her neck. "Find someone else to pester."

"Your girlfriend will do anything for attention," Becky said.

The bell rang. We walked into the school, but as soon as enough students filled the halls, Becky stepped in front of me. She shoved Courtney's questionnaire into my hands. At the top was an envelope addressed to me. I expected a note. Instead, there was a picture of Alice Mae climbing out of the police station's window.

"Lookie what I saw when I was on my way to visit my uncle," Becky said. "Tell that little tramp that I have copies, and if she wants to keep her academic life squeaky clean, a.k.a. not being expelled, then she better make nice."

I asked, "Make nice, how?"

"Option one: Dump you."

"Why would you care if I date Alice Mae?"

"I don't, but Courtney does, and she's my best friend," Becky said.

"Last time I checked, she and John Luke were lockin' lips."

"Just because she's dating the football captain doesn't mean she wants you to be happy," Becky said. "Option two: Tell me why you and your mom skip town so much, and we'll both back off."

"Again, why do you care so much?"

"Because you messed with my friend, so it's my duty as BFF to get justice for her, one way or another," Becky said. "The latest theory is that Lauren had a sex change. She's actually your dad."

"If you start a rumor about my mom, you will pay."

"I'm shaking," Becky mocked and pointed to the incriminating picture. "She will pay."

# Death of the Mad Hatter

As soon as Becky left, I shot a text to Alice Mae. *Meet me in the janitor closet before lit.*

Alice Mae: *I'll be late for class.*

Me: *You'll be expelled if you don't.*

# CHAPTER THIRTY-FIVE

(Ryley: Present Time)

Alice Mae beat me to the closet. The tardy bell rang just as I pulled the door closed behind me. I set my backpack down and flipped over a bucket to use as a seat. Alice Mae leaned against the shelf used for cleaning supplies. I handed her the picture Becky gave me. I noticed the purple painted peacock feathers on her nails. The polish changed hues when the light reflected on it. It was mesmerizing, but I stayed focused.

"You're not good at making friends," I said.

"I thought we already established that neither of us wants to be just friends," Alice Mae said and winked.

"Becky doesn't like you or me for that matter. She's on a mission to get us in trouble," I said, trying to stay on topic. "Do you have any ideas why?"

Alice Mae pressed her lips together in a thin line as she studied the picture. "I should make a confession."

"Go on."

Crickets chirped—well, not actually. But, I could have heard them with as silent as it was in the closet.

"I said that I *should* make a confession, but that's not what I'm going to do."

"Why do you make everything so difficult? Becky wants blood. She will expose your B&E tendencies if we don't break up, or if I don't tell her why my mom and I skipped towns so much."

"First, you've never taken me anywhere except for this closet. So, as far as I'm concerned, we had not officially had a single date. It's a far cry from dating, and I don't remember you ever asking me to be your girlfriend," Alice Mae said. "And second, why did you move so often?"

I crossed my arms. "I ask you questions and get nowhere. Why should I answer any of yours?"

"Because you like to kiss me."

Oh.

"It made you rather hard to find," Alice Mae said and bit her bottom lip. She was right. I did want to kiss her.

"Why were you looking for me?"

"Because Hearts asked me," she said, looking at the photo again. Alice Mae dropped the photo in the mop bucket. The image blurred as it sunk lower. She blew over the water like it was a warm drink she was trying to cool. The water boiled. She grinned as the water turned colors. When she blew over the water again, it turned clear. She pulled out the photo paper. It was absolutely white.

"Becky has more," I said.

"I guess I was wrong about her—she's not a complete idiot," she said, and tossed the photo in the trash. "Good news for mankind, but bad news for me."

"What were you doing in the police station?"

She dusted her hands and placed them on my legs. She leaned close so that I could smell the sweets on her breath. She whispered, "Secretive things."

The closet door opened. Alice Mae jumped back like someone was attacking her with a wet fish. I stood up so fast that I hit my head on the broom rack. Half a dozen brooms and mops fell off, attacking Alice Mae as she raced toward the door.

Bob, the janitor, stood dumbfounded as he blocked the opening. Busted. Within thirty minutes, Alice Mae and I were in the principal, Wittrock's, office. The Maude sisters circled their niece. Alice Mae sat on her hands and kept her face down. I couldn't figure out if her apparent shyness around them was all an act or if she was truly scared of her aunts. Then, there was my mom—my very angry mother. She paced the office like a caged animal, mumbling over and over that she couldn't believe that I'd do such a thing.

I wanted to say, "Mom, I was caught in a janitor's closet with a girl. It wasn't like I killed a man" but I didn't. Everyone was acting like we'd committed a felony. I leaned over to Alice Mae and whispered, "I'll be scrubbing the floors with a toothbrush for a week."

The corners of Alice Mae's mouth twitched. Zola Maude walked in front of her niece and kneeled in front of her. "Keep smiling and I'll tell Hearts that you didn't learn anything from your last floor cleaning."

Wittrock entered and went to his office chair. Zola Maude returned to her position next to Vida Maude, behind Alice Mae. My mom never stopped pacing. He picked up a paper that was on his desk and examined it like it was a disciplinary report of sorts. I knew better. I'd stolen a glance at it. It was the school's lunch menu for next week.

He said, "Your teachers have noted that you've been caught *alone* in classrooms as well as demonstrating irrational behavior, Ryley."

"What teachers?" I asked.

Alice Mae grabbed my hand. The gesture surprised me, thus stopping me from asking any more impromptu questions.

"Does it matter?" Wittrock asked, crossing his arms.

"Of course it matters," I said.

"Ryley Edward Edgar!" Mom exclaimed, "Show some respect, I raised you better than this!"

A.k.a: Shut up. It wasn't hard to read between the lines on that comment. They were as evident as the scowl lines on her face.

"Mrs. Dotson and Mr. Blanch, if you must know who reported repeated instances, Ryley," Wittrock said, blithely. "Any more questions?"

Alice Mae tightened her grip on my hand. "You're making this worse," she whispered.

"I can only imagine how difficult raising a young boy would be, Lauren," Wittrock said, sympathetically. "But, I have to treat Ryley like any other student. One more slip-up, and he'll be suspended. Until then, he'll have afterschool detention."

"I've never gotten into any trouble before now! Don't you think this is a little harsh?" I said, through gritted teeth.

"You're a bright boy, Ryley. You read the news. Too often we read about school shootings and youth stabbings. I don't want that happening at Rockingham."

"You found me in a closet with a girl!" I yelled. Alice Mae's grip was cutting off circulation, but I didn't care. "It wasn't like I was holding a knife to anyone's throat!"

"A wonderful demonstration of *Edgar temper*," Vida Maude said, inspecting her nails like she was bored.

"And it's a good thing Bob found you," Wittrock said. "There are too many teen pregna—"

"We didn't even kiss!" I yelled, standing up. My chair fell over backwards.

"What were you doing then?" Zola Maude asked, nonchalantly.

She may have been pretending not to care, but I could hear the hint of curiosity in her voice. Alice Mae must have heard it too.

"Enough lies, Ryley. We were caught neckin' in a closet. It happens," Alice Mae said and pulled her scarf back. On her neck was a bruise—a bruise that a vacuum could cause or a pair of lips.

"You have a hickey," I said, staring dumbly at her purple skin. I'd never considered myself as the jealous type, but it was in that moment that I understood what envy truly felt like. I wanted Alice Mae all to myself. I hate the idea of her being with other guys.

"It's what happens when *someone* sucks on your neck," she said, and tightened her scarf.

Her purple nail polish was smeared where it was perfect before. Only the feather design was untouched. Had she been scraping her nails when I wasn't watching?

She curled her hands by her sides, hiding her nails. "And my punishment, Mr. Wittrock?"

"You've been absent and late entirely too much this year. You'll be suspended for a week and then a month of in-school-suspension."

I couldn't get my mind off of Alice Mae and that horrid bruise on her neck. We weren't exclusive. We weren't really even dating. So *technically*, I couldn't be mad. No, I wasn't mad. Madness didn't properly describe the level of rage. I was furious! Psychotically enraged.

And what made me even more livid was that I had no right to be. I couldn't even ask the girl out!

So that night, after my mom went to bed, I snuck out of the house and joined Mick, Dax, and Irwin for a frog hunt. It got my mind off of girls for a couple hours.

However, at six forty-two the next morning, I received a pix message. I hoped it was from Alice Mae. I hoped it was some logical reason why she had the markings on her neck from another guy. I hoped it was an apology of some sort that would explain everything. Instead, it was an image of me climbing out my bedroom window. Under it was a text.

Becky: *Happy Hunting?*

# CHAPTER THIRTY-SIX

(Ryley: Present Time)

I glanced at my wrist watch. Seven-oh-five. Way too early to be out of bed, yet there I was, sitting in *Connie's Coffea Shoppe* waiting for the head cheerleader to show. I was armed with the only other person I trusted, Dax. Sleep was still crusted in his eyes. It had only been a few hours since we called it a night from gathering frogs.

"So, we need to bribe Miss Muffin Top to delete that picture," Dax said, blinking at me like he wasn't sure if he was still dreaming or if he was actually awake.

"And figure out why she's so interested in getting me in trouble."

Dressed to the nines, Becky walked in. She had to have been up for hours to look so good. Yet, I had noticed mud under her fingernails. That was all the more evidence I needed to have to know she followed us last night. She ordered a cappuccino and then sat across the table from us.

"You're following me," I stated. I might as well get that obviousness on the table right away. "Why?"

"You really want to know?" she asked and sipped her drink.

"Would we be here at this ungodly hour if we didn't?" Dax said. He didn't do well in the mornings. Maybe I should have asked Irwin to join me instead.

"If you really want to know, ask your *girlfriend*," she said. "Alice Mae is the one who hired me."

"Alice Mae *hired* you to spy on me?" I could barely choke out the question.

"Initially yes, but she made me swear not to tell anyone. In fact, she made me promise that I'd act like I hated her."

"That came naturally," Dax said.

Becky rolled her eyes. "Alice Mae knew I had family in law enforcement and wanted me to find out everything I could about you and your family."

I said, "Do I have to ask the obvious question of why?"

"She never indulged me with the details of her master plan," Becky said. "But, when I found that document about your uncle, she immediately terminated my services. Then, I caught her crawling out of the police station window. So now I'm far too curious about you, and I'm not going to stop until I figure out your secret, Ryley."

Dax nudged my shoulder. "I think you should tell her about your dad, and then find Alice Mae…"

"I know!" I interrupted. He was right. If I was going to get Becky off my back, I had to come clean that he was locked up in an insane asylum. Maybe she'd keep it a secret.

"I'm not going to stop, Ryley. Like I said, I was curious, but then you went and publicly humiliated my best friend by making out with another girl. So, I'm making it my duty to see you disgraced as well."

"If I tell you, will you delete the pictures you have of me sneaking out of the house?" I asked. "Are you spying on me non-stop or did someone tip you off?"

"I knew something was up when your little four-eyed friend blurted out that you guys weren't up to anything yesterday. So, I figured it was an opportunity to get more dirt on you. Glad it worked," she said, and held up her cell phone. She showed me the picture she had of me. "I'll hit the delete button after you tell me your secret."

"My dad is alive," I said.

"Duh, I'm not a moron," she said. "Details."

"He's checked into the West Harbour Psychiatric Treatment Facility for schizophrenia and paranoia," I said, rubbing my eyes. "He thinks that this evil queen from another realm is out to get him and made my mom promise never to stay anywhere for a long period of time."

"So that's why you clammed-up in lit when we were talking about nut jobs," Becky said. "It hit home for you. That makes sense. So why is Alice Mae so interested in you?"

I dug into my backpack and pulled out Mr. Ruth. "Because I took her stupid bunny, and she'll stop at nothing to get it back," I lied.

By lunch time, everyone knew the truth about my dad. I guessed that it didn't matter much because I rapidly became known as the crazy guy who carried around a stuffed bunny, destined to live in a madhouse like his dad. Becky got what she wanted: My public humiliation.

Everyone stared at me when I stepped into the cafeteria. I actually looked up to see if there was an audience monitor telling everyone to be silent. After grabbing my food, I found an open spot next to Irwin and Dax. Mick was sharing a table with his football buddies, but raised his milk container to me in lieu of a greeting. At least he wasn't going to *unfriend* me like most others.

In light of my recent principal visit, threat of suspension, and news of my dad, Irwin suggested that we nix the Senior Prank. "J-just stay out of the s-s-spotlight for-r a w-while."

"No, I need a distraction from this pandemonium," I said. "Let's give everyone something else to talk about."

Dax glance over at Mick. "I'll tell him the timetable moved up to tomorrow."

I'd never been more determined to figure out Alice Mae's secret. Whatever it was, it had to be big—big enough to ruin my life. It was why I sent her a text, saying that it was imperative that we meet tonight, especially since my suspension/expulsion was possible after this stunt.

Alice Mae: *Is this your way of asking me out on a date?*

A little finesse would go a long way if I was going to get what I wanted. So I replied, saying that she should definitely dress up and be prepared to be swept off her feet.

Alice Mae: *I'll wear good shoes then so I don't slip too much...but, don't people usually go on a date at the end of the week?*

There was no winning with her. Me: *Fine, let's meet up on Saturday.*

# CHAPTER THIRTY-SEVEN

(Ryley: Present Time)

During lunch break, the guys and I took off for my house in Dax's Yota. We gathered up the frogs that we'd collected. There were enough to fill three ice cream buckets. We loaded up the frogs and drove back to school. I was positive Irwin was going to have an anxiety attack, but the guy kept his cool as we pulled into the parking lot.

There was no good way to conceal an ice cream bucket. I left the car first. I was to place the bucket in the boys' bathroom. Dax had his in the chemistry room and Mick was going to dump his in the band room, which was on the opposite side of the school from the teachers' lounge.

I was so nervous; I went into the girls' bathroom instead of the boys'. *Smooth move, genius.* I stayed close to the door. The hall was empty, so I cracked the door to leave when someone tapped me on the shoulder. I turned around just in time for Courtney to knee me in the groin.

"You're peeping on me!" Courtney yelled, and kicked me again.

Falling to my knees, I dropped the bucket. The lid popped off. Out hopped a batch of frogs. Courtney screamed and reached for the door. Clutching my damaged goods, I grabbed her waist and kept her from barreling out.

"I'm *so* telling Wittrock! You're chemically imbalanced!" Courtney yelled, wiggling away.

Barricading myself in front of her, (via me on my back and my leg pinned against the door) I said, "Hush Courtney, it's not like they're going to eat your leg. It's not a special batch of zombie frogs. Just chill!"

"Good plan, dummy. Mock me," Courtney said, raising her heeled shoe in the air.

I didn't have to connect the dots to know she would be connecting that pointy heel with my manhood. "I'm sorry!"

"What?"

"I'm sorry… I'm sorry about everything," I said. I knew I should warn her that the crazed blonde secretly poisoned her. I did want Alice Mae to be punished; I wanted to be the one doing it——not the police. "I never meant to hurt your feelings, Courtney. I did like you."

"If you liked me so much, why did you kiss Alice Mae?"

"I wasn't thinking," I said.

"Obviously."

"If it makes you feel any better, she's playing me too. That hickey on her neck wasn't from me."

Courtney lowered her foot to the floor. I scrambled to get up and keep the door closed. Other girls were already knocking on the door to be let in. I was running out of time. Frogs were everywhere, and they weren't quiet. It wasn't long before the chicks on the other side of the door commented about the noise.

Courtney crossed her arms. "I could be convinced to stay quiet about this silly senior prank."

"What do you want? I'll give you anything."

"So dump Alice Mae, and I'll forgive you."

"I will on Saturday." Right after I get my answers...

"Good. And if you don't, I'll convince John Luke that you ruined my reputation. I'm sure his fist and your face will get acquainted," she said.

Gotcha, he'll open up a can of whoopass.

She glanced at the only window in the bathroom. "I'll give you a ten-second head start before I open that door. Don't forget, girls have small bladders and will probably break down the door in a few seconds. Oh and Ryley, don't ever cross me again. I'd simply *hate* for Becky to investigate Lauren."

"Leave my mom out of this."

"Tempt me, Ryley. Tempt me and I'll bring your mom into this so fast she'll be just as confused with reality as your father."

I slammed my hand next to her head. "Wreck my parents' lives—"

"And you'll what?" she said. "Take it out on me? I don't think so because the only thing keeping you from getting expelled is my foot on this door. So run away before it accidently slips open."

I almost broke the window trying to get out before a stampede of girls came barging in. I fell to the ground, spraining my ankle. I swore under my breath, but it was covered up by the multiple shrieks.

# Chapter Thirty-Eight

(Ryley: Present Time)

Midnight on Saturday, I stood outside Alice Mae's house. Her light turned on after I sent her a text saying I had arrived. Normally, I'd dress up for dates, but I didn't tonight, mainly to convince myself that I wasn't trying to impress Alice Mae. I admitted that the girl had stolen my heart, but it didn't mean that she robbed me of my intelligence. For all I knew, she was my enemy. Clearly, she wasn't as into me as I thought, and she was a devious witch who was going to stop at nothing until she got what she wanted—whatever that was. So blue jeans, t-shirt, backpack (with Mr. Ruth and some extras stuffed inside) and a baseball cap completed my outfit.

Ten minutes passed by before Alice Mae's bedroom window opened. She threw a knotted sheet down. A twinge hit my stomach when she climbed from her window. It wasn't butterflies that girls describe when seeing someone they like. It was more like an anvil weighing me down.

Somehow, she still appeared graceful while scaling the house—in heeled boots, no less. She wore a white mink fur coat that stopped at her knees. The hem of a dress peeked out underneath. She wore a beautiful purple hat with a black veil. Her hair was pinned up in the back, forming a messy bun. Her eye shadow shimmered. I didn't know a lot about makeup, but she knew her way around the material. Her black boots stopped just short of her knees.

"Where are we off to?" she asked, retrieving a piece of candy from her coat pocket.

I retrieved a bandana from my backpack. "Close your eyes."

She pushed the bandana away. "No."

"Don't you trust me?"

"No."

"Then take a leap of faith. And, hand over the candy."

"No."

"Then we won't get very far with our date."

She exchanged a few pieces of candy for the blindfold. I didn't press the issue, but I was sure that she still had some candy on her somewhere. After she secured the blindfold over her eyes, I dug into my backpack and pulled out a Coke. The moment I cracked it open, Alice Mae fussed with her blindfold and pushed it onto her forehead.

"Ryley, I can't drink that! It will offset the—"

"Drink it, or I'll end this date here and now. You can call one of your other male-callers to spend Saturday night with."

"What other male-callers?"

I pointed to her neck. The hickey still showed like a bad omen. "Are you a switch hitter or something?"

She rolled her eyes. "A baseball reference? I swear your life exists around that sport!"

Refusing to get sidetracked, I asked, "Who gave you that hickey?"

She blinked at me. Yep, that was her response. I'd accused her of dating other guys, and she managed a blink.

Alice Mae held up her hand. Her purple nail polish was perfectly applied and her peacock design had changed to a sparkling diamond. Swiftly, she rubbed her pointer finger over her neck. The purple polish came off, leaving the impression that she had been used as a lollipop.

"Oh."

"It's just another parlor trick I learned from the Joker."

"The Joker?"

"One of the queen's personal minions who dabbles in fortune telling, but he's not as good as his great, great grandfather," she said, counting the *greats* on her fingers as she spoke.

"Well that makes perfect sense," I said sarcastically and dug out two sets of headphones.

She watched me as I put them in my ears. I plugged it into my phone. I offered her my other set. She set the can down on the sidewalk and pushed them into her ears and then into her phone. Again, she covered her eyes with the bandana. I called her.

"Alice Mae speaking." She spoke like she didn't know who was on the other end.

"It's me." I said dryly and picked up the can. "You are going to ruin your surprise if you don't take a drink."

"But I—"

"You can't see anything strange because you are blindfolded. The ear buds block out most everything else besides my voice. So whatever effects Wonderland causes, you won't notice, even without candy," I said. "Tell me I'm wrong."

She pressed her lips together. She reached out. I handed her the can. Before she took a drink, "Things are not going to go as planned."

"My plan or yours?" I asked before I could stop myself.

She paused in mid-drink. Even with her eyes covered, I could tell she was weighing her responses. "Mine."

After shrugging on my backpack, I took the half-empty can and dumped the rest of the beverage out on the street. I took her hand. She drummed on my hand nervously as I led her away. Her confidence was down to zilch. The longer we walked, the closer she got.

When we reached the chemistry class's window, I popped it open with a screwdriver that I had put in my backpack. I placed both hands on the windowsill and pulled myself up. After straddling the window, I extended my hand down to her. Her fingertips found mine.

"Ryley, I'm not going to break and enter."

"Says the girl who broke into a police station," I said. "Are you going to tell me what you were doing there, yet?"

"No."

She took my hand. I pulled her up to the top. When she was stable, I jumped into the classroom. I could hear the frogs ribbiting.

She jumped onto the floor. I caught her in my arms and caught my breath as well. She smelled good— exorbitantly good. Vanilla covered in cherries. I took her hand again and maneuvered us around the desks.

Occasionally, she'd squeeze my hand harder like something had startled her. I led her to a corner in the library where I'd been busy setting up our date before I showed up in front of her house. Created with books from the last shelf, I made two low-rider chairs and a table. It took about fifty more books than I predicted, but I had a surplus so I wasn't worried.

"Would you like to ditch the jacket or are you still chilly?"

She undid the only button that kept the jacket on, revealing a sequined, midnight blue number. It was a good thing she was still blindfolded because minutes could have passed while I stared at her, and I wouldn't have noticed. It felt like the start of a dirty movie, as I watched her remove her coat. She handed it to me. I tossed it aside without looking where I had thrown it. I couldn't take my eyes off of her.

"Ryley? Is something wrong?"

"Nope." Courtney was right. My brain turned to mush around her.

I helped her onto the seat. She grabbed the edges and burst out laughing when she realized she was sitting on a stack of books. She played with the pages. It was captivating to watch her explore my setup with her fingertips.

"Ryley, did you create an entire table and chairs out of books?"

"You said you liked books."

"Usually I read them, not sit on them."

On the table was a pizza that I'd ordered. I hoped it wouldn't be very cold since I'd picked it up thirty minutes before. I placed a slice in front of her.

"I'm *allergic* to mushrooms," she said and used air quotes.

"Is that your way of saying this better not be a fungus pizza?"

"Sort of," she said. "What kind is it?"

"Your favorite."

"How do you know what my favorite pizza is?" she asked.

"I'm observant," I said, recalling her in the cafeteria as she ate her pizza.

She took a bite. She ate almost half of the pizza before she took out her ear plugs. I didn't comment, but I ended the forty-three minute phone call and took out my ear buds.

"So you fashioned a table and chairs out of books, what other tricks do you have up your sleeve?"

"You're the trickster, not me," I said.

She turned her head in the direction of the door. I assured her that there was nothing there. She nervously tapped the top of my makeshift table.

I gently grabbed her hand, stopping her from tapping. "What is your favorite color?" I asked, hoping to keep her mind in the here-and-now.

"I do enjoy the color orange."

"Orange?"

"It doubles as a fruit. Who wouldn't love it?"

She removed the blindfold and looked around. She squealed when she saw the book I had placed upright on the center of the table. It was a gardening book with a beautiful white rose on the cover.

She eagerly picked up the book and looked through it. "You're quite charming, Ryley. How many girls have you brought to the library before me?"

"Why do you think I've brought anyone else here?"

"Because breaking into a library, reading the written word by people who know how to express love, hate, lust and everything in the middle is far too..." she stopped, taking in the atmosphere.

"Is far too what?"

She smiled that irresistible smile of hers. At the moment, it was a little mischievous mixed with a rare form of shyness that didn't usually reside there.

"Sexy." She whispered the word as if she'd never spoken such a naughty word in front of a boy before. Her hands clenched tight.

"Is that a bad thing?" I reached for her balled up, little fists. She relaxed her hands. Her fingernails had indented half-moon marks into her skin.

"Yes and no."

"Then I'll stop being so sexy, without being any less sexy."

She laughed. I smiled broadly—too much, so I imagined the dorky expression on my face. I turned away and folded the pizza box into my backpack.

She set the book in her lap and closed it, but I could tell that she wanted to look at it more. I took it from her and pulled out the slip. After digging in my bag for a pencil, I wrote her name on the checkout slip.

"It's yours for the week," I said and handed it back to her.

"What's your favorite color, Ryley?" she asked, flipping through the pages.

"The color of your eyes." I wanted to stick my head in the ground like the cartoon ostrich drawn on a children's book that made up a significant portion of the table. Why had I just said that? I sounded like a dork.

"You are like gravity, Ryley. You know that you have that effect on me, don't you?" Gravity? The question must have been written on my face because she answered me without me having to open my mouth. "You draw me in. It makes me nervous. It makes me second guess my… hell, every decision I've made in years."

I stood up and leaned against the side of the table that was closer to her. "Why?"

I waited patiently as she chipped away the fingernail polish on her ring finger. The hours seemed to pass before she answered. When she did, she blinked away tears that were threatening to fall.

"Because I think you are the reason why I will choose Wrong," she said. "A day will come when I must choose to live in Wonderland or here. I won't be able to cross realms anymore. Why or how this is possible, I do not know. I just know that is the truth."

"And this troubles you? Why?" I asked, kindly. Finally, I was getting somewhere with her.

"You were right about me," she said, seemingly changing topics. "I'm not a good person, and that's why I don't fight Hearts anymore. Well, that and if I break another Wrongdoing Law, I'm toast. But it doesn't matter what the law says, I'm just like her. Besides, the last time I went up against her, too many people's lives were ruined. That's why I break-in to places like police stations. That's why I've tracked down your dad. My... my mischief has gotten me into more trouble. And, it's why I have my friend's blood on my hands."

"You killed a man?"

"Not by my blade, but it might as well have been," she said.

"You teamed up with Hearts not because you wanted to, but because she blackmailed you, didn't she?" I asked. My thoughts were rapid. Was Alice Mae to blame for my dad leaving his birthplace? Had she instigated the events that caused my uncle's murder? Who was M.H? Why did she insist on me keeping Mr. Ruth? Was Chez a bigger player in this messed up game Hearts instigated? Why did she put so much clout in the prophecies? So many more question boiled up, but I began with one—the one that always seemed the most important to me. "How do you know my dad, Alice Mae?"

"I was his deliverer before everything went wrong."

"His deliverer? For what? Newspapers? Pizza?"

"Candies." A tear fell from her eye. She quickly wiped it onto her fingers. Holding her breath, she looked at the tear stain like she expected it to grow into this great flood or something. When it didn't, she fidgeted. "Can I please have my candies back? I need one. I can't focus. I can't breathe!"

She began to hyperventilate. I pulled her up next to me and hugged her ferociously—even though I knew I shouldn't. Torn was the perfect word to describe how I felt. I knew I should be level-headed and get to the bottom of her mischief, but all I wanted to do was keep her from shedding another tear.

"You don't need any sweets, Alice Mae—not right now anyway. You just need a distraction from yourself."

"Are you trying to distract me from my past? It's far too haunting. You won't succeed," she said, and took several deep breaths as she fiddled with the collar of my shirt.

"Won't I?" I said.

"It is doubtful."

"Bring me to Wonderland," I said. If I could just get there, perhaps I'd find someone who was more willing to share the secrets Alice Mae kept.

"You can't. I told you that I'd never bring you there, even if you begged me," she said, and then bit her lip. She was contemplating a deep thought. "Your father has forbidden it."

"That's not my dad's decision to make."

"Yet, he made it all the same. If the Queen finds out that I told you any of this, I'll be in so much trouble… Why do I keep telling you the secrets I promised never to speak about?" she said frantically and then kissed me before I could ask any more questions about the dangerous and manipulative World of Wonderland.

We didn't stop kissing until my lips were raw. It just happened to be the exact moment that the fire alarm went off.

# CHAPTER THIRTY-NINE

(Ryley: Present Time)

There were times I just wanted to press rewind in life and start over. This was one of those times. Trapped in the school, the alarms were blaring so loud I could hardly think straight. I was going to get suspended and Alice Mae would probably be expelled if we didn't get out of here quickly. We'd be the only two morons in Rockingham history who had broken *into* the school and got caught. Yep, we were so busted.

"Oh good, you hear bells too?" Alice Mae asked, covering her ears with her hands.

I frantically disassembled the book-table by tossing the novels and textbooks around so it no longer represented a table and chairs. Alice Mae stopped me. She held up her phone and insisted that we capture the moment.

"You want to take a photo *right now*? The cops are probably on their way over!"

"Well, the chance of us getting expelled and never getting to see each other again is most probable. We're likely never to step foot inside this building alone, so we might as well cherish the moment," she said, digging into my pockets to retrieve my phone. "Besides, you have an incriminating

196

photo of me breaking into a police station. Why shouldn't I have one of you committing a crime?"

Like I said, this was one of those times I wished that I could just press rewind. That way, I could suggest us taking a photo-op earlier in the evening so we didn't have the urgency of *capturing the moment* when we were literally minutes from walking out of the school in handcuffs.

Alice Mae held up my phone and smiled blissfully at it. I tried not to throw up. Just as it flashed, I glanced at her. There was no arguing it; Alice Mae was particular. After I promised to text her the picture, she handed the phone back and grabbed her coat off of the floor.

"Don't just stand around, Ryley! We need to hurry, unless your plan for our date included a visit behind bars."

And, there it was—my urge to strangle her *again*. She bent over and retrieved a thin piece of candy from her boot cuff. A Fruit Roll Up. She plopped it in her mouth. I knew she didn't give me all of her sweet stash.

I slapped the checkout slip inside Ms. Taffy's folder. We raced out of the library, only to stop on a dime. I couldn't tell for sure what city officials were walking down the hall towards us, but they were swinging their flashlights right to left, scanning the halls. One shouted out when he saw me.

"Stop!" he ordered.

We bolted.

Alice Mae led the way through the halls like she hadn't just transferred to the school at the start of the year. She maneuvered the twists and turns like she'd studied the layout of the school. I simply kept up, until she turned down the secondary stairwell that led to the lifting room in the basement.

"Alice Mae, there isn't any place to hide down here!"

"Fine, then find your own place to hide."

She ran to the back of the weight room. Originally, the room had been twice as big, but a false wall had been put in to make a storage room.

The leftover and old uniforms for the various sports hung from racks and filled up cardboard boxes. Alice Mae pulled out a bobby pin and fiddled with the lock. Within a split second, she had broken into the storage unit.

"Where did you learn to do that?" I asked.

"Like I said, Wonderland is full of mischievous creatures," she said. "I wouldn't make it very long if I didn't know how to pick a lock. The Joker can attest to that."

I followed her into the makeshift closet. She softly closed the door shut. It clicked, locking us inside. It was dark. Only the exit sign above the door illuminated the room. We weaved to the back of the storage place and hid behind the equipment.

"I swear I saw two kids run in here," an officer said loud enough to hear through the thin wall.

"That's Becky's uncle, Officer Pullman," Alice Mae whispered. "His password for everything is sprinkleddonut."

"Really?"

She rolled her eyes. "His password was his mother's maiden name, which isn't hard to find if you know who to talk to or where to look."

"I wasn't under the impression that you knew much about electronics since you hand crafted all the missing posters."

"You didn't get the impression because I didn't want you to."

I guessed that I was more impressionable than I thought. "What were you looking for in the police station?"

"I wasn't looking," she said. I just stared at her until she explained more fully. "I was there to upload the document indicating Robert Edgar had a brother. It wasn't in the computer systems until then, and it was imperative that it be electronically recorded."

"Why?"

"Well, how else was Becky going to uncover any dirt on your family, if I wasn't the one to put it there? The girl barely knows how to answer her smartphone."

I crossed my arms to keep from wringing her neck. "*Why* did you want Becky snooping around in my family business?"

"To keep you distracted from what I was doing."

Pullman jiggled on the storage room door. It didn't budge. Another voice echoed in the weight room. "We found a window pried open in a science room."

The officers left. We sat in silence for a few minutes, listening for any noise that might indicate that they found us. "I don't know the protocol for B&E, but I think we might have to bunker down here for a while until it's safe to leave."

"Then let's make the most of it," she said, and rummaged through the clothing and tossed me a pair of tight pants. I picked up the baseball pants from the 1960's. There was a rat hole on the side. Tossing me the uniform top she said, "Try them on."

"Here?" *In front of you?*

"Do you want me to wear the blindfold, again?" she said. The shadows cast darkness on her face, appearing ominous.

I didn't answer her, not with words anyway. Instead, I stripped off my shirt and cast it down onto the floor. Her gaze plummeted. Her mouth made an "O" shape.

"Oh dear," she whispered, and then turned around when I reached for my jean's zipper.

"Have you ever seen a guy before?"

"Duh, I have! It's not like male humans are an endangered species, hiding in the furthest corners of the world that only come out during a blue moon! But, if you're asking if I've seen a naked…" her voice trailed off. She fidgeted with a uniform. "It's not like I spend my free time peeping in the boys' locker room, though rumor has it that you enjoy hanging out in the girls' bathroom."

"Who did you hear that from?"

"John Luke. He said you are still infatuated with *his girlfriend.*"

"Are you jealous of her?"

"No," she said a little too fast. "I just don't like rumors about you and her, of any sort. But…were you spying on her in the bathroom?"

"No."

"Prove it," she said, and defiantly crossed her arms.

"Where do you think all the bullfrogs came from? A Froggie fairy?" I leaned in close and whispered in her ear. "My plan was to dump them in the boys' bathroom, not the girls'. Courtney just so happened to be in the room when I emptied my load."

"You're disgusting!" She might have thought I was a gross boy, but her tone of voice gave away her true feelings. She was impressed—or at least amused.

"Not to change the subject, but something you said piqued my interest. Haven't you ever been with someone before?" I said more than asked, slipping on a pair of baseball pants that were five inches too short.

She glanced over her shoulder as I zipped up the pants. Our eyes locked. It was impossible not to see that she was thinking about *it.* So, it was impossible for me to think of anything else as well. She didn't look away when I slipped on the uniform top. The hunger in her eyes made it difficult to keep putting clothes on, but I managed.

"Have *you* ever been naked with a girl before?"

There was no right answer to that question. If I told her I'd been with girls before, the conversation would derail to the most undesirable discussion I dared to have with a girl, but it wasn't like I could just stand there like a mute monk. I needed to say something! Anything!

"I'm experienced."

"Well, then I'm in need of a crash course," she said, and reached for the oh-so-small strap that held up her dress.

Her shoulders were so small and delicate that it would be a small movement to simply brush her strap aside. I imagined it falling to the floor, revealing her... She brushed it off, but the dress stayed on. I didn't have the thought capacity to logically figure out how it stayed up. Why did women wear attire that defied physics? To tease men, I thought. The thin material should have fallen to the ground!

She turned around and moved her hair to the side. "I could use a hand with the zipper, Ryley. It's in the back."

Oh. That's how the dress stayed up.

"It's your turn to turn around," she said after I pulled the tiny zipper down, revealing the curves of her back. She had such a beautiful art-worthy body. To draw the contours of her figure... I let my hands fall to my side, even though I wanted to trace my finger along the small of her back where two perfectly formed dimples interrupted the smooth...

"Ryley?" She clutched her dress in the front to keep it from falling. I finally convinced myself that looking at her face was where my gaze *should* be. *Actually* convincing me of that was another thing entirely.

Alice Mae's grin filled her face, but her cheeks were flushed. "I don't care if you close your eyes or turn around, but I'd like a little privacy, or you won't see the remarkable outfit I picked out for you."

"No problem." I didn't move.

The corners of her mouth twitched. She raised her hand in the air and twirled her finger.

"What?" I asked.

"Privacy?"

Yep, brain to mush. "Turning. Turning," I said, raising my hands in the air as if to say *you caught me.*

I faced away from her. I tried to think about foot fungus, dirty diapers, and rotten watermelons—anything that was unappealing. I heard her dress fall. I grabbed the nearest stack of cardboard boxes for support and tried to think about anything other than her perfectly sculpted ass-ets. Behind me was a half-naked girl, just prancing around in the school's athletic over-sized closet. I lost the battle of my wills. I *had* to steal a peek— just one. I glanced over my shoulder just in time to see her disappear behind a stack of football gear.

"No peeking!"

"You have a knack at temptation, Alice Mae."

"Temptation is a word made up by desperate men, with lustful thoughts, to sound less crude to women."

"Many words have been created to replace crude words like lust."

"Yet, the words to describe love have fewer synonyms."

"If there are fewer words, it is only because men are left speechless at the beauty women bestow," I said, contemplating another glance. "Our puny brains stop working when in the presence of desirable women."

A box fell to the floor with a bang! I turned around in time to see helmets hitting the floor, burying Alice Mae's dress. She was nowhere to be seen.

"Are you hurt?" I called out.

A tap on my shoulder alerted me otherwise. I shouldn't have been surprised when she burned past the cheerleader uniforms and headed for the football pads. I burst out laughing when she paired the shoulder pads with a wrestler's uniform.

"Words escape me in the presence of your beauty."

She pretended to be mad. She even put her hands on her hips and scowled, which made her more attractive. There was no denying Alice Mae's magnificence. She could compete with models in natural beauty, but it wouldn't be a competition when considering her quirky personality. She wasn't definable. She was complicated. She had so many different levels, uncharted territory, to her. She was a mystery, and I wanted to spend all eternity trying to solve her, if I wasn't fighting with her.

Obviously, I couldn't say that. No one ever wants something (or someone) if it's too easy to take. So I added, "You're even more attractive when you pout."

"I'm not pouting," she insisted, even though her bottom lip stuck out enough for me to struggle to keep my thoughts from wandering back to her kiss.

"Then tell me what word you'd use to describe what you're doing to me," I said, stepping closer to the only girl in the world who could pull off wearing a combination wrestler's and football player's uniform and be so damn provocative.

"I'm just being playful." The look in her eyes was anything but innocent.

"Playful?" I closed the distance between us. "I think you need to check out a thesaurus from the library because *playful* isn't the word I'd use."

I pressed my finger against her shoulder pads. I traced my finger down until it fell off the pads. The spandex wrestling uniform accentuated the perfect formed lines of her stomach. I let my finger drift lower until I traced her hip that protruded slightly.

"What word would you use?"

"*Inviting.*" I lifted her chin. I bent forward so my nose traced her cheek. "You are being rather inviting." With my other hand, I tugged on the thin spandex that covered her stomach. "And I want to accept your invitation."

"Ryley, I'm not the kind of a girl who just sends out all sorts of invitations without..."

"You're not the kind of girl who falls in love?"

She pulled away. "It would be tragic if I fell in love."

I let my hands fall by my side. "Would it be tragic to fall in love, period—or just with me?"

Her answer was clear in her eyes. She tried to blink away the truth, but it was too late. I saw it. She dreamed of falling in love, but not with someone like me.

"Read you crystal clear," I said, backing off to look for my clothes. They had to be somewhere under the pile of knocked-over helmets.

She grabbed my arm, stopping me from throwing the football equipment all over, but I didn't look at her. "It's not easy. You don't understand, Ryley."

"That's all I ever wanted—to understand! You accuse me of missing the point but offer little to no explanation!" I jerked my hand out of her grasp. "I want to understand what is so different about you and this magical place you've come from, but you don't tell me anything! You are just this mess of secrets that don't make any sense. I know you have something planned, or the queen does, or…I don't know *something!* But, I'm sick of—"

"Would you cordially accept my invitation?"

Ummm, what? "Stop trying to change the sub—"

"I like you, you big dummy!" She yelled at the top of her lungs.

I covered her mouth. If the officers were close, they *had* to have heard us. When no one pounded down the door with handcuffs, I removed my hand and stepped away from her.

"I'm just scared because things are moving so fast and I don't know what I'm doing. I've never been with anyone like you. Smart. Funny. S-s-sexy," she said, stuttering on the last word. She paced around in the wrestling uniform. "I haven't even kissed anyone until you!"

"Just because you're afraid—" Wait! What? She's never kissed anyone before?

I tried to keep my smile from growing, but it was useless. She made a sound I didn't think girls were capable of making—a noise mimicking a ravenous beast. The malefic sound held a hint of *inviting*. Inviting and, for lack of a better word since my brain wasn't working quite right, enticing.

"One second I want to slap you across the face and the next I want to stop all your worries with a kiss, you big turd face! I don't know the *Rules of Dating*. I've never been in *love* before!" Her mouth hung open. She looked like she had been ready to curse up a storm, until *that* four letter word came out.

She loved me? I knew I should do something—anything, except stand still and hold a random helmet. I dropped it. She turned away when I approached her. I wrapped my arms around her waist. The football pads made it difficult to hold her, but a girl like Alice Mae would always be difficult in some way or another, figuratively speaking.

"I guess we will figure out the rules together," I whispered.

She caught her breath. She placed her trembling hand over mine. We said nothing for one blissful minute. The silence wasn't uncomfortable like it usually was when I was with girls. It was peaceful.

"Ryley, do you *really* want to make the journey to Wonderland?" Alice Mae asked, wiggling out of my embrace. She batted her eyelashes, like she was trying to take attention off of *her* uncertainties. "It's not a world filled with magical rainbows and unicorns—well, it is, but they don't always play nice with others."

"I can handle a few ninja-like critters."

"If the queen hears of your journey, she will be…" Her voice trailed off as she tried to find the right wording.

"Maddened?"

She frowned. "I'm sure there will be feelings of that as well. She has unusual reactions to outside guests."

"So, it's dangerous."

"Quite, but if *you* truly want to go there, then I'll escort you," Alice Mae said. "But the decision has to be yours, not mine."

# CHAPTER FORTY

(Alice Mae: Present Time)

Tears threatened to spill onto my cheeks. They burned my eyes like acid. I looked up at the night's sky as I hurried home. Darkness blanketed the sky, cloaking everything in shadows. Evil could hide in plain sight, just like I could hide in the shadows during nightfall.

Chez was waiting for me, perched on the apple tree. He was pawing at one of the apples that still clung to the branch. Most apples had fallen to the ground. They rotted next to an ordinary looking rabbit hole. His yellow eyes turned gold when he saw me wipe an escaped tear off of my cheek. Just because he couldn't communicate with me via the conventional verbal method in this realm, didn't mean that I couldn't take a guess at what he was thinking… and I didn't need him running to the queen with "false" information.

"I haven't fallen for the boy," I said. "The tears are for show in case anyone is watching. It's all just a part of my plan."

Chez meowed.

"I'm *so* not crying because I feel bad about what I have to do. My plan is in place and is working. It's working so well, in fact, that Ryley actually begged me to bring him to Wonderland," I said, walking past the cat and onto the front steps of my aunts' house.

The cat reappeared in front of me, effectively blocking the entrance. He didn't make a sound, but he stared at the fake hickeys I had created. He jumped on my shoulder and sniffed my neck.

"The hickeys are merely flare. I'm an actress. If he wasn't jealous that would be a bad sign, but he is. He's falling for me, not the other way around," I said, pulling the cat off of me. Chez dug his claws into my shoulder. "You don't believe me?"

The cat hissed.

"Tell the queen to prepare iced tea, just the way Ryley likes it, for he will be in her court by the week's end."

# CHAPTER FORTY-ONE

(Ryley: Present Time)

Screaming that thirteen and a half flamingos would drown in the great flood that had been bestowed upon us, my dad sat on the table's edge with his feet on the chair. He used a spoon as an oar to row himself to safety. A nurse tried to reason with him in an effort to get him sitting upright on the seat, but it was useless.

"Dad, there's no great flood or drowning birds here," I said, fiddling with the candies that Alice Mae had given me before we walked to the school.

"Blasphemous!" he cried.

"Dad, if you sit in the chair, I'll give you some candy," I said. When he didn't budge from his spot, I added that it had a *wondrous* flavor.

He sat his butt down on the chair faster than I could retrieve a rolled candy from my pocket. I tossed it to him. He peeled away the wax paper wrapper, revealing a faint pink Tootsie Roll. He popped it in his mouth. He leaned back in his seat and closed his eyes as he sucked on the candy.

"Why don't you want Ryley to know about Wonderland?" I asked, hoping to sound casual. He wasn't in his right mind and clearly he didn't want *me* to know about it so I pretended to be a random visitor.

"To protect him from the Queen of Hearts."

"Why does he need protection from her?"

"She meddles with lives even though she is not privy to do such. She was not born into royalty, even though she'd let you think such," he said, and then opened his eyes. They weren't unfocused or dilated. He reached out to me and spoke with clarity. "Ryley? Is that really you?"

We stood up and hugged each other. He placed his hands on my shoulders and told me that I'd grown so much.

I said, "Tell me about Wonderla——"

My dad slapped his hand over my mouth. He moved his hand to press his finger over my lips. "How do you know about that place?"

I removed his hand. "A little bird whistled in my ear and told me the secrets of that realm."

"Was it an actual talking bird or was that a metaphor?"

Maybe the candy wasn't working. "Birds don't talk, Dad."

He breathed a sigh of relief. Whatever knowledge he gained from my comment pleased him. The innocent smile turned into a dark smirk. "The birds here aren't much for conversation, are they?"

Dismissing his comment, I said, "I've come to the understanding that you and Hearts weren't the fondest of friends."

"I'm not going to discuss *her,*" my dad spat. **He acted like I had violated some heavenly rule by bringing up the queen. He crossed** his arms. "How is your mother doing?"

I crossed my arms too. Like father like son, I guessed. If he wasn't going to bargain with me, perhaps a little guilt would do the trick. I pulled out my wallet. Inside was a picture of Mom and me that was taken at the church's last photo shoot. I showed it to him.

"Mom misses you."

He handed me the photo back. I shook my head and told him to keep it. I had a hundred different questions brewing about Wonderland, but I kept them to myself for now. Instead, I told my dad about the past few years. I told him about the colleges I wanted to attend. "I'm hoping to get into a school with a decent physics department."

A broad smile spread across his face. "Following your old man's footsteps I see."

I nodded. The questions were burning on my tongue. I couldn't keep them suppressed any longer. "Dad, why don't you just make candy like this and come back home? You could have your old life back."

He sighed one of the sighs a truly broken person is capable of doing. The failure and realization was as evident as the wrinkles in his face. If he was a younger man, he'd look like tears were seconds from forming in his eyes, but he wasn't a young man anymore. All the tears about his situation had already been shed.

"You're not going to stop until you get answers, are you?"

"Nope."

"You're stubborn, like me," he said, and then smiled weakly. "I can't have my old life back, because I can't get my hands on the ever-changing recipe since the Maude sisters took over M.H's candy operation."

"What if I could get you the recipe?" I said, thinking of all the ways to break into the Maude sister's house and steal it.

"It's written in the *Sweets for the Rabbit Hole Voyager*, which is secured in Hearts' master library," my dad said. "Besides, since Wonderland is always changing, thus, the recipe and ingredients change as well."

Of course it did.

"Certainly someone changes the recipe. It's not like the book just knows when to change the recipe," I said.

My dad gave me a look that indicated otherwise.

"What if I could get my hands on the book?" I asked.

My dad waved the idea away like it was a fly in the air. "No, that's a terrible idea. It didn't work out so well last time the candies were delivered, I don't want to think about the repercussion you'd face if you took Hearts' book."

"It's just a candy recipe, Dad," I said. "It's not like I'd get into major trouble if someone caught me."

"If you believe that, then you understand nothing," he said, glancing at the nurses' station. "Care for a walk?"

The medical staff was watching us interact with great curiosity. I suppose it would be a bit odd for a mental patient to suddenly act lucid. So we made our way outside before anyone started asking questions. Dad chose the cement bench furthest from the facility.

"If someone caught you stealing candy for *me*, there would be repercussions to pay to the queen. And she wouldn't give you a slide because you're family," he said. When I didn't react to the news, he commented, "The little bird that told you about Wonderland must have been quite the talker if you already know the queen has a tiny heart."

"It was more like pulling teeth from the little bird," I said, dismissively. "So, why wouldn't my family ties matter?"

"Hearts killed her husband and blamed it on his clumsiness. She claimed that Eddie tripped on a guillotine. I heard the truth come from a grasshopper before a villainous cat did away with the insect," he said. "I publicly accused her of the crime, but had no evidence. Besides, it was a logical explanation given to creatures who don't usually warrant rational thought. Long story short, I was banished—not beheaded—but only because I was next in line to the throne. I would live out my life in this realm, and she would rule from her court. Neither party should pass into each other's chosen realm… which meant I needed a truck full of candies to offset the consequences of living outside of Wonderland."

211

"So when you ran out of sweets, you lost your mind," I said, piecing together the story. "Which is why you needed someone to deliver your candies... What happened to the last *deliverer*?"

"You're skipping ahead in the story," my dad said. "I had an infinite number of sweets, but that was recalled by Hearts after you fell down a rabbit hole. The queen had ordered the rabbits to put in overtime digging. I suspect that she wanted you to wander into her court."

Excuse me? "I've been to Wonderland?"

"As a child. I gave you an Eraser Tracer, an unforgettable-forgettable sweet to make you lose recollection of that night," he said, and then sighed heavily. "Wonderland is a magical world filled with evil creatures who have pretty faces. It's filled with delicate, yet violent, creatures. Hearts is at the top of that list, so when I discovered that she had you, there was no alternative. I had to give up my infinite number of candies to get you back."

He gave up his sanity for me? "And then you needed a delivery person. Which meant you still had loyalties... Who did your deliveries?" I asked even though I had a suspicion. "What went wrong?"

"M.H. befriended Rutherford, a loyal Hare of mine back then, who dug him secret holes so he could travel back and forth, delivering sweets to me." Dad closed his eyes like recalling such memories were painful. "Everything was fine until the Jack gave M.H. a prophecy warning him that the queen would catch on from his Comings and Goings, so he needed an apprentice—someone to carry on with the deliveries. Per M.H's request, Rutherford found an innocent looking child from this realm who had family ties to Wonderland. What better candidate as an apprentice, than a child whose aunts were close allies to the queen? She'd only been to Wonderland a handful of times before you fell down a rabbit hole."

My dad's pupils were dilating—probably because the candy he was sucking on was now gone. I had forgotten how intimidating he could be when lucid. Somewhere inside him, he was still my dad—not just a crazed person. Guilt overcame me. He basically ended his life because I tripped and fell down a rabbit hole.

"You asked me what went wrong. Several things went wrong. A mess of ghastly events rolled into one, forming a great big disaster, creating a wrongful doing," he said. His voice wavered like he didn't trust the words that were coming out. I could tell I was losing him. "So that's not the question you want to ask. You won't like the answer."

"What should I have asked?" I asked and handed him another candy.

He shook his head. I didn't think he wanted to remember anymore. His past life, his life in Wonderland, had to have been quite painful.

"*Who* was Wrong, not *what* went wrong. Rutherford brought a stupid, young girl to M.H. She was to be his apprentice. *She* was the Wrong choice," he said, through gritted teeth.

"Who was the girl?"

"The girl with a boy's name," my dad said and then swatted the air like he was being attacked by kamikaze bees.

# CHAPTER FORTY-TWO

(Ryley: Present Time)

Alice Mae stood outside my bedroom window. She wore an elaborate purple dress with red trim. The ruffles that lined the bottom of her dress were a deep green, so dark they appeared almost black. She wore black and white striped leggings and bright blue boots. In her hand was a basket tied with a faded pink ribbon. She had her hair pinned back. In her other hand was a lime umbrella with purple and white polka dots.

I was wearing gray sweat pants and an old shirt that had been washed so many times it was nearly see-through. We couldn't have looked more like polar opposites.

"You'll be made as an Otherworlder within a clock's ticktock wearing a fashion statement like that," she said, giving me the once over.

"We're going to Wonderland now?" I asked, glancing at the watch my dad had given me. Ten to eight. "What about school? We'll be late, and you hate that."

She smiled that smile of hers—the one that could stop my heart from beating. She set the basket down on the ground, leaned the umbrella against the side of the house, and rested her hands on the windowsill, making her look oh, so innocent.

"Time moves differently in Wonderland. It slows in the morning and speeds up at night, but at different rates daily, of course. No day's length is ever the same," she said. "Anyhoo, we have plenty of time to get there and back before the school bell rings."

Was her innocent nature a lie? Had she tricked my dad? Had she tricked M.H? If so, why did she still befriend Mr. Ruth? She certainly didn't get along well with her aunts, who were friends with Hearts.

"We need to talk," I said. "Would you like to come in?"

"I said time moves differently in Wonderland, not that it stops completely," she said. "We have enough time for you to change and leave. A heart to heart can be done in that realm, not this one."

I leaned on the windowsill. Our hands barely brushed but the touch was enough to send an electrical shock through me. From the look in her eyes, I knew I wasn't the only one feeling the sensation. My dad *had* to be wrong about Alice Mae. I didn't doubt that the Liddell family was allied with Hearts, but Alice Mae looked at me like her world revolved around me. She couldn't betray me. Right?

"Wonderland can wait—a few minutes at least," I said. "I'm not going to ask you how you know my dad anymore."

Her polished smile faltered. "Your curiosity has vanished?"

I shook my head. "The candies you gave me on our date worked quite effectively with my dad. He had a very interesting story to tell."

Instantly, a frown tattooed her face. Her eyes shoved metaphorical daggers through me. She dug in her basket and pulled out the racecar. I didn't know what she saw in the toy, but I suspected it was ensorcelled to my dad's car.

"What *lies* did Robby utter?"

"They weren't lies."

"Just because you believe lies, doesn't make them truths."

"What I *want to believe* is that you're *not* setting me up, like you set

215

up my dad."

Instead of denying it, she turned and walked away from my bedroom window. I nearly broke my neck climbing out of the window and chasing after her. I grabbed her shoulders and twisted her around to face me. I was expecting her to spit on me, slap me across the face, or lecture me about some nonsense I didn't understand. But instead, what I saw was a girl fighting back tears. One slid down her cheek.

"You shouldn't want to come to Wonderland, Ryley. It's dangerous. I'm dangerous. If you had half of a brain, you'd stay far, far away from me."

"So you think I'm a cretin?" I asked, relaxing my grip. "Well, I am. It's absurd to like you when my gut instinct tells me to run away. But here I am, holding you still so I don't have to chase after you. If you are so dangerous, then why are you running away from me?"

"Change of heart?"

That was it! I dropped my grip. If she was going to run, I was done chasing her. But, if my theory was right, then she'd stay. This was a game to her and if I could tell anything from that smirk of hers, she didn't want it to be over.

"What went horribly wrong when you delivered for my dad?"

"You'll hate me if you know the truth."

"Hate is just one of the many feelings I have for you."

"It doesn't matter if I tell you or not." Her blue eyes turned to ice. Risqué and perilous thoughts crossed them. "You want to go to Wonderland. You want to see it. Your curiosity has gotten the best of you."

"That was part of your diabolical plan, was it not? To lure me there on the queen's behalf? I'm not an idiot, Alice Mae. I know that's what the queen wants. Besides, it's high time I met the woman who murdered my uncle and banished my dad. And there is a book in Hearts' library that I need."

That caught her by surprise. "A book?"

*"Sweets for the Rabbit Hole Voyager.* My dad sacrificed his life for me. I'm going to see to it that he gets his life back,*"* I said. "But before I set foot in a rabbit hole, you are going to tell me what happened between you and my dad."

She signed, "Several years ago," she said, counting on her fingers. "on my *umpteenth* visit to Wonderland, M.H. asked me to make my first delivery to a frog that guarded Robby Edgar's house…"

# CHAPTER FORTY-THREE

(Alice Mae: Umpteenth Visit to Wonderland… and back)

…Wonderland wasn't so different from the Otherworld. The Otherworld was just a dull, flat, boring version of Wonderland. The wondrous world was filled with possibilities just like this one. That was the single thought that crossed my mind as I knocked on an ordinary door that belonged to an even more ordinary house, in a cookie cutter development, in a town with a forgettable name. The only extraordinary thing about the gray painted house was the ceramic frog guarding the front door. It was the very frog that guarded the *Waiting Room* door.

Following M.H's instructions, I placed twenty one sugar tarts in the frog's mouth. Closing my eyes, I counted to ten and then opened them. The candy had vanished. I grinned. It worked just like M.H. said it would. He said that sometimes wondrous magic was shy in this realm and needed privacy to work.

In another week, I'd return to this very ordinary house with the ordinary door, in an unremarkable town and place another handful of extraordinary candies in the frog's mouth. That was the plan M.H. had set in place.

We should have had a Plan B.

I knocked on the door ten times, mimicking a tune that Omar the cockatoo had taught me. That being the only notification I was to give and then scamper away before anyone spotted me. But, I hadn't expected the door to open so fast. My delivery had been anticipated.

It was the boy—the son of the rightful king to the Red Court! Ryley gave me the same look that he'd given the queen when she asked him his name. He had the same eyes as his father—dark brown.

"It's not the pizza delivery boy, Dad," Ryley called out.

He stood there with a disappointed and hungry look. His father walked up behind him. Robby sucked the end of a cigar. Pools of smoke twirled from his mouth. The tobacco roll fell out after he got a good look at me and his mouth dropped open. "Go inside, son."

"You're the niece of the Maude sisters, aren't you?" Robby asked, but didn't wait for an answer. "The M.H. is a *fool*! He should have known better than to trust, much less train, a Liddell!"

I asked, timidly, "You know my family?"

"Liddells notoriously side with Hearts. A family of spies," he said. "I thought M.H. was training a *boy!*"

"I go by *Al* in Wonderland," I said, hoping to score points.

"So that's why M.H. was convinced you were the right choice, because you are a girl with a boy's name. He thought you were the child the *Bleeding Hearts Prophecy* mentioned."

"Hearts was positive that my niece was the one who'd stop her reign, until she heard of the name of your son. A boy with a girl's name…" Zola Maude said, creeping from the shadows provided by the ordinary bushes in the front yard. "Imagine my shame when I find my only niece betraying the family name. Delivering candies to a known traitor, the Banished Prince of Spades! You should be ashamed of yourself, Alice Mae!"

I'd never been so scared in my life. "I'm sorry!"

"If you *ever* misbehave again, I'll see that the Joker and you have a play date," Zola Maude threatened. Her teeth sharpened like a snake's. It sent shivers down my spine.

Robby's eyes darkened to match the night sky. "How did you find me, Zola Maude?"

"It was rather easy. It may behoove you to get better at staying 'lost.' Perhaps, if you town-hopped more, it might be more difficult to track you. Just a suggestion," she said, mockingly and held up a racecar. It was identical to the one Robby had in his garage!

"I'll keep that in mind," Robby said, picking up the cigar. When he was bent over, he whispered to the frog. "Send word to the Mad Hatter that he's been made."

There were times when magic needed to be coaxed. There were times magic needed to be taught. But, there were times that magic was just magic—unexplainable and marvelous. The ceramic cracked as the frog came alive. Within seconds the frog was hopping away. Zola Maude let go of me to chase it. I knew at the bottom of my heart that she was going to kill the amphibian.

Robby must have come to the same conclusion because he flicked his cigar at Zola Maude. It landed in her hair, igniting it.

# Chapter Forty-Four

(Ryley: Present Time)

"… Zola Maude's hair burned until there was nothing left," Alice Mae said, recalling the first and only delivery she'd made for my dad. "I'd seen many unspeakable things, in this realm and in Wonderland. Watching my aunt burn wasn't one of them."

I didn't know what to say or do. I'd thought that Alice Mae was this evil creature with a pretty face, who I just so happened to fall in love with. My dad made Alice Mae out to be this scandalous creature when it had only been a series of misfortunate events.

"What did Zola Maude mean when she said that you and the Joker would have a play date?" I asked, hoping that my imagination had gotten the best of me.

Alice Mae's bottom lip trembled. "The Joker is a sadistic child, trapped in an adult's body. I'd rather not talk about our play dates."

"But it's where you learned your magical tricks, isn't it? It was punishment for disobeying your aunts, wasn't it?"

Her eyes turned so icy blue, they looked almost white. "I've been taking lessons from the Joker for years, and have been smuggling his toys for even longer."

She'd been tortured via his toys. Toys! Used for torture! I couldn't imagine how horrible that had to have been for her. I went to hug her, to take her worries away like I would for my mom when she was troubled. Instead of melting into my embrace, Alice Mae pushed me away.

I whispered her name like it was a plea for her to forgive herself. "It wasn't your fault that you were caught."

"I'm no innocent either." Tears glossed over her enchanting blue eyes. "So, are we going to Wonderland or not?"

"Does the queen know I'm coming?"

"*I've* told Hearts nothing about your Comings and Goings."

From the plaid pants to the dress shoes and over jacket that used to be my dad's, I looked preposterous. But, Alice Mae insisted that I would blend in perfectly. So there we were, standing beside the apple tree in her front yard.

"You really shouldn't squeeze Mr. Ruth so tight," Alice Mae said, looking at the stuffed rabbit in my hands.

I loosened my grip. Alice Mae dug inside the basket she carried. She handed me a single cupcake that had the words *Eat Me* written on it with purple frosting.

"If you're feeling small, then eat this," she said.

She flipped open the other side of the basket. Inside was the smallest glass pop bottle I'd ever seen. It was no bigger than my little finger. Written on the glass were the words: *Drink Me.*

"Drink this if you're feeling a bit too big," she said, and then looked back at the house that might as well have been a prison. "My aunts should still be dead to the world for another couple hours, but we should still hurry. Chez gets restless, and I'm never sure where he's going to pop up."

She instructed me to keep my eyes closed. Just as I shut them, she pushed me. I stumbled and intended to catch myself against the tree. I immediately opened my eyes. All the colors of the yard dripped like wet paint. I grabbed the tree, but the bark came off in gooey chunks. I tried to pick up my feet, but it felt like I was trapped in quicksand. It sucked me down until my body was submerged in the dirt. And then, gravity failed. I was no longer stuck to Earth. Instead of floating like one would in outer space, I experienced a free-fall. A gut-check of epic proportions hit me as I tried to remember how to breathe. Up wasn't down, but down was up… and off to the side in a slightly twisted manner.

I was falling down (or up?) a rabbit hole.

# CHAPTER FORTY-FIVE

(Ryley: Present Time in Wonderland)

The *Waiting Room*, as Alice Mae affectionately called it, was a round, black and white checkered chamber. It occupied a different space and time than both Wonderland and my realm. The ceiling was above my head, but not centered—more off to the side, over my ear. The effect was dizzying. In the center of the room was a glass table with a beautiful, glass mermaid holding it.

Something squirmed in my hand. The white rabbit, no longer a stuffed toy, wiggled in my grip. I dropped it. The creature hopped over to Alice Mae and tugged on the edge of her dress. She was leaning against the chamber wall where vines had taken over. Dirt clumped on her clothes, but she still looked polished in an odd way. Maybe it was just my eyes.

"You look worse," she said. "You were flailing your arms like you were drowning."

She was right. I looked like I just got done rolling around in the mud. "Anyone who sees me will know I'm not from around here."

"Then we shall stay hidden," Alice Mae said, dubiously.

The rabbit tugged harder on Alice Mae's dress. "M.H. wouldn't stand for what you are planning to do."

"And what of the queen, Mr. Ruth? She certainly wouldn't stand for *me* if I didn't play nice," Alice Mae said, dismissively.

"What about the prophecy?" Mr. Ruth said, clutching the hem of her dress even tighter. "The Reign of Terror must end!"

"And end it shall, one way or another," Alice Mae said. "But I'm no longer listening to old men who tell stories about the future. Look where it got M.H."

"You need to stop punishing yourself for the things you cannot control, Al!" Mr. Ruth said. "It's not your fault he—"

Alice Mae grabbed the rabbit and covered his mouth. "Listen to me, old friend. I refuse to let another person die because of my actions."

The rabbit thumped his feet on Alice Mae's hand until she loosened them. "What do you think the queen will do to the Heir?"

I hadn't bothered to follow half of what they were saying. I was too busy staring at the real-life animal that had been a stuffed toy seconds before. "Have I lost it, or is that rabbit talking?"

Alice Mae looked startled, like she'd forgotten I was standing in the *Waiting Room* with her. Like always, she quickly recovered and wore a pleasing smile. "Creatures of this realm are not as dumb as the animals of the Otherworld, Ryley. They can talk, just like you and I."

She set the rabbit down. Mr. Ruth scurried to the twisted vines in the far corner of the chamber. He pulled several back, revealing a ceramic frog—*my dad's gift to my mom!* Mr. Ruth thumped the frog on his head.

"Spit it up!" Mr. Ruth said. "Robby's son is here."

The ceramic that held the frog together shattered, revealing a very alive frog that still wore a suit with my dad's initials sewn on it. The ceramic frog burped up a tiny, skeleton key and caught it with his hand. He looked like he'd been awakened from a coma. The moment he saw me, the frog no longer appeared lethargic. He looked at Mr. Ruth, then Alice Mae, and then back to me.

"The boy with the girl's name shall be known as Robby's son no longer," the frog said. "He is the spitting image of M.H!"

"The Mad Hatter?" Mr. Ruth said, looking at me with wide eyes.

"He does have the M.H's flamboyant characteristics," Alice Mae said, softly. All the blood drained from her face.

"Why the grim face?" I said, clearly missing an important piece of information.

"My stomach must just be upset from the fall," Alice Mae said, dismissively. "Ryley, I'd like to formally introduce you to Theodore, the Toad."

"I'm a *frog*, not a toad!" Theodore said, spitting out the "T" word like it was a four-letter curse. "Just because my name starts with a 'T' doesn't mean I'm a toad!"

"My dad gave you to my mom," I said, dumbly.

"It's like having a conversation with a child," Theodore said and shook his head. "I was to watch over you and your mother, you foolish boy. Did you think that the Great Robert Edgar would leave you and Lauren unprotected?"

"He left a toad to protect us?"

"*Frog*, not toad," Theodore spat. "And what are you saying? That I'm not good enough to keep away your enemies? I've been a loyal servant to your father for years, and all you see is a worthless frog. Figures."

"He didn't mean to offend," Alice Mae said. She walked over to me and clung to my arm, like we were a couple. "He's just not used to animals smart enough to talk. Remember, I used to be the same way."

Theodore looked at Alice Mae like she was a poop fly. "Like I said, I have been Robby's loyal servant for years. I don't trust you, Al. I never have, especially after you led Zola Maude to him."

Mr. Ruth nudged Theodore. "Watch your words. Al swears up and down that she didn't know her aunt was following her."

"You're just a naive rumperbabbit. Al is a liar. Everyone knows this," Theodore said and then glared at Alice Mae. "Like I said, I've sworn to protect the Heir as best I can. I don't trust you or your intentions. I've heard rumors of your diabolical plan and won't allow you into Wonderland until you promise that this is not another trick. I'll only permit the Mad Hatter to enter Wonderland if it's by his own accord."

Alice Mae placed her hand over her heart. "I hate Hearts."

"You didn't answer my question, Al," Theodore said, hopping up to her like she was a bug he was going to crush. "I asked you if you were planning more tricks."

"I did not tell her of Ryley's arrival," Alice Mae said.

"I'll be watching you, Al," Theodore said, handing me a bronzed key.

Theodore and Mr. Ruth hopped to a mouse door that had been covered with the vines. I followed their lead and unlocked the door. Mr. Ruth hopped through. I inspected the door that was much too small for me to squeeze through. Just when I was about to ask Theodore what I should do, his green skin and clothing hardened. He was once again ceramic.

"And how are the humans supposed to enter Wonderland?" I asked.

"I already spelled it out for you," she said, glancing at the mangled cupcake and the bottle in my hand.

The frosted words *Eat Me* were no longer legible. I forgot about the little bottle in my hand. The room seemed to grow when I took a swig of the beverage. It tasted like a sugary toenail. Soon I became as small as the door. Clothes twisted around me, forming as I reshaped. Alice Mae took a drink as well and in a manner of seconds she was no bigger than a mouse. Her dress shrank too, fitting to her new miniature size.

She pulled out a pink ribbon from her basket. "You blindfolded me on our first date. I'd like to return the favor. Wonderland takes some time getting used to."

"Am I going to regret this?" I asked as she tied the ribbon around my eyes.

"Probably."

"Theodore doesn't like you," I said, stalling to leave the *Waiting Room*. I needed a minute to talk to Alice Mae, alone.

"Most creatures in Wonderland don't like me anymore."

"Do they blame you because my dad lost his mind?"

She laughed a pitiful laugh that made my heart ache. "No, they blame me for what happened to M.H."

"Which is?"

"A story for another time," she said, and gave me a gentle nudge to the door.

Since I really wanted to see Wonderland, I decided not to press the issue, but I knew something was wrong—very wrong about this whole ordeal. I still couldn't slow my heart from beating so rapidly whenever I was around Alice Mae... even though I was certain she was ordered to bring me to Wonderland to meet with the queen. Since our end goal was the same, I played along. I just wished that Alice Mae would have trusted me enough to tell me the truth. I wished that she could just see how much I cared for her.

I walked through the door, expecting to step out onto the ground. There wasn't any ground under my foot, only what felt like a ladder. I felt around. Bark. We'd come out of a tree. I licked the frosting on my fingers. Just as I shrank, I grew quickly (still blindfolded, mind you).

I felt the sun on my skin. The air smelled fresh, like it was early spring instead of nearly winter. She led me to a secluded place and instructed me to sit. It felt like I was walking in a swamp. Water squished under my feet, but my shoes didn't get wet. It was the oddest sensation. Birds sang. I imagined that the creatures were some kind of cockatoo and penguin hybrid, but I said nothing. She handed me a cup. I sniffed it. It smelled like hot tea, but when I took a sip it was ice cold.

"Don't worry," Alice Mae said. "We're alone, for now. Few creatures come out at night."

At night? "Nice try, but I can feel the sun warming my skin."

"Oh, is that so?"

"I might be extremely disorientated, but I'm still aware of my surroundings."

"Then take off your blindfold, Mad Hatter," Mr. Ruth said.

"Enough of you, Mr. Ruth, into the basket you will go," she said. I could hear her pick up the rabbit and place it inside of the basket. She closed off the lid. "We need a little more privacy anyway."

"Mr. Ruth falls deaf inside a wicker basket?" I asked.

"He gets sleepy in dark, cozy places," she said, and giggled as if I had asked an asinine question.

When I removed the blindfold, I refused to believe that my eyes were working properly. I was on the inside of a cave that had thousands of punch holes, letting the stars shine through. The moon was a hundred times closer than I ever recalled seeing it.

I touched my forearm with my finger. It was hot to the touch.

"Moon burn is a real problem in this world," Alice Mae said.

She was shaded by the umbrella. Shadows cast their darkness on her eyes. She patted a patch of blue and green grass beside her. A blue caterpillar crawled like a slinky across her boot. It shined like a glow worm, expelling a vibrant blue hue that lit the contents that Alice Mae had set out on the quilted blanket.

"How is this possible?" I asked, walking under the protection of the umbrella.

"I told you. The laws of this realm, this world, don't work the same way that they do in yours," she said, tossing out a quilted blanket that she'd pulled from the basket.

She lifted the basket lid and pulled out containers. Some of the

229

containers' dimensions were bigger than the basket itself. Each one contained a different course of a meal—five total.

Trying not to think too hard about this impossible place, I scooted closer to Alice Mae. It seemed all so surreal. She picked up a strawberry, took a bite, and then offered it to me. It was the best strawberry I'd ever had. She tossed the end over her shoulder. It fell to the ground. I watched in disbelief as the green vine wiggled up from the squishy dirt—a strawberry vine.

I picked up a caramel covered apple, took a bite, and then threw it as far as I could. It bounced off the rocky surface a few hundred yards away. I waited, staring at the place where it landed. Alice Mae reached for my hand and rolled her thumb over mine as we stared at the apple. A small tree trunk grew from the fruit. A golden liquid drizzled from the bark, like caramel.

I eyed the ham sandwiches. "If I threw that, would a pig sprout from the ground?"

She grabbed one of them. "I wonder if it would fly."

I grabbed her wrist and redirected the ham sandwich to my mouth. I took a bite and then shook my head. "We might starve if you do such a thing."

"That would be a shame," she said, and grinned wickedly.

"Can I ask you something without you getting angry at me and the curiousness of my question?" I asked.

"Tread carefully with your words, Ryley. They are more powerful than you think."

"Every molecule in my body screams that you are dangerous and that I shouldn't trust you, but every time I look at you, I forget all logic and hope that you can't hear my heart beating out of my chest. I fall into your eyes and swear that I catch a glimpse of your soul. You sound like an angel when you speak. You consume my thoughts. I forget to eat because I day dream about your kiss," I said and brushed her hair out of her face. "I'm going to tell you something I've never told a girl before. I've fallen hard—and not just down a rabbit hole."

She clenched her teeth and held her breath. She opened her mouth only to close it quickly. I reached for her hand and encouraged her to speak her mind.

"Everyone I've ever loved—truly loved—has died, except for Mr. Ruth and he lost his eye because of me," she said, and handed me the torn playing card. On it was the *Madmen's Prophecy*.

"What were you and Mr. Ruth talking about in the *Waiting Room*?" I asked, keeping my voice even. I didn't believe for one second that I was going to die. It was just a silly prophecy that an old man wrote on a card, but it was clear that everyone else thought it to be the unrelenting truth. What had Alice Mae said? Just because we believe lies doesn't make them the truth.

"I've made so many wrong decisions already," Alice Mae said. A tear slipped, but she fought the others back.

"We all make thousands of wrong choices in life. What matters is what you learn from them," I said and kissed her.

The flavor from the strawberry burst in my mouth like I'd never tasted anything so sweet. Unlike her candies, it didn't discombobulate me. So, I pulled her onto my lap and whispered three words I'd never said to a girl before. "I love you."

She pressed her finger over my lips. "I love you too, Ryley, which is why this is so hard."

"What is so hard?"

She wiped her cheeks and stood up, much to my protest. She picked up the basket and locked the lid, trapping Mr. Ruth inside. "I love you. Please, don't forget that."

"Why does this feel like you're telling me good-bye?" I pushed the ground to stand up. But my hand caught on something. The squishy dirt held me in place. I was effectively handcuffed to the dirt.

"The price tag the queen set for my freedom was your head."

Chez appeared beside her. "Oh, I do love a good execution."

"What are you doing, Alice Mae?" I demanded, jerking on my hand to free myself. I stopped when I heard the footsteps of heels on the ground. Standing before me was a midget with red hair and a scarlet heart-shaped pin on her black cloak. *Hearts.*

"It's been quite some time since I've seen an Edgar in Wonderland," Hearts said.

Tears streaked down Alice Mae's cheeks. Teardrops trickled to the ground, pooling together. She picked up the umbrella and held it over her head. As soon as she was covered, thunder broke.

"I was wrong to second-guess you, Al. When Chez said that you would bring me Robby's son today, I didn't believe him. You're almost always late, but it's not even tea time yet. I'm impressed, vaguely impressed anyway."

Alice Mae wouldn't take her attention off her feet. "I do hate being late. There's a dreadfully beautiful story about my timeliness, Ryley. Would you like to hear it?"

# CHAPTER FORTY-SIX

(Alice Mae: Umpteenth plus One visit to Wonderland)

Word spread of M.H's treason against the queen. Many creatures stayed indoors, not wanting to see their beloved candy-maker kneel before a guillotine. However, I had a front seat view. My aunts sat on both sides of me, eating popcorn and talking with delight that the traitor was apprehended. Zola Maude wore a wig——pink, no less. The queen sat high on her throne, petting Chez. Beside her were two bird cages that imprisoned Mr. Ruth and Theodore.

The Joker pulled up on the guillotine's ropes, and the blade rose higher and higher. The sadistic creature acted like the over-sized knife was going to slip from his grasp each time he caught me looking at M.H. As the blade drove toward the ground, he managed to grab the end. M.H's neck was nicked, just enough for red to soak into his white collared shirt.

When the queen stood up, Chez disappeared. She cleared her throat. She sounded like she was trying to rid a frog from her throat. "M.H. I hereby sentence you…"

The sentencing didn't matter, not when my dear friend looked at me. He always wore a smile, even in the direst times. The creatures were right about him. He was certifiably nuts, but he was happy. Even in the last minutes of his life, he managed a smile. He looked up at his hat. I knew without having to be told, there was something in there that he wanted.

"I'm not Wrong about you, Al. Even if Robby, even if the entire court, loses faith in you, I believe that you are the one that will end the Reign of Terro—"

The Joker's blade came down, silencing M.H. for good. A part of me died with him. All the air escaped from my lungs. I could hear my screams, but couldn't do anything to stop them. Vida Maude covered my mouth. My tears stained her hand. I shook free and fell to my knees, a couple feet in front of M.H's bodiless head. With the greatest care, I removed his hat. Taped inside was a two of hearts playing card. The Jack's prophecy was written on it. The *HATed fool will die twice before the MADness stops*. I didn't understand the Jack's logic. A person could only die once, unless there were two Mad Hatters?

In the end it didn't matter. M.H. was dead. It was my fault. I slipped the card back inside the hat and clutched it against my chest. I pressed my lips together, trapping my screams inside as card soldiers dragged away M.H's body.

The Joker picked up M.H's head. He tossed it to one of the card soldiers and sang merrily, "Come and Go. Go and Come. Two pieces forever and never one!"

Queen reached inside the bird cage and retrieved Mr. Ruth. She held him up by the ears.

Clapping his hands, the Joker joined the queen. He circled Theodore's cage, dancing with glee. I hated that he could be so cheerful. The world should have ended with M.H's last breath. Strapped to the Joker's hip was a sheath. When he pulled it out, I had been expecting to see a long sword. Instead there was a knife meant for a mouse. He pointed the knife against Mr. Ruth's neck.

"White rabbit, I sentence you to death by association!" Hearts yelled and held the rumperbabbit up high enough for the court to see.

I couldn't bear it! "Spare him!"

My scream didn't stop the Joker from piercing Mr. Ruth, but it was successful enough in startling him enough that the Joker missed Mr. Ruth's neck. He managed to nick Mr. Ruth's eye. Mr. Ruth clutched his face and gave a horrifying yell. I felt like throwing up. I'd never heard a rabbit squeal before.

"You have no right to utter a word, stupid girl!" The Queen said, putting her hands on her hips with the rabbit still in tow.

"Yet, I plea on his behalf! Spare him! I'll take his place if I have to!" I yelled loud enough for the court to hear. I glanced around. The creatures who showed looked at me with empty eyes. They blamed me for M.H's death. They blamed me for the cruelty bestowed upon Robert Edgar. They blamed me for everything, as did I.

I couldn't see Chez, but when bloody footprints trailed from the pool of blood on the guillotine to me, I knew the cat was nearby. He appeared by my feet, licking his paw. It was everything I could do to not kick him like a football.

"You'd offer your life for a bunny's?" Chez asked.

"I'm more responsible than he," I said. "I'll offer my life if you spare the frog's and the rabbit's lives."

"You will be punished, too, for your insubordination!" The Queen dropped Mr. Ruth when she screamed at me. "Your head will be placed next to M.H's."

Popcorn went flying as Vida and Zola Maude jumped out of their seats. They stood up next to me.

"Our niece is no longer protected by the Rightdoing Law because she has already committed a crime—dousing your roses with pesticide. So, she is subject to the Wrongdoing Law and is punishable by death. However, she is still a child. Every child is protected until they reach the age of adulthood," Zola Maude said, adjusting her wig. "You can sentence her to death, but you cannot kill her until she's eighteen, if you choose so at that time. It is still many years away."

The Joker dragged his mouse knife across Theodore's bird cage, demanding our attention. "As a toy maker of untraditional toys, I would promise the court that the girl with the boy's name is punished, if it so pleases the queen?"

"It *is* against the laws to execute a child," Hearts said, pondering the idea.

"But what of the *Bleeding Hearts Prophecy*? It is said that a girl with a boy's name or a boy with a girl's name will end your reign," Chez said, appearing in front of the queen. "You should rewrite the laws and finish the girl off now and then chase down the boy to do the same."

"If I rewrite a law, it has to go to the committee, and then there is a lot of frivolous paperwork. It's all quite boring." The queen smiled a vicious little smile. "No, I'll allow the Joker and the girl to have regular play dates. And then, when the time comes, Al will find Robert's son, the boy with the girlish name, and bring him to Wonderland."

"What makes you think Al will be able to bring him here?"

"M.H had dumb faith in the girl," Hearts said. "And, she likes the chase—she kept up with the white rabbit in order to follow it to Wonderland."

I swallowed a lump in my throat. "I'll never do it."

"Then I shall put an end to the madness by locking you in a high tower until you are of killing age, following the Wrongdoing Law verbatim. But, I won't stop there. I'll seek out everyone you have ever loved or had association with and end their puny, little lives as well," Hearts ordered.

Everyone would die? I couldn't bear it! "That's against the Rightdoing Law! You can't punish creatures until they have committed their first crime. You're allowed one crime without punishment. You'd be breaking the rules!"

"My dear, stupid girl, do you really think that I don't know all the creatures' dirtiest, darkest secrets? I have dirt on everyone. Few are protected by the Rightdoing Law. So you can swear fidelity to me and promise never to dabble with time-stopping, and I'll spare your life," Hearts said. "You'll live and only *one* other person may die."

I could hardly get the words off of my tongue. They felt sticky and suffocating. "Then I shall serve you until the boy returns."

The queen dismissed the court. As everyone filed out of the court,

I fell to my knees in front of the pool of blood. I set the Mad Hatter's Hat down beside me. What had I done?

"I wish I could turn back time," I whispered, looking at my reflection in the red pool.

"Words like that will get you killed," the Joker said, standing over me. No compassion lingered in his voice. He sounded cold and dead. "But enough with that. You promised that you wouldn't meddle with the time-stopping business. And, you're late for a dance lesson. You will soon understand the importance of being timely!"

"A dance lesson?"

"Yes, don't you think it is an excellent idea for a play date? Don't answer that. We'll have plenty of time for other childish games later," he said. His smile widened across his face so I could see his dark, stained teeth. "You may have sworn loyalty, but the queen did entrust me to teach you the error of your ways. So, our first play date will not end until *you* need candy to see straight in the Otherworld. A fitting punishment, don't you think?"

I danced until my feet bled.

# CHAPTER FORTY-SEVEN

(Alice Mae: Present Time in Wonderland)

The cave's glowworms made it just bright enough to illuminate Ryley's dark eyes. There was no doubt he hated me. He didn't bother trying to unstick his hand from the ground. He just sat there, glaring at me. I was a deceitful creature, and I never told him otherwise. Even so, I expected it to be easier to give him up to the queen. Of course, that was before I fell in love with him.

Ryley's life would spare countless others. I told myself that it was better this way. But, even I couldn't pretend to convince myself that was the truth.

"What a lovely story," Hearts said, pacing around Ryley.

Her heels clicked when she walked on the marshy ground, defying physics. The rain sprinkled from the sky. Thunder clouds rolled in. A storm would soon come. Rain drops would fall from the sky with each tear I shed. I tried to keep them from spilling. Everyone didn't need to be soaking wet because I was upset.

"But that's just what it is—a story. Just because that's what you believe doesn't mean it's the truth. I have no intention of killing Ryley. He's just a boy."

"Should I rejoice?" Ryley's voice was thick with sarcasm.

"If you knew what was good for you, you would," Chez said. The proverbial bad cat vanished, all except for his eyes. They blended in with the glow worms. "Enough of the damsel in distress two-bit act, Al. Leave before you bestow another great flood and wash everyone away. Go back up through the rabbit hole where you came from and don't come back unless you are summoned. The queen and the boy have some catching up to do—alone."

# CHAPTER FORTY-EIGHT

(Ryley: Present Time in Wonderland)

Giant soldier cutouts escorted me to the castle. They looked like knights in shining armor but had no faces. If I didn't know better, it would appear that shadows animated the bronze armor. A playing card imprint was just over their heart, like a badge. A number two, five, seven, eight, and a ten circled around a granite table. There were two chairs decorated to appear like there were snakes were crawling up the legs and armrests.

Two women, who looked like they'd been dipped in white paint, stood by the queen's side, eyeing me like I'd personally insulted them. Giant red hearts were painted on their faces. They were the queen's personal guards, no doubt.

The queen motioned for me to sit while she attended a fire that a fire breathing lizard had started when we arrived, dripping wet from the rain. Once the flames turned blue, she turned her attention to a frazzled porcupine, holding a tea tray. She acted like I was a guest, but I knew I was merely getting the royal treatment for a prisoner.

When I reached for the back of the chair, it moved. I just stood there and watched the chair move back all on its own. Disbelieving my eyes, I examined it. The table and chairs weren't made of granite. They were snakes painted to look like the rock. When I refused to sit, the soldier with number seven of spades poked me with his paper mache sword. I shouldn't have been surprised that it drew blood. There was no logic in this world.

I raised my hands and sat down on the chair. The snakes slithered back into the table. Their tails tickled my skin, curling around my ankles and legs. They'd tighten and relax in sync with the gigantic ticking clock that hung next to a portrait on the wall. The picture of the fellow looked like my dad, but he was a little older. He had to be my uncle Eddie.

"Edward was a glorious king until having a misfortunate accident involving one of my toys. I really shouldn't have left that guillotine lying around. Thankfully, we have a wise and forgiving queen. She spared my life," said a man wearing a dunce hat.

He sat on a crimson red carpet beside me. He pulled a box of matches from his tall socks. Lining up a match to the strike box, he flicked matches in the air and let them burn.

"You must be the Joker," I said.

"You must be the boy—"

"With the girl's name," I interrupted. "Yes, I know. It was a cruel joke my dad played."

"Oh, but the cruelest of jokes are usually the best," the Joker said in a not-so-pleasant way. "Usually people don't get my humor. Glad you do."

The porcupine that Hearts had been speaking to walked over to the table. He stayed as far away as possible from the snake chair but managed to place a tea cup in front of me and pour me a cup of steaming tea. The cup had a black heart with a red tear drop painted on it—the Bleeding Heart. Speaking of Hearts, she sat down across from me.

"Please, drink. It's the finest blend the court has to offer," the queen said, watching me closely.

"I prefer my tea cold," I said.

Without a word, the porcupine took off running toward the door. In less than five seconds, he returned with an ice tray in his hands.

"What took you so long?" The queen asked the porcupine. Before he could answer, she turned to me. "It's so hard to find good help these days."

The porcupine offered me the tray. I took a few cubes from the tray and plopped them in my cup but didn't bother taking a sip.

"Please, drink," the queen said, again.

"I'll wait until the ice melts first," I said and crossed my arms. "Why did you banish my dad from Wonderland?"

"Oh goodie, I've been meaning to have such a conversation with you, ever since I realized you existed," Hearts said. She still hadn't taken a drink of the tea.

"Joker, could you be a dear and give Ryley and I some seclusion. We have private matters to discuss," Hearts said. "Take LeDee and LeDum with you."

The Joker pulled a smoke bomb from his pocket. He flicked a match in the air and threw the bomb at the match, lighting the fuse. Smoke exploded. When it cleared, the Joker was gone along with the two white painted women.

I pointed to the card soldiers. "What about them? Won't they hear our *private discussion?*"

"They won't be telling anyone my secrets."

"Because they have no tongues?" I asked.

"Because they have no heads."

Oh.

"Your Uncle Eddie is amongst them, but it's not like it's *him* anymore. He's just an emotionless, headless drone who looks no different than number eight," she said, indifferently and pointed to the random soldier with an eight on its badge.

"How many soldiers do you have?"

"I have many minions, but enough of that. Let's get down to business. You father proclaimed false witness to your uncle, my late husband's murder. Robert actually had the audacity to accuse me of being Edward's murderer. Can you imagine?"

"Why did he accuse you of murder?"

"Because a lying grasshopper told Robby that it was me who pushed Edward onto the guillotine when in fact I just watched in horror," Hearts said. "I was made out to be this scandalous witch of a queen. And, with the awful news that had just been leaked, many creatures were determined to see me booted from the throne."

"What news was leaked?"

"Word spreads fast in Wonderland, Ryley. Lies catch wind even faster. Rumor had it that King Edward had fallen in love with a seamstress named Genevine. The king was going to leave me for her, renounce his throne to be with her. He told me in a love-letter. I have never been more ashamed. But, his death was bad timing—a coincidence. Surely you can understand why the creatures of my court were suspicious. Robert wouldn't quit ranting about my crime so I had him banished. People will believe lies if they are convincing enough, but, it doesn't mean it's the truth," Hearts said, holding the tea cup in her hand. She still had yet to take a drink. "I hope you can forgive me for what I was forced to do to your father, because it is my hope that we are to be great friends."

"So why is Alice Mae positive that you are going to behead me?"

"Al hasn't ever been very bright," the queen said. "She hears one thing and exaggerates it to another. Stupid girl."

"So you didn't request that she find me and bring me here?" I asked and then took a sip of the tea.

Hearts watched me with an intense stare. When I didn't fall over dead, she sipped her own. "I did ask that she find you, but not with the intentions of killing you. I offer the opposite, if you'll have it. Edward left me childless, which means there is no Heir to the throne of the Red Court when you come of age. When do you turn eighteen?"

"One week," I said.

"Only one week! Then it seems you've returned just in time! If you want to rule, be something bigger than yourself, you could rule this court. The choice is yours. I would ensure that it's the greatest ceremony the Red Court has ever bared witness to, if it would please you. The choice is yours, but it would be misfortunate if you choose wrong."

# CHAPTER FORTY-NINE

(Ryley: Present Time)

Crawling up the rabbit hole was about as feasible as squeezing through a crack in the sidewalk. Nevertheless, I trusted the white rabbit to lead me out of the forsaken world. Wiggling and pulling as I pried myself out of the alternate dimension left me gasping for air. Rain and mud clung to my clothes. Mr. Ruth was once again a stuffed animal, making me think that I'd just been on a bad trip and not really traveled anywhere.

Alice Mae was waiting for me. She leaned against the apple tree, holding a dirty top hat. Her makeup was smudged from the tears she'd cried. When I looked at her, it felt like a disease had crawled its way into my heart and poisoned my veins. There were so many things we had to discuss. She brought me to Wonderland to die—at least that was what she thought. Even though it was wrong, it didn't mean that she didn't believe it. Could I really have fallen for someone who would sacrifice my life?

"Hearts doesn't want to kill me," I said.

"She lies."

"She wants me in Wonderland as Heir to the throne."

Alice Mae stood up. Even though I towered over her, it didn't matter. She was on a mission to convince me that a lie was the truth. "She's up to something, Ryley. She has a plan for you, and it doesn't involve you sitting on the throne."

"You belong in a straightjacket instead of a pretty dress."

A tear drizzled down her cheek. I hated that my heart ached as I watched more slide down her polished skin. Each tear washed away a bit of dirt still on her face. She grabbed my hand. I didn't move it away, but I kept it stiff in hers.

"I meant what I said, Ryley. I do love you."

"You would see me dead! I know now that my death was the endgame in your devious plan. You tricked me, Alice Mae. You made me fall in love with you just so you could save your own skin!"

"What would you have me do!" she yelled. "Hearts wouldn't just come for me. She'd kill everyone I've ever loved. It would be a massacre."

"So sacrificing my life was your solution?"

"I was just a girl when I agreed to Hearts' terms," Alice Mae said. Her breaths became rapid. She was hyperventilating. Struggling for air, she admitted it was a poor decision to make, and it was wrong. "You aren't alone in your feelings," she said. "Everything I told you wasn't a lie. My heart burns when I see you. I can't even describe the way my soul turns to fire when we kiss, but I don't—"

"Don't you get it? I'm breaking up with you! You brought me to Wonderland to die! Luckily, Hearts had something else in mind. I draw the line at death! I'd be a bonehead to stay with you!"

# CHAPTER FIFTY

(Alice Mae: Present Time)

Eighteen days marked off the calendar, and Ryley was the first person I thought of when I woke up in the morning. He was the only person that wiggled into my thoughts during my leisure classes, like advanced chemistry or microbiology. When my aunts finished off a batch of candies, I didn't linger around the kitchen, waiting for the pieces to cool just enough to gobble them up. Even my dancing couldn't distract me from the breaking of my heart. Every class was just another hour of torture that I had to endure. Nothing the Joker did to me compared to sitting next to Ryley in class and not being able to speak to him. Every note I slipped him, he crumpled without reading. Every text went un-read (I think). He wanted nothing to do with me. I couldn't blame him.

However, I couldn't hide from the tear stained pillows anymore. I knew I had to make things right. In the middle of the night, I crawled out of bed. I grabbed three pointy jacks that I'd stolen from the Joker during one of our many play dates and shoved them in my pocket. I didn't trust many things in Wonderland, and the queen was at the top of that list. I cracked the door. Chez must have been sleeping against my door because he jumped onto his feet suddenly. He looked up with sleepy, grumpy eyes. I imagined him telling me that I was ruining his beauty sleep.

"I need to see Hearts," I whispered, afraid to wake my aunts at this late hour. "You need to convince the queen to see me, tonight."

Chez yawned. Lying back on the ground, he closed his eyes.

"Fine, I'll go back to Wonderland by myself," I said, and tiptoed down the stairs. I moved quickly so that even if my aunts saw me, I'd be out the door in a few seconds; thus, free of any of their endless questions.

I raced to the rabbit hole next to the apple tree in the front yard. Chez was out there waiting for me. He batted his paw at me and then disappeared.

*She did not summon you, Al. She's not going to be happy about this midnight interruption.*

I ignored his warning and stepped toward the apple tree. And so I fell down the rabbit hole again. Mr. Ruth met up with me in the *Waiting Room*. No matter how many times I told him to stay safe in hiding, he refused.

"You're not going to get rid of me so easy, my friend."

I kneeled beside him. "Then promise you won't interfere. Just know that having you stand by my side has been one of the greatest honors."

Within the hour, I was in the queen's private chambers. The room was deceptively striking. For such heinous crimes committed in this place, I thought it would be more fitting if it looked like a dungeon, but it didn't. Climbing red roses covered the walls and dangled from the ceiling. The balcony was chiseled from black granite. Huge drapes blew in the breeze. On the wall, next to yet another picture of the late Edward Edgar was a clock. The numbers were drawn over painted white roses. The entire room was a picturesque spring scene, except for the guard standing at the entrance. I could almost believe it to be beautiful, if such a vicious woman didn't occupy it.

Hearts appeared about as thrilled to see me as one would be to get a colonoscopy. She sat in the chair by the balcony, holding her Bleeding Heart cup as a mouse poured a warm, dark beverage into it. After filling it, he poured a thimble for himself. He drank it quickly—so quickly he probably burned his tongue. When he didn't knock over dead, the queen sipped from her cup.

"Well, get on with it. Why are you here? I don't recall summoning you," Hearts said, looking at the clock on the wall.

Mr. Ruth, who was glued to my leg, tugged on my clothing. He didn't have to speak to let me know he was worried. I could see it in his precious eye.

"Don't kill Ryley," I said to the queen.

"Didn't you hear? The queen has no intentions of killing him," Chez said, curled up at the queen's feet.

"You truly want Ryley to be next in line for the throne?" I asked.

"It's his decision to make," she said. "He's of age to take over if that is what he wants."

"He's also of killing age now," I said. "When I brought him here a couple weeks ago, he wasn't."

"Inconvenient timing," Chez said.

The queen took a sip from her cup and then set it on the nightstand. "Why did you wake me up at this hour, Al? Did you really think telling me a heart-wrenching story wouldn't bore me? I knew you had fallen for him the day you told me of your plan to lure him here."

"You knew?"

Hearts exchanged a look with Chez. It was one of those looks that people give when they think you're too dumb to follow the conversation.

"If I promise you that I won't attempt to keep time from ticking, will you spare Ryley's life?" I asked, desperate to set things right. I couldn't bear to know another loved one died because of me.

"No," Hearts said. "You already promised that you wouldn't dabble in time meddling the day M.H. died."

"Take my life instead of Ryley's," I begged. "You won't have to worry about me ending your reign."

"But, you can't guarantee that Ryley won't end her reign either," Chez said, bored with the conversation.

I wished that damn cat would stay out of my business.

"But wouldn't he do just that? If he is Heir to the throne, he would only end your reign when you die—of old age or of natural causes," Mr. Ruth said, frantically. He paced nervously, back and forth, as he spoke. I couldn't blame him. The last time he was so close to the queen, he lost an eye. "You wouldn't have to worry about assassinations or the *Bleeding Heart Prophecy* coming true."

"Go back to your world, Al, and take the rumperbabbits with you. Hearts will summon you if she's interested in any service you may provide," Chez said. "It's getting late, and I haven't gotten a sufficient amount of beauty sleep yet."

"What if I could convince Ryley *not* to come back to Wonderland?" I said out of sheer desperation. "I know that you wanted Ryley here so you could end his life. It would take care of your little prophecy problem about a boy with a girl's name ending your reign, and it would be a final blow to Robert for telling… for spreading all those rumors about you."

Hearts picked up her tea and took a sip. "You really don't think I killed Edward?"

"No," I lied.

"Then you are a stupid girl," Hearts said under her breath. "But you have enough wit to know that I'm not going to let anyone tell lies about me. Robert should have died for his insubordination, but I guess his son's death will suffice."

"You can't kill Ryley!"

"Oh, I can. I can, and I will. *When* he comes to Wonderland to claim the throne, his head will become… detachable," Hearts laughed. "Perhaps you can make one last delivery to Robert, for old time's sake, and give him his son's head on a platter?"

Enraged, I grabbed the jacks from my pocket and flung them at Hearts. Chez disappeared as the pointed metal hurled closer. One jack pierced Hearts' neck, but the others missed. They hit the clock behind her. The pointy ends stuck through the glass and pinned the second hand so that it could only move forward a few ticks. Then, discouraged with its lack of progress, the second hand ticked backwards. It repeated random ticking so that time moved forward and then backward—forever stuck in a proverbial time warp.

"The Jack was right," Mr. Ruth whispered. He saw the second hand acting up as well.

The prophecy rang in my mind. *A strong-Willed child shall set the time-stalemate into motion, but only if a tWo-eyed hare can lure her to the Wonderful World of Wonderland. She Will be given a choice to live Wondrously forever or be banished to Weep in her homeland. Seconds Will tick forWard and backWards until her decision no longer Wavers. HoWever, she Will choose Wrong.*

Hearts picked the jack out from her neck. She inspected it like the blood on it intrigued her. "I should kill you for that, but I won't. I'm a fair and merciful queen, Al. So, I'll make you a deal. I'll spare the boy's life *if* he never steps foot in this realm."

"Done." I said. "I only need to return to the Otherworld once more to convince him."

"I wasn't finished speaking," Hearts said. "He *never* returns, but you will, and you will never leave. The Joker has been positively lonely and needs a playmate."

"You want me to make my decision to live here or in the Otherworld?"

"The decision is yours. Time is ticking."

# CHAPTER FIFTY-ONE

(Alice Mae: Present Time in Wonderland)

I wasn't necessarily surprised when I woke up the next morning to garbage being flung onto my bed (with me still in it). Zola Maude held the trashcan like it was a gun. Chez circled her feet, smiling as I pushed the sludge off me and crawled out of bed. As I gathered the pieces of rubbish, Zola Maude lectured me on the importance of *not* sticking a queen's neck with a jack—a stolen jack at that.

"The Joker wants all of his toys back," Zola Maude had said, eyeing my collection.

She had banished me to the kitchen for additional cleaning. With a toothbrush in hand, I scrubbed the interior of the oven. Burnt candy had caked onto the sides for years. Even though I was deep in elbow grease, cleaning the oven was a much easier punishment than any the Joker had ever given me. Scraping off the grub was almost relaxing... if Vida Maude hadn't insisted on supervising.

"Hearts should have ordered us to return you to Wonderland!" Vida Maude screamed for the umpteenth time. "You should be thanking her for not receiving a harsher chastisement!"

"Shall I write her a letter?" I muttered, under my breath.

After that comment she tacked on cleaning all the bathrooms in the house, including Chez's litter box. "You're lucky you have someone to make you sweets so you don't lose your mind, but I promise you that I'll stop giving them to you if the queen requests it."

"Nice to see where your loyalties lie," I said and then looked up at my aunt. It'd been years since I'd gotten the strength to look up at either of them. "You know Hearts is a bitter, old hag. Yet, you are still loyal to her, even when you know she killed the king."

"She did no such thing!" Vida Maude protested. "And, if you had any common sense, you'd be thanking your dear sweet aunts for bailing you out every time you got into trouble!"

"Bailing me out?" I said, in disbelief. "When M.H was beheaded, you agreed for the Joker to—"

"Torture is still a better punishment than death!"

"That, my dear, sweet aunt, depends on who you ask. Death would have been sweeter than any of the candy I've eaten."

# CHAPTER FIFTY-TWO

(Alice Mae: Present Time)

Forty eight pieces of candy devoured, and I haven't even made it to my locker. If I were diabetic, I would be in danger of going into a coma by now, but my nerves were going bonkers, and I was seeing creatures that rarely came out in Wonderland. I popped a stick of raspberry gum in my mouth and hoped to stop seeing things that weren't really there.

Never in my wildest dreams did I consider the possibility that I could fall for *the boy with the girl's name*. Why couldn't Ryley have bacne, chronic case of nose bleeds, genetic baldness, or uncontrollable gingivitis? Oh no, he had to be perfect in every way. And, that body... Nuff said. It was all I could do to convince my knees not to weaken at the sight of him. Forming coherent words when he spoke my name was dang near impossible. Perhaps if his frontal lobe was a teensy weensy smaller, I might have been able to convince myself that he wasn't so intellectually stimulating. But, he was *stimulating,* in more ways than one; there was no denying that; no matter how badly I tried to hate him.

But I didn't hate him—that was the problem.

I never wanted to fall in love, ever. And, then Ryley changed that. I couldn't imagine falling in love, but now that I had, it was painful not to be *his girl,* much less just stand back and watch as he flirted with one of the sophomore girls that Mick had introduced him to.

Plus, I still had to figure out a way to keep him from accepting Hearts' false offer—not that he'd believe anything I said now. But, I owed him. I had to get him to listen.

It was a difficult thought to process when he had the girl pinned against the wall. She blinked up at him with her overrated brown eyes. I hoped her false eyelashes fell out in her lunch. She giggled and walked her fingers up his shirt. Seriously! What did guys see in her? I was sure that she was a snotty, little—

"Sucks to be old news, doesn't it?" Courtney said, in passing.

A legitimate comeback failed to come out. So instead I spit out my gum and flicked it in her hair when her back was turned. I didn't even try to hide my smile when it tangled into her hair. I wondered how long it'd take her to notice. I bet it would be on the first hair flip.

I popped another candy on my tongue, and focused on the grape flavor instead of how Ryley's hand came dangerously close to the girl he had pinned against the locker. I closed my eyes and tried to forget the library date—my first date.

"Well, at least I know he was lying when he said he loved me," I said, talking to myself since no one else had befriended me since I'd transferred to this school.

"Ryley said that he loved you?" Dax leaned against a locker. He appeared comfortable, like he'd been watching me for a while. "He actually said the words *I love you?*"

I looked at my feet, hoping to buy time in order to figure out how to respond. "He regrets it now."

Dax rolled his eyes. "Duh, he regrets it now! He's literally been a nomad for years, bouncing from town to town when anyone got too close to him or when things got rough. What did you think was going to happen when he finally admitted that he liked you?"

I shrugged my shoulders. There was a limited amount of knowledge I could impart to Dax that wouldn't get me a psych assessment if he told anyone with authority. "I made a horribly bad decision at his expense."

"I thought you had Ryley figured out, Alice Mae. I figured you for a pro, not the type that would sit around and pout because a guy didn't call you back."

"You don't understand, Dax. I did something bad—unforgivably bad. I don't blame him for being mad."

"If he can still swing a bat and ace a test, there wasn't anything that you could have done that was so unforgivable." Dax walked up to me and nudged my shoulder. "Ryley likes the chase, but you stopped running. He'd follow you to the end of the world, Alice Mae. Ryley isn't the type of guy who cares how much money he has in his bank account or what car he drives. Heck, he still bums around in his dad's old POS. He wants adventure and a lifetime of memories to carry him through old age. Besides, I've seen how he looks at you, and that look isn't in his eyes right now."

I nodded to Ryley and the girl. It sure looked like he'd forgotten about me. They were practically making out in the hallway!

"He's looking for a distraction," Dax said, after the girl pulled out her cell phone to enter the digits Ryley had to be giving her. "Do you love him?"

"Love is one of the many feelings I have for him," I said as jealousy raged in my heart.

# CHAPTER FIFTY-THREE

(Ryley: Present Time)

Distractions. I needed all the distractions I could get. It'd been a few weeks since I discovered that Alice Mae wasn't actually playing hard to get. She acted like she didn't want me to go to Wonderland, just to make me want it more. And then, it turns out I have royal blood raging through my veins. Hearts didn't want to kill me. She offered me the throne. Maybe the paranoia that the candy was supposed to offset wasn't working as well as Alice Mae hoped.

The worst thing about the whole ordeal was that I couldn't get her out of my head, no matter how hard I tried. And, just when I thought I was finally getting over her, I'd find another of her many notes in my locker. I tried not to read them… the last one was her ranting that Hearts still wanted to off me. Yeah, right.

*She* was why I was chit chatting with the brown-eyed girl in the hall. I think her name was Jessica, or Jenny? It didn't matter. As I rattled off my phone number, J-girl put it in her phone. I hoped that she'd call me so I wouldn't have to spend another weekend pacing around my room thinking about *her*. I glanced over my shoulder to see if Alice Mae was still staring at me.

She was still chomping on her gum, but she wasn't alone. My would-be best friend was chatting with her. I turned my attention back to the J-girl. I was just telling her that I would be a lucky guy if she called soon, when Alice Mae walked up to her and grabbed J-girl's phone, like it was socially acceptable to go through someone else's stuff.

"Hey! That's mine!" J-girl said. "Give it back!"

Alice Mae deleted my number and then tossed it back. "Trust me, darling. You don't want Ryley's number. He gave me herpes."

My mouth dropped. Looking back, I suppose it was the best reaction I could have had. J-girl looked from Alice Mae and then to me.

"You're lying," J-girl said.

"Am I? Then ask Ryley for his number again, I dare you," Alice Mae said, and walked away like she didn't care one way or another.

I quickly rattled off my phone number to J-girl and swore on my uncle's grave that I didn't have *any* STD's. I raced up to Alice Mae. I didn't grab her arm to stop her like I wanted to. There were so freaking many things I wanted to do to this girl! Touching, especially in anger, would be detrimental.

"So, I don't text you back or reply to your notes, so you are going to start rumors about me and ruin my reputation," I scoffed. "Should I start calling you Becky?"

"If you'd just listen to me, and be remotely unbiased, then I'll leave you alone to do whatever you want."

I stopped walking. I wasn't going to encourage her behavior. She was doing it again—tricking me into talking to her. "The great thing about starting a nasty rumor about me having *The Herp* means you have it too."

By the second period, everyone in school thought that Alice Mae and I had nasty Uglies. By the third period, I *might* have started a rumor that she used to be three hundred pounds. She had her stretch-marks lasered off. The rumor retaliation was in full swing by fourth period. I heard one that I *had* been recruited by a D-1 college, but it fell through because of my steroid problem. After hearing that little number slip, I mentioned (to Becky, The Gossip Queen) that Alice Mae had been born with a tail.

By the time the lunch ladies got their serve on, everyone considered me a leper. No one wanted to sit beside me, not even Dax. But, that might have had something to do with him betraying me by talking to Alice Mae before first bell. I think he felt guilty, or knew that I'd seen him, and would want to have a little chat about loyalties.

I spotted Alice Mae. She sat in the corner by herself—surprise, surprise. I slammed my tray down beside hers and chomped away on my food, hoping she'd be disgusted by my loud eating. When she made no move and hadn't reacted, I glared at her. Like always, her hair and makeup were pristine, but her nails were past mutilation. The nail beds were downright bloody.

"I know I messed up," Alice Mae said, looking in the opposite direction. "I'm not asking you to take me back. I don't even blame you for getting all PMS-y, but it is imperative that you hear what I have to say."

"Says the lying liar."

"You don't get it, do you? Hearts offered you the throne so you'd be tempted to come back to Wonderland… where she'd kill you. The throne was just bait."

Got it. If I returned to Wonderland, my hopes of ruling the cockamamie place will be smashed with a guillotine. But, I didn't care. I didn't want the throne or anything that came with it. Living in Wonderland wasn't realistic. Deep down, I'd rather follow in my dad's footsteps and become a professor, teaching theoretical physics. This world made sense. Wonderland didn't.

"If Hearts wanted me dead, I would be. I was sitting in a snake chair. One bite and I'd die from their venom."

Alice Mae was with me until I made the snake comment. Then, her eyes dilated. She popped in another candy. Whatever I'd said distracted her.

"Snake venom, I wonder if M.H. ever thought about using that as a poison to kill the queen. Maybe Genevine can find a way... I'll send Mr. Ruth..."

I snapped my fingers in front of her face. *Just keep staying mad at her—otherwise those ridiculous feelings of affection will come pouring back.*

"You're paranoid, Alice Mae. Hearts wasn't out to get you—or me—or anyone. She's just a lonely, old woman whose husband died."

Alice Mae dug into her pocket and pulled out a playing card, a price tag, and a crumpled piece of paper.

"I'm not paranoid, Ryley. I believe the Jack wrote these three prophecies about us. Everything set into motion when the king was beheaded... A girl will choose Wrong. Time will stop." She took a deep breath and said, "And, a HATed fool will die twice."

*A strong-Willed child shall set the time-stalemate into motion, but only if a tWo-eyed hare can lure her to the Wonderful World of Wonderland. She Will be given a choice to live Wondrously forever or be banished to Weep in her homeland. Seconds Will tick forWard and backWards until her decision no longer Wavers. HoWever, she Will choose Wrong.*

"Mr. Ruth only has one eye," I pointed out.

"He had both when he lured me to Wonderland the first time. The Joker didn't poke out his eye until much later," she said, and pointed to the *Bleeding Hearts Prophecy.*

The Jack prophesied: *If the King loses his head, then the Queen with a bleeding Heart would rule the Red Court until Time ceased to move forward. When a second carried on for infinity, every creature in Wonderland would tip their Hat to the misfit girl with a boy's name (or was it a boy with a Girl's name?) who'd end the Reign of Terror. However, it all hinged on the One-Eyed Hare being able to convince an uninspirable Heir that the impossible was indeed possible—like stopping time—and that insane Love was worth a Beheading.*

"Falling in love with you was like stumbling down a rabbit hole and seeing a magical world. Whereas, your betrayal was like tripping on a guillotine." I said. "I fell for you, and it *wasn't* worth a beheading."

"I hope the Hare can change your mind," she said, and slid the last prophecy in front of me.

The *HATed fool will die twice before the MADness stops.* "Hat and mad are capitalized. I think it was a reference to the Mad Hatter," she said. "And I think you are the second Mad Hatter."

"You still think the Jack saw into the future?" I asked, still not buying what Alice Mae was putting down. "Because if this is true, I'm a man who can defy death."

"The Joker predicted that the hated fool would die *twice.* So I don't hold much clout in that word. He isn't as talented in his fortune telling as his great-great grandfather, and he sometimes gets predictions wrong. But you should still be cautious."

I crossed my arms. "You're doing it again. You're playing with my curiosity to get me to do what you want."

"I am."

That was it! I grabbed my tray, stood up, and walked away. I made it as far as the garbage cans before Alice Mae grabbed my arm. I hated that her touch set my skin ablaze and garbled my thoughts so that I could only think of her, feel her, want her. I desperately needed more space between us.

"I use manipulation because of the effectiveness." She let go of my arm. "But, I was wrong, so wrong to deliver you to Hearts with the assumption that she'd whack you. I should have known my imagination was getting the best of me. I probably wasn't eating enough candy and paranoia snuck up on me. Just please promise me you won't go back there."

Alice Mae looked defeated—crushed, more like it. The weight of her words seemed more important than their face value. I could tell without asking that if she returned to Wonderland, something very horrible would happen to her.

"You should go back to Wonderland, Alice Mae. You belong in that upside-down place, not me."

I regretted the words as soon as they came out of my mouth. But, Alice Mae knew I fell in love with her, and she'd use it to get what she wanted. I just didn't know what she wanted now.

"So you won't go back to Wonderland if I'm there?" Her eyes were filled with tears. One trickled down her cheek. Her lips pressed into a thin line. She held her breath, waiting for my answer.

"I'm not going to promise that," I said. "There is still something I need from that world. And if I have to tell the queen I'll be her Heir to get it, I will."

"You want the recipe book," she said. "If I can get you the book, will you stay in this world, forever?"

"Yes."

# CHAPTER FIFTY-FOUR

(Ryley: Present Time)

Alice Mae didn't come to school the next day or the day after that, but there was a note taped to my locker. Another love-letter from Alice Mae, no doubt.

I was wrong.

It was a page that looked like it was torn from a very old book. It was a faded recipe. The more closely I inspected it, the more the ingredient list appeared to change. It was an optical illusion. One second it appeared to be a recipe for chocolates and then the next it was for sweet tarts. The candy recipe changed every few seconds. I just hoped that my dad could decipher it.

Scribbled in Alice Mae's handwriting was a note: *Hearts wasn't the only one who had a copy of his novel. One other man, the author, kept the original. Since I was his apprentice, I knew where he kept all his candy recipes, the poisonous ones and the yummy ones.*

*Good bye, R.*

She'd kissed the letter. I traced the faint, blue lipstick. The halls were empty. Well, actually they were filled with students, but it was short one blonde.

I was finally rid of that girl—the wench who stole my heart and stomped on it. There was an emptiness in my heart when I realized she'd taken my advice and left this world. I may care for the girl, but that wasn't a good enough reason to be together. Right?

At least I could put Wonderland behind me, until I went home. The frogs that my friends and I had released in the school appeared to have regrouped. They were hopping around my house. My mom was chasing them around with a broom.

"Ryley, thank goodness you're home," she said, sweeping the varmints outside. "They're everywhere! I swear they are coming up through the floor!"

I ran up the steps but tripped over the ceramic frog. Theodore appeared the same, except for its smirk. I looked back at the house to make sure my mom was inside. Water blasted the window of the door. She ditched the broom for the sink sprayer.

"Theodore, did you do this?"

The ceramic frog didn't move. It just kept on smiling.

"Was this Alice Mae's doing?"

Again, no answer. I was half tempted to tell Theodore that I was going to smash its ceramic body by dropping it off of the porch when I recalled what my mom said.

*...they are coming up through the floor!*

I dropped my backpack on the kitchen table, squishing a few frogs in the process. I raced to my room. It was an amphibian nightmare. They were everywhere: On my television, bed, and on my dresser. Yet, I couldn't figure out where they were coming from, until I looked under the bed.

A rabbit hole.

I could still hear my mom screaming at the things from the kitchen. I knew I was going to regret it, but I grabbed my baseball bat, held onto my ball cap, and pushed myself into the hole.

The *Waiting Room* was empty of any green hopping creatures. The vines still clung to the walls. The checkered floor still disorientated me, but I was prepared this time.

"Hello?" I called out.

There was a creak behind me. Raising my bat, I turned to face it. A scared looking rabbit looked up at me—the One-Eyed Hare, Mr. Ruth.

"Sending an army of frogs to my house—was that a strategic move in the game Alice Mae is playing with me?" I demanded, keeping the bat held high.

"The frogs and frogs alike have hated Al since the first M.H. was beheaded. They are merely celebrating because Al is 'entertaining' the queen, second Mad Hatter," Mr. Ruth said, glancing at my hat. "I truly didn't think it'd go this far, but the prophecy about her was true. I saw the second hand dance back and forth, like time is no longer a linear force—"

"What did she do?"

"She made a deal with the queen," Mr. Ruth said, timidly. He walked back and forth. "Guilt coats her soul. It has since she got her best friend killed. No one blames her more than she does. She made me promise to keep my good eye on you, never let you out of my sight until it's safe. So, I cannot let you into Wonderland. It's for your safety. You will die if you step through the mouse door."

I dropped the bat. "And what happens to her if I don't cross into Wonderland?"

"You must understand that I believe the prophecies to be true. The HATed fool will die twice before the MADness stops. Ryley, that card was split in half and given to you and M.H. The prediction about Al has commenced as well. She will Weep in the Otherworld or live Wondrously. She thinks that living Wondrously means that she will be forgiven in death—a death given to her by Wonderland's queen."

I swung my bat down on the mermaid table. Mr. Ruth took off running while the glass shattered. He hid behind the vines and watched me cautiously.

"Tell me about the deal she made!"

The rabbit swallowed a lump in his throat. "Hearts wouldn't have to fret about her reign ending if she could ensure that you'd never come back to Wonderland... and if she met death."

"She's going to die for me?"

"To ensure your safety, which I promised her I'd do. You cannot enter Wonderland, or you'll prove the prophecy right."

I fell to my knees. Glass ground into my skin. "I wish I'd never met her."

Mr. Ruth gasped. He hopped from out of the vines. He moved quickly but with precision, missing every piece of glass on the floor, until he was standing directly in front of me.

"She's made many mistakes, Mad Hatter. But she's doing this because she loves you. For Al, meeting you saved her from the bitterness residing in her soul."

I gripped the bat tight in my hand. Could I do it? Could I walk away? Could I live with myself year-in and year-out? Did I even know what love meant, if I could bear to walk away and let her die?

"I hate Alice Mae, but I love her more," I said. "Did my dad think the impossible was possible?"

Mr. Ruth shifted nervously. "I don't like where this conversation is going."

"Until my dad lost track of reality, he was working as a physics depart—"

266

"Your father loved your mother, he still does. From afar, which is what you now have to learn to do," Mr. Ruth said. "Hearts might not kill Alice Mae right away. Besides, I can't let you enter Wonderland. I made a promise to Al. It might as well have been her dying wish."

"No, you promised her that you'd never take your good eye off me until it was safe," I said. "She didn't specify whose safety."

# CHAPTER FIFTY-FIVE

(Ryley: Present Time in Wonderland)

"She once danced until her feet bled," the Joker said, standing on a wooden platform. "Now that she's all grown up, she'll dance until her body can no longer carry her to center stage."

The boards were uneven and splintered. Lights strung all around the stage. Lanterns floated in the air. It looked like a little girl threw a tea party and invited all her stuffed animals. However, these creatures were animated. They chatted pleasantly with one another, like this wasn't a ballet that ended only when a girl collapsed. The Maude sisters were there—nibbling on saltwater taffy! Adjacent to the stage was Hearts, perched on her throne. She smiled a pleasant little smile. I hated when people said nothing and just smiled. It hid their true feelings.

I kept to the protection of the white magnolia tree even though it was a moonless night. Mr. Ruth kept to my side, doing precisely what he promised Alice Mae.

"Start the ceremony," Hearts said, seemingly bored already.

Half past midnight, Alice Mae took to the stage. Her light blue shoes flickered when her toe came into contact with the stage. It appeared as if she'd captured a thousand fireflies and trapped them in her

268

grandmother's glass slippers. The taut, golden ballerina outfit accentuated her willowy figure. Her gait was so light she seemed to float on stage. On her head was a purple hat that my dad had worn on his wedding day—a hat belonging to her late friend. It was a hat that belonged to a hated fool.

She tipped her hat to the crowd. "Tonight, I dance for my late friend, the infamous M.H."

There were no claps. No one shouted with glee. They gave her hateful looks. I couldn't imagine the strength it took to walk in her shoes. If I hadn't been watching for it, I'd never have seen the tear slip from her eye as she stood in a pose. It rolled down her perfect porcelain face, leaving only a faint line to show that she'd shed a tear for her loved ones. Weeks had lapsed since she once danced in a classroom, when no one watched but me. Now, her audience consisted of people who didn't know, weren't aware of her strength.

The music resonated. It began slow and wispy. Yet, it quickly turned retro, complimenting Alice Mae's particular taste in music. She danced as if a puppeteer was moving her. She was so graceful. I'd never seen anyone more beautiful—or haunting. This dance she choreographed was a dance of her life. The beauty. The shame. Every Wrong she ever made, and the few rights—this dance represented her undying nature to fight when it would have been easier to give up.

I couldn't believe that she could twist and turn her dance lessons with the Joker and make them into a thing of haunting splendor. He sat at the edge of the stage, chucking smoke bombs at Alice Mae. They exploded as she moved. Still, she didn't flinch. I wondered how many times the man tormented her while she twirled in circles around him.

Our gazes met when she completed a jump. **Her light blue eyes were dazzling, even though they were icy. She never stumbled, even though I could see that she wasn't happy to see me.** She glanced at Mr. Ruth and shook her head in disappointment.

The music blasted, drowning out the rest of the world. The spotlight showed only one girl in the world. The entire world could have taken five, and I wouldn't have noticed because I couldn't take my eyes off of Alice Mae.

Mr. Ruth tugged on my pants. He pointed to Alice Mae's shoes.

They were no longer all light blue. Red stained them.

Pushing away from the tree, I walked through the crowd with my baseball bat still in hand. Alice Mae became more and more panicked the closer I came. She even tossed the hat off to me, which I promptly put on my head. When I was blocked from the queen's sight by an elephant, she whispered for me to leave.

"I didn't realize you would be having a speaking part," Hearts commented. "Who are you telling to leave? As queen, I claim exclusive rights to tell people when to come and go."

Alice Mae stopped dancing and stared at me. She threw her hands up in the air. "Why did you come? You promised you wouldn't once you had the recipe!"

There was so much I wanted to say. There was so much left unsaid. But, privacy was not going to be given. The creatures watched us like our conversation was a part of the show.

"Because, I'll follow you anywhere, Alice Mae, even down a muddy rabbit hole."

"All those hurtful things you said—"

"If you jotted down all of my ill-thought out comments, you could write a book entitled, *Guide to Getting Punched in the Throat for Boneheads.*"

"You weren't supposed to come here!"

"Yet, I'm here all the same."

The Joker got one good look at me and alerted the queen. Hearts actually got off her chair and walked across the stage to see for herself. "My-oh-my, Ryley Edward Edgar, the Heir with the One-Eyed Hare has graced us with his presence."

# CHAPTER FIFTY-SIX

(Ryley: Present Time in Wonderland)

Hearts walked off the stage. Each creature took a step back when their queen walked closer. The spotlight moved off Alice Mae and onto the queen the moment her foot hit the ground. As soon as Alice Mae was in the dark, the Joker stepped in front of her, blocking her from my sight completely.

I supposed it was for the better that I couldn't see her. She distracted me enough as it was, and if I ever needed to mind my words, tonight was crucial.

"I must say, I'm rather curious why you are here," Hearts said, smugly. "A small feat since I'm usually quite aware of everyone's Comings and Goings, young Mr. Edgar."

The crowd gasped. A few creatures pointed at me. "Edgar? Robby's son?" "The Banished Prince's child?" and the "son of the notorious Prince of Spades?" could be heard amongst the murmurs. Mr. Ruth stepped even closer to me, which I didn't think possible. His nerves were making mine jump.

"You made me a rather enticing offer. I'd be a dope not to consider it. And what kind of person would I be not to discuss the

271

possibilities of my reign in person?" I asked.

"Reign?" A frazzled egret repeated in disbelief. It dipped down from its perch on the tree to get a better look at me. "You plan to end Hearts' reign?"

"What's your name, boy?" A purple colored caterpillar shouted out. It was so small I hadn't noticed it before. It took a drag from a tiny hookah and then blew the smoke at me.

"Ryley Edward Edgar," I stated.

Word of the *Bleeding Heart Prophecy* lingered amongst the crowd. Their heads were on swivels, looking at me and the queen. The chaos the crowd generated agreed with Hearts.

A lizard stepped forward, eyeing the watch that belonged to my dad. "Where do your loyalties lay, Mr. Edgar? With your father or with the queen?"

"That very question is what I intend to discuss with the queen, in private," I said, addressing Hearts.

"Come, join me by my throne. We can discuss anything you like while Al entertains us," Hearts said and turned her back to me.

Following the queen, Mr. Ruth and I walked onto the stage but stopped in front of the Joker. He looked at me like I was a bug he could squash with his ridiculous, oversized shoes.

"I'd like a word with the girl," I said.

"That traitorous girl is performing for the queen," the Joker said. "Surely you don't want Hearts to wait."

I gripped my bat with both hands. "Alice Mae told me you like to play games. She spoke *fondly* about your play dates. Perhaps you and I could play a game of baseball later?"

"Ryley, don't!" Alice Mae warned. "The Joker is a far better trickster than I."

The Joker grinned. I don't know if he practiced in the mirror, but when he lowered his face, shadows cast on his face made him appear absolutely evil. "Only if I can bring the equipment."

"Sure, now please step aside, I have something very important to discuss with Alice Mae before I can give the queen an answer. By keeping me from speaking with her, *you* are making the queen wait more."

"Then you should proceed," the Joker said and bowed. He dropped a marble. When it hit the stage, a flash of light burst. He was gone.

"What are you doing here?" All the blood had drained from Alice Mae's face. "Mr. Ruth was supposed to keep you safe."

"Keep me safe?" I said, mockingly. "That Hare *convinced* me to come here."

"I did no such thing!" Mr. Ruth exclaimed. "I did the exact opposite! I tried to get him to stay in the Otherworld."

"He convinced me with what he didn't say. My dad loved my mom, but from afar. It was painful for both of them, and I *refuse* to do the same, especially if the girl is worth the trouble. And, boy-oh-boy are you troublesome, Alice Mae. But you're worth it."

"You should have listened to Mr. Ruth," Alice Mae said. "It's not safe for you here."

"And it's safe for you? Word has it that you are going to dance to your death."

Alice Mae swallowed a lump in her throat. "I am."

"For me?"

She whimpered, which was as painful as gutting me with a dull knife. Dropping that bat, I gently cupped her cheek and directed her attention back to me. "You have a way with words, Alice Mae. You twist them upon themselves, and you tell the truth only when you don't think anyone will believe you! You manipulated me to do what you want, and…" I took a deep breath. "And, I've never been sorrier for what I've said then I am right now. I never should have made you feel worthless, even if I have every single right to be catastrophically outraged at you. But, no matter how hard I tried—and believe me, I've tried—I can't *not* love you!"

"Love and hate are rather similar emotions for being polar opposites. Perhaps you are confusing the two."

Out of everything she could have said, that comment hadn't made the Top Ten. "Did you ever love me, or were you just toying with me?"

"I'm not toying with you," she said, sliding her trembling hand along mine. "I love you."

"I want a future with you—a real future," I said. "I'm sick of going back and forth between love and hate, between friends and not friends, between being enemies and lovers."

"If all this wondrous nonsense hadn't interfered, we might have had a future," she said. "But, it did, and we can't change the past, no matter how hard we try."

"But we can control our future."

"Our future has been foretold." A tear slipped from her eye. She pushed away from me. "Goodbye, Ryley."

As she turned her back to me, I grabbed her wrist and jerked her against me. She caught herself against my chest. I didn't need a memo to know she was telling me the lies she believed to be true. Even if the prophecies were true, I'd still fight for her. As much of a nuisance as she was, she was worth fighting for—even if she'd already given up.

"Kiss me," I said. "Kiss me, and if you can still tell me goodbye, then I'll back off."

"It's not that easy."

"Anything worth fighting for usually isn't."

Standing inches from her, I never felt so far away. I lifted her chin and guided her lips to mine. Part of me expected her to bite my tongue, but I hoped she'd kiss me back, and *oh*, did she kiss back. Her body slid up against mine, moving like she did when she danced. She wrapped her arms around my neck when I pulled her against me. I kissed her like I've never kissed another girl in my life. I drank in her lips as I pulled her close. She broke the kiss in a sudden gasp when I slipped my hands around her waist. When I looked into her breathtaking eyes, I knew my question no longer warranted an answer. She wasn't going to tell me goodbye. I'd finally left her speechless.

"Run," I whispered. "Run far, far away and don't come back until I send the white rabbit for you."

She trembled in my arms. "I *won't* leave you."

"That wasn't a request," I said, memorizing how she looked.

"How romantic," Hearts said, sarcastically. "The boy and girl tripped into each other's arms and fell in love."

"It's better than tripping onto a guillotine blade," I said.

Mr. Ruth passed out. He hit the stage, making the only sound in the entire court for a solid minute. Everyone looked at me like they couldn't believe I'd say such a thing (even Alice Mae). I kissed her on the forehead and told her to take off as soon as I caused a big enough distraction.

"I had a few questions before I take you up on the offer to end your reign, *Sweet Heart*," I said, ensuring I laid the sarcasm on thick. I grabbed my bat and flipped it in the air before handing it to Alice Mae. "It's no sword, but it'll pack a good punch if you swing hard enough."

"You want something that will pack a good punch?" the Joker said and flung a tiny, black toy-bomb (with two plastic legs) on stage next to me. It walked forward, edging closer and closer until it hit my foot...

I didn't remember the explosion.

# CHAPTER FIFTY-SEVEN

(Alice Mae: Present Time in the Waiting Room)

I awoke on a checkered floor that was covered in shattered glass. My clothes were torn, least of my worries. My skin was scratched and my legs burned. But, it didn't compare to the stabbing pain in my feet. They were bruised and bloody.

I pushed myself into a sitting position. The glass ground into my palms. I tried to stand, but my feet refused to carry me. I remembered an explosion… and then, nothing. Everything went blank.

"Good, I thought you'd never wake."

I recognized that voice anywhere, even in the dimly lit *Waiting Room*. "Did you decide that you couldn't wait for me to dance myself into an early grave, Joker?" I asked, looking around for the man in the dunce hat.

He lit a sparkler and put it in his mouth like a cigarette. The sparks lit enough of the room that I could only make him out. Everything else bled into blackness.

"Actually, if I had my way, the Mad Hatter would have front row seats as you danced yourself to death, but the queen had a better idea," the Joker said, kneeling in front of me.

"His name is Ryley, not the Mad Hatter!"

His beady eyes could always pierce their way into my soul. It was like I could feel him clawing his way through me, seeing into the darkest parts, and forcing me to act upon them. "Oh, how I missed our play dates, Al."

"What do you want?"

The Joker stood up suddenly, like he was a puppet and his puppeteer yanked on his cords. "It's been months since I've played a good Guessing Game," the Joker said, twirling around on his feet like I did in my ballet shoes. "The Mad Hatter's punishment is... Blank. Would you like a hint or do you think you can fill in the blank all by yourself?"

I fought back tears. I hated that I cried so easily. It made me feel like a little girl. Tears made me feel weak. "Is he de-dead?" I asked, choking on the last word.

"This game is getting boring!" The Joker clapped his hands together. "I'd be more worried about you, my dear, stupid girl."

"What about me?" I asked, pushing away from him.

"We're setting up picket pool. I'm betting you'll go kooky with grief. Perchance there is a vacant room in the psych ward where Robby calls home. Chez says you'll take your own life," he said, prancing around the room with his sparkler in his hand. He wrote the words: *Want a Hint yet?*

"Just tell me!"

He lit another sparkler and handed it to me. It was everything I could do not to poke him with it.

He whispered, "Death is not in your immediate future, Al. But, I cannot say the same for that boy you were kissing. His expiration date is coming soon enough."

I grabbed his collar and pulled him close. "If Hearts hurts him in any way—"

"You'll what? If you return to Wonderland, *for longer than a second*, your head is mine! I'll add it to the collection of others. So unless you find a way to stop time, you can never return, unless you like being hunted," the Joker said and laughed giddily. He cleared his throat and spoke like he did when announcing the news to the court. "The best part is that any creature who merely *sees* you in this realm again and doesn't report it will have their *eyes* scooped out, regardless if they are still protected by the Rightdoing Law. Hearts says she'll send the traitor—which is you if you're wondering—the eyes. And, anyone who actually helps the traitor will be subject to punishment via play dates with me, yours truly, the Joker."

I couldn't hold back my tears any longer. They poured from my eyes like they were coming from a spigot. The Joker jerked my hand from his clothing. He took out the watch that belonged to Ryley and tossed it to me.

"A token of the *time* we spent together. Get it?" he said, chuckling at the pun of his joke. "I really should get going. I'll be late if I stay much longer. The Mad Hatter and I have a very important date. Cheerio!"

# CHAPTER FIFTY-EIGHT

(Ryley: Present Time in Wonderland)

The Red Court's dungeon wasn't the stereotypical dungeon. It wasn't concrete or made of stone. Water didn't drip from cracks in the ceiling. Chains didn't dangle from the walls—scratch that. They did. I just spotted one across the room next to the bird cages. One was big enough for me to fit in. I thanked my lucky stars that I wasn't occupying it. My hands were tied behind my back and my legs were shackled. Given that my body was burned and my clothes were tattered, I looked the part of a common criminal.

The underground room looked more like a demented children's room rather than a place to keep prisoners. A painting of a circus scene was drawn on the floor, but it was difficult to make out the picture entirely due to the fact that it was covered with large piles of sand. Three bases and a home plate were laid out, making it appear like a baseball field. The bases and home plate were nailed down with railroad spikes that jutted up from the floor. Toys lay on the floor. I counted eleven different size balls, including a bowling ball, a yo-yo, countless cards, jacks, toy soldiers, and a bungee cord that hung from the ceiling. The bungee cord hung close to a red fire pole that dropped down from a circular hole in the ceiling. Other than that hole, I saw no other way out of the room.

279

On one side of the room was a theatrical stage. The black curtains were drawn. A bouncy-castle holding hundreds of red balls was next to it. Spider webs made up nets that extended to the ceiling. The entire ball pit was crawling with spiders. It was my nightmare: trapped in a hole surrounded by spiders. Sitting in a rocking chair next to it was an old hag knitting a blue scarf. I had to blink several times to make out what she was using for thread—spider's silk.

"Miss, can you free me?" I asked, raising my feet in the air so she could see the shackles.

The hag set her knitting down and walked over to me, dragging a ball and chain behind her. "His locks are impervious to everyone unless he teaches them how to break it, Mad Hatter."

"Name's Ryley."

"But you are known by many other names, boy with the girl's name," she said, coming closer. "The Heir. The, *second*, Mad Hatter. Nicknames and aliases are just as important as true names, maybe even more important."

"What's your name?"

"Genevine. I'm the infamous seamstress."

Her clothes were stained; they had some resemblance of what Alice Mae would wear. The cloth appeared expensive, minus the stains. Spiders crawled from her hair and crept over her clothes. I shuddered in disgust, but managed to keep the repulsed thoughts from being expressed on my face.

"After the beheading of M.H, Hearts decided she wanted to keep a closer watch on me. I've been living in this place ever since." Her wild hair hid much of her face, but a glimpse of sorrow showed in her eyes. "You would have liked your uncle, Eddie. It's a pity Hearts killed him before you were born. But, I suppose if you ever want to see him, all you have to do is look in the mirror."

"You knew my uncle?"

"He's about as bright as that girl," said a spider riding on her shoulder.

"Oh hush, Alfred. He knows nothing about the love Eddie and I had before the queen killed him," Genevine said to the spider.

"You are the reason that the king lost his head?" I asked.

"See, I told you that Robby told him nothing about Wonderland," Genevine said. "Any information he knows is only because Al told him."

"Where is Alice Mae?" I asked, hoping she fended better than I had. At least she had the bat for protection. Hopefully, it did her a little bit of good.

A clang drove my attention to the floor below the circular hole in the ceiling. My bat, "slightly" altered, lay on the floor. Rusty nails had been hammered through the bat, sticking out in all directions. Only a narrow spot at the end was nail-free.

"No point in wondering where Al is at now," Genevine whispered. "You have a date with destiny."

"I'm not going to die in this madhouse," I said.

"That will be a true tragedy then," Alfred said. "Because then the madness will never stop."

"Bottom's up!" The Joker yelled from the ceiling.

Genevine looked up at the ceiling and cursed. I liked her a little more because of that. "Do you love Al—really love her?"

"Enough to come to this hell-hole and keep her from dancing to her death," I replied.

"The Hare convinced you then, that the impossible was possible—like stopping time or that love was worth a beheading?" Genevine asked, watching the Joker slid down the pole.

I rolled my eyes. Why did everyone insist on talking in riddles? "I swear that loving Alice Mae is impossible."

"Yet, you do?" Alfred said, looking at me with all his eyes.

"Yes."

"Then I shall tell the others."

"Tell the others what?"

"That the impossible has been done," Genevine said and hurried away to her place by the bouncy castle.

When the Joker reached the floor, he raised his hands in the air as if to say *ta-da*. He pranced around in a baseball uniform that could have been on exhibit at a museum.

"That was a nifty trick you did, flipping the bat in the air, care to show me?" the Joker asked.

"I would, but my hands are in shackles."

"Oh, I can fix that," he said, pulling a bobby pin from his sleeve.

As he picked the lock, I contemplated climbing the pole to escape, which didn't sound enjoyable since my hands were burned. I glanced over at the chair where Genevine had been sitting. She was gone, as was every single spider from the bouncy castle. Where had they gone?

The Joker leaned in close and whispered in my ear. "I can practically hear your screaming thoughts of escape. It's been quite some time since I had such an enthusiastic playmate. Genevine refuses to play with me. She'd rather hide in the castle I made for her. So please, try to escape. I have so many neglected toys I've been dying to play with."

"Why did you make her a bouncy castle?" I asked, hoping to distract him.

"Well, she wanted to be queen, after all. Bump Hearts off the throne and marry Eddie. So, I thought it only fitting she should have a castle to live in when she's not making exquisite dresses for Hearts."

"She makes dresses for Hearts?"

"Well, she is the most talented seamstress since M.H. choked on a blade."

The lock clicked. My hands were free. Before standing up, I weighed my options. The madman clearly wanted someone to torture, and I had no intention of being said person. I pointed to the shackles around my feet.

"Think you could work your magic on these?"

"I could," he said. His smile lost its charm when he snarled. "But I won't. Odds won't be in my favor."

He walked over to the staged area and pulled back the curtain. It revealed a large collection of knives, swords, and disfigured blades. *The Wall of Weapons* was written across the top. He unveiled an object the size of a piano. Underneath it was a large chopping blade—the guillotine.

I shuffled over to my deformed bat. I picked it up, testing the weight.

"Do you like the modifications?" the Joker asked, watching me with curiosity.

"I don't think a ball will recoil quite as nice when hit," I said.

"Shall we test it out?" the Joker asked and threw a pink bouncy ball.

Instinctually, I got into batting stance and swung at the ball. Pink gel burst from the ball, covering me in jelly. It burned upon contact. It ate through my clothes, but I was more concerned about the gel melting my skin. Swearing under my breath, I charged the Joker. The madman laughed and wiggled his finger at me, encouraging me to strike him.

When he was an arm's reach away, I swung. He chucked a smoke bomb by his feet and disappeared. My bat hit nothing. He reappeared on the third base and waved.

Even though I didn't know where Alice Mae was, she still managed to crawl into my mind. I couldn't imagine her playing in this demented place with the Joker. I recalled that he kept her here long enough that she couldn't return home without having to rely on candies to function. He tortured her! Ruined her life! Wrecked her childhood! He manipulated her!

I never thought myself to be a killer, but I promised that I would end this madman's life. I could do that for Alice Mae... if it was the last thing I'd do.

"You're going to have to be much faster than that if you're going to catch me, Mad Hatter."

"I AM NOT THE MAD HATTER!"

"Then you should return his hat," the Joker said, nodding to the purple hat still on my head. "It's not very polite to wear the clothing of a deadman."

I pointed the bat at the Joker. "*You* are the deadman."

"It's not in the cards," he said, revealing a tarot card from his sleeve and flinging it at me.

As it spun in the air, it grew bigger. The paper transformed into metal. The damn thing was a blade, and it was spinning head height.

I ducked, throwing the bat at the Joker as I fell. It stuck in his shoulder. He laughed wildly and jerked it out. Then, he flipped it in the air and grabbed the non-pointy end. He threw another smoke bomb on the floor. He disappeared and reappeared above me.

I had a second to react before he swung the bat down on me. I grabbed the sand and threw it in his face as I kicked my feet up to stop the bat. The nails drove into my feet. Yelling out in pain, I shoved my feet into the Joker's chest.

"You're never going to sit on the throne!" the Joker yelled, scrambling to get away from me. "Hearts never wanted you there. It was all a ploy to kill you once you were of age. Your death will torture your father, no matter where he calls home."

"Yeah, I figured that one out myself," I said, jerking the bat from my feet. It burned like a mother!

"Have you figured out the best part yet? Al is banished from Wonderland. And, she thinks you're dead! She will live out her life thinking she's responsible for your demise when in fact you get to be my play toy for all eternity! Isn't it grand! She will be tortured with that thought!" he exclaimed giddily. "It is notable to mention that if she steps foot in this realm, for even a second, I have permission to kill her, so even if you manage to send word that you are still alive and she tries to rescue you, I have Hearts' blessing to kill her! Anyone who sees her, or aides her in any way, will be tortured to the full extent of the law. And down here, there are no laws, Mad Hatter."

The Joker just made my hit list. But, I could breathe a little easier knowing that Alice Mae was safe in the Otherworld. At least I didn't have to search this entire castle looking for her.

"Where is Hearts, anyway?"

"Probably bossing her cats around, but don't worry about her. She cannot help you here," he said. "Hearts may Reign the Red Court, but it is I who specializes in Terror. However, I assure you that she'll hear about our first play date."

"Lovely," I said, sarcastically. "It's a rather fine date we are having, isn't it?"

"Yes, but it doesn't measure up to the dates I had with Al as a young girl," the Joker said, circling me. "She tried so hard not to shed a tear, but that made it all the more satisfying when she did finally break down. Do you know what was the most rewarding?"

"Enlighten me," I said, and stood on my feet. Stabbing pains shot through me. Blood pooled around me. My body was weak. My head was throbbing. But, my mind was raging.

The Joker grabbed a yo-yo from the ground. He tested out the recoil once before bothering to look up at me. "That she's exactly like me even though she fights her manipulative nature. She's like a daughter."

I charged him again, swinging the bat like a lunatic. The Joker walked backwards, light on his toes as he anticipated my moves. We edged closer and closer to the Wall of Weapons. On the follow-through I released the bat—this time at his feet. It hit his ankles, tripping him. Just as he collided into the weapons, he released the yo-yo. The string wrapped around my neck. Falling to my knees, I grabbed at the string, but it kept sinking deeper and deeper into my skin.

My body went limp. The world felt weightless as my head teetered on my shoulders. The last person I saw before darkness clouded my vision was the Joker, dead against the wall looking much like a pin-cushion.

# CHAPTER FIFTY-NINE

(Alice Mae: Present Time)

Just like the prophecy predicted: I wept, banished in my homeland. Nothing good would happen if I returned to Wonderland, but then again I wasn't good. I was all Wrong.

Mr. Ruth appeared on my bed with a note secured to his belly by a rubber band. *Read Me* was written on the outside. On the inside was a message, written on a page torn from a book so old the pages turned yellow. On the top was the title of the book *Sweets for the Slithering Kind*, a M.H. novel. It was the Jack's handwriting.

*The Mad Hatter, the Joker Slayer, lost his head, like every man of that family. But, rest assured, Wonderland is a place where the impossible is possible. Just because a heart no longer beats, doesn't mean the love is lost.*

The news brought me to my knees, but there was a sliver of hope that piggybacked that tragedy—Ryley killed the Joker. I snuck as much candy as possible into my backpack, but I knew it was pointless. One day I'd have to learn to live in this world without them, and then I'd embrace my straightjacket.

I thought about stopping by Ryley's house. Lauren would be frazzled, not knowing what happened to her son. But, I couldn't do it. I couldn't tell her. What was I to say? Your son was killed by an evil queen in a magical world you don't ever want to find yourself in? I just hoped that one day the recipe I'd given Ryley would find its way to his father.

I never went back to the school. My uncompleted homework never left my backpack. Dax, Irwin, Mick, even Becky and Courtney and the rest of the school would never know what happened to their classmates.

The West Harbour Psychiatric Treatment Facility was my first and only stop. Robby Edgar was in the game room, playing with red paint. He'd created a series of lines that didn't line up quite correctly. Moving slowly, so as not to startle him, I sat down across the table. Robby didn't acknowledge my presence until I slid the worn, bronze watch in front of him.

He took the watch, handling it with the greatest care. Some red paint got on the metal. I suppose it was fitting. His son's blood was spilt. My throat refused to work properly. His big, brown eyes turned black as tears filled them.

"Why do you have Ryley's watch?" Robby asked, coldly.

I swallowed the lump in my throat. It took me several times to speak before any words came out. When my voice returned, I only managed to say, "It *was* his watch. Time has no meaning to the dead."

Robby never spoke again after that. He beat the watch against the table. The metal dented. The glass shattered. Red bled onto the papers, but it wasn't just paint anymore. The hour hand was the first to stop, but it was when the second hand stopped ticking that I willed death to come swiftly for the both of us. Even when the nurses and doctors raced to stop him, Robby didn't stop beating his fists against the watch until it was completely destroyed. Time no longer ticked.

*… Time ceased to move forward. A second carried on for infinity…*

# CHAPTER SIXTY

(Alice Mae: Present Time in the Waiting Room)

31,536,000 seconds—equivalent to approximately one year—ticked away in one, infinite drawn-out moment in time. It was in that never-ending moment that I fully embraced my metaphorical straightjacket. That also just so happened to be the exact amount of time it took me to instigate my revenge. It was a naive to think death was the sweetness that I craved. Oh no, I was oh so wrong. Vengeance was what I wanted all along.

M.H's legacy revolved around making a poison taste so sweet that Hearts wouldn't suspect that she was dying. He chose me to be his apprentice and do what he couldn't. Every day that I did nothing, I failed him. In my rational thoughts, I decided to un-fail him once and for all.

The *Waiting Room* appeared exactly as it had the last time I found myself in the forsaken chamber, except for the thick layer of dust. The mermaid table still lay in ruins. Vines wiggled through the mouse door and grew up the walls. The black and white checkered tile was still just as disorienting. A few sparklers lay on the ground. The sulfur scent was just as fresh as it had been when the Joker lit them. Down was up, but up was still a little off to the side.

The only addition in the *Waiting Room* was the sledge hammer that still had the price tag. That was instrumental if Plan "A" fell through because Genevine forgot to put on her big girl panties. If she bailed on me, that meant I no longer had the means to get my hands on *Drink Me* juice. I'd need something to widen the mouse door, wouldn't I?

While I waited for my company, I twirled around on my toes, reenacting the last dance I performed on stage. Instead of the disgruntled audience, I imagined an audience captivated by my recital.

Mr. Ruth pushed the door open, nearly knocking over the ceramic toad that guarded it. I glanced at the timepiece that I'd taped together after Robby had his way with it. The hour and second hand had been restored but the hands never moved. One can never be late if time did not tick forward.

Mr. Ruth said, "There is something you should know. It's a secret which has been haunting me for a year and—"

"No need to share secrets, not here, not today." I brought my finger to my lips and glanced at Theodore, just to make sure they knew I was serious about this beautifully haunting act of treason was on a *need to know* basis.

"I've misplaced my straightjacket in Wonderland." I hoped he understood. My revenge consumed me, driving me mad. I wanted to— needed to—do something before it finished me off completely. "I have to get it back before time gets impatient with me and starts ticking again."

"There's nothing wrong with being a *little* mad."

"Little mad, good. Lots mad, blissfully dangerous."

"Ah-ha! You admit it! Madness is bliss." He nervously thumped his foot when I rolled my eyes. "Wonderland welcomes crazies, but there has to be other places to find refuge before time catches up with you."

"I'm logically impared." I shrugged my shoulders and tried not to focus on just how messed up my life had gotten. I handed him a note that was addressed to Genevine. "I belong in Wonderland. But, let's not focus on that. This will be my last request of you, old friend. Please, don't make me beg. Tell Genevine to follow the ingredients and instructions to the 'T.' I'll be waiting in this room until she sends word that the tonic is ready."

# CHAPTER SIXTY-ONE

(Alice Mae: Present Time in Wonderland)

When the moon scared away the sun, I cracked the mouse door after someone continued to knock on it with much persistence. I expected to see Mr. Ruth standing on the other side. However, when I opened the door, I realized quite quickly that it wasn't a knocking I heard, for no one was there. The knocking was actually the tick from a clock. But it wasn't just one clock. There was a hallway of clocks. Old stopwatches, modern wrist watches, grandfather clocks, elaborate hanging ones. They all told a different time, but their ticks were synchronized.

Just inside the hallway were two bottles and a tiny box that was no bigger than a thumbnail. I lifted the lid. Inside was a miniature red velvet cupcake, wrapped in black tissue paper. *Eat Me.* I tucked it in my pocket, saving it for later.

The first bottle didn't have a *Drink Me* etched on the glass, but rather there was a skull and crossbones. A snake slithered around them. I popped the cork top and sniffed the tonic. Nothing, but then again snake repellent was odorless.

I tucked the bottle inside my pocket and reached for the *Drink Me* one. I took a swig. Today, it tasted like blueberries and cotton candy. After a nauseating shrinkage, I stepped into the hallway. As soon as my foot touched the tile, all the clocks began ticking at a different rate. Some of the clocks became loud and obnoxious while others ticked as if they were the bass drum to a song. Nevertheless, as I neared the end of the hallway, one thing was obvious. The ticks slowed.

When I reached the end of the hallway, there was a massive door. It wasn't made of wood or metal or any other substance that would make for good doorway material. It was card stock designed much like a playing card, but it wasn't any of the number cards. It was a face card, but it wasn't the joker, queen, or king. It was a sketch drawing of a two faced man—M.H. and the second Mad Hatter—my Ryley.

I swung it open and marveled at the place I'd never been in—a house of cards. Sheets were thrown over the furniture. The drapes were pulled so that no light showed through. I dug in my pocket and pulled out a flare that I'd stolen from the Joker during one of our many play dates.

Just as I was going to strike the flare, someone lit a candle. Sitting in a chair in front of the coffee table was the Jack, Genevine, Mr. Ruth, and a man I never hoped to see again. Robby Edgar. He kept his head down, staring at the floorboards like the answers of the universe were hidden in the woodwork. When I walked closer, he lowered his head even more and pulled the top hat that belonged to M.H. over his eyes. For a brief moment, I wondered when he got it. Last I knew, the hat was worn by his son.

"You look half dead," Robby whispered. His voice sounded rougher than I remembered. He wore a fancy, black ballroom tux—cufflinks and a fancy silk scarf included. He had his collar popped and his shirt was pulled up high.

"Death is a friend whom I have been late to meet," I said.

And, then it dawned on me that I couldn't remember the last time I bothered to look presentable. My torn leggings would have looked punk-rocker, if I hadn't paired it with my plaid skirt. My ruffled shirt would have been nice, if I hadn't slept in it the past couple of days. The black fingernail polish on my nails brought out the pasty white in my skin. At least the polish hid the dirt under my nails. My hair was pulled back low on my neck, in a messy bun. I remembered twisting it back before I fell down the rabbit hole. Now, locks fell over my face. I touched my cheek and wondered when I last applied lipstick. For a moment, I felt naked in front of Genevine—the woman who'd shown me the power of makeup. But, the seamstress didn't fare much better than me. She appeared much like an old hag, with her wild hair and pretty, but torn, clothes. Looking at her was like staring into a looking glass, minus the ball and chain and cluster of spiders.

"That's a pity," Robby said, stealing my attention.

"Is it a pity I haven't yet died, or that I am alive?" I said. I knew he blamed me for his son's death. Hell, I blamed me for Ryley's demise.

"When was the last time you had any sweets?" he asked.

He was measuring my intelligence? Perhaps my level of paranoia intrigued him. "I don't crave the sweet-stuff anymore. Vengeance will taste much sweeter than any candy I've ever sucked on, even if it kills me."

Keeping his hat pulled down, Robby stood up abruptly, turning so his back was to me. He began pacing around the room. My deathly comment had bothered him. I wanted to tell him he was being a wuss, but his opinion of me no longer mattered. I couldn't bring his son back, but I could avenge him.

Mr. Ruth followed Robby back and forth. They kept their voices low and argued about something——it didn't matter to me, not in the least.

"Where are we, Genevine?" I asked.

"A house of cards, hidden deep within the mushroom patch. Few people know this place even exists or that Edgar resides here. If the queen found out, she'd stop at nothing to kill him," she said. On her lap was a beautiful, black night robe with a perfect white rose emblem embroidered on the front in the finest, white silk. She handed it to me. "I finished it last night."

I inspected the white rose. "And the tonic?"

"Edgar made the liquid sweet himself and the concoction is in the skull and bones bottle," Alfred said. Like always, he was perched on Genevine's shoulder. He patted his belly. "And then every spider drank the tonic, I assure you."

"Edgar made the tonic?" I asked, glancing at Robby.

Sarah J. Pepper

"He took over M.H's candy operation," Genevine said. "But all trades go through Mr. Ruth so no one knows he's here. It keeps rumors about his existence from getting back to the queen."

"And if I succeed in killing Hearts, is he to rule?"

Genevine looked at him and then back to me. Judging from her frown, I figured that she wasn't totally on board with the decision rendered. "I will rule in his place, unless a time comes when he is needed to reign."

"Are you going to ditch your over-sized bracelet?" I asked, nodding to her ball and chain. "You know the Joker taught me how to pick a lock. I could free you."

"Ask me again if you survive," Genevine said. "There's no point in getting rid of it unless the queen is dead. I've seen her storage closet, and she's got more where that came from."

Mr. Ruth cursed at Robby, interrupting our conversation. "Names are important! She must know yours, you idiotic, irrational fool!"

Yep, Genevine would make a more fitting queen than Robby as king. She didn't make a habit of kicking the wall out of frustration, like he just did.

Robby kneeled beside the white rabbit. "Is that so, *Rutherford?*"

I thought Mr. Ruth might punch Robby in the chest for calling him by his actual name, but he didn't. Although, Mr. Ruth did pull on the scarf wrapped around Robby's neck, revealing a thick scar underneath. It wrapped around his neck and had fresh stitches.

Mr. Ruth yelled, "You push my buttons, Mad—"

Robby cupped his hand over the rabbit's mouth. "What shall you do, if you survive this suicide mission, Alice Mae? Will you return to the Otherworld or stay here."

"I've always preferred living in Wonderland. I'm in sync here, whereas I'm out of step in the Otherworld." I tilted my head to the side. "Why do you care?"

Before he could answer, Mr. Ruth bit down on his hand hard enough to draw blood. Robby released him and cradled his hand. With Robby otherwise engaged, Mr. Ruth snatched his hat and took off running. Robby scrambled to catch the white rabbit, but it soon became clear that he was never going to capture the bunny. Stopping the chase, Robby pulled the scarf off his neck and wrapped his hand wound.

"I should leave," I said, checking the time on the broken watch that once belonged to Ryley. "I don't have time to watch an old man try to capture a rumperbabbit while they argue about names. M.H. once thought that names were important and look where that got him."

Gathering the robe, I double-checked to make sure I had the bottle with the skull and snakes etched into the glass. I crossed the room and tried the doorknob. As I opened it, Robby stopped me by placing his injured hand over mine. I stared at his hand, trying to figure out in what realm he'd ever want to physically touch me.

"Have you fallen in love?" he whispered. "Do you still dance? Are you... happy?"

"What would you need—? Why do you—? Does it really—"

When I met his gaze, all the air was sucked from my lungs. A squeak escaped my throat. I dropped the robe and the bottle, and the strength in my knees failed.

*He* caught me. *Ryley* caught me. A part of me was sure his hands would slip through me, like a ghost's. But, they didn't. He held me in his arms. He looked as if he'd aged ten years, making him look more like his father than the young man I had fallen for. Small wrinkles lined his face. Strands of his hair were turning gray.

I pushed away from him. He was far older than I recalled. Even if he'd lived, he would still be in his late teens. "The Ryley I knew couldn't grow facial hair," I managed to say to the impersonator.

"Time moves differently here." The mystery-man stepped closer to me and kept his hands raised in the air. He acted like I was a rabid animal. "I nick myself shaving now."

Genevine pressed her lips into a thin line. I screamed for her to tell me the truth, but she didn't speak a word. Mr. Ruth hid in the shadows.

"You wrote that he lost his head!" I screamed at the Jack. I wished I had a bat or something to keep the impersonator from stepping closer to me. Surely, this scenario was a figment of my imagination! It had to be a schizophrenic episode. I closed my eyes and pressed my hands over my eyes.

"I'm going to wake up now. I'm going to wake up and find myself in some white room in some random hospital. The nurses will give me yummy drugs and make this nightmare disappear. I never escaped to the rabbit hole. I made all this up. There is no such thing as a rumperbabbit," I said and then hyperventilated. "It's not real. It's not real. It'snotreal. It'snotreal.It'snotreal.It'snotreal."

"I'm not a nightmare," the impersonator said, pulling my hands away from my eyes. His dark eyes never appeared so fierce. He was in control and spoke in a calm voice. "The Jack wrote you as a favor to me. It was my deepest hope that you'd go on and live your life in the Otherworld. I hoped you'd find your *happily ever after*."

"You're really here. You're really alive?" I asked.

"Sort of."

"You should have told me you were alive!" I screamed. "You could have come for me! It is a special kind of cruel to make me believe you were dead!"

He covered my mouth with his hand. "Don't speak. Just listen. If I could have come for you, I would have. Don't you think I'd kill to see my family and friends again?" Ryley whispered, removing his hand from my mouth. "Don't you think I wished my heart to stop beating because loving you from afar was killing me—killed me?"

I couldn't take my eyes off of his scar. "Kill*ed* you?"

# CHAPTER SIXTY-TWO

(Ryley: One year ago in Wonderland)

A cluster of spiders were loosening the yo-yo's string from around my neck. Their proximity made me want to gag. One day I would get over my irrational fear of spiders, but today wasn't that day. Their webs were everywhere. The silk shimmered different colors, depending on how the light hit them. My headache pounding was almost crippling. I'd kill for an aspirin. I reached up to rub my temples when someone slapped my hand out of the way.

"If you move too much, Genevine won't be able to finish."

A spider sat on the hag's shoulder with its butt to me. Genevine pulled a thin silk thread from the spider, slid it through a needle, and lowered it to my neck. Genevine pulled back on the string. I felt a tug on my neck.

"What are you doing?" I asked. My voice didn't sound like me. It was far too rough and deep, but I was still too out of it to think straight. Everything seemed backwards but moving in fast-forward.

"I'm doing the impossible," she said. "If you can, then so can I."

I tried to think of what had happened before I lost consciousness.

297

Sarah J. Pepper

There was the fight with the Joker. I recalled the Wall of Weapons and watching the Joker's body go limp. Knives, swords, and other pointy "toys" stuck out from him.

A smaller spider—daddy long leg—held up a mirror for me to see. Genevine was cutting a string that was attached to my horribly bloody neck!

"Impossible," I muttered, moving my neck. The slightest movement hurt, but I wasn't dead.

"This is a world of impossibilities," the daddy long leg said, giving me the mirror. "Life after death may not be possible in the Otherworld, but nothing is impossible in Wonderland."

I cringed at the idea of being so close to a spider, and I tried not to think that their webs were holding me in place. I studied Genevine's handiwork. I should be dead. Right? Still, I was moving, talking, and breathing.

"You should be careful though, the stitching could tear at any moment. I'd hate for you to turn your head too quickly and have the darn thing fall off. All you boys in the Edgar family are far too handsome to be headless."

"How is this possible?"

"Magic," Genevine replied. "You don't get the title of MTS—Most Talented Seamstress—in the court for nothing."

I sat up. The movement was nauseating. I held my wobbling head for a moment before looking for an escape. The fire pole would be my best bet. I could get out of this demented place and——

"Where is Alice Mae?" I asked, speaking so quickly my question was barely audible.

Genevine grabbed my hand, stopping me from my attempt to stand. "You have to let her go."

"Like hell I do!"

"I'm a seamstress, not a doctor," she stated, calmly. "The yo-yo's

298

string cut deep into your neck. The spiders were able to remove it before it severed everything… but, even though I stitched you up, it doesn't mean I'm a doctor. I don't have medical training."

"What does that mean?" I asked, looking from her to the spiders for an explanation.

"Well, the Joker did slit your throat with that nasty yo-yo," Alfred said. "In the Otherworld, does a person live long after his head is semi-detached?"

# CHAPTER SIXTY-THREE

(Alice Mae: Present time in Wonderland)

"For most of your life, you've been guilt-ridden. I couldn't bear the thought of you punishing yourself because of what happened to me, so I didn't want you to hear about my unconventional survival," Ryley said, tucking a straggly piece of my hair behind my ear. He smiled one of those infuriating, sexy smiles. "I stay in this house of cards where no one will look for a deadman, thus, I stay under Hearts' radar. I've taken over M.H's candy operation since everyone referred to me as the second Mad Hatter anyway. It seemed like a self-fulfilling prophecy so I didn't fight it. Anyway, when Genevine showed me the recipe you wrote, I knew you were planning to return. You were taking some kind of barbaric risk when it would be easier to just stay away. So that meant it was useless to hide from you too."

*For a year I thought he was dead!* I slapped his hand away from me. I pushed away from him. His eyes were wide and wild, not knowing what I'd do next.

"Next time you think you're doing me a favor, don't!" I planned on kicking him with my pointy shoes, except he kept backing away from me. So, I took off my shoe and threw it at him. The heel of the shoe stuck into the playing card wall next to the Jack.

"I thought the Joker predicted that the HATed fool would die *twice!"* I screamed at the old man.

"You act like you're upset that I'm *not* dead! Sorry to disappoint you," Ryley mocked. "Besides, you're the one who said I shouldn't hold much clout in the Joker's predictions. You said that he's not as gifted in seeing the future as his great-great grandfather! You insisted that he often gets his predictions wrong!"

For a *year—a freaking year—*I believed he was dead! I was half-tempted to kill him to prove a point! "You could have told me the truth, Mad Hatter!"

"Don't call me that, *ever again."* Ryley said in a tone so ominous that shivers enveloped my body. Yet, I couldn't care more about what he wanted. I'd shiver all day long if he could feel one ounce of suffering I had felt.

"Mad Hatter! Mad Hatter! Mad Hatter!"

"Why do you insist on talking when you should just shut-up and listen, *stupid girl?"*

"The walking, talking DEADMAN wants me to shut up?"

"I like to think of my situation as *living-impaired."*

"Splitting hairs, aren't we?"

"As long as I stay in this realm, I can live. My death is permanent if I venture into the Otherworld."

My other shoe didn't drop—I kicked it off at him. He dodged it. When it hit the floor, he charged me. Grabbing my arms, he kept his body pressed up hard against mine.

"Get off me you inconsiderate dead freak!"

"Don't you ever stop talking?"

Before I could answer, he kissed me…

... I held *nothing* back. I made sure he could feel just how peeved I was with my lips. I didn't have to scream insults at him, but I used my tongue to get my point across. Biting helped too.

And then it was as if someone flipped a switch inside me. As angry as I was, my fears bubbled up. I don't know how he did it, but Ryley made me feel every single emotion I had for him at the same time. All my anger, sorrow, fear, and love rose out of me. They came out in the form of tears, trickling down my cheeks and onto our lips. Ryley drank them in as he kept me close in his embrace.

I imagined that Ryley and I would have spent the rest of the night either screaming at each other, or doing other things with our lips, but Genevine coughed one of those, *you're not alone* kind of coughs.

"We still have a queen to kill," she said.

# CHAPTER SIXTY-FOUR

(Alice Mae: Present time in Wonderland)

"*You* don't have to do this," Ryley said. "I would do it for you."

"No, you can't," Genevine said, stealing the words I was to say.

Even though she was fighting for my cause, I couldn't help but to be curious. "Why can't he?" I asked.

She picked up the robe and the bottle that I'd dropped by the door. She handed them to me. I peeled myself away from Ryley to take them. It was more difficult than I imagined. Being an inch away from him made me queasy and dizzy simultaneously. I shoved the bottle in my pocket before Ryley could snatch it away from me.

"Because, I have to make a few stitches in the Mad Hatter's neck every couple of days to keep his head from rolling off his shoulders. Since the spiders' thread is what I used, it means that the tonic they drank, at your request, is in the threads around his neck," Genevine said, inspecting Ryley's scar. "And you tore some stitches in your tussle with Alice Mae."

"No matter," Ryley said. "I can still take Alice Mae's place."

"No, you can't," Mr. Ruth said, handing back his hat. "I promised

Alice Mae a long time ago that I would keep you safe. I technically failed, but I'm not one to repeat mistakes."

"They are right. You cheated death once," I said, clutching the robe. "I've already lived one year *knowing* that you were dead. Call me selfish, call me insane, call me *stupid*, but I don't want to live like that *ever* again. If anyone is going to die, it's going to be me."

"Woo'ld yo i'ike t'tho k'now?" the Jack said, quietly. He was still sitting on the couch, blending into the shadows, long forgotten. He clutched a deck of tarot cards. "Woo'ld yo I'ike t'tho k'now if yo wil'l i'ive t'tho see t'tho'omorrow?"

No, I would not like to know the future! I couldn't shake my head fast enough. Conversely, I couldn't say the same about Ryley. He looked exactly how I imagined a mouse would appear, gawking at a piece of cheese on a trap.

"If we know, for sure, that you will die on this vendetta, then I will volunteer to take your place," Ryley said.

"It doesn't work that way, Ryley. The prophecies never make any sense until it happens. Just because our future is predicted doesn't mean I want to know it. I lived my whole life knowing I was Wrong, according to the *BackWards Wanderer Prophecy*. But, the thing is, everyone makes 'wrong' decisions. To predict that someone would do wrong is like saying someone will eventually die. I've been chased by the ghosts of my past. I thought M.H. would suddenly wake from the dead, but it was he and *you* that the *Madmen's Prophecy* was regarding," I said.

Standing on my tiptoes, I gave him a quick peck on the cheek and stole his hat. The fabric was old and worn, but it felt good in my hands. And, it smelled like him—like home with a faint aroma of sweets. I turned to leave, but he held onto my hand.

"Let's run away together," he said. "I don't want to let you out of my sight again, and if you don't survive…"

I pressed my finger over his lips. "Death is a friend I've been waiting a very long time to see. Besides, if I'm to die, then I'll haunt you until the end of time."

# CHAPTER SIXTY-FIVE

(Ryley: Present time in Wonderland)

Even in the desolate, run-down, dark room that screamed *crypt*, Alice Mae stood defiantly graceful. Even though she was dressed in rags, her beauty couldn't be hidden. There was a spark of crazy in her eye that only came when someone lost everything, but residing in there was her overwhelming sense of intelligence. I had no doubt she'd kill the queen, sacrifice herself if it came to it—that was what terrified me.

"The queen will awake soon," I said and kissed her hand.

She smiled again—a twisted, sly smile that sent chills down my spine. Her blue eyes turned as cold as ice. After turning on her heel, she walked out of the room I'd made entirely of cards. She walked so soundlessly, I could trick myself to believe she was a ghost. As soon as the door shut behind her, I turned to the Jack.

"Will she survive?" I would chase her down, tackle her if I had to, and kill the queen myself if it meant she would be safe.

The corner of the old man's lips twitched. He reached up and plucked a blonde hair off of my jacket, Alice Mae's. He pulled out a red one from his pocket. It had to be Hearts'. Twisting them around each other, he held them over the candle's flame. It sizzled, leaving a puff of white smoke. He gestured to my scarf that I'd used to bandage my hand. I unraveled it and handed it to him. On a single thread he wrote: *ONLY ONE SHaLL SURVIVE. The one wHosE heArt bleeds the most will peRsevere buT a full recovery iS unlikely.*

I paid close attention to the capital letters and lower case. H.E.A.R.T.S was capitalized. AL was not. "What does this mean? AL will survive? Will Hearts bleed?"

"The *She Prophecy* is about Al and Hearts. You asked if *she* shall survive. One *she* will watch the other *she* die. That much is certain, but the length of said survival is uncertain," the Jack said, speaking without trouble.

"Your tongue—I thought it had been cut out," I said.

"What you think is the truth, and what is reality is not the same."

I grabbed the Jack's collar and pulled the old man up so we were face to face. The red wool clothing felt as slippery as silk in my hands so I twisted it around my fist. The more fabric I gathered, the more loose his clothing became, like it was peeling away from him. The color of his skin wavered, like he was made of water. The tighter I pulled his clothing, the more that slipped through my fingers. He turned his back to me and walked away. A ball of clothing was wadded in my fist, draping from his collar.

"Enough parlor tricks!" I said through gritted teeth and chased after him. "If Alice Mae is to die, I'll take her place!"

"One *she* will come out alive, but it is *certain* that if you go anywhere near the tonic Alice Mae carries, *many* deaths will follow."

He traced the spider web stitching along my neck. He didn't have to point out that the tonic that the spiders drank was laced in their webbing. I would become the target, just like the queen.

I shoved him away. He collapsed onto the furniture and chuckled, amplifying to a full-blown laugh. A dreadful feeling burst in the pit of my stomach. I raced to the door. Locked. I turned back to the Jack, planning to demand that he unlock it, but the old man was gone. Only Genevine and the white rabbit stood in the house of cards.

"You may have ended the Terror plaguing this court when you took the Joker's life, but in the end he was still family, and I loved him regardless of his faults," the Jack's voice echoed even though he wasn't visible. "Tit-for-tat. One will die, but will it be the *she* who wears the mad man's hat?"

I beat the door well after the shards shredded my hands.

# CHAPTER SIXTY-SIX

(Alice Mae: Present Time in Wonderland)

Death by poison—it was the best I could hope for as I sat at the snake table and waited for Hearts to wake. The slithering creatures wrapped their tails around my ankles and legs. The sun had long since risen before she crawled out of bed and put on her robe. I raised my glass when she saw me. She didn't look the least bit surprised to see me. The thought made me smile. I wondered how many nights had passed while she tossed and turned, waiting for me to return, *if* I returned.

"Guards!" she screamed.

I put my elbows on the table and leaned forward to whisper my secret. "I've locked the doors with one of the late Joker's impermeable locks. I do admit his locking toys are high quality. The only way in or out is to break down the door."

Hearts looked half-panicked, but recovered quickly. Wearing a deceitful smile, she wrapped herself in the robe Genevine sewed last night. Eyeing the food and drink on the table, she stood back like she was unsure if she should wait until her guards could dispose of me or attack me herself.

"Are you scared of a *stupid* girl?" I asked, laying the sarcasm on thick. I crossed my legs, making sure she'd get an eyeful of my torn clothing.

That got me the glare of the century. "To what do I owe this pleasure, Al?"

"I wanted you to be the first to hear that after a long hiatus, I've decided to stay in Wonderland," I said and took a sip of the tea. I closed my eyes and enjoyed the natural flavor as it hit my tongue. "But, if I'm to live in this nightmarish place, I do have a list of demands."

That comment got the queen laughing. "You are in no position to make demands! You have been banished to the Otherworld!"

"Yes, I chose to live there to keep everyone safe. I was considered a traitor and anyone who helped me would have their eyes removed. So, for a year I never came back here, but it was the Wrong decision. I should never have left."

She eased up and sat down across the table from me. The snakes' tails tightened their grip, but I did not react to the tension. Instead, I set my tea cup down and listened to the queen laugh.

"Even if the Joker is dead, you still have a price on your head."

"I do hope it's a high price," I said, holding up a spoon. I fussed with my hair. "I like expensive things."

The tension tightened around my legs. My feet had already gone numb. I could tell that the creatures were desperately trying not to react to the tonic.

"My demands are as follows," I said. "Robby Edgar is to have his banishment lifted. He can live here or in the Otherworld. If he chooses to stay in the Otherworld, Genevine is to be announced as queen. Oh, and every single red rose in the court shall be painted white."

Chez appeared on top of the table, next to the sugar cubes. He tilted his head as he inspected my spoon before knocking it off of the table. "We might as well rename it the White Court," he said dully.

"What a fabulous idea!" I exclaimed.

The door handle shook. The guards had arrived. Not a second had passed and the door rattled from their pounding.

"Is that all?" Hearts said. Her tone of voice was dry.

I smacked my head. "Oh, heavens, I forgot. That price tag you put on my head shall be lifted. It is not my intention to die… well, not today anyway."

I took another sip of the tea. Hearts watched me carefully. I forced a smile. I set the tea cup down on the saucer and giggled. My laughs weren't for the queen's everlasting paranoia from eating poisoned food—it was that the snakes had recoiled from my legs. They moved so slowly that the cat didn't even hear them.

"And if I refuse your extensive list of demands?" Hearts asked and took a sip of her tea.

I dug in my pocket and pulled out the bottle. Popping off the cork, I raised it above my head and waited for them to get a good look at it.

"Is that snake repellent?" Chez asked. His hair stood on end when he noticed my now snake-less chair. "Where are the four legless ones?"

The queen stood up so quickly her chair fell over. She stepped back; looking at the floor like the tiles themselves may come up and bite her. I'd give up all my worldly possessions to have captured Hearts' expression on camera the moment she saw the four snakes coming after her.

"If you refuse my demands, it will be the last decision you make, Hearts," I said, tilting the bottle so a splash of the tonic dripped out. "All you have to do is play nice, and I'll give you the repellent."

"I'd rather die than agree to your terms," she said, running toward the door.

"And so you shall…" I drizzled out the tonic onto the tablecloth. When it was empty, I took out Ryley's pocket watch. The hands lay still. They were still as broken as my heart. "When a second carries on for infinity, the Reign of Terror shall end. I'm adlibbing, but I think you get the idea."

The guards beat at the door more profusely, the louder their queen screamed for help. Splinters flew as they took their battle axes to the wood. Their paper weapons packed a punch after all. In desperation, Hearts shook the handle as the snakes nipped at her ankles.

Chez appeared by Hearts' legs. With his sharp claws, he pawed at the snakes. It didn't slow the creepy crawlies. Covered in claw marks, the snakes slithered up her legs, around her body, until they reached the rose emblem. It was then that Chez made his exit and disappeared while all four snakes circled around the queen's neck. They bit at the rose emblem. Blood spattered the white rose, until it looked like the flower bled.

"Poison was always a part of M.H's plan. But, all of his plans had one main glitch. You see, I knew if anyone poisoned your food, they would succumb to death because you always waited to eat or drink until someone else does first. So I had to come up with another idea, which Ryley gave me when he told me about your snaky chair. To honor M.H. I kept his poisonous theme in mind when I made my plan, but it wouldn't come from me. Oh, no. The poison came from the venom. And since he was the best candy-maker the court had ever known, I thought it only fitting to collaborate sweets into my plan... Isn't it positively perfect?"

I memorized the look of horror on the queen's face. Straightjacket—that one word echoed in my mind. I should really be tied up somewhere, locked away, and have the key thrown away. Yes, yes, all of those choices would be completely acceptable. But, deep down in the darkest cracks of my heart, I had never had more of a reason to smile— really smile.

"How did I incorporate the candy tonic, you may ask. Genevine's spiders drank that snake tonic and then the seamstress used their silk to sew that beautiful heart on your robe," I said, leaning back in my chair.

A single tear fell, but it wasn't for Hearts. I took off the hat that belonged to a candy-making conspirator, a banished Heir, and, my beloved. Tucked in the top was a photo of Ryley and me when we committed our first crime of breaking and entering. He looked at me like I was his world. I pressed the photo over my chest and prayed that he knew how deeply I loved him. Killing the queen didn't make my heart any less broken or my soul any less destroyed, but it finally felt like I was doing something Right.

The queen fell to her knees as the paper mache soldiers barged through the door. LeDee and LeDum followed after. They opened their mouths to scream, but only shrill gibberish came out. The air circled around them as they breathed in and out, sucking the oxygen from the air. Red tears stained their cheeks as they grabbed at the snakes. But the slitherings had already clamped down on the robe, sucking the candy from the very fibers of the silk in the rose emblem. The soldiers didn't know what to do now that Hearts was dead, but I didn't fault them for that. They were headless. Unhurriedly, I stood up, smoothed my shirt, and walked to the broken down door until I saw Ryley standing amongst the soldiers, pushing his way to the front.

"Run!" I screamed at Ryley.

But, it was too late. The snakes had already caught whiff of the sweet scent laced in the stitching of his neck! Grabbing a battle axe from a dumbfounded soldier, he flipped it in the air and swung as the venomous snakes attacked.

Everything happened so fast.

# CHAPTER SIXTY-SEVEN

(Alice Mae: Present Time in Wonderland)

Blood spattered everything. Ryley swung the weapon so quickly I could hardly follow, but there were four snakes and only one of him. They twisted around his arms and legs, moving quickly as they tried to get at his neck. Wrapped in their grip, he didn't stop swinging until four snakes lay dead at his feet. *So many deaths...*

I raced over to him, stepping over the queen. Tears burned my eyes. Four snakes lay dead at Ryley's feet, but he was not without injury. Bruises lined his arms, and blood coated his hands. Ryley dropped the battle axe in a pool of red and embraced me. My tears drizzled over his lacerated hands when he cupped my face.

"You're hurt!" I said, wishing death wouldn't take him from me again. I didn't want to say good-bye. I couldn't say good-bye, not again. I'd rather die.

"I'll survive, Alice Mae."

I shook my head and grabbed his hands, inspecting them thoroughly. There was just so much blood! Maybe if I could suck the poison from his wounds he wouldn't die on me—again.

He clutched my hands and forced me to look up at him. "The snakes didn't bite me, but I did have to beat down a couple of doors to get to you."

He smiled, encouraging me to believe him. But I learned long ago not to trust a smile. I searched for fanged tooth marks on his neck. There were none. He brought my hand up to his lips and kissed it sweetly, like we were on a romantic date instead of standing in a pool of blood.

Mr. Ruth peered around the corner. His legs wobbled and he looked like he was seconds from fainting. "He refused to listen to me! I swear I did everything I could to keep him safe. But he kept bulldozing down doors until he found you," Mr. Ruth said and then peered around us. "Is she really dead?"

LeDee and LeDum wailed. Their incoherent reply was answer enough.

"It's so strange that those snakes just went crazy and killed the queen, isn't it?" Ryley asked, glancing at the queen's entourage.

I fought back an off kilter grin. "Yes, we should let everyone know the Queen of Hearts had a *misfortunate accident* involving her pet snakes."

Genevine and her spiders were waiting at the castle's gate. Mr. Ruth raced out in front of us to deliver the news. When Ryley and I emerged, walking hand in hand, every creature in the court gathered near the gate, looking up at Genevine for direction. She would be a wonderful ruler of the court. I pulled a bobby pin from my hair and went to work unlocking the heavy weight from around her ankle. It took some coaxing, but eventually the clasp unlocked. For the first time in decades, she was truly free.

Ryley knelt down next to Mr. Ruth. "If you wouldn't mind doing a favor for me, I'd be much obliged."

"Anything," Mr. Ruth said.

Ryley pulled a worn page with a mirage recipe. My handwriting was written on the edge along with faded blue lipstick; it was the note I'd taped to his locker last year. Instinctively, I brought my hand up to my bare lips. So much had changed in a year. I'd changed so much.

He handed it to Mr. Ruth. "I would have personally given this to my dad, but I'm bound to Wonderland."

Mr. Ruth thumped his foot nervously. "Robby's mind is truly lost, Mad Hatter, and it's not because he is missing his sweets. News of your death did him in."

"Then give it to my mom. She'll know what to do," Ryley said.

"And if I can't find her?"

I dug in my pocket and pulled out a few dice, eleven crumpled cards, a jack, and the old racecar. I handed it to the rabbit. "If you are close enough to Robby's vehicle, the racecar's headlights will light up, and the wheels will spin. It will lead you to it. You might be able to track Lauren if she still drives it."

"In the meantime, if my dad's mind can handle it, deliver a message for me. Tell him that I am… doing well. Explain what happened. Let him know that it is safe to return to Wonderland," he said, and glanced back up at me.

There was a weight to his gaze that held little meaning to anyone else but me. He acted like he could see my diseased soul, my bleeding heart, and my broken mind. He knew about the not-so-good-parts of me, and loved me anyway. I didn't know if I brought out the good in him, or if I just made him want to pull his hair out, but nevertheless, I had stolen his heart when he was running away with mine. Our love ran deep—deep enough to kill, deep enough to die.

Ryley turned back to the white rabbit. "And let him know that Alice Mae will be with me—as long as she stays in Wonderland."

Mr. Ruth saluted him and scampered off. Ryley stood up next to me and took in the sight of all the creatures in the court. There was no cheering or clapping. They were rendered silent by the news of the queen's death. No one stopped us. No one arrested us. No one voiced a protest. Instead, they tipped their hats to us as we walked past them. Ryley's hand found mine.

"A long time ago, you told me that you wondered what it'd be like to be so small that you could hide from all life's problems in a house made up of cards," Ryley said. "Would you like to come home with me, and see what it's like?"

"Nothing has ever sounded so sweet."

Wonderland was an intoxicating, magical world where the most far-fetched dreams could come true and the impossible was possible. Conversely, it was a realm where the most daunting nightmares could haunt us until the end of time.

*Heads would Roll...*

*Hearts would Break...*

*In the end, did it (really) matter who Reigned?*

# About the Author

Sarah J. Pepper lives in South Dakota with her real-life prince charming. At a young age, she fell for paranormal books and now incorporates that genre with the romance that thrives in the hearts of us all. When she's not storytelling, she's most likely biking, hoarding chocolate, or taking a bubble bath. Get a glimpse inside her head at www.sarahjpepper.com
@sarahjpepper

CPSIA information can be obtained at www.ICGtesting.com
Printed in the USA
LVOW11s0315210714

395259LV00017B/280/P

9 781492 823919